SO BIG

edna ferber

SO BIG

PERENNIAL 🏭 CLASSICS

HarperCollins books may be purchased for educational, business, or sales promotional use. For information please write: Special Markets Department, HarperCollins Publishers Inc., 10 East 53rd Street, New York, NY 10022.

First Perennial Classics edition published 2000.
Perennial Classics are published by Perennial, an imprint of HarperCollins Publishers.

Library of Congress Cataloging-in-Publication Data has been applied for.
ISBN 0-06-095669-0

00 01 02 03 04 ❖/RRD 10 9 8 7 6 5 4 3 2 1

SO BIG

1

Until he was almost ten the name stuck to him. He had literally to fight his way free of it. From So Big (of fond and infantile derivation) it had been condensed into Sobig. And Sobig DeJong, in all its consonantal disharmony, he had remained until he was a ten-year-old schoolboy in that incredibly Dutch district southwest of Chicago known first as New Holland and later as High Prairie. At ten, by dint of fists, teeth, copper-toed boots and temper, he earned the right to be called by his real name, Dirk DeJong. Now and then, of course, the nickname bobbed up and had to be subdued in a brief and bitter skirmish. His mother, with whom the name had originated, was the worst offender. When she lapsed he did not, naturally, use schoolyard tactics on her. But he sulked and glowered portentously and refused to answer, though her tone, when she called him So Big, would have melted the heart of any but that natural savage, a boy of ten.

The nickname had sprung from the early and idiotic question invariably put to babies and answered by them, with infinite patience, through the years of their infancy.

Selina DeJong, darting expertly about her kitchen, from washtub to baking board, from stove to table, or, if at work in the fields of the truck farm, straightening the numbed back for a moment's respite from the close-set rows of carrots, turnips, spinach, or beets over which she was labouring, would wipe the sweat beads from nose and forehead with a quick duck of her head in the crook of her bent arm.

Those great fine dark eyes of hers would regard the child perched impermanently on a little heap of empty potato sacks, one of which comprised his costume. He was constantly detaching himself from the parent sack heap to dig and burrow in the rich warm black loam of the truck garden. Selina DeJong had little time for the expression of affection. The work was always hot at her heels. You saw a young woman in a blue calico dress, faded and earth-grimed. Between her eyes was a driven look as of one who walks always a little ahead of herself in her haste. Her dark abundant hair was skewered into a utilitarian knob from which soft loops and strands were constantly escaping, to be pushed back by that same harried ducking gesture of head and bent arm. Her hands, for such use, were usually too crusted and inground with the soil into which she was delving. You saw a child of perhaps two years, dirt-streaked, sunburned, and generally otherwise defaced by those bumps, bites, scratches, and contusions that are the common lot of the farm child of a mother harried by work. Yet, in that moment, as the woman looked at the child there in the warm moist spring of the Illinois prairie land, or in the cluttered kitchen of the farmhouse, there quivered and vibrated between them and all about them an aura, a glow, that imparted to them and their surroundings a mystery, a beauty, a radiance.

"How big is baby?" Selina would demand, senselessly. "How big is my man?"

The child would momentarily cease to poke plump fingers into the rich black loam. He would smile a gummy though slightly weary smile and stretch wide his arms. She, too, would open her tired arms wide, wide. Then they would say in a duet, his mouth a puckered pink petal, hers quivering with tenderness and a certain amusement, "*So-o-o-o big!*" with the voice soaring on the prolonged vowel and dropping suddenly with the second word. Part of the game. The child became so habituated to this question that sometimes, if Selina happened to glance round at him suddenly in the midst of her task, he would take his cue without the familiar question being put and would squel his "So-o-o-o big!" rather absently, in dutiful solo. Then he would throw back his head and laugh a triumphant laugh, his open mouth a coral orifice. She would run to him, and swoop down upon him, and bury her flushed face in the warm moist creases of his neck, and make as though to devour him. "So big!"

But of course he wasn't. He wasn't as big as that. In fact, he never became as big as the wide-stretched arms of her love and imagination would have had him. You would have thought she should have been satisfied when, in later years, he was the Dirk DeJong whose name you saw (engraved) at the top of heavy cream linen paper, so rich and thick and stiff as to have the effect of being starched and ironed by some costly American business process; whose clothes were made by Peter Peel, the English tailor; whose roadster ran on a French chassis; whose cabinet held mellow Italian vermouth and Spanish sherry; whose wants were served by a Japanese houseman; whose life, in short, was that of the successful citizen of the Republic. But she wasn't. Not only was she dissatisfied: she was at once remorseful and indignant, as though she, Selina DeJong, the vegetable peddler, had been partly to blame for this success of his, and partly cheated by it.

When Selina DeJong had been Selina Peake she had lived in Chicago with her father. They had lived in many other cities as well. In Denver during the rampant '80s. In New York when Selina was twelve. In Milwaukee briefly. There was even a San Francisco interlude which was always a little sketchy in Selina's mind and which had ended in a departure so hurried as to bewilder even Selina who had learned to accept sudden comings and abrupt goings without question. "Business," her father always said. "Little deal." She never knew until the day of his death how literally the word deal was applicable to his business transactions. Simeon Peake, travelling the country with his little daughter, was a gambler by profession, temperament, and natural talents. When in luck they lived royally, stopping at the best hotels, eating strange, succulent sea-viands, going to the play, driving in hired rigs (always with two horses. If Simeon Peake had not enough money for a two-horse equipage he walked). When fortune hid her face they lived in boarding houses, ate boarding-house meals, wore the clothes bought when Fortune's breath was balmy. During all this time Selina attended schools, good, bad, private, public, with surprising regularity considering her nomadic existence. Deep-bosomed matrons, seeing this dark-eyed serious child seated alone in a hotel lobby or boarding-house parlour, would bend over her in solicitous questioning.

"Where is your mamma, little girl?"

"She is dead," Selina would reply, politely and composedly.

"Oh, my poor little dear!" Then, with a warm rush, "Don't you want to come and play with my little girl? She loves little girls to play with. H'm?" The "m" of the interrogation held hummingly, tenderly.

"No, thank you very much. I'm waiting for my father. He would be disappointed not to find me here."

These good ladies wasted their sympathy. Selina had a beautiful time. Except for three years, to recall which was to her like entering a sombre icy room on leaving a warm and glowing one, her life was free, interesting, varied. She made decisions usually devolving upon the adult mind. She selected clothes. She ruled her father. She read absorbedly books found in boarding-house parlours, in hotels, in such public libraries as the times afforded. She was alone for hours a day, daily. Frequently her father, fearful of loneliness for her, brought her an armful of books and she had an orgy, dipping and swooping about among them in a sort of gourmand's ecstasy of indecision. In this way, at fifteen, she knew the writings of Byron, Jane Austen, Dickens, Charlotte Bronte, Felicia Hemans. Not to speak of Mrs. E. D. E. N. Southworth, Bertha M. Clay, and that good fairy of the scullery, the *Fireside Companion,* in whose pages factory girls and dukes were brought together as inevitably as steak and onions. These last were, of course, the result of Selina's mode of living, and were loaned her by kind-hearted landladies, chambermaids, and waitresses all the way from California to New York.

Her three dark years—from nine to twelve—were spent with her two maiden aunts, the Misses Sarah and Abbie Peake, in the dim, prim Vermont Peake house from which her father, the black sheep, had run away when a boy. After her mother's death Simeon Peake had sent his little daughter back east in a fit of remorse and temporary helplessness on his part and a spurt of forgiveness and churchly charity on the part of his two sisters. The two women were incredibly drawn in the pattern of the New England spinster of fiction. Mitts, preserves, Bible, chilly best room, solemn and kittenless cat, order, little-girls-mustn't. They smelled of apples—of withered apples that have rotted at the core. Selina had once found such an apple in a corner of a disorderly schooldesk, had sniffed it, regarded its wrinkled, sapless pink cheek, and had bitten into it adventuresomely, only to spit out the mouthful in an explosive and unladylike spray. It had been all black and mouldy at its heart.

Something of this she must have conveyed, in her desperation, to her father in an uncensored letter. Without warning he had come for her, and at sight of him she had been guilty of the only fit of hysteria that marked her life, before or after the episode.

So, then, from twelve to nineteen she was happy. They had come to Chicago in 1885, when she was sixteen. There they remained. Selina attended Miss Fister's Select School for Young Ladies. When her father brought her there he had raised quite a flutter in the Fister breast—so soft-spoken was he, so gentle, so sad-appearing, so winning as to smile. In the investment business, he explained. Stocks and that kind of thing. A widower. Miss Fister said, yes, she understood.

Simeon Peake had had nothing of the look of the professional gambler of the day. The wide slouch hat, the flowing mustache, the glittering eye, the too-bright boots, the gay cravat, all were missing in Simeon Peake's makeup. True, he did sport a singularly clear white diamond pin in his shirt front; and his hat he wore just a little on one side. But then, these both were in the male mode and quite commonly seen. For the rest he seemed a mild and suave man, slim, a trifle diffident, speaking seldom and then with a New England drawl by which he had come honestly enough, Vermont Peake that he was.

Chicago was his meat. It was booming, prosperous. Jeff Hankins's red plush and mirrored gambling house, and Mike McDonald's, too, both on Clark Street, knew him daily. He played in good luck and bad, but he managed somehow to see to it that there was always the money to pay for the Fister schooling. His was the ideal poker face—bland, emotionless, immobile. When he was flush they ate at the Palmer House, dining off chicken or quail and thick rich soup and the apple pie for which the hostelry was famous. Waiters hovered solicitously about Simeon Peake, though he rarely addressed them and never looked at them. Selina was happy. She knew only such young people—girls—as she met at Miss Fister's school. Of men, other than her father, she knew as little as a nun—less. For those cloistered creatures must, if only in the conning of their Bible, learn much of the moods and passions that sway the male. The Songs of Solomon alone are a glorious sex education. But the Bible was not included in Selina's haphazard reading, and the Gideonite was not then a force in the hotel world.

Her chum was Julie Hempel, daughter of August Hempel, the Clark Street butcher. You probably now own some Hempel stock, if you're lucky; and eat Hempel bacon and Hempel hams cured in the hickory, for in Chicago the distance from butcher of 1885 to packer of 1890 was only a five-year leap.

Being so much alone developed in her a gift for the make-believe. In a comfortable, well-dressed way she was a sort of mixture of Dick Swiveller's Marchioness and Sarah Crewe. Even in her childhood she extracted from life the double enjoyment that comes usually only to the creative mind. "Now I'm doing this. Now I'm doing that," she told herself while she was doing it. Looking on while she participated. Perhaps her theatre-going had something to do with this. At an age when most little girls were not only unheard but practically unseen, she occupied a grown-up seat at the play, her rapt face, with its dark serious eyes, glowing in a sort of luminous pallor as she sat proudly next her father. Simeon Peake had the gambler's love of the theatre, himself possessing the dramatic quality necessary to the successful following of his profession.

In this way Selina, half-hidden in the depths of an orchestra seat, wriggled in ecstatic anticipation when the curtain ascended on the grotesque rows of Haverly's minstrels. She wept (as did Simeon) over the agonies of The Two Orphans when Kitty Blanchard and McKee Rankin came to Chicago with the Union Square Stock Company. She witnessed that startling innovation, a Jewish play, called Samuel of Posen. She was Fanny Davenport in Pique. Simeon even took her to a performance of that shocking and delightful form of new entertainment, the Extravanganza. She thought the plump creature in tights and spangles, descending the long stairway, the most beautiful being she had ever seen.

"The thing I like about plays and books is that anything can happen. Anything! You never know," Selina said, after one of these evenings.

"No different from life," Simeon Peake assured her. "You've no idea the things that happen to you if you just relax and take them as they come."

Curiously enough, Simeon Peake said this, not through ignorance, but deliberately and with reason. In his way and day he was a very modern father. "I want you to see all kinds," he would say to her. "I want you to realize that this whole thing is just a grand adventure. A fine show. The trick is to play in it and look at it at the same time."

"What whole thing?"

"Living. All mixed up. The more kinds of people you see, and the more things you do, and the more things that happen to you, the richer you are. Even if they're not pleasant things. That's living. Remember, no matter what happens, good or bad, it's just so much"—he used the gambler's term, unconsciously—"just so much velvet."

But Selina, somehow, understood. "You mean that anything's better than being Aunt Sarah and Aunt Abbie."

"Well—yes. There are only two kinds of people in the world that really count. One kind's wheat and the other kind's emeralds."

"Fanny Davenport's an emerald," said Selina, quickly, and rather surprised to find herself saying it.

"Yes. That's it."

"And—and Julie Hempel's father—he's wheat."

"By golly, Sele!" shouted Simeon Peake. "You're a shrewd little tyke!"

It was after reading "Pride and Prejudice" that she decided to be the Jane Austen of her time. She became very mysterious and enjoyed a brief period of unpopularity at Miss Fister's owing to her veiled allusions to her "work"; and an annoying way of smiling to herself and tapping a ruminative toe as though engaged in visions far too exquisite for the common eye. Her chum Julie Hempel, properly enough, became enraged at this and gave Selina to understand that she must make her choice between revealing her secret or being cast out of the Hempel heart. Selina swore her to secrecy.

"Very well, then. Now I'll tell you. I'm going to be a novelist." Julie was palpably disappointed, though she said, "Selina!" as though properly impressed, but followed it up with: "Still, I don't see why you had to be so mysterious about it."

"You just don't understand, Julie. Writers have to study life at first hand. And if people know you're studying them they don't act natural. Now, that day you were telling me about the young man in your father's shop who looked at you and said——"

"Selina Peake, if you dare to put that in your book I'll never speak——"

"All right. I won't. But that's what I mean. You see!"

Julie Hempel and Selina Peake, both finished products of Miss Fister's school, were of an age—nineteen. Selina, on this September day had been spending the afternoon with Julie, and now, adjusting her hat preparatory to leaving, she clapped her hands over her ears to shut out the sounds of Julie's importunings that she stay to supper. Certainly the prospect of the usual Monday evening meal in Mrs. Tebbitt's boarding house (the Peake luck was momentarily low) did not present sufficient excuse for Selina's refusal. Indeed, the Hempel supper as sketched dish for dish by the urgent Julie brought little greedy groans from Selina.

"It's prairie chickens—three of them—that a farmer west of town brought Father. Mother fixes them with stuffing, and there's currant jell. Creamed onions and baked tomatoes. And for dessert, apple roll."

Selina snapped the elastic holding her high-crowned hat under her chignon of hair in the back. She uttered a final and quavering groan. "On Monday nights we have cold mutton and cabbage at Mrs. Tebbitt's. This is Monday."

"Well then, silly, why not stay!"

"Father comes home at six. If I'm not there he's disappointed."

Julie, plump, blonde, placid, forsook her soft white blandishments and tried steel against the steel of Selina's decision.

"He leaves you right after supper. And you're alone every night until twelve and after."

"I don't see what that has to do with it," Selina said, stiffly.

Julie's steel, being low-grade, melted at once and ran off her in rivulets. "Of course it hasn't, Selie dear. Only I thought you might leave him just this once."

"If I'm not there he's disappointed. And that terrible Mrs. Tebbitt makes eyes at him. He hates it there."

"Then I don't see why you stay. I never could see. You've been there four months now, and I think it's horrid and stuffy; and oilcloth on the stairs."

"Father has had some temporary business setbacks."

Selina's costume testified to that. True, it was modish, and bustled, and basqued, and flounced; and her high-crowned short-rimmed hat, with its trimming of feathers and flowers and ribbons had come from New York. But both were of last spring's purchasing, and this was September.

In the course of the afternoon they had been looking over the pages of Godey's *Ladies' Book* for that month. The disparity between Selina's costume and the creations pictured there was much as the difference between the Tebbitt meal and that outlined by Julie. Now Julie, fond though defeated, kissed her friend good-bye.

Selina walked quickly the short distance from the Hempel house to Tebbitt's, on Dearborn Avenue. Up in her second-floor room she took off her hat and called to her father, but he had not yet come in. She was glad of that. She had been fearful of being late. She regarded her hat now with some distaste, decided to rip off the faded spring roses, did rip a stitch or two, only to discover that the hat material was more faded than the roses, and that the uncovered surface showed up a dark splotch like a wall-spot when a picture, long hung, is removed. So she got a needle and prepared to tack the offending rose in its accustomed place.

Perched on the arm of a chair near the window, taking quick deft stitches, she heard a sound. She had never heard that sound before—that peculiar sound—the slow, ominous tread of men laden with a heavy inert burden; bearing with infinite care that which was well beyond hurting. Selina had never heard that sound before, and yet, hearing it, she recognized it by one of those pangs, centuries old, called woman's instinct. Thud—shuffle—thud—shuffle—up the narrow stairway, along the passage. She stood up, the needle poised in her hand. The hat fell to the floor. Her eyes were wide, fixed. Her lips slightly parted. The listening look. She knew.

She knew even before she heard the hoarse man's voice saying, "Lift 'er up there a little on the corner, now. Easy—e-e-easy." And Mrs. Tebbitt's high shrill clamour: "You can't bring it in there! You hadn't ought to bring it in here like this!"

Selina's suspended breath came back. She was panting now. She had flung open the door. A flat still burden partially covered with an overcoat carelessly flung over the face. The feet, in their square-toed boots, wobbled listlessly. Selina noticed how shiny the boots were. He was always very finicking about such things.

Simeon Peake had been shot in Jeff Hankins's place at five in the afternoon. The irony of it was that the bullet had not been intended for him at all. Its derelict course had been due to feminine aim. Sped by one of those over-dramatic ladies who, armed with horsewhip or pistol in tardy defence of their honour, spangled Chicago's dull '80s with their doings, it had been meant for a well-known newspaper publisher usually mentioned (in papers other than his own) as a bon vivant. The lady's leaden remonstrance was to have been proof of the fact that he had been more vivacious than bon.

It was, perhaps, because of this that the matter was pretty well hushed up. The publisher's paper—which was Chicago's foremost—scarcely mentioned the incident and purposely misspelled the name.

The lady, thinking her task accomplished, had taken truer aim with her second bullet, and had saved herself the trouble of trial by human jury.

Simeon Peake left his daughter Selina a legacy of two fine clear blue-white diamonds (he had had the gambler's love of them) and the sum of four hundred and ninety-seven dollars in cash. Just how he had managed to have a sum like this put by was a mystery. The envelope containing it had evidently once held a larger sum. It had been sealed, and then slit. On the outside was written, in Simeon Peake's fine, almost feminine hand: "For my little daughter Selina Peake in case anything should happen to me." It bore a date seven years old. What the original sum had been no one ever knew. That any sum remained was evidence of the almost heroic self-control practised by one to whom money—ready money in any sum at all—meant only fuel to feed the flames of his gaming fever.

To Selina fell the choice of earning her own living or of returning to the Vermont village and becoming a withered and sapless dried apple, with black fuzz and mould at her heart, like her aunts, the Misses Sarah and Abbie Peake. She did not hesitate.

"But what kind of work!" Julie Hempel demanded. "What kind of work can you do?" Women—that is, the Selina Peakes—did not work.

"I—well, I can teach."

"Teach what?"

"The things I learned at Miss Fister's."

Julie's expression weighed and discredited Miss Fister. "Who to?" Which certainly justified her expression.

"To children. People's children. Or in the public schools."

"You have to do something fun—go to Normal, or teach in the country, don't you?—before you can teach in the public schools. They're mostly old. Twenty-five or even thirty—or more!" with nineteen's incapacity to imagine an age beyond thirty.

That Julie was taking the offensive in this conversation, and Selina the defensive, was indicative of the girl's numbed state. Selina did not then know the iron qualities her friend was displaying in being with her at all. Mrs. Hempel had quite properly forbidden Julie ever to see the dead dissolute gambler's daughter again. She had even sent a note to Miss Fister expressing her opinion of a school which would, by admitting such unselected ladies to its select circle, expose other pupils to contamination.

Selina rallied to Julie's onslaught. "Then I'll just teach a country school. I'm good at arithmetic. You know that." Julie should have known it, having had all her Fister sums solved by Selina. "Country schools are just arithmetic and grammar and geography."

"You! Teaching a country school!"

She looked at Selina.

She saw a misleadingly delicate face, the skull small and exquisitely formed. The cheek bones rather high—or perhaps they looked so because of the fact that the eyes, dark, soft, and luminous, were unusually deep-set in their sockets. The face, instead of narrowing to a soft curve at the chin, developed unexpected strength in the jaw line. That line, fine, steel-strong, sharp and clear, was of the stuff of which pioneer women are made. Julie, inexperienced in the art of reading the human physiognomy, did not decipher the meaning of it. Selina's hair was thick, long, and fine, so that she piled it easily in the loops, coils, and knots that fashion demanded. Her nose, slightly pinched at the nostrils, was exquisite. When she laughed it had the trick of wrinkling just a little across the narrow bridge; very engaging, and mischievous. She was thought a rather plain little thing, which she wasn't. But the eyes were what you marked and remembered. People to whom she was speaking had a way of looking into them deeply. Selina was often embarrassed to discover that they were not hearing what she had to say. Perhaps it was this velvety softness of the eyes that caused one to overlook the firmness of the lower face. When the next ten years had done their worst to her, and Julie had suddenly come upon her stepping agilely out of a truck gardener's wagon on Prairie Avenue, a tanned, weather-beaten, toil-worn woman, her abundant hair skewered into a knob and held by a long gray hairpin, her full calico skirt grimed with the mud of the wagon wheel, a pair of men's old side-boots on her slim feet, a grotesquely battered old felt hat (her husband's) on her head, her arms full of ears of sweet corn, and carrots, and radishes, and bunches of beets; a woman with bad teeth, flat breasts, a sagging pocket in her capacious skirt—even then Julie, staring, had known her by her eyes. And she had run to her in her silk suit and her fine silk shirtwaist and her hat with the plume and had cried, "Oh, Selina! My dear! My dear!"—with a sob of horror and pity—"My dear." And had taken Selina, carrots, beets, corn, and radishes, in her arms. The vegetables lay scattered all about them on the sidewalk in front of Julie Hempel Arnold's great stone house on Prairie Avenue. But strangely enough it had been Selina who had done the comforting, patting Julie's silken shoulder and saying, over and over, "There, there! It's all right, Julie. It's all right. Don't cry. What's there to cry for! Sh! . . . It's all right."

2

Selina had thought herself lucky to get the Dutch school at High Prairie, ten miles outside Chicago. Thirty dollars a month! She was to board at the house of Klaas Pool, the truck farmer. It was August Hempel who had brought it all about; or Julie, urging him. Now, at forty-five, August Hempel, the Clark Street butcher, knew every farmer and stockman for miles around, and hundreds besides scattered throughout Cook County and the State of Illinois.

To get the Dutch school for Selina Peake was a simple enough matter for him. The High Prairie district school teacher had always, heretofore, been a man. A more advantageous position presenting itself, this year's prospective teacher had withdrawn before the school term had begun. This was in September. High Prairie school did not open until the first week in November. In that region of truck farms every boy and girl over six was busy in the fields throughout the early autumn. Two years of this, and Selina would be qualified for a city grade. August Hempel indicated that he could arrange that, too, when the time came. Selina thought this shrewd red-faced butcher a wonderful man, indeed. Which he was.

At forty-seven, single-handed, he was to establish the famous Hempel Packing Company. At fifty he was the power in the yards, and there were Hempel branches in Kansas City, Omaha, Denver. At sixty you saw the name of Hempel plastered over packing sheds, factories, and canning plants all the way from Honolulu to Portland. You read:

Don't Say Ham: Say Hempel's.

Hempel products ranged incredibly from pork to pineapple; from grease to grape-juice. An indictment meant no more to Hempel, the packer, than an injunction for speeding to you. Something of his character may be gleaned from the fact that farmers who had known the butcher at forty still addressed this millionaire, at sixty, as Aug. At sixty-five he took up golf and beat his son-in-law, Michael Arnold, at it. A magnificent old pirate, sailing the perilous commercial seas of the American '90s before commissions, investigations, and inquisitive senate insisted on applying whitewash to the black flag of trade.

Selina went about her preparations in a singularly clear-headed fashion, considering her youth and inexperience. She sold one of the blue-white diamonds, and kept one. She placed her inheritance of four hundred and ninety-seven dollars, complete, in the bank. She bought stout sensible boots, two dresses, one a brown lady's-cloth which she made herself, finished with white collars and cuffs, very neat (the cuffs to be protected by black sateen sleevelets, of course, while teaching); and a wine-red cashmere (mad, but she couldn't resist it) for best.

She eagerly learned what she could of this region once known as New Holland. Its people were all truck gardeners, and as Dutch as the Netherlands from which they or their fathers had come. She heard stories of wooden shoes worn in the wet prairie fields; of a red-faced plodding Cornelius Van der Bilt living in placid ignorance of the existence of his distinguished New York patronymic connection; of sturdy, phlegmatic, industrious farmers in squat, many-windowed houses patterned after the north Holland houses of their European memories. Many of them had come from the town of Schoorl, or near it. Others from the lowlands outside Amsterdam. Selina pictured it another Sleepy Hollow, a replica of the quaint settlement in Washington Irving's delightful tale. The deserting schoolmaster had been a second Ichabod Crane, naturally; the farmer at whose house she was to live a modern Mynheer Van Tassel, pipe, chuckle, and all. She and Julie Hempel read the tale over together on an afternoon when Julie managed to evade the maternal edict. Selina, picturing mellow golden corn fields; crusty crullers, crumbling oly-koeks, toothsome wild ducks, sides of smoked beef, pumpkin pies; country dances, apple-cheeked farmer girls, felt sorry for poor Julie staying on in the dull gray commonplaceness of Chicago.

The last week in October found her on the way to High Prairie, seated beside Klaas Pool in the two-horse wagon with which he brought his garden stuff to the Chicago market. She sat perched next him on the high seat like a saucy wren beside a ruminant Holstein. So they jolted up the long Halsted road through the late October sunset. The prairie land just outside Chicago had not then been made a terrifying and epic thing of slag-heaps, smoke-stacks, and blast furnaces like a Pennell drawing. To-day it stretched away and away in the last rays of the late autumn sunlight over which the lake mist was beginning to creep like chiffon covering gold. Mile after mile of cabbage fields, jade-green against the earth. Mile after mile of red cabbage, a rich plummy Burgundy veined with black. Between these, heaps of corn were piled-up sunshine. Against the horizon an occasional patch of woods showed the last russet and bronze of oak and maple. These things Selina saw with her beauty-loving eye, and she clasped her hands in their black cotton gloves.

"Oh, Mr. Pool!" she cried. "Mr. Pool! How beautiful it is here!"

Klaas Pool, driving his team of horses down the muddy Halsted road, was looking straight ahead, his eyes fastened seemingly on an invisible spot between the off-horse's ears. His was not the kind of brain that acts quickly, nor was his body's mechanism the sort that quickly responds to that brain's message. His eyes were china-blue in a round red face that was covered with a stubble of stiff golden hairs. His round moon of a head was set low and solidly between his great shoulders, so that as he began to turn it now, slowly, you marvelled at the process and waited fearfully to hear a creak. He was turning his head toward Selina, but keeping his gaze on the spot between his horse's ears. Evidently the head and the eyes revolved by quite distinct processes. Now he faced Selina almost directly. Then he brought his eyes around, slowly, until they focussed on her cameo-like face all alight now with her enjoyment of the scene around her; with a certain elation at this new venture into which she was entering; and with excitement such as she used to feel when the curtain rose with tantalizing deliberateness on the first act of a play which she was seeing with her father. She was well bundled up against the sharp October air in her cloak and muffler, with a shawl tucked about her knees and waist. The usual creamy pallor of her fine clear skin showed an unwonted pink, and her eyes were wide, dark, and bright. Beside this sparkling delicate girl's face Klaas Pool's heavy features seemed carved from the stuff of another clay and race. His pale blue eyes showed incomprehension.

"Beautiful!" he echoed, in puzzled interrogation. "What is beautiful?"

Selina's slim arms flashed out from the swathings of cloak, shawl, and muffler and were flung wide in a gesture that embraced the landscape on which the late afternoon sun was casting a glow peculiar to that lake region, all rose and golden and mist-shimmering.

"This! The—the cabbages."

A slow-dawning film of fun crept over the blue of Klaas Pool's stare. This film spread almost imperceptibly so that it fluted his broad nostrils, met and widened his full lips, reached and agitated his massive shoulders, tickled the round belly, so that all Klaas Pool, from his eyes to his waist, was rippling and shaking with slow, solemn, heavy Dutch mirth.

"Cabbages is beautiful!" his round pop eyes staring at her in a fixity of glee. "Cabbages is beautiful!" His silent laughter now rose and became audible in a rich throaty chortle. It was plain that laughter, with Klaas Pool, was not a thing to be lightly dismissed, once raised. "Cabbages——" he choked a little, and spluttered, overcome. Now he began to shift his gaze back to his horses and the road, by the same process of turning his head first and then his eyes, so that to

Selina the mirthful tail of his right eye and his round cheek with the golden fuzz on it gave him an incredibly roguish brownie look.

Selina laughed, too, even while she protested his laughter. "But they are!" she insisted. "They *are* beautiful. Like jade and Burgundy. No, like—uh—like—what's that in—like chrysoprase and porphyry. All those fields of cabbages and the corn and the beet-tops together look like Persian patches."

Which was, certainly, no way for a new school teacher to talk to a Holland truck gardener driving his team along the dirt road on his way to High Prairie. But then, Selina, remember, had read Byron at seventeen.

Klaas Pool knew nothing of chrysoprase and porphyry. Nor of Byron. Nor, for that matter, of jade and Burgundy. But he did know cabbages, both green and red. He knew cabbage from seed to sauerkraut; he knew and grew varieties from the sturdy Flat Dutch to the early Wakefield. But that they were beautiful; that they looked like jewels; that they lay like Persian patches, had never entered his head, and rightly. What has the head of a cabbage, or, for that matter, of a robust, soil-stained, toiling Dutch truck farmer to do with nonsense like chrysoprase, with jade, with Burgundy, with Persian patterns!

The horses clopped down the heavy country road. Now and again the bulk beside Selina was agitated silently, as before. And from between the golden fuzz of stubble beard she would hear, "Cabbages! Cabbages is——" But she did not feel offended. She could not have been offended at anything to-day. For in spite of her recent tragedy, her nineteen years, her loneliness, the terrifying thought of this new home to which she was going, among strangers, she was conscious of a warm little thrill of elation, of excitement—of adventure! That was it. "The whole thing's just a grand adventure," Simeon Peake had said. Selina gave a little bounce of anticipation. She was doing a revolutionary and daring thing; a thing that the Vermont and now, fortunately, inaccessible Peakes would have regarded with horror. For equipment she had youth, curiosity, a steel-strong frame; one brown lady's-cloth, one wine-red cashmere; four hundred and ninety-seven dollars; and a gay, adventuresome spirit that was never to die, though it led her into curious places and she often found, at the end, only a trackless waste from which she had to retrace her steps, painfully. But always, to her, red and green cabbages were to be jade and Burgundy, chrysoprase and porphyry. Life has no weapons against a woman like that.

So now, as they bumped and jolted along the road Selina thought herself lucky, though she was a little terrified. She turned her gaze from the flat prairie land to the silent figure beside her. Hers was a lively, volatile nature, and his uncommunicativeness made her vaguely uncomfortable. Yet there was nothing glum about his face. Upon it there even lingered, in the corners of his eyes and about his mouth, faint shadows of merriment.

Klaas Pool was a school director. She was to live at his house. Perhaps she should not have said that about the cabbages. So now she drew herself up primly and tried to appear the school teacher, and succeeded in looking as severe as a white pansy.

"Ahem!" (or nearly that). "You have three children, haven't you, Mr. Pool? They'll all be my pupils?"

Klaas Pool ruminated on this. He concentrated so that a slight frown marred the serenity of his brow. In this double question of hers, an attempt to give the conversation a dignified turn, she had apparently created some difficulty for her host. He was trying to shake his head two ways at the same time. This gave it a rotary motion. Selina saw, with amazement, that he was attempting to nod negation and confirmation at once.

"You mean you haven't—or they're not?—or——?"

"I have got three children. All will not be your pupils." There was something final, unshakable in his delivery of this.

"Dear me! Why not? Which ones won't?"

This fusillade proved fatal. It served permanently to check the slight trickle of conversation which had begun to issue from his lips. They jogged on for perhaps a matter of three miles, in silence. Selina told herself then, sternly, that she must not laugh. Having told herself this, sternly, she began to laugh because she could not help it; a gay little sound that flew out like the whir of a bird's wing on the crisp autumnnal sunset air. And suddenly this light sound was joined by a slow rumbling that swelled and bubbled a good deal in the manner of the rich glubby sounds that issue from a kettle that has been simmering for a long time. So they laughed together, these two; the rather scared young thing who was trying to be prim, and the dull, unimaginative truck farmer because this alert, great-eyed, slim white creature perched birdlike on the wagon seat beside him had tickled his slow humour-sense.

Selina felt suddenly friendly and happy. "Do tell me which ones will and which won't."

"Geertje goes to school. Jozina goes to school. Roelf works by the farm."

"How old is Roelf?" She was being school teacherly again.

"Roelf is twelve."

"Twelve! And no longer at school! But why not!"

"Roelf he works by the farm."

"Doesn't Roelf like school?"

"But sure."

"Don't you think he ought to go to school?"

"But sure."

Having begun, she could not go back. "Doesn't your wife want Roelf to go to school any more?"

"Maartje? But sure."

She gathered herself together; hurled herself behind the next question. "Then why *doesn't* he go to school, for pity's sake!"

Klaas Pool's pale blue eyes were fixed on the spot between the horse's ears. His face was serene, placid, patient.

"Roelf he works by the farm."

Selina subsided, beaten.

She wondered about Roelf. Would he be a furtive, slinking boy, like Smike? Geertje and Jozina. Geertje—Gertrude, of course. Jozina? Josephine. Maartje?—m-m-m-m—Martha, probably. At any rate, it was going to be interesting. It was going to be wonderful! Suppose she had gone to Vermont and become a dried apple!

Dusk was coming on. The lake mist came drifting across the prairie and hung, a pearly haze, over the frost-nipped stubble and the leafless trees. It caught the last light in the sky, and held it, giving to fields, trees, black earth, to the man seated stolidly beside the girl, and to the face of the girl herself an opalescent glow very wonderful to see. Selina, seeing it, opened her lips to exclaim again; and then, remembering, closed them. She had learned her first lesson in High Prairie.

3

The Klaas Pools lived in a typical High Prairie house. They had passed a score like it in the dusk. These sturdy Holland-Americans had built here in Illinois after the pattern of the squat houses that dot the lowlands about Amsterdam, Haarlem, and Rotterdam. A row of pollards stood stiffly by the roadside. As they turned in at the yard Selina's eye was caught by the glitter of glass. The house was many-windowed, the panes the size of pocket-handkerchiefs. Even in the dusk Selina thought she had never seen windows sparkle so. She did not then know that spotless window-panes were a mark of social standing in High Prairie. Yard and dwelling had a geometrical neatness like that of a toy house in a set of playthings. The effect was marred by a clothes-line hung with a dado of miscellaneous wash—a pair of faded overalls, a shirt, socks, a man's drawers carefully patched and now bellying grotesquely in the breeze like a comic tramp turned bacchanal. Selina was to know this frieze of nether garments as a daily decoration in the farm-wife's yard.

Peering down over the high wheel she waited for Klaas Pool to assist her in alighting. He seemed to have no such thought. Having jumped down, he was throwing empty crates and boxes out of the back of the wagon. So Selina, gathering her shawls and cloak about her, clambered down the side of the wheel and stood looking about her in the dim light, a very small figure in a very large world. Klaas had opened the barn door. Now he returned and slapped one of the horses smartly on the flank. The team trotted obediently off to the barn. He picked up her little hide-bound trunk. She took her satchel. The yard was quite dark now. As Klaas Pool opened the kitchen door the red mouth that was the open draught in the kitchen stove grinned a toothy welcome at them.

A woman stood over the stove, a fork in her hand. The kitchen was clean, but disorderly, with the disorder that comes of pressure of work. There was a not unpleasant smell of cooking. Selina sniffed it hungrily. The woman turned to face them. Selina stared.

This, she thought, must be some other—an old woman—his mother perhaps. But: "Maartje, here is school teacher," said Klaas Pool. Selina put out her hand to meet the other woman's hand, rough, hard, calloused. Her own, touching it, was like satin against a pine board. Maartje smiled, and you saw her broken discoloured teeth. She pushed back the sparse hair from her high forehead, fumbled a little, shyly, at the collar of her clean blue calico dress.

"Pleased to meet you," Maartje said, primly. "Make you welcome." Then, as Pool stamped out to the yard, slamming the door behind him, "Pool he could have come with you by the front way, too. Lay off your things." Selina began to remove the wrappings that swathed her—the muffler, the shawl, the cloak. Now she stood, a slim, incongruously elegant little figure in that kitchen. The brown lady's-cloth was very tight and basqued above, very flounced and bustled below. "My, how you are young!" cried Maartje. She moved nearer, as if impelled, and fingered the stuff of Selina's gown. And as she did this Selina suddenly saw that she, too, was young. The bad teeth, the thin hair, the careless dress, the littered kitchen, the harassed frown— above all these, standing out clearly, appeared the look of a girl.

"Why, I do believe she's not more than twenty-eight!" Selina said to herself in a kind of panic. "I do believe she's not more than twenty-eight."

She had been aware of the two pigtailed heads appearing and vanishing in the doorway of the next room. Now Maartje was shooting her into this room. Evidently her hostess was distressed because the school teacher's formal entrance had not been made by way of parlour instead of kitchen. She followed Maartje Pool into the front room. Behind the stove, tittering, were two yellow-haired little girls. Geertje and Jozina, of course. Selina went over to them, smiling. "Which is Geertje?" she asked. "And which Jozina?" But at this the titters became squeals. They retired behind the round black bulwark of the wood-burner, overcome. There was no fire in this shining ebon structure, though the evening was sharp. Above the stove a length of pipe, glittering with polish as was the stove itself, crossed the width of the room and vanished through a queer little perforated grating in the ceiling. Selina's quick glance encompassed the room. In the window were a few hardy plants in pots on a green-painted wooden rack. There were geraniums, blossomless; a cactus with its thick slabs of petals like slices of gangrenous ham set up for beauty in a parlour; a plant called Jacob's ladder, on a spindling trellis. The bony scaffolding of the green-painted wooden stand was turned toward the room. The flowers blindly faced the dark square of the window. There was a sofa with a wrinkled calico cover; three rocking chairs; some stark crayons of incredibly hard-featured Dutch ancients on the wall. It was all neat, stiff, unlovely. But Selina had known too many years of boarding-house ugliness to be offended at this.

Maartje had lighted a small glass-bowled lamp. The chimney of this sparkled as had the window panes. A steep, uncarpeted stairway, enclosed, led off the sitting room. Up this Maartje Pool, talking, led the way to Selina's bedroom. Selina was to learn that the farm woman, often inarticulate through lack of companionship, becomes a torrent of talk when opportunity presents itself. They made quite a little procession. First, Mrs. Pool with the lamp; then Selina with the satchel; then, tap-tap, tap-tap, Jozina and Geertje, their heavy hob-nailed shoes creating a great clatter on the wooden stairs, though they were tip-toeing in an effort to make themselves unheard by their mother. There evidently had been an arrangement on the subject of their invisibility. The procession moved to the accompaniment of Maartje's, "Now you stay downstairs didn't I tell you!" There was in her tone a warning; a menace. The two pigtails would hang back a moment, only to come tap-tapping on again, their saucer eyes at once fearful and mischievous.

A narrow, dim, close-smelling hallway, uncarpeted. At the end of it a door opening into the room that was to be Selina's. As its chill struck her to the marrow three objects caught her eye. The bed, a huge and not unhandsome walnut mausoleum, reared its sombre height almost to the room's top. Indeed, its apex of grapes did actually seem to achieve a meeting with the whitewashed ceiling. The mattress of straw and cornhusks was unworthy of this edifice, but over it Mrs. Pool had mercifully placed a feather bed, stitched and quilted, so that Selina lay soft and warm through the winter. Along one wall stood a low chest so richly brown as to appear black. The front panel of this was curiously carved. Selina stooped before it and for the second time that day said: "How beautiful!" then looked quickly round at Maartje Pool as though fearful of finding her laughing as Klaas Pool had laughed. But Mrs. Pool's face reflected the glow in her own. She came over to Selina and stooped with her over the chest, holding the lamp so that its yellow flame lighted up the scrolls and tendrils of the carved surface. With one discoloured forefinger she traced the bold flourishes on the panel. "See? How it makes out letters?"

Selina peered closer. "Why, sure enough! This first one's an S!"

Maartje was kneeling before the chest now. "Sure an S. For Sophia. It is a Holland bride's chest. And here is K. And here is big D. It makes Sophia Kroon DeVries. It is anyways two hundred years. My mother she gave it to me when I was married, and her mother she gave it to her when she was married, and her mother gave it to her when she was married, and her——"

"I should think so!" exclaimed Selina, rather meaninglessly; but stemming the torrent. "What's in it? Anything? There ought to be bride's clothes in it, yellow with age."

"It is!" cried Maartje Pool and gave a little bounce that imperilled the lamp.

"No!" The two on their knees sat smiling at each other, wide-eyed, like schoolgirls. The pigtails, emboldened, had come tap-tapping nearer and were peering over the shoulders of the women before the chest.

"Here—wait." Maartje Pool thrust the lamp into Selina's hand, raised the lid of the chest, dived expertly into its depths amidst a great rustling of old newspapers and emerged red-faced with a Dutch basque and voluminous skirt of silk; an age-yellow cap whose wings, stiff with embroidery, stood out grandly on either side; a pair of wooden shoes, stained terra-cotta like the sails of the Vollendam fishing boats, and carved from toe to heel in a delicate and intricate pattern. A bridal gown, a bridal cap, bridal shoes.

"Well!" said Selina, with the feeling of a little girl in a rich attic on a rainy day. She clasped her hands. "May I dress up in it some time?"

Maartje Pool, folding the garments hastily, looked shocked and horrified. "Never must anybody dress up in a bride's dress only to get married. It brings bad luck." Then, as Selina stroked the stiff silken folds of the skirt with a slim and caressing forefinger: "So you get married to a High Prairie Dutchman I let you wear it." At this absurdity they both laughed again. Selina thought that this school-teaching venture was starting out very well. She would have *such* things to tell her father—then she remembered. She shivered a little as she stood up now. She raised her arms to take off her hat, feeling suddenly tired, cold, strange in this house with this farm woman, and the two staring little girls, and the great red-faced man. There surged over her a great wave of longing for her father—for the gay little dinners, for the theatre treats, for his humorous philosophical drawl, for the Chicago streets, and the ugly Chicago houses; for Julie, for Miss Fister's school; for anything and any one that was accustomed, known, and therefore dear. Even Aunt Abbie and Aunt Sarah had a not unlovely aspect, viewed from this chill farmhouse bedroom that had suddenly become her home. She had a horrible premonition that she was going to cry, began to blink very fast, turned a little blindly in the dim light and caught sight of the room's third arresting object. A blue-black cylinder of tin sheeting, like a stove and yet unlike. It was polished like the length of pipe in the sitting room below. Indeed, it was evidently a giant flower of this stem.

"What's that?" demanded Selina, pointing.

Maartje Pool, depositing the lamp on the little wash-stand preparatory to leaving, smiled pridefully. "Drum."

"Drum?"

"For heat your room." Selina touched it. It was icy. "When there is fire," Mrs. Pool added, hastily. In her mind's eye Selina traced the tin tube below running along the ceiling in the peaceful and orderly path of a stove-pipe, thrusting its way through the cylindrical hole in the ceiling and here bursting suddenly into swollen and monstrous bloom like an unthinkable goitre on a black neck. Selina was to learn that its heating powers were mythical. Even when the stove in the sitting room was blaring away with a cheerful roar none of the glow communicated itself to the drum. It remained as coolly indifferent to the blasts breathed upon it as a girl hotly besieged by an unwelcome lover. This was to influence a number of Selina's habits, including nocturnal reading and matutinal bathing. Selina was a daily morning bather in a period which looked upon the daily bath as an eccentricity, or, at best, an affectation. It would be charming to be able to record that she continued the practice in the Pool household; but a morning bath in the arctic atmosphere of an Illinois prairie farmhouse would not have been eccentric merely, but mad, even if there had been an available kettle of hot water at 6:30 A.M., which there emphatically was not. Selina was grateful for an occasional steaming basin of water at night and a hurried piecemeal bath by the mythical heat of the drum.

"Maartje!" roared a voice from belowstairs. The voice of the hungry male. There was wafted up, too, a faint smell of scorching. Then came sounds of a bumping and thumping along the narrow stairway.

"Og heden!" cried Maartje, in a panic, her hands high in air. She was off, sweeping the two pigtails with her in her flight. There were sounds of scuffling on the stairway, and Maartje's voice calling something that sounded like hookendunk to Selina. But she decided that

that couldn't be. The bumping now sounded along the passage outside her room. Selina turned from her satchel to behold a gnome in the doorway. Below, she saw a pair of bow-legs; above, her own little hide-bound trunk; between, a broad face, a grizzled beard, a lacklustre eye in a weather-beaten countenance.

"Jakob Hoogendunk," the gnome announced, briefly, peering up at her from beneath the trunk balanced on his back.

Selina laughed delightedly. "Not really! Do come in. This is a good place, don't you think? Along the wall? Mr.—Mr. Hoogendunk?"

Jakob Hoogendunk grunted and plodded across the room, the trunk lurching perilously above his bow-legged stride. He set it down with a final thump, wiped his nose with the back of his hand—sign of a task completed—and surveyed the trunk largely, as if he had made it. "Thank you, Mr. Hoogendunk," said Selina, and put out her hand. "I'm Selina Peake. How"—she couldn't resist it—"how did you leave Rip?"

It was characteristic of her that in this grizzled hired man, twisted with rheumatism, reeking of mould and manure, she should see a direct descendant of those gnarled and bearded bowlers so mysteriously encountered by Rip Van Winkle on that fatal day in the Kaatskills. The name, too, appealed to her in its comic ugliness. So she laughed a soft little laugh; held out her hand. The man was not offended. He knew that people laughed when they were introduced. So he laughed, too, in a mixture of embarrassment and attempted ease, looking down at the small hand extended to him. He blinked at it curiously. He wiped his two hands down his thighs, hard; then shook his great grizzled head. "My hand is all muck. I ain't washed up yet," and lurched off, leaving Selina looking rather helplessly down at her own extended hand. His clatter on the wooden stairway sounded like cavalry on a frozen road.

Left alone in her room Selina unlocked her trunk and took from it two photographs—one of a mild-looking man with his hat a little on one side, the other of a woman who might have been a twenty-five-year-old Selina, minus the courageous jaw-line. Looking about for a fitting place on which to stand these leather-framed treasures she considered the top of the chill drum, humorously, then actually placed them there, for lack of better refuge, from which vantage point they regarded her with politely interested eyes. Perhaps Jakob Hoogendunk would put up a shelf for her. That would serve for her little stock of books and for the pictures as well. She was enjoying that little flush of exhilaration that comes to a woman, unpacking. There was about her trunk, even though closed but this very day, the element of surprise that gilds familiar objects when disclosed for the first time in unfamiliar surroundings. She took out her neat pile of warm woollen underwear, her stout shoes. She shook out the crushed folds of the wine-coloured cashmere. Now, if ever, she should have regretted its purchase. But she didn't. No one, she reflected, as she spread it rosily on the bed, possessing a wine-coloured cashmere could be altogether downcast.

The wine cashmere on the bed, the photographs on the drum, her clothes hanging comfortably on wall-hooks with a calico curtain on a cord protecting them, her stock of books on the closed trunk. Already the room wore the aspect of familiarity.

From belowstairs came the hiss of frying. Selina washed in the chill water of the basin, took down her hair and coiled it again before the swimmy little mirror over the wash-stand. She adjusted the stitched white bands of the severe collar and patted the cuffs of the brown lady's-cloth. The tight basque was fastened with buttons from throat to waist. Her fine long head rose above this trying base with such grace and dignity as to render the stiff garment beautiful. The skirt billowed and puffed out behind, and was drawn in folds across the front. It was a day of appalling bunchiness and equally appalling tightness in dress; of panniers, galloons, plastrons, reveres, bustles, and all manner of lumpy bedevilment. That Selina could appear in this disfiguring garment a creature still graceful, slim, and pliant was a sheer triumph of spirit over matter.

She blew out the light now and descended the steep wooden stairway to the unlighted parlour. The door between parlour and kitchen was closed. Selina sniffed sensitively. There was pork for supper. She was to learn that there always was pork for supper. As the winter wore on she developed a horror of this porcine fare, remembering to have read somewhere that one's diet was in time reflected in one's face; that gross eating made one gross looking. She would examine her features fearfully in the swimmy mirror—the lovely little white nose—was it coarsening? The deep-set dark eyes—were they squinting? The firm sweet lips—were they broadening? But the reflection in the glass reassured her.

She hesitated a moment there in the darkness. Then she opened the kitchen door. There swam out at her a haze of smoke, from which emerged round blue eyes, guttural talk, the smell of frying grease, of stable, of loam, and of woollen wash freshly brought in from the line. With an inrush of cold air that sent the blue haze into swirls the outer kitchen door opened. A boy, his arm piled high with stove-wood, entered; a dark, handsome sullen boy who stared at Selina over the armload of wood. Selina stared back at him. There sprang to life between the boy of twelve and the woman of nineteen an electric current of feeling.

"Roelf," thought Selina; and even took a step toward him, inexplicably drawn.

"Hurry then with that wood there!" fretted Maartje at the stove. The boy flung the armful into the box, brushed his sleeve and coat-front mechanically, still looking at Selina. A slave to the insatiable maw of the wood-box.

Klaas Pool, already at table, thumped with his knife. "Sit down! Sit down, teacher." Selina hesitated, looked at Maartje. Maartje was holding a frying pan aloft in one hand while with the other she thrust and poked a fresh stick of wood into the open-lidded stove. The two pigtails seated themselves at the table, set with its red-checked cloth and bone-handled cutlery. Jakob Hoogendunk, who had been splashing, snorting, and puffing porpoise-fashion in a corner over a hand-basin whose cubic contents were out of all proportion to the sounds extracted therefrom, now seated himself. Roelf flung his cap on a wall-hook and sat down. Only Selina and Maartje remained standing. "Sit down! Sit down!" Klaas Pool said again, jovially. "Well, how is cabbages?" He chuckled and winked. Jakob Hoogendunk snorted. A duet of titters from the pigtails. Maartje at the stove smiled; but a trifle grimly, one might have thought, watching her. Evidently Klaas had not hugged his joke in secret. Only the boy Roelf remained unsmiling. Even Selina, feeling the red mounting her cheeks, smiled a little, nervously, and sat down with some suddenness.

Maartje Pool now thumped down on the table a great bowl of potatoes fried in grease; a platter of ham. There was bread cut in chunks. The coffee was rye, roasted in the oven, ground, and taken without sugar or cream. Of this food there was plenty. It made Mrs. Tebbitt's Monday night meal seem ambrosial. Selina's visions of chickens, oly-koeks, wild ducks, crusty crullers, and pumpkin pies vanished, never to return. She had been very hungry, but now, as she talked, nodded, smiled, she cut her food into infinitesimal bites, did not chew them so very well, and despised herself for being dainty. A slight, distinctive little figure there in the yellow lamplight, eating this coarse fare bravely, turning her soft dark glance on the woman who was making countless trips from stove to table, from table to stove; on the sullen handsome boy with his purplish chapped hands and his sombre eyes; on the two round-eyed, red-cheeked little girls; on the great red-faced full-lipped man eating his supper noisily and with relish; on Jakob Hoogendunk, grazing greedily. . . .

"Well," she thought, "it's going to be different enough, that's certain. . . . This is a vegetable farm, and they don't eat vegetables. I wonder why. . . . What a pity that she lets herself look like that, just because she's a farm woman. Her hair screwed into that knob, her skin rough and neglected. That hideous dress. Shapeless. She's not bad looking, either. A red spot on either cheek, now; and her eyes so blue. A little like those women in the Dutch pictures Father took me to see in—where?—where?—New York, years ago?—yes. A woman in a kitchen, a dark sort of room with pots of brass on a shelf; a high mullioned window. But that woman's face was placid. This one's strained. Why need she look like that, frowsy, harried, old! . . . The boy is, somehow, foreign looking—Italian. Queer. . . . They talk a good deal like some German neighbours we had in Milwaukee. They twist sentences. Literal translations from the Dutch, I suppose. . . ."

Jakob Hoogendunk was talking. Supper over, the men sat relaxed, pipe in mouth. Maartje was clearing the supper things, with Geertje and Jozina making a great pretense at helping. If they giggled like that in school, Selina thought, she would, in time, go mad, and knock their pigtailed heads together.

"You got to have rich bottom land," Hoogendunk was saying, "else you get little tough stringy stuff. I seen it in market Friday, laying. Stick to vegetables that is vegetables and not new-fangled stuff. Celery! What is celery! It ain't rightly a vegetable, and it ain't a yerb. Look how Voorhees he used as much as one hundred fifty pounds nitrate of sody, let alone regular fertilizer, and what comes from it? Little stringy stuff. You got to have rich bottom land."

Selina was interested. She had always thought that vegetables grew. You put them in the ground—seeds or something—and pretty soon things came popping up—potatoes, cabbages, onions, carrots, beets. But what was this thing called nitrate of soda? It must have had something to do with the creamed cabbage at Mrs. Tebbitt's. And she had never known it. And what was regular fertilizer? She leaned forward.

"What's a regular fertilizer?"

Klaas Pool and Jakob Hoogendunk looked at her. She looked at them, her fine intelligent eyes alight with interest. Pool then tipped back his chair, lifted a stove-lid, spat into the embers, replaced the lid and rolled his slow gaze in the direction of Jakob Hoogendunk. Hoogendunk rolled his slow gaze in the direction of Klaas Pool. Then both turned to look at this audacious female who thus interrupted men's conversation.

Pool took his pipe from his mouth, blew a thin spiral, wiped his mouth with the back of his hand. "Regular fertilizer is—regular fertilizer."

Jakob Hoogendunk nodded his solemn confirmation of this.

"What's in it?" persisted Selina.

Pool waved a huge red hand as though to waft away this troublesome insect. He looked at Maartje. But Maartje was slamming about her work. Geertje and Jozina were absorbed in some game of their own behind the stove. Roelf, at the table, sat reading, one slim hand, chapped and gritty with rough work, outspread on the cloth. Selina noticed, without knowing she noticed, that the fingers were long, slim, and the broken nails thin and fine. "But what's in it?" she said again. Suddenly life in the kitchen hung suspended. The two men frowned. Maartje half turned from her dishpan. The two little girls peered out from behind the stove. Roelf looked up from his book. Even the collie, lying in front of the stove half asleep, suddenly ran his tongue out, winked one eye. But Selina, all sociability, awaited her answer. She could not know that in High Prairie women did not brazenly intrude thus on men's weighty conversation. The men looked at her, unanswering. She began to feel a little uncomfortable. The boy Roelf rose and went to the cupboard in the kitchen corner. He took down a large green-bound book, and placed it in Selina's hand. The book smelled terribly. Its covers were greasy with handling. On the page margins a brown stain showed the imprint of fingers. Roelf pointed at a page. Selina followed the line with her eye.

Good Basic Fertilizer for Market-Garden Crops.

Then, below:

Nitrate of soda.
Ammonium sulfate.
Dried blood.

Selina shut the book and handed it back to Roelf, gingerly. Dried blood! She stared at the two men. "What does it mean by dried blood?"

Klaas answered stubbornly, "Dried blood is dried blood. You put in the field dried blood and it makes grow. Cabbages, onions, squash." At sight of her horrified face he grinned. "Well, cabbages is anyway beautiful, huh?" He rolled a facetious eye around at Jakob. Evidently this joke was going to last him the winter.

Selina stood up. She wasn't annoyed; but she wanted, suddenly, to be alone in her room—in the room that but an hour before had been a strange and terrifying chamber with its towering bed, its chill drum, its ghostly bride's chest. Now it had become a refuge, snug, safe, infinitely desirable. She turned to Mrs. Pool. "I—I think I'll go up to my room. I'm very tired. The ride, I suppose. I'm not used . . ." Her voice trailed off.

"Sure," said Maartje, briskly. She had finished the supper dishes and was busy with a huge bowl, flour, a baking board. "Sure go up. I got my bread to set yet and what all."

"If I could have some hot water—"

"Roelf! Stop once that reading and show school teacher where is hot water. Geertje! Jozina! Never in my world did I see such." She cuffed a convenient pigtail by way of emphasis. A wail arose.

"Never mind. It doesn't matter. Don't bother." Selina was in a sort of panic now. She wanted to be out of the room. But the boy Roelf, with quiet swiftness, had taken a battered tin pail from its hook on the wall, had lifted an iron slab at the back of the kitchen stove. A mist of steam arose. He dipped the pail into the tiny reservoir thus revealed. Then, as Selina made as though to take it, he walked past her. She heard him ascending the wooden stairway. She wanted to be after him. But first she must know the name of the book over which he had been poring. But between her and the book outspread on the table were Pool, Hoogendunk, dog, pigtails, Maartje. She pointed with a determined forefinger. "What's that book Roelf was reading?"

Maartje thumped a great ball of dough on the baking board. Her arms were white with flour. She kneaded and pummelled expertly. "Woorden boek."

Well. That meant nothing. Woorden boek. Woorden b—— Dimly the meaning of the Dutch words began to come to her. But it couldn't be. She brushed past the men in the tipped-back chairs, stepped over the collie, reached across the table. Woorden—word. Boek—book. Word book. "He's reading the dictionary!" Selina said, aloud. "He's reading the dictionary!" She had the horrible feeling that she was going to laugh and cry at once; hysteria.

Mrs. Pool glanced around. "School teacher he gave it to Roelf time he quit last spring for spring planting. A word book. In it is more as a hundred thousand words, all different."

Selina flung a good-night over her shoulder and made for the stairway. He should have all her books. She would send to Chicago for books. She would spend her thirty dollars a month buying books for him. He had been reading the dictionary!

Roelf had placed the pail of hot water on the little wash-stand, and had lighted the glass lamp. He was intent on replacing the glass chimney within the four prongs that held it firm. Downstairs, in the crowded kitchen, he had seemed quite the man. Now, in the yellow lamplight, his profile sharply outlined, she saw that he was just a small boy with tousled hair. About his cheeks, his mouth, his chin one could even see the last faint traces of soft infantile roundness. His trousers, absurdly cut down from a man's pair by inexpert hands, hung grotesquely about his slim shanks.

"He's just a little boy," thought Selina, with a quick pang. He was about to pass her now, without glancing at her, his head down. She put out her hand; touched his shoulder. He looked up at her, his face startlingly alive, his eyes blazing. It came to Selina that until now she had not heard him speak. Her hand pressed the thin stuff of his coat sleeve.

"Cabbages—fields of cabbages—what you said—they *are* beautiful," he stammered. He was terribly in earnest. Before she could reply he was out of the room, clattering down the stairs.

Selina stood, blinking a little.

The glow that warmed her now endured while she splashed about in the inadequate basin; took down the dark soft masses of her hair; put on the voluminous long-sleeved, high-necked nightgown. Just before she blew out the lamp her last glimpse was of the black drum stationed like a patient eunuch in the corner; and she could smile at that; even giggle a little, what with weariness, excitement, and a general feeling of being awake in a dream. But once in the vast bed she lay there utterly lost in the waves of terror and loneliness that envelop one at night in a strange house amongst strange people. She lay there, tensed and tight, her toes curled with nervousness, her spine

hunched with it, her leg muscles taut. She peeked over the edge of
the covers looking a good deal like a frightened brownie, if one could
have seen her; her eyes very wide, the pupils turned well toward the
corners with the look of listening and distrust. The sharp November
air cut in from the fields that were fertilized with dried blood. She
shivered, and wrinkled up her lovely little nose and seemed to sniff
this loathsome taint in the air. She listened to the noises that came
from belowstairs; voices gruff, unaccustomed; shrill, high. These
ceased and gave place to others less accustomed to her city-bred ears;
a dogs bark and an answering one; a far-off train whistle; the dull thud
of hoofs stamping on the barn floor; the wind in the bare tree
branches outside the window.

Her watch—a gift from Simeon Peake on her eighteenth birth-
day—with the gold case all beautifully engraved with a likeness of a
gate, and a church, and a waterfall and a bird, linked together with
spirals and flourishes of the most graceful description, was ticking
away companionably under her pillow. She felt for it, took it out and
held it in her palm, under her cheek, for comfort.

She knew she would not sleep that night. She knew she would
not sleep——

She awoke to a clear, cold November dawn; children's voices;
the neighing of horses; a great sizzling and hissing, and scent of frying
bacon; a clucking and squawking in the barnyard. It was six o'clock.
Selina's first day as a school teacher. In a little more than two hours
she would be facing a whole roomful of round-eyed Geertjes and Jozi-
nas and Roelfs. The bedroom was cruelly cold. As she threw the bed-
clothes heroically aside Selina decided that it took an appalling
amount of courage—this life that Simeon Peake had called a great
adventure.

4

Every morning throughout November it was the same. At six o'clock:
"Miss Peake! *Oh,* Miss Peake!"

"I'm up!" Selina would call in what she meant to be a gay voice, through chattering teeth.

"You better come down and dress where is warm here by the stove."

Peering down the perforations in the floor-hole through which the parlour chimney swelled so proudly into the drum, Selina could vaguely descry Mrs. Pool stationed just below, her gaze upturned.

That first morning, on hearing this invitation, Selina had been rocked between horror and mirth. "I'm not cold, really, I'm almost dressed. I'll be down directly."

Maartje Pool must have sensed some of the shock in the girl's voice; or, perhaps, even some of the laughter. "Pool and Jakob are long out already cutting. Here back of the stove you can dress warm."

Shivering and tempted though she was, Selina had set her will against it. A little hardening of the muscles around her jaw so that they stood out whitely beneath the fine-grained skin. "I won't go down," she said to herself, shaking with the cold. "I won't come down to dressing behind the kitchen stove like a—like a peasant in one of those dreadful Russian novels. . . . That sounds stuck up and horrid. . . . The Pools are good and kind and decent. . . . But I *won't* come down to huddling behind the stove with a bundle of underwear in my arms. Oh, *dear,* this corset's like a casing of ice."

Geertje and Jozina had no such maidenly scruples. Each morning they gathered their small woollen garments in a bundle and scudded briskly to the kitchen for warmth, though their bedroom just off the parlour had by no means the degree of refrigeration possessed by Selina's clammy chamber. Not only that, the Misses Pool slept snugly in the woollen nether garments that invested them by day and so had only mounts of wollen petticoats, woolen stockings, and mysterious grimy straps, bands, and fastenings with which to struggle. Their intimate flannels had a cactus quality that made the early martyrs' hair shirts seem, in comparison, but a fleece-lined cloud. Dressing behind the kitchen stove was a natural and universal custom in High Prairie.

By the middle of December as Selina stuck her nose cautiously out of the covers into the midnight blackness of early morning you might have observed, if it had been at all light, that the tip of that elegant and erstwhile alabaster feature had been encarmined during the night by a mischievous brush wielded by that same wight who had been busy painting fronds and lacy ferns and gorgeous blossoms of silver all over the bedroom window. Slowly, inch by inch, that bedroom window crept down, down. Then, too, the Pools objected to the icy blasts which swept the open stairway and penetrated their hermetically sealed bedrooms below. Often the water in the pitcher on her washstand was frozen when Selina awoke. Her garments, laid out the night before so that their donning next morning might occupy a minimum of time, were mortuary to the touch. Worst of all were the steel-stiffened, unwieldy, and ridiculous stays that encased the female form of that day. As Selina's numbed fingers struggled with the fastenings of this iciest of garments her ribs shrank from its arctic embrace.

"But I won't dress behind the kitchen stove!" declared Selina, glaring meanwhile at that hollow pretense, the drum. She even stuck her tongue out at it (only nineteen, remember!). For that matter, it may as well be known that she brought home a piece of chalk from school and sketched a demon face on the drum's bulging front, giving it a personal and horrid aspect that afforded her much satisfaction.

When she thought back, years later, on that period of her High Prairie experience, stoves seemed to figure with absurd prominence in her memory. That might well be. A stove changed the whole course of her life.

From the first, the schoolhouse stove was her bête noir. Out of the welter of that first year it stood, huge and menacing, a black tyrant. The High Prairie schoolhouse in which Selina taught was little more than a mile up the road beyond the Pool farm. She came to know that road in all its moods—ice-locked, drifted with snow, wallowing in mud. School began at half-past eight. After her first week Selina had the mathematics of her early morning reduced to the least common denominator. Up at six. A plunge into the frigid garments; breakfast of bread, cheese, sometimes bacon, always rye coffee without cream or sugar. On with the cloak, muffler, hood, mittens, galoshes. The lunch box in bad weather. Up the road to the schoolhouse, battling the prairie wind that whipped the tears into the eyes, ploughing the drifts, slipping on the hard ruts and icy ridges in dry weather. Excellent at nineteen. As she flew down the road in sun or rain, in wind or snow, her mind's eye was fixed on the stove. The schoolhouse reached, her numbed fingers wrestled with the rusty lock. The door opened, there smote her the schoolroom smell—a mingling of dead ashes, kerosene, unwashed bodies, dust, mice, chalk, stovewood, lunch crumbs, mould, slate that has been washed with saliva. Into this Selina rushed, untying her muffler as she entered. In the little vestibule there was a box piled with chunks of stove-wood and another heaped with dried corncobs. Alongside this a can of kerosene. The cobs served as kindling. A dozen or more of these you soaked with kerosene and stuffed into the maw of the rusty iron pot-bellied stove. A match. Up flared the corn-cobs. Now was the moment for a small stick of wood; another to keep it company. Shut the door. Draughts. Dampers. Smoke. Suspense. A blaze, then a crackle. The wood has caught. In with a chunk now. A wait. Another chunk. Slam the door. The schoolhouse fire is started for the day. As the room thawed gradually Selina removed layers of outer garments. By the time the children arrived the room was livable.

Naturally, those who sat near this monster baked; those near the windows froze. Sometimes Selina felt she must go mad beholding the writhings and contortions of a roomful of wriggling bodies scratching at backs, legs, and sides as the stove grew hotter and flesh rebelled against the harsh contact with the prickling undergarments of an over-cautious day.

Selina had seen herself, dignified, yet gentle, instructing a room-ful of Dutch cherubs in the simpler elements of learning. But it is difficult to be dignified and gracious when you are suffering from chil-blains. Selina fell victim to this sordid discomfort, as did every child in the room. She sat at the battered pine desk or moved about, a little ice-wool shawl around her shoulders when the wind was wrong and the stove balky. Her white little face seemed whiter in contrast with the black folds of this sombre garment. Her slim hands were rough and chapped. The oldest child in the room was thirteen, the youngest four and a half. From eight-thirty until four Selina ruled this grubby domain; a hot-and-cold roomful of sneezing, coughing, wriggling, shuffling, dozing children, toe scuffling on agonized heel, and heel scrunching on agonized toe, in a frenzy of itching.

"Aggie Vander Sijde, parse this sentence: The ground is wet because it has rained."

Miss Vander Sijde, eleven, arises with a switching of skirts and a tossing of pigtail. " 'Ground' the subject; 'is wet' the predicate; 'because' . . ."

Selina is listening with school-teacherly expression indicative of encouragement and approval. "Jan Snip, parse this sentence: The flower will wither if it is picked."

Brown lady's-cloth; ice-wool shawl; chalk in hand. Just a phase; a brief chapter in the adventure. Something to remember and look back on with a mingling of amusement and wonder. Things were going to happen. Such things, with life and life and life stretching ahead of her! In five years—two—even one, perhaps, who knows but that she might be lying on lacy pillows on just such a bleak winter morning, a satin coverlet over her, the morning light shaded by soft rose-coloured hangings. (Early influence of the *Fireside Companion*.)

"What time is it, Celeste?"

"It is now eleven o'clock, madame."

"Is that all!"

"Would madame like that I prepare her bath now, or later?"

"Later, Celeste. My chocolate now. My letters."

". . . and if is the conjunction modifying . . ."

Early in the winter Selina had had the unfortunate idea of opening the ice-locked windows at intervals and giving the children five minutes of exercise while the fresh cold air cleared brains and room at once. Arms waved wildly, heads wobbled, short legs worked vigorously. At the end of the week twenty High Prairie parents sent protests by note or word of mouth. Jan and Cornelius, Katrina and Aggie went to school to learn reading and writing and numbers, not to stand with open windows in the winter.

On the Pool farm the winter work had set in. Klaas drove into Chicago with winter vegetables only once a week now. He and Jakob and Roelf were storing potatoes and cabbages underground; repairing fences; preparing frames for the early spring planting; sorting seedlings. It had been Roelf who had taught Selina to build the school-house fire. He had gone with her on that first morning, had started the fire, filled the water pail, initiated her in the rites of corn-cobs, kerosene, and dampers. A shy, dark, silent boy. She set out deliberately to woo him to friendship.

"Roelf, I have a book called 'Ivanhoe.' Would you like to read it?"

"Well, I don't get much time."

"You wouldn't have to hurry. Right there in the house. And there's another called 'The Three Musketeers'."

He was trying not to look pleased; to appear stolid and Dutch, like the people from whom he had sprung. Some Dutch sailor ancestor, Selina thought, or fisherman, must have touched at an Italian port or Spanish and brought back a wife whose eyes and skin and feeling for beauty had skipped layer on layer of placid Netherlanders to crop out now in this wistful sensitive boy.

Selina had spoken to Jakob Hoogendunk about a shelf for her

books and her photographs. He had put up a rough bit of board, very crude and ugly, but it had served. She had come home one snowy afternoon to find this shelf gone and in its place a smooth and polished one, with brackets intricately carved. Roelf had cut, planed, polished, and carved it in many hours of work in the cold little shed off the kitchen. He had there a workshop of sorts, fitted with such tools and implements as he could devise. He did man's work on the farm, yet often at night Selina could faintly hear the rasp of his handsaw after she had gone to bed. He had built a doll's house for Geertje and Jozina that was the black envy of every pigtail in High Prairie. This sort of thing was looked upon by Klaas Pool as foolishness. Roelf's real work in the shed was the making and mending of coldframes and hotbeds for the early spring plants. Whenever possible Roelf neglected this dull work for some fancy of his own. To this Klaas Pool objected as being "dumb." For that matter, High Prairie considered Pool's boy "dumb like." He said such things. When the new Dutch Reformed Church was completed after gigantic effort—red brick, and the first brick church in High Prairie—bright yellow painted pews—a red and yellow glass window, most handsome—the Reverend Vaar-werk brought from New Haarlem to preach the first sermon—Pool's Roelf was heard to hint darkly to a group of High Prairie boys that some night he was going to burn the church down. It was ugly. It hurt you to look at it, just.

Certainly, the boy was different. Selina, none too knowledgeous herself, still recognized that here was something rare, something precious to be fostered, shielded, encouraged.

"Roelf, stop that foolishness, get your ma once some wood. Carving on that box again instead finishing them coldframes. Some day, by golly, I show you. I break every stick . . . dumb as a Groningen . . ."

Roelf did not sulk. He seemed not to mind, particulary, but he came back to the carved box as soon as chance presented itself. Maartje and Klaas Pool were not cruel people, nor unkind. They were a little bewildered by this odd creature that they, inexplicably enough, had produced. It was not a family given to demonstration of affection.

Life was too grim for the flowering of this softer side. Then, too, they had sprung from a phlegmatic and unemotional people. Klaas toiled like a slave in the fields and barn; Maartje's day was a treadmill of cooking, scrubbing, washing, mending from the moment she arose (four in the summer, five in the winter) until she dropped with a groan in her bed often long after the others were asleep. Selina had never seen her kiss Geertje or Jozina. But once she had been a little startled to see Maartje, on one of her countless trips between stove and table, run her hand through the boy's shock of black hair, down the side of his face to his chin which she tipped up with an indescribably tender gesture as she looked down into his eyes. It was a movement fleeting, vague, yet infinitely compassionate. Sometimes she even remonstrated when Klaas berated Roelf. "Leave the boy be, then, Klaas. Leave him be, once."

"She loves him best," Selina thought. "She'd even try to understand him if she had time."

He was reading her books with such hunger as to cause her to wonder if her stock would last him the winter. Sometimes, after supper, when he was hammering and sawing away in the little shed Selina would snatch Maartje's old shawl off the hook, and swathed in this against draughty chinks, she would read aloud to him while he carved, or talk to him above the noise of his tools. Selina was a gay and volatile person. She loved to make this boy laugh. His dark face would flash into almost dazzling animation. Sometimes Maartje, hearing their young laughter, would come to the shed door and stand there a moment, hugging her arms in her rolled apron and smiling at them, uncomprehending but companionable.

"You make fun, h'm?"

"Come in, Mrs. Pool. Sit down on my box and make fun, too. Here, you may have half the shawl."

"Og Heden! I got no time to sit down," She was off.

Roelf slid his plane slowly, more slowly, over the surface of a satin-smooth oak board. He stopped, twined a curl of shaving about his finger. "When I am a man, and earning, I am going to buy my mother a silk dress like I saw in a store in Chicago and she should put it on every day, not only for Sunday; and sit in a chair and make little fine stiches like Widow Paarlenberg."

"What else are you going to do when you grow up?" She waited, certain that he would say something delightful.

"Drive the team to town alone to market."

"Oh, Roelf!"

"Sure. Already I have gone five times—twice with Jakob and three times with Pop. Pretty soon, when I am seventeen or eighteen, I can go alone. At five in the afternoon you start and at nine you are in the Haymarket. There all night you sleep on the wagon. There are gas lights. The men play dice and cards. At four in the morning you are ready when they come, the commission men and the peddlers and the grocery men. Oh, it's fine, I tell you!"

"Roelf!" She was bitterly disappointed.

"Here. Look." He rummaged around in a dusty box in a corner and, suddenly shy again, laid before her a torn sheet of coarse brown paper on which he had sketched crudely, effectively, a mêlée of great-haunched horses; wagons piled high with garden truck; men in overalls and corduroys; flaring gas torches. He had drawn it with a stub of pencil exactly as it looked to him. The result was as startling as that achieved by the present-day disciple of the impressionistic school.

Selina was enchanted.

Many of her evenings during November were spent thus. The family life was lived in a kitchen blue with pipe smoke, heavy with the smell of cooking. Sometimes—though rarely—a fire was lighted in the parlour stove. Often she had school papers to correct—grubby sheaves of arithmetic, grammar, or spelling lessons. Often she longed to read; wanted to sew. Her bedroom was too cold. The men sat in the kitchen or tramped in and out. Geertje and Jozina scuffled and played. Maartje scuttled about like a harried animal, heavy-footed by incredibly swift. The floor was always gritty with the sandy loam tracked in by the men's heavy boots.

Once, early in December, Selina went into town. The trip was born of sudden revolt against her surroundings and a great wave of nostalgia for the dirt and clamour and crowds of Chicago. Early Saturday morning Klaas drove her to the railway station five miles distant. She was to stay until Sunday. A letter had been written Julie Hempel ten days before, but there had been no answer. Once in town she went straight to the Hempel house. Mrs. Hempel, thin-lipped, met her in the hall and said that Julie was out of town. She was visiting her friend Miss Arnold, in Kansas City. Selina was not asked to stay to dinner. She was not asked to sit down. When she left the house her great fine eyes seemed larger and more deep-set than ever, and her jaw-line was set hard against the invasion of tears. Suddenly she hated this Chicago that wanted none of her; that brushed past her, bumping her elbow and offering no apology; that clanged, and shrieked, and whistled, and roared in her ears now grown accustomed to the prairie silence.

"I don't care," she said, which meant she did. "I don't care. Just you wait. Some day I'm going to be—oh, terribly important. And people will say, 'Do you know that wonderful Selina Peake? Well, they say she used to be a country school teacher and slept in an ice-cold room and ate pork three times a . . .' There! I know what I'm going to do. I'm going to have luncheon and I'll order the most delicious things. I think I'll go to the Palmer House where Father and I . . . no, I couldn't stand that. I'll go to the Auditorium Hotel restaurant and have ice cream; and chicken broth in a silver cup; and cream puffs, and all kinds of vegetables and little lamb chops in paper panties. And orange pekoe tea."

She actually did order all these things and had a group of amazed waiters hovering about her table waiting to see her devour this meal, much as a similar group had stared at David Copperfield when he was innocent of having bolted the huge dinner ordered in the inn on his way to London.

She ate the ice cream and drank the orange pekoe (mainly because she loved the sound of its name; it made her think of chrysanthemums and cherry blossoms, spices, fans, and slant-eyed maidens). She devoured a crisp salad with the avidity of a canary pecking at a lettuce leaf. She flirted with the lamb chops. She remembered the size of her father's generous tips and left a sum on the table that temporarily dulled the edge of the waiter's hatred of women diners. But the luncheon could not be said to have been a success. She thought of dinner, and her spirit quailed. She spent the time between one and three buying portable presents for the entire Pool household—including bananas for Geertje and Jozina, for whom that farinaceous fruit had the fascination always held for the farm child. She caught a train at four thirty-five and actually trudged the five miles from the station to the farm, arriving half frozen, weary, with aching arms and nipped toes, to a great welcome of the squeals, grunts, barks, and gutturals that formed the expression of the Pool household. She was astonished to find how happy she was to return to the kitchen stove, to the smell of frying pork, to her own room with the walnut bed and the book shelf. Even the grim drum had taken on the dear and comforting aspect of the accustomed.

5

High Prairie swains failed to find Selina alluring. She was too small, too pale and fragile for their robust taste. Naturally, her coming had been an event in this isolated community. She would have been surprised to know with what eagerness and curiosity High Prairie gathered crumbs of news about her; her appearance, her manner, her dress. Was she stuck up? Was she new fangled? She failed to notice the agitation of the parlour curtains behind the glittering windows of the farmhouses she passed on her way to school. With no visible means of communication news of her leaped from farm to farm as flame leaps the gaps in a forest fire. She would have been aghast to learn that High Prairie, inexplicably enough, knew all about her from the colour of the ribbon that threaded her neat little white corset covers to the number of books on her shelf. She thought cabbage fields beautiful; she read books to that dumb-acting Roelf Pool; she was making over a dress for Maartje after the pattern of the stylish brown lady's-cloth she wore (foolishly) to school. Now and then she encountered a team on the road. She would call a good-day. Sometimes the driver answered, tardily, as though surprised. Sometimes he only stared. She almost never saw the High Prairie farm women, busy in their kitchens.

On her fifth Sunday in the district she accompanied the Pools to the morning service at the Dutch Reformed Church. Maartje seldom had the time for such frivolity. But on this morning Klaas hitched up the big farm wagon with the double seat and took the family complete—Maartje, Selina, Roelf, and the pigtails. Maartje, out of her kitchen calico and dressed in her best black, with a funereal bonnet made sadder by a sparse and drooping feather whose listless fronds emerged surprisingly from a faded red cotton rose, wore a new strange aspect to Selina's eyes, as did Klaas in his clumsy sabbaticals. Roelf had rebelled against going, had been cuffed for it, and had sat very still all through the service, gazing at the red and yellow glass church window. Later he confided to Selina that the sunlight filtering through the crude yellow panes had imparted a bilious look to the unfortunates seated within its range, affording him much secret satisfaction.

Selina's appearance had made quite a stir, of which she was entirely unaware. As the congregation entered by twos and threes she thought they resembled startlingly a woodcut in an old illustrated book she once had seen. The men's Sunday trousers and coats had a square stiff angularity, as though chopped out of a block. The women, in shawls and bonnets of rusty black, were incredibly cut in the same pattern. The unmarried girls, though, were plump, red-cheeked, and not uncomely, with high round cheek-bones on which sat a spot of brick-red which imparted no glow to the face. Their foreheads were prominent and meaningless.

In the midst of this drab assemblage there entered late and rustlingly a tall, slow-moving woman in a city-bought cloak and a bonnet quite unlike the vintage millinery of High Prairie. As she came down the aisle Selina thought she was like a full-sailed frigate. An ample woman, with a fine fair skin and a ripe red mouth; a high firm bosom and great thighs that moved rhythmically, slowly. She had thick, insolent eyelids. Her hands, as she turned the leaves of her hymn book, were smooth and white. As she entered there was a little rustle throughout the congregation; a craning of necks. Though she was bustled and flounced and panniered, you thought, curiously enough, of those lolling white-fleshed and unconventional ladies whom the sixteenth century painters were always portraying as having their toe nails cut with nothing on.

"Who's that?" whispered Selina to Maartje.

"Widow Paarlenberg. She is rich like anything."

"Yes?" Selina was fascinated.

"Look once how she makes eyes at him."

"At him? Who? Who?"

"Pervus DeJong. By Gerrit Pon he is sitting with the blue shirt and sad looking so."

Selina craned, peered. "The—oh—he's very good looking, isn't he?"

"Sure. Widow Paarlenberg is stuck on him. See how she—Sh-sh-sh!—Reverend Dekker looks at us. I tell you after."

Selina decided she'd come to church oftener. The service went on, dull, heavy. It was in English and Dutch. She heard scarcely a word of it. The Widow Paarlenberg and this Pervus DeJong occupied her thoughts. She decided, without malice, that the widow resembled one of the sleekest of the pink porkers rooting in Klaas Pool's barnyard, waiting to be cut into Christmas meat.

The Widow Paarlenberg turned and smiled. Her eyes were slippery (Selina's term). Her mouth became loose and wide with one corner sliding down a trifle into something very like a leer.

With one surge the Dutch Reformed congregation leaned forward to see how Pervus DeJong would respond to his public mark of favour. His gaze was stern, unsmiling. His eyes were fixed on that extremely dull gentleman, the Reverend Dekker.

"He's annoyed," thought Selina, and was pleased at the thought. "Well, I may not be a widow, but I'm sure that's not the way." And then: "Now I wonder what it's like when *he* smiles."

According to fiction as Selina had found it in the *Fireside Companion* and elsewhere, he should have turned at this moment, irresistibly drawn by the magnetism of her gaze, and smiled a rare sweet smile that lighted up his stern young face. But he did not. He yawned suddenly and capaciously. The Reformed Dutch congregation leaned back feeling cheated. Handsome, certainly, Selina reflected. But then, probably Klaas Pool, too, had been handsome a few years ago.

The service ended, there was much talk of the weather, seedlings, stock, the approaching holiday season. Maartje, her Sunday dinner heavy on her mind, was elbowing her way up the aisle. Here and there she introduced Selina briefly to a woman friend. "Mrs. Vander Sijde, meet school teacher."

"Aggie's mother?" Selina would begin, primly, only to be swept along by Maartje on her way to the door. "Mrs. Von Mijnen, meet school teacher. Is Mrs. Von Mijnen." They regarded her with a grim gaze. Selina would smile and not rather nervously, feeling you, frivolous, and somehow guilty.

When, with Maartje, she reached the church porch Pervus DeJong was unhitching the dejected horse that was harnessed to his battered and lopsided cart. The animal stood with four feet bunched together in a drooping and pathetic attitude and seemed inevitably meant for mating with this decrepit vehicle. DeJong untied the reins quickly, and was about to step into the sagging conveyance when the Widow Paarlenberg sailed down the church steps with admirable speed for one so amply proportioned. She made straight for him, skirts billowing, flouncies flying, plumes waving. Maartje clutched Selina's arm. "Look how she makes! She asks him to eat Sunday dinner I bet you! See once how he makes with his head no."

Selina—and the whole congregation unashamedly watching—could indeed see how he made with his head no. His whole body seemed set in negation—the fine head, the broad patient shoulders, the muscular powerful legs in their ill-fitting Sunday blacks. He shook his head, gathered up the reins, and drove away, leaving the Widow Paarlenberg to carry off with such bravado as she could muster this public flouting in full sight of the Dutch Reformed congregation of High Prairie. It must be said that she actually achieved this feat with a rather magnificent composure. Her round pink face, as she turned away, was placid; her great cowlike eyes mild. Selina abandoned the pink porker smile for that of a great Persian cat, full-fed and treacherous, its claws all sheathed in velvet. The widow stepped agilely into her own neat phaeton with its sleep horse and was off down the hard snowless road, her head high.

"Well!" exclaimed Selina, feeling as though she had witnessed the first act of an exciting play. And breathed deeply. So, too, did the watching congregation, so that the widow could be said to have driven off in quite a gust.

As they jogged home in the Pool farm wagon Maartje told her tale with a good deal of savour.

Pervus DeJong had been left a widower two years before. Within a month of that time Leendert Paarlenberg had died, leaving to his widow the richest and most profitable farm in the whole community. Pervus DeJong, on the contrary, through inheritance from his father, old Johannes, possessed a scant twenty-five acres of the worst low-land—practically the only lowland—in all High Prairie. The acreage was notoriously barren. In spring, the critical time for seedlings and early vegetable crops, sixteen of the twenty-five were likely to be under water. Pervus DeJong patiently planted, sowed, gathered crops, hauled them to market; seemed still never to get on in this thrifty Dutch community where getting on was so common a trait as to be no longer thought a virtue. Luck and nature seemed to work against him. His seedlings proved unfertile; his stock was always ailing; his cabbages were worm-infested; snout-beetle bored his rhubarb. When he planted largely of spinach, hoping for a wet spring, the season was dry. Did he turn the following year to sweet potatoes, all auguries pointing to a dry spring and summer, the summer proved the wettest in a decade. Insects and fungi seemed drawn to his fields as by a malevolent force. Had he been small, puny, and insignificant his bad luck would have called forth contemptuous pity. But there was about him the lovableness and splendour of the stricken giant. To complete his discomfort, his household was inadequately ministered by an elderly and rheumatic female connection whose pies and bread were the scandal of the neighbouring housewives.

It was on this Pervus DeJong, then, that the Widow Paarlenberg of the rich acres, the comfortable farmhouse, the gold neck chain, the silk gowns, the soft white hands and the cooking talents, had set her affections. She wooed him openly, notoriously, and with a Dutch vehemence that would have swept another man off his feet. It was known that she sent him a weekly baking of cakes, pies, and bread. She urged upon him choice seeds from her thriving fields; seedlings from her hotbeds; plants, all of which he steadfastly refused. She tricked, cajoled, or nagged him into eating her ample meals. She even asked his advice—that subtlest form of flattery. She asked him about sub-soiling, humus, rotation—she whose rich land yielded, under her shrewd management, more profitably to the single acre than to any ten of Pervus's. One Jan Bras managed her farm admirably under her supervision.

DeJong's was a simple mind. In the beginning, when she said to him, in her deep, caressing voice, "Mr. DeJong, could I ask you a little advice about something? I'm a woman alone since I haven't got Leendert any more, and strangers what do they care how they run the land! It's about my radishes, lettuce, spinach, and turnips. Last year, instead of tender, they were stringy and full of fibre on account that Jan Bras. He's for slow growing. Those vegetables you've got to grow quick. Bras says my fertilizer is the fault, but I know different. What you think?"

Jan Bras, getting wind of this, told it abroad with grim humour. Masculine High Prairie, meeting Pervus DeJong on the road, greeted him with: "Well, DeJong, you been giving the Widow Paarlenberg any good advice here lately about growing?"

It had been a particularly bad season for his fields. As High Prairie poked a sly thumb into his ribs thus he realized that he had been duped by the wily widow. A slow Dutch wrath rose in him against her; a male resentment at being manipulated by a woman. When next she approached him, cajolery in her voice, seeking guidance about tillage, drainage, or crops, he said, bluntly: "Better you ask Harm Tien his advice." Harm Tien was the district idiot, a poor witless creature of thirty with the mind of a child.

Knowing well that the entire community was urging him toward this profitable match with the plump, rich, red-lipped widow, Pervus set his will like a stubborn steer and would have none of her. He was uncomfortable in his untidy house; he was lonely, he was unhappy. But he would have none of her. Vanity, pride, resentment were all mixed up in it.

The very first time that Pervus DeJong met Selina he had a

chance to protect her. With such a start, the end was inevitable. Then, too, Selina had on the wine-colored cashmere and was trying hard to keep the tears back in full view of the whole of High Prairie. Urged by Maartje (and rather fancying the idea) Selina had attended the great meeting and dance at Adam Oom's hall above the general store near the High Prairie station. Farmer families for miles around were there. The new church organ—that time-hallowed pretext for sociability—was the excuse for this gathering. There was a small admission charge. Adam Ooms had given them the hall. The three musicians were playing without fee. The women were to bring supper packed in boxes or baskets, these to be raffled off to the highest bidder whose privilege it then was to sup with the fair whose basket he had bought. Hot coffee could be had at so much the cup. All the proceeds were to be devoted to the organ. It was understood, of course, that there was to be no lively bidding against husbands. Each farm woman knew her own basket as she knew the countenance of her children, and each farmer, as that basket came up at auction, named a cautious sum which automatically made him the basket's possessor. The larger freedom had not come to High Prairie in 1890. The baskets and boxes of the unwed women were to be the fought-for prizes. Maartje had packed her own basket at noon and had driven off at four with Klaas and the children. She was to serve on one of those bustling committees whose duties ranged from coffee making to dish washing. Klaas and Roelf were to be pressed into service. The pigtails would slide up and down the waxed floor of Ooms's hall with other shrieking pigtails of the neighbourhood until the crowd began to arrive for the auction and supper. Jakob Hoogendunk would convey Selina to the festivities when his chores were done. Selina's lunch basket was to be a separate and distinct affair, offered at auction with those of the Katrinas and Linas and Sophias of High Prairie. Not a little apprehensive, she was to pack this basket herself. Maartje, departing, had left copious but disjointed instructions.

"Ham . . . them big cookies in the crock . . . pickles . . . watch how you don't spill . . . plum preserves . . ."

Maartje's own basket was of gigantic proportions and staggering content. Her sandwiches were cubic blocks; her pickles clubs of cucumber; her pies vast plateaus.

The basket provided for Selina, while not quite so large, still was of appalling size as Selina contemplated it. She decided, suddenly, that she would have none of it. In her trunk she had a cardboard box such as shoes come in. Certainly this should hold enough lunch for two, she thought. She and Julie Hempel had used such boxes for picnic lunches on their Saturday holidays. She was a little nervous about the whole thing; rather dreaded the prospect of eating her supper with a High Prairie swain unknown to her. Suppose no one should bid for her box! She resolved to fill it after her own pattern, disregarding Maartje's heavy provender.

She had the kitchen to herself. Jakob was in the fields or out-houses. The house was deliciously quiet. Selina rummaged for the shoe box, lined it with a sheet of tissue paper, rolled up her sleeves, got out mixing bowl, flour, pans. Cup cakes were her ambition. She baked six of them. They came out a beautiful brown but somewhat leaden. Still, anything was better than a wedge of soggy pie, she told herself. She boiled eggs very hard, halved them, devilled their yolks, filled the whites neatly with this mixture and clapped the halves together again, skewering them with a toothpick. Then she rolled each egg separately in tissue paper twisted at the ends. Daintiness, she had decided, should be the keynote of her supper box. She cut bread paper-thin and made jelly sandwiches, scorning the ubiquitous pork. Bananas, she knew, belonged in a lunch box, but these were unobtain-able. She substituted two juicy pippins, polished until their cheeks glittered. The food neatly packed she wrapped the box in paper and tied it with a gay red ribbon yielded by her trunk. At the last moment she whipped into the yard, twisted a brush of evergreen from the tree at the side of the house, and tucked this into the knot of ribbon atop the box. She stepped back and thought the effect enchanting.

She was waiting in her red cashmere and her cloak and hood when Hoogendunk called for her. They were late arrivals, for outside Ooms's hall were hitched all manner of vehicles. There had been a heavy snowfall two days before. This had brought out bob-sleds, cutters, sleighs. The horse sheds were not large enough to shelter all. Late comers had to hitch where they could. There was a great jangling of bells as the horses stamped in the snow.

Selina, balancing her box carefully, opened the door that led to the wooden stairway. The hall was on the second floor. The clamour that struck her ears had the effect of a physical blow. She hesitated a moment, and if there had been any means of returning to the Pool farm, short of walking five miles in the snow, she would have taken it. Up the stairs and into the din. Evidently the auctioning of supper baskets was even now in progress. The roar of voices had broken out after the sale of a basket and now was subsiding under the ear-splitting cracks of the auctioneer's hammer. Through the crowded doorway Selina could catch a glimpse of him as he stood on a chair, the baskets piled before him. He used a barrel elevated on a box as his pulpit. The auctioneer was Adam Ooms who himself had once been the High Prairie school teacher. A fox-faced little man, bald, falsetto, the village clown with a solid foundation of shrewdness under his clowning and a tart layer of malice over it.

High and shrill came his voice. "What am I bid! What am I bid! Thirty cents! Thirty-five! Shame on you, gentlemen. What am I bid! Who'll make it forty!"

Selina felt a little thrill of excitement. She looked about for a place on which to lay her wraps. Every table, chair, hook, and rack in the hallways was piled with clothing. She espied a box that appeared empty, rolled her cloak, muffler, and hood into a neat bundle and, about to cast it into the box, saw, upturned to her from its depths, the round pink faces of the sleeping Kuyper twins, aged six months. From the big hall now came a great shouting, clapping of hands, stamping, cat-calls. Another basket had been disposed of. Oh, dear! In desperation Selina placed her bundle on the floor in a corner, smoothed down the red cashmere, snatched up her lunch box and made for the doorway with the childish eagerness of one out of the crowd to be in it. She wondered where Maartje and Klaas Pool were in this close-packed roomful; and Roelf. In the doorway she found that broad black-coated backs shut off sight and ingress. She had writ-

ten her name neatly on her lunch box. Now she was at a loss to find a
way to reach Adam Ooms. She eyed the great-shouldered expanse just
ahead of her. In desperation she decided to dig into it with a corner
of her box. She dug, viciously. The back winced. Its owner turned.
"Here! What——!"

Selina looked up into the wrathful face of Pervus DeJong. Pervus
DeJong looked down into the startled eyes of Selina Peake. Large
enough eyes at any time; enormous now in her fright at what she had
done.

"I'm sorry! I'm—sorry. I thought if I could—there's no way of
getting my lunch box up there—such a crowd——"

A slim, appealing, lovely little figure in the wine-red cashmere,
amidst all those buxom bosoms, and overheated bodies, and flushed
faces. His gaze left her reluctantly, settled on the lunch box, became,
if possible, more bewildered. "That? Lunch box?"

"Yes. For the raffle. I'm the school teacher. Selina Peake."

He nodded. "I saw you in church Sunday."

"You did! I didn't think you. . . . Did you?"

"Wait here. I'll come back. Wait here."

He took the shoe box. She waited. He ploughed his way through
the crowd like a Juggernaut, reached Adam Ooms's platform and
placed the box inconspicuously next a colossal hamper that was one
of a dozen grouped awaiting Adam's attention. When he had made
his way back to Selina he again said, "Wait," and plunged down the
wooden stairway. Selina waited. She had ceased to feel distressed at
her inability to find the Pools in the crowd, a-tiptoe though she was.
When presently he came back he had in his hand an empty wooden
soap-box. This he up-ended in the doorway just behind the crowd
stationed there. Selina mounted it; found her head a little above the
level of his. She could survey the room from end to end. There were
the Pools. She waved to Maartje; smiled at Roelf. He made as though
to come toward her; did come part way, and was restrained by Maartje
catching at his coat tail.

Selina wished she could think of something to say. She looked
down at Pervus DeJong. The back of his neck was pink, as though

with effort. She thought, instinctively, "My goodness, he's trying to think of something to say, too." That, somehow, put her at her ease. She would wait until he spoke. His neck was now a deep red. The crowd surged back at some disturbance around Adam Ooms's elevation. Selina teetered perilously on her box, put out a hand blindly, felt his great hard hand on her arm, steadying her.

"Quite a crowd, ain't it?" The effort had reached its apex. The red of his neck began to recede.

"Oh, quite!"

"They ain't all High Prairie. Some of 'em's from Low Prairie way. New Haarlem, even."

"Really!"

A pause. Another effort.

"How goes it school teaching?"

"Oh—it goes pretty well."

"You are little to be school teacher, anyway, ain't you?"

"Little!" She drew herself up from her vantage point of the soapbox. "I'm bigger than you are."

They laughed at that as at an exquisite piece of repartee.

Adam Oom's gavel (a wooden potato masher) crashed for silence. "Ladies!" [Crash!] "And gents!" [Crash!] "Gents! Look what basket we've got here!" Look indeed. A great hamper, grown so plethoric that it could no longer wear its cover. Its contents bellied into a mound smoothly covered with a fine white cloth whose glistening surface proclaimed it damask. A Himalaya among hampers. You knew that under that snowy crust lay gold that was fowl done crisply, succulently; emeralds in the form of gherkins; rubies that melted into strawberry preserves; cakes frosted like diamonds; to say nothing of such semi-precious jewels as potato salad; cheeses; sour cream to be spread on rye bread and butter; coffee cakes; crullers.

Crash! "The Widow Paarlenberg's basket, ladies—*and* gents! The Widow Paarlenberg! I don't know what's in it. You don't know what's in it. We don't have to know what's in it. Who has eaten Widow Paarlenberg's chicken once don't have to know. Who has eaten Widow Paarlenberg's cake once don't have to know. What am

I bid on Widow Paarlenberg's basket! What am I bid! WhatmIbid-whatmIbidwhatmIbid!" [Crash!]

The widow herself, very handsome in black silk, her gold neck chain rising and falling richly with the little flurry that now agitated her broad bosom, was seated in a chair against the wall not five feet from the auctioneer's stand. She bridled now, blushed, cast down her eyes, cast up her eyes, succeeded in looking as unconscious as a complaisant Turkish slave girl on the block.

Adam Ooms's glance swept the hall. He leaned forward, his foxlike face fixed in a smile. From the widow herself, seated so prominently at his right, his gaze marked the young blades of the village; the old bucks; youths and widowers and bachelors. Here was the prize of the evening. Around, in a semi-circle, went his keen glance until it reached the tall figure towering in the doorway—reached it, and rested there. His gimlet eyes seemed to bore their way into Pervus DeJong's steady stare. He raised his right arm aloft, brandishing the potato masher. The whole room fixed its gaze on the blond head in the doorway. "Speak up! Young men of High Prairie! Heh, you, Pervus DeJong! WhatmIbidwhatmIbidwhatmIbid!"

"Fifty cents!" The bid came from Gerrit Pon at the other end of the hall. A dashing offer, as a start, in this district where one dollar often represented the profits on a whole load of market truck brought to the city.

Crash! went the potato masher. "Fifty cents I'm bid. Who'll make it seventy-five? Who'll make it seventy-five?"

"Sixty!" Johannes Ambuul, a widower, his age more than the sum of his bid.

"Seventy!" Gerrit Pon.

Adam Ooms whispered it—hissed it. "S-s-s-seventy. Ladies and gents, I wouldn't repeat out loud sucha figger. I would be ashamed. Look at this basket, gents, and then you can say . . . s-s-seventy!"

"Seventy-five!" the cautious Ambuul.

Scarlet, flooding her face, belied the widow's outward air of composure. Pervus DeJong, standing beside Selina, viewed the proceedings with an air of detachment. High Prairie was looking at him expectantly, openly. The widow bit her red lip, tossed her head. Pervus DeJong returned the auctioneer's meaning smirk with the mild gaze of a disinterested outsider. High Prairie, Low Prairie, and New Haarlem sat tense, like an audience at a play. Here, indeed, was drama being enacted in a community whose thrills were all too rare.

"Gents!" Adam Ooms's voice took on a tearful note—the tone of one who is more hurt than angry. "Gents!" Slowly, with infinite reverence, he lifted one corner of the damask cloth that concealed the hamper's contents—lifted it and peered within as at a treasure. At what he saw there he started back dramatically, at once rapturous, despairing, amazed. He rolled his eyes. He smacked his lips. He rubbed his stomach. The sort of dumb show that, since the days of the Greek drama, has been used to denote gastronomic delight.

"Eighty!" was wrenched suddenly from Goris Von Vuuren, the nineteen-year-old fat and gluttonous son of a prosperous New Haarlem farmer.

Adam Ooms rubbed brisk palms together. "Now then! A dollar! A dollar! It's an insult to this basket to make it less than a dollar." He lifted the cover again, sniffed, appeared overcome. "Gents, if it wasn't for Mrs. Ooms sitting there I'd make it a dollar myself and a bargain. A dollar! Am I bid a dollar!" He leaned far forward over his improvised pulpit. "Did I hear you say a dollar, Pervus DeJong?" DeJong stared, immovable, unabashed. His very indifference was contagious. The widow's bountiful basket seemed to shrink before one's eyes. "Eighty-eighty-eighty-eighty-gents! I'm going to tell you something. I'm going to whisper a secret." His lean face was veined with craftiness. "Gents. Listen. It isn't chicken in this beautiful basket. It isn't chicken. It's"—a dramatic pause—"it's *roast duck!*" He swayed back, mopped his brow with his red handkerchief, held one hand high in the air. His last card.

"Eighty-five!" groaned the fat Goris Von Vuuren.

"Eighty-five! Eighty-five! Eightyfiveeightyfiveeightyfive eighty-five! Gents! Gen-tle-men! Eight-five once! Eighty-five—twice!" [Crash!] "Gone to Goris Von Vuuren for eighty-five."

A sigh went up from the assemblage; a sigh that was the wind

before the storm. There followed a tornado of talk. It crackled and
thundered. The rich Widow Paarlenberg would have to eat her supper
with Von Vuuren's boy, the great thick Goris. And there in the doorway, talking to teacher as if they had known each other for years, was
Pervus DeJong with his money in his pocket. It was as good as a play.

Adam Ooms was angry. His lean, fox-like face became pinched
with spite. He prided himself on his antics as auctioneer; and his chef
d'oeuvre had brought a meagre eight-five cents, besides doubtless
winning him the enmity of that profitable store customer, the Widow
Paarlenberg. Goris Von Vuuren came forward to claim his prize
amidst shouting, clapping, laughter. The great hamper was handed
down to him; an ample, rich-looking burden, its handle folded comfortably over its round stomach, its white cover so glistening with
starch and ironing that it gave back the light from the big lamp above
the auctioneer's stand. As Goris Von Vuuren lifted it his great shoulders actually sagged. Its contents promised satiety even to such a
feeder as he. A grin, half sheepish, half triumphant, creased his plump
pink face.

Adam Ooms scuffled about among the many baskets at his feet.
His nostrils looked pinched and his skinny hands shook a little as he
searched for one small object.

When he stood upright once more he was smiling. His little eyes
gleamed. His wooden sceptre pounded for silence. High in one hand,
balanced daintily on his finger tips, he held Selina's little white shoe
box, with its red ribbon binding it, and the plume of evergreen stuck
in the ribbon. Affecting great solicitude he brought it down then to
read the name written on it; held it aloft again, smirking.

He said nothing. Grinning, he held it high. He turned his body
at the waist from side to side, so that all might see. The eyes of those
before him still held a mental picture of the huge hamper, food-
packed, that had just been handed down. The contrast was too
absurd, too cruel. A ripple of laughter swept the room; rose; swelled
to a roar. Adam Ooms drew his mouth down solemnly. His little finger elegantly crooked, he pendulumed the box to right and left. He
swerved his beady eyes from side to side. He waited with a nice sense

of the dramatic until the laughter had reached its height, then held up a hand for silence. A great scraping "Ahem!" as he cleared his throat threatened to send the crowd off again. "Ladies—*and* gents! Here's a dainty little tidbit. Here's something not only for the inner man, but a feast for the eye. Well, boys, if the last lot was too much for you this lot ought to be just about right. If the food ain't quite enough for you, you can tie the ribbon in the lady's hair and put the posy in your buttonhole and there you are. *There* you are! What's more, the lady herself goes with it. You don't get a country girl with this here box, gents. A city girl, you can tell by looking at it, just. And who is she? Who did up this dainty little box just big enough for two?" He inspected it again, solemnly, and added, as an afterthought, "If you ain't feeling specially hungry. Who?——" He looked about, apishly.

Selina's cheeks matched her gown. Her eyes were wide and dark with the effort she was making to force back the hot haze threatening them. Why had she mounted this wretched soap-box! Why had she come to this hideous party! Why had she come to High Prairie! Why! . . .

"Miss Selina Peake, that's who. Miss Se-li-na Peake!"

A hundred balloon faces pulled by a single cord turned toward her as she stood there on the box for all to see. They swam toward her. She put up a hand to push them back.

"What'm I bid! What'm I bid! What'm I bid for this here lovely little toothful, gents! Start her up!"

"Five cents!" piped up old Johannes Ambuul, with a snicker. The tittering crowd broke into a guffaw. Selina was conscious of a little sick feeling at the pit of her stomach. Through the haze she saw the widow's face, no longer sulky, but smiling now. She saw Roelf's dear dark head. His face was set, like a man's. He was coming toward her, or trying to, but the crowd wedged him in, small as he was among those great bodies. She lost sight of him. How hot it was! how hot . . . An arm at her waist. Some one had mounted the little box and stood teetering there beside her, pressed against her slightly, reassuringly. Pervus DeJong. Her head was on a level with his great shoulder now. They stood together in the doorway, on the soap-box, for all High Prairie to see.

"Five cents I'm bid for this lovely little mouthful put up by the school teacher's own fair hands. Five cents! Five——"

"One dollar!" Pervus DeJong.

The balloon faces were suddenly punctured with holes. High Prairie's jaw dropped with astonishment. Its mouth stood open.

There was nothing plain about Selina now. Her dark head was held high, and his fair one beside it made a vivid foil. The purchase of the wine-coloured cashmere was at last justified.

"And ten!" cackled old Johannes Ambuul, his rheumy eyes on Selina.

Art and human spitefulness struggled visibly for mastery in Adam Ooms's face—and art won. The auctioneer triumphed over the man. The term "crowd psychology" was unknown to him, but he was artist enough to sense that some curious magic process, working through this roomful of people, had transformed the little white box, from a thing despised and ridiculed, into an object of beauty, of value, of infinite desirability. He now eyed it in a catalepsy of admiration.

"One-ten I'm bid for this box all tied with a ribbon to match the gown of the girl who brought it. Gents, you get the ribbon, the lunch, *and* the girl. And only one-ten bid for that. Gents! Gents! Remember, it ain't only a lunch—it's a picture. It pleases the eye. Do I hear one——"

"Five bits!" Barend DeRoo, of Low Prairie, in the lists. A strapping young Dutchman, the Brom Bones of the district. Aaltje Huff, in a fit of pique at his indifference, had married to spite him. Cornelia Vinke, belle of New Haarlem, was said to be languishing for love of him. He drove to the Haymarket with his load of produce and played cards all night on the wagon under the gas torches while the street girls of the neighbourhood assailed him in vain. Six feet three, his red face shone now like a harvest moon above the crowd. A merry, mischievous eye that laughed at Pervus DeJong and his dollar bid.

"Dollar and a half!" A high clear voice—a boy's voice. Roelf.

"Oh, no!" said Selina aloud. But she was unheard in the gabble.

Roelf had once confided to her that he had saved three dollars and fifty cents in the last three years. Five dollars would purchase a set of tools that his mind had been fixed on for months past. Selina saw Klaas Pool's look of astonishment changing to anger. Saw Maartje Pool's quick hand on his arm, restraining him.

"Two dollars!" Pervus DeJong.

"Twotwotwotwotwotwo!" Adam Ooms in a frenzy of salesman-ship.

"And ten." Johannes Ambuul's cautious bid.

"Two and a quarter." Barend DeRoo.

"Two-fifty!" Pervus DeJong.

"Three dollars!" The high voice of the boy. It cracked a little on the last syllable, and the crowd laughed.

"Three-three-three-three-threethreethree. Three once——"

"And a half." Pervus DeJong.

"Three sixty."

"Four!" DeRoo.

"And ten."

The boy's voice was heard no more.

"I wish they'd stop," whispered Selina.

"Five!" Pervus DeJong.

"Six!" DeRoo, his face very red.

"And ten."

"Seven!"

"It's only jelly sandwiches," said Selina to DeJong, in a panic.

"Eight!" Johannes Ambuul, gone mad.

"Nine!" DeRoo.

"Nine! Nine I'm bid! Nine-nine-nine! Who'll make it——"

"Let him have it. The cup cakes fell a little. Don't——"

"Ten!" said Pervus DeJong.

Barend DeRoo shrugged his great shoulders.

"Ten-ten-ten. Do I hear eleven? Do I hear ten-fifty! Ten-ten-ten-ten-tententtentententen! Gents! Ten once. Ten twice! Gone!—for ten dollars to Pervus DeJong. And a bargain." Adam Ooms mopped his bald head and his cheeks and the damp spot under his chin.

Ten dollars. Adam Ooms knew, as did all the countryside, this was not the sum of ten dollars merely. No basket of food, though it contained nightingales' tongues, the golden apple of Atalanta, wines of rare vintage, could have been adequate recompense for these ten dollars. They represented sweat and blood; toil and hardship; hours under the burning prairie sun at mid-day; work doggedly carried on through the drenching showers of spring; nights of restless sleep snatched an hour at a time under the sky in the Chicago market place; miles of weary travel down the rude corduroy road between High Prairie and Chicago, now up to the hubs in mud, now blinded by dust and blowing sand.

A sale at Christie's, with a miniature going for a million, could not have met with a deeper hush, a more dramatic babble following the hush.

They ate their lunch together in one corner of Adam Ooms's hall. Selina opened the box and took out the devilled eggs, and the cup cakes that had fallen a little, and the apples, and the sandwiches sliced very, very thin. The coldly appraising eye of all High Prairie, Low Prairie, and New Haarlem watched this sparse provender emerge from the ribbon-tied shoe box. She offered him a sandwich. It looked infinitesimal in his great paw. Suddenly all Selina's agony of embarrassment was swept away, and she was laughing, not wildly or hysterically, but joyously and girlishly. She sank her little white teeth into one of the absurd sandwiches and looked at him, expecting to find him laughing, too. But he wasn't laughing. He looked very earnest, and his blue eyes were fixed hard on the bit of bread in his hand, and his face was very red and clean-shaven. He bit into the sandwich and chewed it solemnly. And Selina thought: "Why, the dear thing! The great big dear thing! And he might have been eating breast of duck . . . Ten dollars!" Aloud she said, "What made you do it?"

"I don't know. I don't know." Then, "You looked so little. And they were making fun. Laughing." He looked very earnest, and his blue eyes were fixed hard on the sandwich, and his face was very red.

"That's a very foolish reason for throwing away ten dollars," Selina said, severely.

He seemed not to hear her; bit ruminantly into one of the cup cakes. Suddenly: "I can't hardly write at all, only to sign my name and like that."

"Read?"

"Only to spell out the words. Anyways I don't get time for reading. But figuring I wish I knew. 'Rithmetic. I can figger some, but those fellows in Haymarket they are too sharp for me. They do numbers in their head—like that, so quick."

Selina leaned toward him. "I'll teach you. I'll teach you."

"How do you mean, teach me?"

"Evenings."

He looked down at his great calloused palms, then up at her. "What would you take for pay?"

"Pay! I don't want any pay." She was genuinely shocked.

His face lighted up with a sudden thought. "Tell you what. My place is just this side the school, next to Bouts's place. I could start for you the fire, mornings, in the school. And thaw the pump and bring in a pail of water. This month, and January and February and part of March, even, now I don't go to market on account it's winter, I could start you the fire. Till spring. And I could come maybe three times a week, evenings, to Pool's place, for lessons." He looked so helpless, so humble, so huge; and the more pathetic for his hugeness.

She felt a little rush of warmth toward him that was at once impersonal and maternal. She thought again, "Why, the dear thing! The great helpless big thing! How serious he is! And funny." He was indeed both serious and funny, with the ridiculous cup cake in his great hand, his eyes wide and ruminant, his face ruddier than ever, his forehead knotted with earnestness. She laughed, suddenly, a gay little laugh and he, after a puzzled pause, joined her companionably.

"Three evenings a week," repeated Selina, then, from the depths of her ignorance. "Why, I'd love to. I'd—love to."

6

The evenings turned out to be Tuesdays, Thursdays, and Saturdays. Supper was over by six-thirty in the Pool household. Pervus was there by seven, very clean as to shirt, his hair brushed till it shone; shy, and given to dropping his hat and bumping against chairs, and looking solemn. Selina was torn between pity and mirth. If only he had blustered. A blustering big man puts the world on the defensive. A gentle giant disarms it.

Selina got out her McBride's Grammar and Duffy's Arithmetic, and together they started to parse verbs, paper walls, dig cisterns, and extract square roots. They found study impossible at the oilcloth-covered kitchen table, with the Pool household eddying about it. Jakob built a fire in the parlour stove and there they sat, teacher and pupil, their feet resting cosily on the gleaming nickel railing that encircled the wood burner.

On the evening of the first lesson Roelf had glowered throughout supper and had disappeared into the work-shed, whence issued a great sound of hammering, sawing, and general clatter. He and Selina had got into the way of spending much time together, in or out of doors. They skated on Vander Sijde's pond; together with the shrieking pigtails they coasted on the little slope that led down from Kuyper's woods to the main road, using sleds that had been put together by Roelf. On bad days they read or studied. Not Sundays merely, but many weekday evenings were spent thus. Selina was determined that

Roelf should break away from the uncouth speech of the countryside; that he should at least share with her the somewhat sketchy knowledge gained at Miss Fister's select school. She, the woman of almost twenty, never talked down to this boy of twelve. The boy worshipped her inarticulately. She had early discovered that he had a feeling for beauty—beauty of line, texture, colour, and grouping—that was rare in one of his years. The feel of a satin ribbon in his fingers; the orange and rose of a sunset; the folds of the wine-red cashmere dress; the cadence of a spoken line, brought a look to his face that startled her. She had a battered volume of Tennyson. When first she read him the line beginning, "Elaine the fair, Elaine the lovable, Elaine, the lily maid of Astolat——" he had uttered a little exclamation. She, glancing up from her book, had found his eyes wide, bright, and luminous in his lean dark face.

"What is it, Roelf?"

He had flushed. "I didn't say nothing—anything. Start over again how it goes, 'Elaine——' "

She had begun again the fragrant lines, "Elaine the fair, Elaine the lovable . . ."

Since the gathering at Ooms's hall he had been moody and sullen; had refused to answer when she spoke to him of his bid for her basket. Urged, he would only say, "Oh, it was just fun to make old Ooms mad."

Now, with the advent of Pervus DeJong, Roelf presented that most touching and miserable of spectacles, a small boy jealous and helpless in his jealousy. Selina had asked him to join the tri-weekly evening lessons; had, indeed, insisted that he be a pupil in the class round the parlour stove. Maartje had said, on the night of Pervus DeJong's first visit, "Roelf, you sit, too, and learn. Is good for you to learn out of books the way teacher says." Klaas Pool, too, had approved the plan, since it would cost nothing and, furthermore, would in no way interfere with Roelf's farm work. "Sure; learn," he said, with a large gesture.

Roelf would not. He behaved very badly; slammed doors, whistled, scuffled on the kitchen floor, made many mysterious trips through the parlour up the stairs that led off that room, ascending with a clatter; incited Geertje and Jozina to quarrels and tears; had the household in a hubbub; stumbled over Dunder, the dog, so that that anguished animal's yelps were added to the din.

Selina was frantic. Lessons were impossible amidst this uproar. "It has never been like this before," she assured Pervus, almost tearfully. "I don't know what's the matter. It's awful."

Pervus had looked up from his slate. His eyes were calm, his lips smiling. "Is all right. In my house is too still, evenings. Next time it goes better. You see."

Next time it did go better. Roelf disappeared into his work-shed after supper; did not emerge until after DeJong's departure.

There was something about the sight of this great creature bent laboriously over a slate, the pencil held clumsily in his huge fingers, that moved Selina strangely. Pity wracked her. If she had known to what emotion this pity was akin she might have taken away the slate and given him a tablet, and the whole course of her life would have been different. "Poor lad," she thought. "Poor lad." Chided herself for being amused at his childlike earnestness.

He did not make an apt pupil, though painstaking. Usually the top draught of the stove was open, and the glow of the fire imparted to his face and head a certain roseate glory. He was very grave. His brow wore a troubled frown. Selina would go over a problem or a sentence again and again, patiently, patiently. Then, suddenly, like a hand passed over his face, his smile would come, transforming it. He had white strong teeth, too small, and perhaps not so white as they seemed because of his russet blondeur. He would smile like a child, and Selina should have been warned by the warm rush of joy that his smile gave her. She would smile, too. He was as pleased as though he had made a fresh and wonderful discovery.

"It's easy," he would say, "when you know it once." Like a boy.

He usually went home by eight-thirty or nine. Often the Pools went to bed before he left. After he had gone Selina was wakeful. She would heat water and wash; brush her hair vigorously; feeling at once buoyant and depressed.

Sometimes they fell to talking. His wife had died in the second year of their marriage, when the child was born. The child, too, had died. A girl. He was unlucky, like that. It was the same with the farm.

"Spring, half of the land is under water. My piece, just. Bouts's place, next to me, is high and rich. Bouts, he don't even need deep ploughing. His land is quick land. It warms up in the spring early. After rain it works easy. He puts in fertilizer, any kind, and his plants jump, like. My place is bad for garden truck. Wet. All the time, wet; or in summer baked before I can loosen it again. Muckland."

Selina thought a moment. She had heard much talk between Klaas and Jakob, winter evenings. "Can't you do something to it—fix it—so that the water will run off? Raise it, or dig a ditch or something?"

"We-e-ell, maybe. Maybe you could. But it costs money, draining."

"It costs money not to, doesn't it?"

He considered this, ruminatively. "Guess it does. But you don't have to have ready cash to let the land lay. To drain it you do."

Sellina shook her head impatiently. "That's a very foolish, short-sighted way to reason."

He looked helpless as only the strong and powerful can look. Selina's heart melted in pity. He would look down at the great calloused hands; up at her. One of the charms of Pervus DeJong lay in the things that his eyes said and his tongue did not. Women always imagined he was about to say what he looked, but he never did. It made otherwise dull conversation with him most exciting.

His was in no way a shrewd mind. His respect for Selina was almost reverence. But he had this advantage: he had married a woman, had lived with her for two years. She had borne him a child. Selina was a girl in experience. She was a woman capable of a great deal of passion, but she did not know that. Passion was a thing no woman possessed, much less talked about. It simply did not exist, except in men, and then was something to be ashamed of, like a violent temper, or a weak stomach.

By the first of March he could speak a slow, careful, and fairly grammatical English. He could master simple sums. By the middle of March the lessons would cease. There was too much work to do about the farm—night work as well as day. She found herself trying not to think about the time when the lessons should cease. She refused to look ahead to April.

One night, late in February, Selina was conscious that she was trying to control something. She was trying to keep her eyes away from something. She realized that she was trying not to look at his hands. She wanted, crazily, to touch them. She wanted to feel them about her throat. She wanted to put her lips on his hands—brush the backs of them, slowly, moistly, with her mouth, lingeringly. She was terribly frightened. She thought to herself: "I am going crazy. I am losing my mind. There is something the matter with me. I wonder how I look. I must look queer."

She said something to make him look up at her. His glance was mild, undismayed. So this hideous thing did not show in her face. She kept her eyes resolutely on the book. At half-past eight she closed her book suddenly. "I'm tired. I think it's the spring coming on." She smiled a little wavering smile. He rose and stretched himself, his great arms high above his head. Selina shivered.

"Two more weeks," he said, "is the last lesson. Well, do you think I have done pretty good—well?"

"Very well," Selina replied, evenly. She felt very tired.

The first week in March he was ill, and did not come. A rheumatic affliction to which he was subject. His father, old Johannes DeJong, had had it before him. Working in the wet fields did it, they said. It was the curse of the truck farmer. Selina's evenings were free to devote to Roelf, who glowed again. She sewed, too; read; helped Mrs. Pool with the housework in a gust of sympathy and found strange relief therein; made over an old dress; studied; wrote all her letters (few enough), even one to the dried-apple aunts in Vermont. She no longer wrote to Julie Hempel. She had heard that Julie was to be married to a Kansas man named Arnold. Julie herself had not written. The first week in March passed. He did not come. Nor did he come the following Tuesday or Thursday. After a terrific battle with herself Selina, after school on Thursday, walked past his house, busily, as though bent on an errand. Despised herself for doing it, could not help herself, found a horrible and tortuous satisfaction in not looking at the house as she passed it.

She was bewildered, frightened. All that week she had a curious feeling—or succession of feelings. There was the sensation of suffocation followed by that of emptiness—of being hollow—boneless—bloodless. Then, at times, there was a feeling of physical pain; at others a sense of being disemboweled. She was restless, listless, by turns. Period of furious activity followed by days of inertia. It was the spring, Maartje said. Selina hoped she wasn't going to be ill. She had never felt like that before. She wanted to cry. She was irritable to the point of waspishness with the children in the schoolroom.

On Saturday—the fourteenth of March—he walked in at seven. Klaas, Maartje, and Roelf had driven off to a gathering at Low Prairie, leaving Selina with the pigtails and old Jakob. She had promised to make taffy for them, and was in the midst of it when his knock sounded at the kitchen door. All the blood in her body rushed to her head; pounded there hotly. He entered. There slipped down over her a complete armour of calmness, of self-possession; of glib how do you do Mr. DeJong and how are you feeling and won't you sit down and there's no fire in the parlour we'll have to sit here.

He took part in the taffy pulling. Selina wondered if Geertje and Jozina would ever have done squealing. It was half-past eight before she bundled them off to bed with a plate of chipped taffy lozenges between them. She heard them scuffling and scrimmaging about in the rare freedom of their parents' absence.

"Now, children!" she called. "You know what you promised your mother and father."

She heard Geertje's tones mimicking her mincingly, "You know what you promised your mother and father." Then a cascade of smothered giggles.

Pervus had been to town, evidently, for he now took from his coat pocket a bag containing half a dozen bananas—that delicacy of delicacies to the farm palate. She half peeled two and brought them in to the pigtails. They ate them thickly rapturous, and dropped off to sleep immediately, surfeited.

Pervus DeJong and Selina sat at the kitchen table, their books spread out before them on the oilcloth. The sweet heavy scent of the fruit filled the room. Selina brought the parlour lamp into the kitchen, the better to see. It was a nickel-bellied lamp with a yellow glass shade that cast a mellow golden glow.

"You didn't go to the meeting," primly. "Mr. and Mrs. Pool went."

"No. No, I didn't go."

"Why not?"

She saw him swallow. "I got through too late. I went to town, and I got through too late. We're fixing to sow tomato seeds in the hotbeds to-morrow."

Selina opened McBride's Grammar. "Ahem!" a school-teacherly cough. "Now, then, we'll parse this sentence: Blucher arrived on the field of Waterloo just as Wellington was receiving the last onslaught of Napoleon. 'Just' may be treated as a modifier of the dependent clause. That is: 'Just' means: at the time *at which*. Well. *Just* here modified *at the time*. And Wellington is the . . ."

This for half an hour. Selina kept her eyes resolutely on the book. His voice went on with the dry business of parsing and its deep resonance struck a response from her as a harp responds when a hand is swept over its strings. Upstairs she could hear old Jakob clumping about in his preparations for bed. Then there was only stillness overhead. Selina kept her eyes resolutely on the book. Yet she saw, as though her eyes rested on them, his large, strong hands. On the backs of them was a fine golden down that deepened at his wrists. Heavier and darker at the wrists. She found herself praying a little for strength—for strength against this horror and wickedness. This sin, this abomination that held her. A terrible, stark, and pitiful prayer, couched in the idiom of the Bible.

"Oh, God, keep my eyes and my thoughts away from him. Away from his hands. Let me keep my eyes and my thoughts away from the golden hairs on his wrists. Let me not think of his wrists. . . . "The owner of the southwest $1/4$ sells a strip 20 rods wide along the south side of his farm. How much does he receive at $150 per acre?"

He triumphed in this transaction, began the struggle with the square root of 576. Square roots agonized him. She washed the slate clean with her little sponge. He was leaning close in his effort to comprehend the fiendish little figures that marched so tractably under Selina's masterly pencil.

She took it up, glibly. "The remainder must contain twice the product of the tens by the units plus the square of the units." He blinked. Utterly bewildered. "*And,*" went on Selina, blithely, "twice the tens, times the units, plus the square of the units, is the same as the sum of twice the tens, and the units, times the units. *Therefore*"— with a flourish—"add 4 units to the 40 and multiply the result by 4. *Therefore*"—in final triumph—"the square root of 576 is 24."

She was breathing rather fast. The fire in the kitchen stove snapped and cracked. "Now, then, suppose you do that for me. We'll wipe it out. There! What must the remainder contain?"

He took it up, slowly, haltingly. The house was terribly still except for the man's voice. "The remainder . . . twice . . . product . . . tens . . . units . . ." A something in his voice—a note—a timbre. She felt herself swaying queerly, as though the whole house were gently rocking. Little delicious agonizing shivers chased each other, hot and cold, up her arms, down her legs, over her spine. . . . "plus the square of the units is the same as the sum twice the tens . . . twice . . . the tens . . . the tens . . ." His voice stopped.

Selina's eyes leaped from the book to his hands, uncontrollably. Something about them startled her. They were clenched into fists. Her eyes now leaped from those clenched fists to the face of the man beside her. Her head came up, and back. Her wide startled eyes met his. His were a blaze of blinding blue in his tanned face. Some corner of her mind that was still working clearly noted this. Then his hands unclenched. The blue blaze scorched her, enveloped her. Her cheek knew the harsh cool feel of a man's cheek. She sensed the potent, terrifying, pungent odour of close contact—a mixture of tobacco smoke, his hair, freshly laundered linen, an indefinable body smell. It was a mingling that disgusted and attracted her. She was at once repelled and drawn. Then she felt his lips on hers and her own, incredibly, responding eagerly, wholly to that pressure.

7

They were married the following May, just two months later. The High Prairie school year practically ended with the appearance of the first tender shoots of green that meant onions, radishes, and spinach above the rich sandy loam. Selina's classes broke, dwindled, shrank to almost nothing. The school became a kindergarten of five-year-old babies who wriggled and shifted and scratched in the warm spring air that came from the teeming prairie through the open windows. The schoolhouse stove stood rusty-red and cold. The drum in Selina's bedroom was a black genie deprived of his power now to taunt her.

Selina was at once bewildered and calm; rebellious and content. Over-laying these emotions was something like grim amusement. Beneath them, something like fright. High Prairie, in May, was green and gold and rose and blue. The spring flowers painted the fields and the roadside with splashes of yellow, of pink, of mauve, and purple. Violets, buttercups, mandrakes, marsh-marigolds, hepatica. The air was soft and cool from the lake. Selina had never known spring in the country before. It made her ache with an actual physical ache. She moved with a strange air of fatality. It was as if she were being drawn inexorably, against her will, her judgment, her plans, into something sweet and terrible. When with Pervus she was elated, gay, voluble. He talked little; looked at her dumbly, worshippingly. When he brought her a withered bunch of trilliums, the tears came to her eyes. He had walked to Updike's woods to get them because he had heard her say she loved them, and there were none nearer. They were limp and listless from the heat, and from being held in his hand. He looked up at her from where he stood on the kitchen steps, she in the doorway. She took them, laid her hand on his head. It was as when some great gentle dog brings in a limp and bedraggled prize dug from the yard and, laying it at one's feet, looks up at one with soft asking eyes.

There were days when the feeling of unreality possessed her. She, a truck farmer's wife, living in High Prairie the rest of her days! Why, no! No! Was this the great adventure that her father had always spoken of? She, who was going to be a happy wayfarer down the path of life—any one of a dozen things. This High Prairie winter was to have been only an episode. Not her life! She looked at Maartje. Oh, but she'd never be like that. That was stupid, unnecessary. Pink and blue dresses in the house, for her. Frills on the window curtains. Flowers in bowls.

Some of the pangs and terrors with which most prospective brides are assailed she confided to Mrs. Pool while that active lady was slamming about the kitchen.

"Did you ever feel scared and—and sort of—scared when you thought about marrying, Mrs. Pool?"

Maartje Pool's hands were in a great batch of bread dough which she pummelled and slapped and kneaded vigorously. She shook out a handful of flour on the baking board while she held the dough mass in the other hand, then plumped it down and again began to knead, both hands doubled into fists.

She laughed a short little laugh. "I ran away."

"You did! You mean you really ran—but why? Didn't you lo—like Klaas?"

Maartje Pool kneaded briskly, the colour high in her cheeks, what with the vigorous pummelling and rolling, and something else that made her look strangely young for the moment—girlish, almost. "Sure I liked him. I liked him."

"But you ran away?"

"Not far. I came back. Nobody ever knew I ran, even. But I ran. I knew."

"Why did you come back?"

Maartje elucidated her philosophy without being in the least aware that it could be called by any such high-sounding name. "You can't run away far enough. Except you stop living you can't run away from life."

The girlish look had fled. She was world-old. Her strong arms ceased their pounding and thumping for a moment. On the steps just outside Klaas and Jakob were scanning the weekly reports preparatory to going into the city late that afternoon.

Selina had the difficult task of winning Roelf to her all over again. He was like a trusting little animal, who, wounded by the hand he has trusted, is shy of it. She used blandishments on this boy of thirteen such as she had never vouchsafed the man she was going to marry. He had asked her, bluntly, one day: "Why are you going to marry with him?" He never spoke the name.

She thought deeply. What to say? The answer ready on her tongue would have little meaning for this boy. There came to her a line from Lancelot and Elaine. She answered, "To serve him, and to follow him through the world." She thought that rather fine-sounding until Roelf promptly rejected it. "That's no reason. An answer out of a book. Anyway, to follow him through the world is dumb. He stays right here in High Prairie all his life."

"How do you know!" Selina retorted, almost angrily. Startled, too.

"I know. He stays."

Still, he could not withstand her long. Together they dug and planted flower beds in Pervus's dingy front yard. It was too late for tulips now. Pervus had brought her some seeds from town. They ranged all the way from poppies to asters; from purple iris to morning glories. The last named were to form the back-porch vine, of course, because they grew quickly. Selina, city-bred, was ignorant of varieties, but insisted she wanted an old-fashioned garden—marigolds, pinks, mignonette, phlox. She and Roelf dug, spaded, planted. The DeJong place was markedly ugly even in that community of squat houses. It lacked the air of sparkling cleanliness that saved the other places from sordidness. The house, even then, was thirty years old—a gray, weather-beaten frame box with a mansard roof and a flat face staring out at the dense willows by the roadside. It needed paint; the fences sagged; the window curtains were awry. The parlour was damp, funereal. The old woman who tended the house for Pervus slopped about all day with a pail and a wet gray rag. There was always a crazy campanile of dirty dishes stacked on the table, and the last meal seemed never to catch up with the next. About the whole house there was a starkness, a bareness that proclaimed no woman who loved it dwelt therein.

Selina told herself (and Pervus) that she would change all that. She saw herself going about with a brush and a can of white paint, leaving beauty in her wake, where ugliness had been.

Her trousseau was of the scantiest. Pervus's household was already equipped with such linens as they would need. The question of a wedding gown troubled her until Maartje suggested that she be married in the old Dutch wedding dress that lay in the bride's chest in Selina's bedroom.

"A real Dutch bride," Maartje said. "Your man will think that is fine." Pervus was delighted. Selina basked in his love like a kitten in the sun. She was, after all, a very lonely little bride with only two photographs on the shelf in her bedroom to give her courage and counsel. The old Dutch wedding gown was many inches too large for her. The skirt-band overlapped her slim waist; her slender little bosom did not fill out the generous width of the bodice; but the effect of the whole was amazingly quaint as well as pathetic. The wings of the stiffly embroidered coif framed the white face from which the eyes looked out, large and dark. She had even tried to wear the hand-carved shoes, but had to give that up. In them her feet were as lost as minnows in a rowboat. She had much difficulty with the queer old buttons and fastenings. It was as though the dead and gone Sophia Kroon were trying, with futile ghostly fingers, to prevent this young thing from meeting the fate that was to be hers.

They were married at the Pools'. Klaas and Maartje had insisted on furnishing the wedding supper—ham, chickens, sausages, cakes,

pickles, beer. The Reverend Dekker married them and all through the ceremony Selina chided herself because she could not keep her mind on his words in the fascination of watching his short stubby beard as it waggled with every motion of his jaw. Pervus looked stiff, solemn, and uncomfortable in his wedding blacks—not at all the handsome giant of the everyday corduroys and blue shirt. In the midst of the ceremony Selina had her moment of panic when she actually saw herself running shrieking from this company, this man, this house, down the road, on, on toward—toward what? The feeling was so strong that she was surprised to find herself still standing there in the Dutch wedding gown answering "I do" in the proper place.

The wedding gifts were few. The Pools had given them a "hanging lamp," coveted of the farmer's wife; a hideous atrocity in yellow, with pink roses on its shade and prisms dangling and tinkling all around the edge. It was intended to hang suspended from the parlour ceiling, and worked up and down on a sort of pulley chain. From the Widow Paarlenberg came a water set in red frosted glass shading to pink—a fat pitcher and six tumblers. Roelf's gift, the result of many weeks' labour in the work-shed, was a bride's chest copied from the fine old piece that had saved Selina's room from sheer ugliness. He had stained the wood, polished it. Had carved the front of it with her initials—very like those that stood out so boldly on the old chest upstairs—S.P.D. And the year—1890. The whole was a fine piece of craftsmanship for a boy of thirteen—would not have discredited a man of any age. It was the one beautiful gift among Selina's clumsy crude wedding things. She had thanked him with tears in her eyes. "Roelf, you'll come to see me often, won't you? Often!" Then, as he had hesitated, "I'll need you so. You're all I've got." A strange thing for a bride to say.

"I'll come," the boy had said, trying to make his voice casual, his tone careless. "Sure, I'll come oncet in a while."

"Once, Roelf. *Once* in a while."

He repeated it after her, dutifully.

After the wedding they went straight to DeJong's house. In May the vegetable farmer cannot neglect his garden even for a day. The

house had been made ready for them. The sway of the old house-keeper was over. Her kitchen bedroom was empty.

Throughout the supper Selina had had thoughts which were so foolish and detached as almost to alarm her.

"Now I am married. I am Mrs. Pervus DeJong. That's a pretty name. It would look quite distinguished on a calling card, very spidery and fine:

Mrs. Pervus DeJong

At Home Fridays

She recalled this later, grimly, when she was Mrs. Pervus DeJong, at home not only Fridays, but Saturdays, Sundays, Mondays, Tuesdays, Wednesdays, and Thursdays.

They drove down the road to DeJong's place. Selina thought, "Now I am driving home with my husband. I feel his shoulder against mine. I wish he would talk. I wish he would say something. Still, I'm not frightened."

Pervus's market wagon was standing in the yard, shafts down. He should have gone to market to-day; would certainly have to go tomorrow, starting early in the afternoon so as to get a good stand in the Haymarket. By the light of his lantern the wagon seemed to Selina to be a symbol. She had often seen it before, but now that it was to be a part of her life—this the DeJong market wagon and she Mrs. DeJong—she saw clearly what a crazy, disreputable, and poverty-

proclaiming old vehicle it was, in contrast with the neat strong wagon in Klaas Pool's yard, smart with green paint and red lettering that announced, "Klaas Pool, Garden Produce." With the two sleek farm horses the turnout looked as prosperous and comfortable as Klaas himself.

Pervus swung her down from the seat of the buggy, his hand about her waist, and held her so for a moment, close. Selina said, "You must have that wagon painted, Pervus. And the seat-springs fixed and the sideboard mended."

He stared. "Wagon!"

"Yes. It looks a sight."

The house was tidy enough, but none too clean. Old Mrs. Voorhees had not been minded to keep house too scrupulously for a man who would be unlikely to know whether or not it was clean. Pervus lighted the lamps. There was a fire in the kitchen stove. It made the house seem stuffy on this mild May night. Selina thought that her own little bedroom at the Pools', no longer hers, must be deliciously cool and still with the breeze fanning fresh from the west. Pervus was putting the horse into the barn. The bedroom was off the sitting room. The window was shut. This last year had taught Selina to prepare the night before for next morning's rising, so as to lose the least possible time. She did this now, unconsciously. She took off her white muslin underwear with its frills and embroidery—the three stiff petticoats, and the stiffly starched corset-cover, and the high-bosomed corset and put them into the bureau drawer that she herself had cleaned and papered neatly the week before. She brushed her hair, laid out tomorrow's garments, put on her high-necked, long-sleeved nightgown and got into this strange bed. She heard Pervus DeJong shut the kitchen door; the latch clicked, the lock turned. Heavy quick footsteps across the bare kitchen floor. This man was coming into her room . . . "You can't run far enough," Maartje Pool had said. "Except you stop living you can't run away from life."

Next morning it was dark when he awakened her at four. She started up with a little cry and sat up, straining her ears, her eyes. "Is that you, Father?" She was little Selina Peake again, and Simeon Peake had come in, gay, debonair, from a night's gaming. Pervus DeJong was already padding about the room in stocking feet. "What—what time is it? What's the matter, Father? Why are you up? Haven't you gone to bed . . ." Then she remembered.

Pervus DeJong laughed and came toward her. "Get up, little lazy bones. It's after four. All yesterday's work I've got to do, and all today's. Breakfast, little Lina, breakfast. You are a farmer's wife now."

8

By October High Prairie housewives told each other that Mrs. Pervus DeJong was "expecting." Dirk DeJong was born in the bedroom off the sitting room on the fifteenth day of March, of a bewildered, somewhat resentful, but deeply interested mother; and a proud, foolish, and vainglorious father whose air of achievement, considering the really slight part he had played in the long, tedious, and racking business, was disproportionate. The name Dirk had sounded to Selina like something tall, straight, and slim. Pervus had chosen it. It had been his grandfather's name.

Sometimes, during those months, Selina would look back on her first winter in High Prairie—that winter of the icy bedroom, the chill black drum, the schoolhouse fire, the chilblains, the Pool pork—and it seemed a lovely dream; a time of ease, of freedom, of careless happiness. That icy room had been her room; that mile of road traversed on bitter winter mornings a mere jaunt; the schoolhouse stove a toy, fractious but fascinating.

Pervus DeJong loved his pretty young wife, and she him. But young love thrives on colour, warmth, beauty. It becomes prosaic and inarticulate when forced to begin its day at four in the morning by reaching blindly, dazedly, for limp and obscure garments dangling from bedpost or chair, and to end that day at nine, numb and sodden with weariness, after seventeen hours of physical labour.

It was a wet summer. Pervus's choice tomato plants, so carefully set out in the hope of a dry season, became draggled gray spectres in a waste of mire. Of fruit the field bore one tomato the size of a marble.

For the rest, the crops were moderately successful on the DeJong place. But the work necessary to make this so was heartbreaking. Pervus and his hired helper, Jan Steen, used the hand sower and hand cultivator. It seemed to Selina that they were slaves to these buds, shoots, and roots that clamoured with a hundred thousand voices, "Let me out! Let me out!" She had known, during her winter at the Pools', that Klaas, Roelf, and old Jakob worked early and late, but her months there had encompassed what is really the truck farmer's leisure period. She had arrived in November. She had married in May. From May until October it was necessary to tend the fields with a concentration amounting to fury. Selina had never dreamed that human beings toiled like that for sustenance. Toil was a thing she had never encountered until coming to High Prairie. Now she saw her husband wrenching a living out of the earth by sheer muscle, sweat, and pain. During June, July, August, and September the good black prairie soil for miles around was teeming, a hotbed of plenty. There was born in Selina at this time a feeling for the land that she was never to lose. Perhaps the child within her had something to do with this. She was aware of a feeling of kinship with the earth; an illusion of splendour, or fulfilment. Sometimes, in a moment's respite from her work about the house, she would stand in the kitchen doorway, her flushed face turned toward the fields. Wave on wave of green, wave on wave, until the waves melted into each other and became a verdant sea.

As cabbages had been cabbages, and no more, to Klaas Pool, so, to Pervus, these carrots, beets, onions, turnips, and radishes were just so much produce, to be planted, tended, gathered, marketed. But to Selina, during that summer, they became a vital part in the vast mechanism of a living world. Pervus, earth, sun, rain, all elemental forces that laboured to produce the food for millions of humans. The sordid, grubby little acreage became a kingdom; the phlegmatic Dutch-American truck farmers of the region were high priests consecrated to the service of the divinity, Earth. She thought of Chicago's children. If they had red cheeks, clear eyes, nimble brains it was because Pervus brought them the food that made them so. It was before the day when glib talk of irons, vitamines, arsenic entered into all discussion pertaining to food. Yet Selina sensed something of the meaning behind these toiling, patient figures, all unconscious of meaning, bent double in the fields for miles throughout High Prairie. Something of this she tried to convey to Pervus. He only stared, his blue eyes wide and unresponsive.

"Farm work grand! Farm work is slave work. Yesterday, from the load of carrots in town I didn't make enough to bring you the goods for the child so when it comes you should have clothes for it. It's better I feed them to the livestock."

Pervus drove into the Chicago market every other day. During July and August he sometimes did not have his clothes off for a week. Together he and Jan Steen would load the wagon with the day's garnering. At four he would start on the tedious trip into town. The historic old Haymarket on west Randolph Street had become the stand for market gardeners for miles around Chicago. Here they stationed their wagons in preparation for the next day's selling. The wagons stood, close packed, in triple rows, down both sides of the curb and in the middle of the street. The early comer got the advantageous stand. There was no regular allotment of space. Pervus tried to reach the Haymarket by nine at night. Often bad roads made a detour necessary and he was late. That usually meant bad business next day. The men, for the most part, slept on their wagons, curled up on the wagon-seat or stretched out on the sacks. Their horses were stabled and fed in nearby sheds, with more actual comfort than the men themselves. One could get a room for twenty-five cents in one of the ramshackle rooming houses that faced the street. But the rooms were small, stuffy, none too clean; the beds little more comfortable than the wagons. Besides, twenty-five cents! You got twenty-five cents for half a barrel of tomatoes. You got twenty-five cents for a sack of potatoes. Onions brought seventy-five cents a sack. Cabbages went a hundred heads for two dollars, and they were five-pound heads. If you drove home with ten dollars in your pocket it represented a profit of exactly zero. The sum must go above that. No; one did not pay out twenty-five cents for the mere privilege of sleeping in a bed.

One June day, a month or more after their marriage, Selina drove into Chicago with Pervus, an incongruous little figure in her bride's finery perched on the seat of the vegetable wagon piled high with early garden stuff. They had started before four that afternoon, and reached the city at nine, though the roads were still heavy from the late May rains. It was, in a way, their wedding trip, for Selina had not been away from the farm since her marriage. The sun was bright and hot. Selina held an umbrella to shield herself from the heat and looked about her with enjoyment and interest. She chattered, turned her head this way and that, exclaimed, questioned. Sometimes she wished that Pervus would respond more quickly to her mood. A gay, volatile creature, she frisked about him like a friendly bright-eyed terrier about a stolid, ponderous St. Bernard.

As they jogged along now she revealed magnificent plans that had been forming in her imagination during the past four weeks. It had not taken her four weeks—or days—to discover that this great broad-shouldered man she had married was a kindly creature, tender and good, but lacking any vestige of initiative, of spirit. She marvelled, sometimes, at the memory of his boldness in bidding for her lunch box that evening of the raffle. It seemed incredible now, though he frequently referred to it, wagging his head doggishly and grinning the broadly complacent grin of the conquering male. But he was, after all, a dull fellow, and there was in Selina a dash of fire, of wholesome wickedness, of adventure, that he never quite understood. For her flashes of flame he had a mingled feeling of uneasiness and pride.

In the manner of all young brides, Selina started bravely out to make her husband over. He was handsome, strong, gentle; slow, conservative, morose. She would make him keen, daring, successful, buoyant. Now, bumping down the Halsted road, she sketched some of her plans in large dashing strokes.

"Pervus, we must paint the house in October, before the frost sets in, and after the summer work is over. White would be nice, with green trimmings. Though perhaps white isn't practical. Or maybe

green with darker green trimmings. A lovely background for the hol-
lyhocks." (Those that she and Roelf had planted showed no signs of
coming up.) "Then that west sixteen. We'll drain it."

"Yeh, drain," Pervus muttered. "It's clay land. Drain and you
have got yet clay. Hard clay soil."

Selina had the answer to that. "I know it. You've got to use tile
drainage. And—wait a minute—humus. I know what humus is. It's
decayed vegetables. There's always a pile by the side of the barn; and
you've been using it on the quick land. All the west sixteen isn't clay.
Part of it's muckland. All it needs is draining and manure. With potash, too, and phosphoric acid."

Pervus laughed a great hearty laugh that Selina found surprisingly infuriating. He put one great brown hand patronizingly on her
flushed cheek; pinched it gently.

"Don't!" said Selina, and jerked her head away. It was the first
time she had ever resented a caress from him.

Pervus laughed again. "Well, well, well! School teacher is a
farmer now, huh? I bet even Widow Paarlenberg don't know as much
as my little farmer about"—he exploded again—"about this, now,
potash and—what kind of acid? Tell me, little Lina, from where did
you learn all this about truck farming?"

"Out of a book," Selina said, almost snappishly. "I sent to Chicago for it."

"A book! A book!" He slapped his knee. "A vegetable farmer
out of a book."

"Why not! The man who wrote it knows more about vegetable
farming than anybody in all High Prairie. He knows about new ways.
You're running the farm just the way your father ran it."

"What was good enough for my father is good enough for me."

"It isn't!" cried Selina, "It isn't! The book says clay loam is all
right for cabbages, peas, and beans. It tells you how. It tells you how!"
She was like a frantic little fly darting and pricking him on to accelerate
the stolid sluggishness of his slow plodding gait.

Having begun, she plunged on. "We ought to have two horses
to haul the wagon to market. It would save you hours of time that

you could spend on the place. Two horses, and a new wagon, green and red, like Klaas Pool's."

Pervus stared straight ahead down the road between his horse's ears much as Klaas Pool had done so maddeningly on Selina's first ride on the Halsted road. "Fine talk. Fine talk."

"It isn't talk. It's plans. You've got to plan."

"Fine talk. Fine talk."

"Oh!" Selina beat her knee with an impotent fist. It was the nearest they had ever come to quarrelling. It would seem that Pervus had the best of the argument, for when two years had passed the west sixteen was still a boggy clay mass, and unprolific; and the old house stared out shabby and paintless, at the dense willows by the roadside.

They slept that night in one of the twenty-five-cent rooming houses. Rather, Pervus slept. The woman lay awake, listening to the city noises that had become strange in her ears; staring out into the purple-black oblong that was the open window, until that oblong became gray. She wept a little, perhaps. But in the morning Pervus might have noted (if he had been a man given to noting) that the fine jaw-line was set as determinedly as ever with an angle that spelled inevitably paint, drainage, humus, potash, phosphoric acid, and a horse team.

She rose before four with Pervus, glad to be out of the stuffy little room with its spotted and scaly green wall paper, its rickety bed and chair. They had a cup of coffee and a slice of bread in the eating house on the first floor. Selina waited while he tended the horse. The night-watchman had been paid another twenty-five cents for watching the wagonload through the night as it stood in a row with the hundreds of others in the Haymarket. It was scarcely dawn when the trading began. Selina, watching it from the wagon seat, thought that this was a ridiculously haphazard and perilous method of distributing the food for whose fruition Pervus had toiled with aching back and tired arms. But she said nothing.

She kept, perforce, to the house that first year, and the second. Pervus declared that his woman should never work in the fields as did many of the High Prairie wives and daughters. Of ready cash there was almost none. Pervus was hard put to it to pay Jan Steen his monthly wage during May, June, July, and August, when he was employed on the DeJong place, though Steen got but a pittance, being known as a poor hand, and "dumb." Selina learned much that first year, and the second, but she said little. She kept the house in order—rough work, and endless—and she managed, miraculously, to keep herself looking fresh and neat. She understood now Maartje Pool's drab garments, harrassed face, heavily swift feet, never at rest. The idea of flowers in bowls was abandoned by July. Had it not been for Roelf's faithful tending, the flower beds themselves, planted with such hopes, would have perished for lack of care.

Roelf came often to the house. He found there a tranquillity and peace never known in the Pool place, with its hubbub and clatter. In order to make her house attractive Selina had actually rifled her precious little bank hoard—the four hundred and ninety-seven dollars left her by her father. She still had one of the clear white diamonds. She kept it sewed in the hem of an old flannel petticoat. Once she had shown it to Pervus.

"If I sell this maybe we could get enough money to drain and tile."

Pervus took the stone, weighed it in his great palm, blinked as he always did when discussing a subject of which he was ignorant. "How much could you get for it? Fifty dollars, maybe. Five hundred is what I would need."

"I've got that. I've got it in the bank!"

"Well, maybe next spring. Right now I got my hands full, and more."

To Selina that seemed a short-sighted argument. But she was too newly married to stand her ground; too much in love; too ignorant still of farm conditions.

The can of white paint and the brush actually did materialize. For weeks it was dangerous to sit, lean, or tread upon any paintable thing in the DeJong farmhouse without eliciting a cry of warning from Selina. She would actually have tried her hand at the outside of the house with a quart can and three-inch brush if Pervus hadn't intervened. She hemmed dimity curtains, made slip-covers for the hideous parlour sofa and the ugliest of the chairs. Subscribed for a magazine called *House and Garden*. Together she and Roelf used to pore over this fascinating periodical. Terraces, lily-pools, leaded casements, cretonne, fireplaces, yew trees, pergolas, fountains—they absorbed them all, exclaimed, admired, actually criticized. Selina was torn between an English cottage with timbered porch, bay window, stone flagging, and an Italian villa with a broad terrace on which she would stand in trailing white with a Russian wolf-hound. If High Prairie had ever overheard one of these conversations between the farm woman who would always be a girl and the farm boy who had never been quite a child, it would have raised palms high in an "Og heden!" of horror. But High Prairie never heard, and wouldn't have understood if it had. She did another strange thing: She placed the fine hand-carved oak chest Roelf had given her in a position so that her child should see it as soon as he opened his eyes in the morning. It was the most beautiful thing she possessed. She had, too, an incomplete set of old Dutch luster ware. It had belonged to Pervus's mother, and to her mother before her. On Sunday nights Selina used this set for supper, though Pervus protested. And she always insisted that Dirk drink his milk out of one of the lovely jewel-like cups. Pervus thought this a piece of madness.

Selina was up daily at four. Dressing was a swift and mechanical covering of the body. Breakfast must be ready for Pervus and Jan when they came in from the barn. The house to clean, the chickens to tend, sewing, washing, ironing, cooking. She contrived ways of minimizing her steps, of lightening her labour. And she saw clearly how the little farm was mismanaged through lack of foresight, imagination, and—she faced it squarely—through stupidity. She was fond of this great, kindly, blundering, stubborn boy who was her husband. But she saw him with amazing clearness through the mists of her love. There was something prophetic about the way she began to absorb knowledge of the farm work, of vegetable culture, of marketing. Listening, seeing, she learned about soil, planting, weather, selling. The daily talk of the house and fields was of nothing else. About this little twenty-five-acre garden patch there was nothing of the majesty of the Iowa, Illinois, and Kansas grain farms, with their endless billows of wheat and corn, rye, alfalfa, and barley rolling away to the horizon. Everything was done in diminutive here. An acre of this. Two acres of that. A score of chickens. One cow. One horse. Two pigs. Here was all the drudgery of farm life with none of its bounteousness, fine sweep, or splendour. Selina sensed that every inch of soul should have been made to yield to the utmost. Yet there lay the west sixteen, useless during most of the year; reliable never. And there was no money to drain it or enrich it; no ready cash for the purchase or profitable neighbouring acreage. She did not know the term intensive farming, but this was what she meant. Artificial protection against the treacherous climate of the Great Lakes region was pitifully lacking in Pervus's plans. Now it would be hot with the humid, withering, sticky heat of the district. The ground was teeming, smoking, and the green things seemed actually to be pushing their way out of the earth so that one could almost see them growing, as in some absurd optical illusion. Then, without warning, would come the icy Lake Michigan wind, nipping the tender shoots with fiendish fingers. There should have been hotbeds and coldframes, forcing-hills, hand-boxes. There were almost none.

These things Selina saw, but not quite clearly. She went about her housework, now dreamily, now happily. Her physical condition swayed her mood. Sometimes, in the early autumn, when the days became cooler, she would go to where Pervus and Jan were working in the fields in the late afternoon gathering the produce for that night's trip to market. She would stand there, a bit of sewing in her hand, perhaps, the wind ruffling her hair, whipping her skirts, her face no longer pale, tilted a little toward the good sun like a lovely tawny flower. Sometimes she sat perched on a pile of empty sacks, or on an up-ended crate, her sewing in her hand. She was happiest at such times—most content—except for the pang she felt at sight of the great dark splotch on the blue of Pervus's work-shirt where the sweat stained it.

She had come out so one autumn afternoon. She was feeling

particularly gay, buoyant. In one of his rare hours of leisure Roelf Pool had come to help her with her peony roots which Pervus had brought her from Chicago for fall planting. Roelf had dug the trench, deep and wide, mulched it with cow-manure, banked it. They were to form a double row up the path to the front of the house, and in her mind's eye Selina already saw them blooming when spring should come, shaggy balls of luscious pink. Now Roelf was lending a hand to Pervus and Jan as they bent over the late beets and radishes. It was a day all gold and blue and scarlet; warm for the season with a ripe mellow warmth like yellow chartreuse. There were stretches of seal-black loam where the vegetables had been uprooted. Bunches of them, string-tied, lay ready for gathering into baskets. Selina's eye was gladdened by the clear coral of radishes flung against the rich black loam.

"A jewel, Pervus!" she cried. "A jewel in an Ethiop's ear!"

"What?" said Pervus, looking up, amiable but uncomprehending. But the boy smiled. Selina had left him that book for his own when she went away. Suddenly Selina stooped and picked up one of the scarlet and green clusters tied with its bits of string. Laughing, she whipped out a hairpin and fastened the bunch in her hair just behind her ear. An absurd thing to do, and childish. It should have looked as absurd as it was, but it didn't. Instead it was like a great crimson flower there. Her cheeks were flushed with the hot sun. Her fine dark hair was windblown and a little loosened, her dress open at the throat. Her figure was fuller, her breast had a richer curve, for the child was four months on the way. She was laughing. At a little exclamation from Roelf, Pervus looked up, as did Jan. Selina took a slow rhythmic step, and another, her arms upraised, a provocative lovely bacchic little figure there in the fields under the hot blue sky. Jan Steen wiped the sweat from his brown face, a glow in his eyes.

"You are like the calendar!" cried Roelf, "on the wall in the parlour." A cheap but vivid and not unlovely picture of a girl with cherries in her hair. It hung in the Pool farmhouse.

Pervus DeJong showed one of his rare storms of passion. Selina had not seen that blaze of blue in his eyes since the night, months ago, in the Pools' kitchen. But that blaze had been a hot and burning blue, like the sky of to-day. This was a bitter blue, a chill and freezing thing, like the steel-blue of ice in the sun.

"Take them things out of your hair now! Take shame to yourself!" He strode over to her and snatched the things from her hair and threw them down and ground them into the soft earth with his heavy heel. A long coil of her fine dark hair came rippling over her shoulder as he did so. She stood looking at him, her eyes wide, dark, enormous in her face now suddenly white.

His wrath was born of the narrow insular mind that fears gossip. He knew that the hired man would tell through the length and width of High Prairie how Pervus DeJong's wife pinned red radishes in her hair and danced in the fields like a loose woman.

Selina had turned, fled to the house. It was their first serious quarrel. For days she was hurt, ashamed, moody. They made it up, of course. Pervus was contrite, abject almost. But something that belonged to her girlhood had left her that day.

During that winter she was often hideously lonely. She never got over her hunger for companionship. Here she was, a gregarious and fun-loving creature, buried in a snow-bound Illinois prairie farmhouse with a husband who looked upon conversation as a convenience, not a pastime. She learned much that winter about the utter sordidness of farm life. She rarely saw the Pools; she rarely saw any one outside her own little household. The front room—the parlour—was usually bitterly cold but sometimes she used to slip in there, a shawl over her shoulders, and sit at the frosty window to watch for a wagon to go by, or a chance pedestrian up the road. She did not pity herself, nor regret her step. She felt, physically, pretty well for a child-bearing woman; and Pervus was tender, kindly, sympathetic, if not always understanding. She struggled gallantly to keep up the small decencies of existence. She loved the glow in Pervus's eyes when she appeared with a bright ribbon, a fresh collar, though he said nothing and perhaps she only fancied that he noticed. Once or twice she had walked the mile and a half of slippery road to the Pools', and had sat in Maartje's warm bright bustling kitchen for comfort. It seemed to her incredible that a little more than a year ago she had first stepped into this kitchen in her modish brown lady's-cloth dress, muffled in wraps, cold but elated, interested, ready for adventure, surprise, discomfort—anything. And now here she was in that same kitchen, amazingly, unbelievably Mrs. Pervus DeJong, truck farmer's wife, with a child soon to be born. And where was adventure now? And where was life? And where the love of chance bred in her by her father?

The two years following Dirk's birth were always somewhat vague in Selina's mind, like a dream in which horror and happiness are inextricably blended. The boy was a plump hardy infant who employed himself cheerfully in whatever spot Selina happened to deposit him. He had his father's blond exterior, his mother's brunette vivacity. At two he was a child of average intelligence, sturdy physique, and marked good humour. He almost never cried.

He was just twelve months old when Selina's second child—a girl—was born dead. Twice during those two years Pervus fell victim to his so-called rheumatic attacks following the early spring planting when he was often forced to stand in water up to his ankles. He suffered intensely and during his illness was as tractable as a goaded bull. Selina understood why half of High Prairie was bent and twisted with rheumatism—why the little Dutch Reformed church on Sunday mornings resembled a shrine to which sick and crippled pilgrims creep.

High Prairie was kind to the harried household. The farm women sent Dutch dainties. The men lent a hand in the fields, though they were hard put to it to tend their own crops at this season. The Widow Paarlenberg's neat smart rig was frequently to be seen waiting under the willows in the DeJong yard. The Paarlenberg, still widow, still Paarlenberg, brought soups and chickens and cakes which never stuck in Selina's throat because she refused to touch them. The Widow Paarlenberg was what is known as good-hearted. She was happiest when some one else was in trouble. Hearing of an illness, a catastrophe, "Og heden!" she would cry, and rush off to the scene with sustaining soup. She was the sort of lady bountiful who likes to see her benficiaries benefit before her very eyes. If she brought them soup at ten in the morning she wanted to see that soup consumed.

"Eat it all," she would urge. "Take it now, while it is hot. See, you are looking better already. Just another spoonful."

In the DeJongs' plight she found a grisly satisfaction, cloaked by commiseration. Selina, white and weak following her tragic second confinement, still found strength to refuse the widow's sustaining positions. The widow, her silks making a gentle susurrus in the bare little bedroom, regarded Selina with eyes in which pity and triumph made horrid conflict. Selina's eyes, enormous now in her white face, were twin pools of Peake pride.

"It's most kind of you, Mrs. Paarlenberg, but I don't like soup."

"A whole chicken boiled in it."

"Especially chicken soup. Neither does Pervus. But I'm sure Mrs. Voorhees will enjoy it." This being Pervus's old housekeeper pressed now into temporary emergency service.

It was easy to see why the DeJong house still was unpainted two years after Selina's rosy plans began to form; why the fences still sagged, the wagon creaked, the single horse hauled the produce to market.

Selina had been married almost three years when there came to her a letter from Julie Hempel, now married. The letter had been sent to the Klaas Pool farm and Jozina had brought it to her. Though she had not seen it since her days at Miss Fister's school, Selina recognized with a little hastening heart-beat the spidery handwriting with the shading and curleycues. Seated on her kitchen steps in her calico dress she read it.

DARLING SELINA:—

I thought it was so queer that you didn't answer my letter and now I know you must have thought it queer that I did not answer yours. I found your letter to me, written long ago, when I was going over Mother's things last week. It was the letter you must have written when I was in Kansas City. Mother had never given it to me. I am not reproaching her. You see, I had written you from Kansas City, but had sent my letter to Mamma to mail because I never could remember that funny address of yours in the country.

Mamma died three weeks ago. Last week I was going over her things—a trying task, you may imagine—and there were your two letters addressed to me. She had never destroyed them. Poor Mamma . . .

Well, dear Selina, I suppose you don't even know that I'm married. I married Michael Arnold of Kansas City. The Arnolds were in the packing business there, you know. Michael has gone into business with Pa here in Chicago and I suppose you have heard of Pa's success. Just all of a sudden he began to make a great deal of money after he left the butcher business and went into the yards—the stockyards, you know. Poor Mamma was so happy these last few years, and had everything that was beautiful. I have two children. Eugene and Pauline.

I am getting to be quite a society person. You would laugh to see me. I am on the Ladies' Entertainment Committee of the World's Fair. We are supposed to entertain all the visiting big bugs—that is the lady bugs. There! How is that for a joke?

I suppose you know about the Infanta Eulalie. Of Spain, you know. And what she did about the Potter Palmer ball. . . .

Selina, holding the letter in her work-stained hand, looked up and across the fields and away to where the prairie met the sky and closed in on her; her world. The Infanta Eulalie of Spain. . . . She went back to the letter.

Well, she came to Chicago for the Fair and Mrs. Potter Palmer was to give a huge reception and ball for her. Mrs. P. is head of the whole committee, you know, and I must say she looks queenly with her white hair so beautifully dressed and her diamond dog-collar and her black velvet and all. Well, at the very last minute the Infanta refused to attend the ball because she had just heard that Mrs. P. was an innkeeper's wife. Imagine! The Palmer House, of course.

Selina, holding the letter in her hand, imagined.

It was in the third year of Selina's marriage that she first went into the fields to work. Pervus had protested miserably, though the vegetables were spoiling in the ground.

"Let them rot," he said. "Better the stuff rots in the ground. DeJong women folks they never worked in the fields. Not even in Holland. Not my mother or my grandmother. It isn't for women."

Selina had regained health and vigour after two years of wretchedness. She felt steel-strong and even hopeful again, sure sign of physical well-being. Long before now she had realized that this time must inevitably come. So she answered briskly, "Nonsense, Pervus. Working in the field's no harder than washing or ironing or scrubbing or standing over a hot stove in August. Women's work! Housework's the hardest work in the world. That's why men won't do it."

She would often take the boy Dirk with her into the fields, placing him on a heap of empty sacks in the shade. He invariably crawled off this lowly throne to dig and burrow in the warm black dirt. He even made as though to help his mother, pulling at the rooted things with futile fingers, and sitting back with a bump when a shallow root did unexpectedly yield to his tugging.

"Look! He's a farmer already," Pervus would say.

But within Selina something would cry, "No! No!"

During May, June, and July Pervus worked not only from morning until night, but by moonlight as well, and Selina worked with him. Often their sleep was a matter of three hours only, or four.

So two years went—three years—four. In the fourth year of Selina's marriage she suffered the loss of her one woman friend in all High Prairie. Maartje Pool died in childbirth, as was so often the case in this region where a Gampish midwife acted as obstetrician. The child, too, had not lived. Death had not been kind to Maartje Pool. It had brought neither peace nor youth to her face, as it so often does. Selina, looking down at the strangely still figure that had been so active, so bustling, realized that for the first time in the years she had known her she was seeing Maartje Pool at rest. It seemed incredible that she could lie there, the infant in her arms, while the house was filled with people and there were chairs to be handed, space to be cleared, food to be cooked and served. Sitting there with the other

High Prairie women Selina had a hideous feeling that Maartje would suddenly rise up and take things in charge; rub and scratch with capable fingers the spatters of dried mud on Klaas Pool's black trousers (he had been in the yard to see to the horses); quiet the loud wailing of Geertje and Jozina; pass her gnarled hand over Roelf's wide-staring tearless eyes; wipe the film of dust from the parlour table that had never known a speck during her regime.

"You can't run far enough," Maartje had said. "Except you stop living you can't run away from life."

Well, she had run far enough this time.

Roelf was sixteen now, Geertje twelve, Jozina eleven. What would this household do now, Selina wondered, without the woman who had been so faithful a slave to it? Who would keep the pig-tails—no longer giggling—in clean ginghams and decent square-toed shoes? Who, when Klaas broke out in rumbling Dutch wrath against what he termed Roelf's "dumb" ways, would say, "Og, Pool, leave the boy alone once. He does nothing." Who would keep Klaas himself in order; cook his meals, wash his clothes, iron his shirts, take pride in the great ruddy childlike giant?

Klaas answered these questions just nine months later by marrying the Widow Paarlenberg. High Prairie was rocked with surprise. For months this marriage was the talk of the district. They had gone to Niagara Falls on a wedding trip; Pool's place was going to have this improvement and that; no, they were going to move to the Widow Paarlenberg's large farmhouse (they would always call her that); no, Pool was putting in a bathroom with a bathtub and running water; no, they were going to buy the Stikker place between Pool's and Paarlenberg's and make one farm of it, the largest in all High Prairie, Low Prairie, or New Haarlem. Well, no fool like an old fool.

So insatiable was High Prairie's curiosity that every scrap of fresh news was swallowed at a gulp. When the word went round of Roelf's flight from the farm, no one knew where, it served only as sauce to the great dish of gossip.

Selina had known. Pervus was away at the market when Roelf had knocked at the farmhouse door one night at eight, had turned the knob and entered, as usual. But there was nothing of the usual about his appearance. He wore his best suit—his first suit of store clothes, bought at the time of his mother's funeral. It never had fitted him; now was grotesquely small for him. He had shot up amazingly in the last eight or nine months. Yet there was nothing of the ridiculous about him as he stood before her now, tall, lean, dark. He put down his cheap yellow suitcase.

"Well, Roelf."

"I am going away. I couldn't stay."

She nodded. "Where?"

"Away. Chicago maybe." He was terribly moved, so he made his tone casual. "They came home last night. I have got some books that belong to you." He made as though to open the suitcase.

"No, no! Keep them."

"Good-bye."

"Good-bye, Roelf." She took the boy's dark head in her two hands and, standing on tiptoe, kissed him. She turned to go. "Wait a minute. Wait a minute." She had a few dollars—in quarters, dimes, half dollars—perhaps ten dollars in all—hidden away in a canister on the shelf. She reached for it. But when she came back with the box in her hand he was gone.

9

✯

Dirk was eight; Little Sobig DeJong, in a suit made of beansacking sewed
together by his mother. A brown blond boy with mosquito bites on
his legs and his legs never still. Nothing of the dreamer about this lad.
The one-room schoolhouse of Selina's day had been replaced by a
two-story brick structure, very fine, of which High Prairie was vastly
proud. The rusty iron stove had been dethroned by a central heater.
Dirk went to school from October until June. Pervus protested that
this was foolish. The boy could be of great help in the fields from the
beginning of April to the first of November, but Selina fought sav-
agely for his schooling, and won.

"Reading and writing and figgering is what a farmer is got to
know," Pervus argued. "The rest is all foolishness. Constantinople is
the capital of Turkey he studies last night and uses good oil in the
lamp. What good does it do a truck farmer when he knows Constantinople is the capital of Turkey? That don't help him raise turnips."

"Sobig isn't a truck farmer."

"Well, he will be pretty soon. Time I was fifteen I was running
our place."

Verbally Selina did not combat this. But within her every force
was gathering to fight it when the time should come. Her Sobig a
truck farmer, a slave to the soil, bent by it, beaten by it, blasted by it,
so that he, in time, like the other men of High Prairie, would take on
the very look of the rocks and earth among which they toiled!

Dirk, at eight, was a none too handsome child, considering his father and mother—or his father and mother as they had been. He had, though, a "different" look. His eyelashes were too long for a boy. Wasted, Selina said as she touched them with a fond forefinger, when a girl would have been so glad of them. He had developed, too, a slightly aquiline nose, probably a long-jump inheritance from some Cromwellian rapscallion of the English Peakes of a past century. It was not until he was seventeen or eighteen that he was to metamorphose suddenly into a graceful and aristocratic youngster with an indefinable look about him of distinction and actual elegance. It was when Dirk was thirty that Peter Peel the English tailor (of Michigan Avenue north) said he was the only man in Chicago who could wear English clothes without having them look like Halsted Street. Dirk probably appeared a little startled at that, as well he might, west Halsted Street having loomed up so large in his background.

Selina was a farm woman now, nearing thirty. The work rode her as it had ridden Maartje Pool. In the DeJong yard there was always a dado of washing, identical with the one that had greeted Selina's eye when first she drove into the Pool yard years before. Faded overalls, a shirt, socks, a boy's drawers grotesquely patched and mended, towels of rough sacking. She, too, rose at four, snatched up shapeless garments, invested herself with them, seized her great coil of fine cloudy hair, twisted it into a utilitarian knob and skewered it with a hairpin from which the varnish had long departed, leaving it a dull gray; thrust her slim feet into shapeless shoes, dabbed her face with cold water hurried to the kitchen stove. The work was always at her heels, its breath hot on her neck. Baskets of mending piled up, threatened to overwhelm her. Overalls, woollen shirts, drawers, socks. Socks! They lay coiled and twisted in an old market basket. Sometimes as she sat late at night mending them, in and out, in and out, with quick fierce stabs of the needle in her work-scarred hand, they seemed to writhe and squirm and wriggle horribly, like snakes. One of her bad dreams was that in which she saw herself overwhelmed, drowned, swallowed up by a huge welter and boiling of undarned, unmended nightshirts, drawers, socks, aprons, overalls.

Seeing her thus one would have thought that the Selina Peake of the wine-red cashmere, the fun-loving disposition, the high-spirited courage, had departed forever. But these things still persisted. For that matter, even the wine-red cashmere clung to existence. So hopelessly old-fashioned now as to be almost picturesque, it hung in Selina's closet like a rosy memory. Sometimes when she came upon it in an orgy of cleaning she would pass her rough hands over its soft folds and by that magic process Mrs. Pervus DeJong vanished in a pouf and in her place was the girl Selina Peake perched a-tiptoe on a soap-box in Adam Ooms's hall while all High Prairie, open-mouthed, looked on as the impecunious Pervus DeJong threw ten hard-earned dollars at her feet. In thrifty moments she had often thought of cutting the wine-red cashmere into rag-rug strips; of dyeing it a sedate brown or black and remodeling it for a much-needed best dress; of fashioning it into shirts for Dirk. But she never did.

It would be gratifying to be able to record that in these eight or nine years Selina had been able to work wonders on the DeJong farm; that the house glittered, the crops thrived richly, the barn housed sleek cattle. But it could not be truthfully said. True, she had achieved some changes, but at the cost of terrific effort. A less indomitable woman would have sunk into apathy years before. The house had a coat of paint—lead-gray, because it was cheapest. There were two horses—the second a broken-down old mare, blind in one eye, that they had picked up for five dollars after it had been turned out to pasture for future sale as horse-carcass. Piet Pon, the mare's owner who drove a milk route, had hoped to get three dollars for the animal, dead. A month of rest and pasturage restored the mare to usefulness. Selina had made the bargain, and Pervus had scolded her roundly for it. Now he drove the mare to market, saw that she pulled more sturdily than the other horse, but had never retracted. It was no quality of meanness in him. Pervus merely was like that.

But the west sixteen! That had been Selina's most heroic achievement. Her plan, spoken of to Pervus in the first month of her marriage, had taken years to mature; even now was but a partial triumph. She had even descended to nagging.

"Why don't we put in asparagus?"

"Asparagus!" considered something of a luxury, and rarely included in the High Prairie truck farmer's products. "And wait three years for a crop!"

"Yes, but then we'd have it. And a plantation's good for ten years, once it's started."

"Plantation! What is that? An asparagus plantation? Asparagus I've always heard of in beds."

"That's the old idea. I've been reading up on it. The new way is to plant asparagus in rows, the way you would rhubarb or corn. Plant six feet apart, and four acres anyway."

He was not even sufficiently interested to be amused. "Yeh, four acres where? In the clay land, maybe." He did laugh then, if the short bitter sound he made could be construed as indicating mirth. "Out of a book."

"In the clay land," Selina urged, crisply. "And out of a book. Every farmer in High Prairie raises cabbage, turnips, carrots, beets, beans, onions, and they're better quality than ours. That west sixteen isn't bringing you anything, so what difference does it make if I am wrong! Let me put my own money into it, I've thought it all out, Pervus. Please. We'll under-drain the clay soil. Just five or six acres, to start. We'll manure it heavily—as much as we can afford—and then for two years we'll plant potatoes there. We'll put in our asparagus plants the third spring—one-year-old seedlings. I'll promise to keep it weeded—Dirk and I. He'll be a big boy by that time."

"How much manure?"

"Oh, twenty to forty tons to the acre—"

He shook his head in slow Dutch opposition.

"—but if you'll let me use humus I won't need that much. Let me try it, Pervus. Let me try."

In the end she had her way, partly because Pervus was too occupied with his own endless work to oppose her; and partly because he was, in his undemonstrative way, still in love with his vivacious, nimble-witted, high-spirited wife, though to her frantic goadings and proddings he was as phlegmatically oblivious as an elephant to a pin prick. Year in, year out, he maintained his slow-prodding gait, content to do as his father had done before him; content to let the rest of High Prairie pass him on the road. He rarely showed temper. Selina often wished he would. Sometimes, in a sort of hysteria of hopelessness, she would rush at him, ruffle up his thick coarse hair, now beginning to be threaded with gray; shake his great impassive shoulders.

"Pervus! Pervus! if you'd only get mad—real mad! Fly into a rage. Break things! Beat me! Sell the farm! Run away!" She didn't mean it, of course. It was the vital and constructive force in her resenting his apathy, his acceptance of things as they were.

"What is that for dumb talk?" He would regard her solemnly through a haze of smoke, his pipe making a maddening putt-putt of sleepy content.

Though she worked as hard as any woman in High Prairie, had as little, dressed as badly, he still regarded her as a luxury; an exquisite toy which, in a moment of madness, he had taken for himself. "Little Lina"—tolerantly, fondly. You would have thought that he spoiled her, pampered her. Perhaps he even thought he did.

When she spoke of modern farming, of books on vegetable gardening, he came very near to angry impatience, though his amusement at the idea saved him from it. College agricultural courses he designated as foolishness. Of Linnaeus he had never heard. Burbank was, for him, non-existent, and he thought head-lettuce a silly fad. Selina sometimes talked of raising this last named green as a salad, with marketing value. Everyone knew that regular lettuce was leaf lettuce which you ate with vinegar and a sprinkling of sugar, or with hot bacon and fat sopping its wilted leaves.

He said, too, she spoiled the boy. Back of this may have been a lurking jealousy. "Always the boy; always the boy," he would mutter when Selina planned for the child; shielded him; took his part (sometimes unjustly). "You will make a softy of him with your always babying." So from time to time he undertook to harden Dirk. The result was generally disastrous. In one case the process termi-

nated in what was perilously near to tragedy. It was during the mid-
summer school vacation. Dirk was eight. The woody slopes about
High Prairie and the sand hills beyond were covered with the rich
blue of huckleberries. They were dead ripe. One shower would spoil
them. Geertje and Jozina Pool were going huckleberrying and had
consented to take Dirk—a concession, for he was only eight and
considered, at their advanced age, a tagger. But the last of the tomatoes on the DeJong place were also ripe and ready for picking. They
hung, firm, juicy scarlet globes, prime for the Chicago market. Pervus meant to haul them to town that day. And this was work in
which the boy could help. To Dirk's, "Can I go berrying? The huckleberries are ripe. Geert and Jozina are going," his father shook a negative head.

"Yes, well tomatoes are ripe, too, and that comes before huckle-
berries. There's the whole patch to clean up this afternoon by four."
Selina looked up, glanced at Pervus's face, at the boy's, said nothing.
The look said, "He's a child. Let him go, Pervus."

Dirk flushed with disappointment. They were at breakfast. It was
barely daybreak. He looked down at his plate, his lip quivered, his
long lashes lay heavy on his cheeks. Pervus got up, wiped his mouth
with the back of his hand. There was a hard day ahead of him. "Time
I was your age, Sobig, I would think it was an easy day when all I had
to do was pick a tomato patch clean."

Dirk looked up then, quickly. "If I get it all picked can I go?"

"It's a day's job."

"But if I do pick the patch—if I get through early enough—can
I go?"

In his mind's eye Pervus saw the tomato patch, more scarlet than
green, so thick hung the fruit upon the bushes. He smiled. "Yes. You
pick them tomatoes and you can go. But no throwing into the baskets
and getting 'em all softed up."

Secretly Selina resolved to help him, but she knew that this could
not be until afternoon. The berry patches were fully three miles from
the DeJong farm. Dirk would have to finish by three o'clock, at the
latest, to get there. Selina had her morning full with the housework.

He was in the patch before six; fell to work, feverishly. He picked, heaped the fruit into hillocks. The scarlet patches glowed, blood-red, in the sun. The child worked like a machine, with an economy of gesture calculated to the fraction of an inch. He picked, stooped, heaped the mounds in the sultry heat of the August morning. The sweat stood out on his forehead, darkened his blond hair, slid down his cheeks that were pink, then red, then tinged with a purplish tone beneath the summer tan. When dinner time came he gulped a dozen alarming mouthfuls and was out again in the broiling noonday glare. Selina left her dinner dishes unwashed on the table to help him but Pervus intervened. "The boy's got to do it alone," he insisted.

"He'll never do it, Pervus. He's only eight."

"Time I was eight ——"

He actually had cleared the patch by three. He went to the well and took a huge draught of water; drank two great dippersful, lipping it down thirstily, like a colt. It was cool and delicious beyond belief. Then he sloshed a third and a fourth dipperful over his hot head and neck, took an empty lard pail for berries and was off down the dusty road and across the fields, running fleetly in spite of the quivering heat waves that seemed to dance between fiery heaven and parched earth. Selina stood in the kitchen doorway a moment, watching him. He looked very small and determined.

He found Geertje and Jozina, surfeited with fruit, berry stained and bramble torn, lolling languidly in Kuyper's woods. He began to pick the plump blue balls but he ate them listlessly, though thriftily, because that was what he had come for and his father was Dutch. When Geertje and Jozina prepared to leave not an hour after he had come he was ready to go, yet curiously loath to move. His lard pail was half filled. He trotted home laboriously through the late afternoon, feeling giddy and sick, with horrid pains in his head. That night he tossed in delirium, begged not to be made to lie down, came perilously near to death.

Selina's heart was an engine pumping terror, hate, agony through her veins. Hate for her husband who had done this to the boy.

"You did it! You did it! He's a baby and you made him work like a man. If anything happens to him! If anything happens to him! ——"

"Well, I didn't think the kid would go for to do it. I didn't ask him to pick and then go berrying. He said could he and I said yes. If I had said no it would have been wrong, too, maybe."

"You're all alike. Look at Roelf Pool! They tried to make a farmer of him, too. And ruined him."

"What's the matter with farming? What's the matter with a farmer? You said farm work was grand work, once."

"Oh, I did. It is. It could be. It —— Oh, what's the use of talking like that now! Look at him! Don't, Sobig! Don't, baby. How hot his head is! Listen! Is that Jan with the doctor? No. No, it isn't. Mustard plasters. Are you sure that's the right thing?"

It was before the day of the omnipresent farmhouse telephone and the farmhouse Ford. Jan's trip to High Prairie village for the doctor and back to the farm meant a delay of hours. But within two days the boy was again about, rather pale, but otherwise seeming none the worse for his experience.

That was Pervus. Thrifty, like his kind, but unlike them in shrewdness. Penny wise, pound foolish; a characteristic that brought him his death. September, usually a succession of golden days and hazy opalescent evenings on the Illinois prairie land, was disastrously cold and rainy that year. Pervus's great frame was racked by rheumatism. He was forty now, and over, still of magnificent physique, so that to see him suffering gave Selina the pangs of pity that one has at sight of the very strong or the very weak in pain. He drove the weary miles to market three times a week, for September was the last big month of the truck farmer's season. After that only the hardier plants survived the frosts—the cabbages, beets, turnips, carrots, pumpkins, squash. The roads in places were morasses of mud into which the wheels were likely to sink to the hubs. Once stuck you had often to wait for a friendly passing team to haul you out. Pervus would start early, detour for miles in order to avoid the worst places. Jan was too stupid, too old, too inexpert to be trusted with the Haymarket trading. Selina would watch Pervus drive off down the road in the creaking old market wagon, the green stuff protected by canvas, but Pervus wet before ever he climbed into the seat. There never seemed to be enough waterproof canvas for both.

"Pervus, take it off those sacks and put it over your shoulders."

"That's them white globe onions. The last of 'em. I can get a fancy price for them but not if they're all wetted down."

"Don't sleep on the wagon to-night, Pervus. Sleep in. Be sure. It saves in the end. You know the last time you were laid up for a week."

"It'll clear. Breaking now over there in the west."

The clouds did break late in the afternoon; the false sun came out hot and bright. Pervus slept out in the Haymarket, for the night was close and humid. At midnight the lake wind sprang up, cold and treacherous, and with it came the rain again. Pervus was drenched by morning, chilled, thoroughly miserable. A hot cup of coffee at four and another at ten when the rush of trading was over stimulated him but little. When he reached home it was mid-afternoon. Beneath the bronze wrought by the wind and sun of many years the gray-white of sickness shone dully, like silver under enamel. Selina put him to bed against his half-hearted protests. Banked him with hot water jars, a hot iron wrapped in flannel at his feet. But later came fever instead of the expected relief of perspiration. Ill though he was he looked more ruddy and hale than most men in health; but suddenly Selina, startled, saw black lines like gashes etched under his eyes, about his mouth, in his cheeks.

In a day when pneumonia was known as lung fever and in a locality that advised closed windows and hot air as a remedy, Pervus's battle was lost before the doctor's hooded buggy was seen standing in the yard for long hours through the night. Toward morning the doctor had Jan Steen stable the horse. It was a sultry night, with flashes of heat lightning in the west.

"I should think if you opened the windows," Selina said to the old High Prairie doctor over and over, emboldened by terror, "it would help him to breathe. He—he's breathing so—he's breathing so ——" She could not bring herself to say so terribly. The sound of the words wrung her as did the sound of his terrible breathing.

10

Perhaps the most poignant and touching feature of the days that followed was not the sight of this stricken giant, lying majestic and aloof in his unwonted black; nor of the boy Dirk, mystified but elated, too, with the unaccustomed stir and excitement; nor of the shabby little farm that seemed to shrink and dwindle into further insignificance beneath the sudden publicity turned upon it. No; it was the sight of Selina, widowed, but having no time for decent tears. The farm was there; it must be tended. Illness, death, sorrow—the garden must be tended, the vegetables pulled, hauled to market, sold. Upon the garden depended the boy's future, and hers.

For the first few days following the funeral one or another of the neighbouring farmers drove the DeJong team to market, aided the blundering Jan in the fields. But each had his hands full with his own farm work. On the fifth day Jan Steen had to take the garden truck to Chicago, though not without many misgivings on Selina's part, all of which were realized when he returned late next day with half the load still on his wagon and a sum of money representing exactly zero in profits. The wilted left-over vegetables were dumped behind the barn to be used later as fertilizer.

"I didn't do so good this time," Jan explained, "on account I didn't get no right place in the market."

"You started early enough."

"Well, they kind of crowded me out, like. They see I was a new hand and time I got the animals stabled and come back they had the wagon crowded out, like."

Selina was standing in the kitchen doorway, Jan in the yard with the team. She turned her face toward the fields. An observant person (Jan Steen was not one of these) would have noted the singularly determined and clear-cut jaw-line of this drably calicoed farm woman.

"I'll go myself Monday."

Jan stared. "Go? Go where, Monday?"

"To market."

At this seeming pleasantry Jan Steen smiled uncertainly, shrugged his shoulders, and was off to the barn. She was always saying things that didn't make sense. His horror and unbelief were shared by the rest of High Prairie when on Monday Selina literally took the reins in her own slim work-scarred hands.

"To market!" argued Jan as excitedly as his phlegmatic nature would permit. "A woman she don't go to market. A woman——"

"This woman does." Selina had risen at three in the morning. Not only that, she had got Jan up, grumbling. Dirk had joined them in the fields at five. Together the three of them had pulled and bunched a wagon load. "Size them," Selina ordered, as they started to bunch radishes, beets, turnips, carrots. "And don't let them loose like that. Tie them tight at the heads, like this. Twice around with the string, and through. Make bouquets of them, not bunches. And we're going to scrub them."

High Prairie washed its vegetables desultorily; sometimes not at all. Higgledy piggledy, large and small, they were bunched and sold as vegetables, not objets d'art. Generally there was a tan crust of good earth coating them which the housewife could scrub off at her own kitchen sink. What else had housewives to do!

Selina, scrubbing the carrots vigorously under the pump, thought they emerged from their unaccustomed bath looking like clustered spears of pure gold. She knew better, though, than to say this in Jan's hearing. Jan, by now, was sullen with bewilderment. He refused to believe that she actually intended to carry out her plan. A woman—a High Prairie farmer's wife—driving to market like a man!

Alone at night in the market place—or at best in one of the cheap rooming houses! By Sunday somehow, mysteriously, the news had filtered through the district. High Prairie attended the Dutch Reformed church with a question hot on its tongue and Selina did not attend the morning services. A fine state of things, and she a widow of a week! High Prairie called at the DeJong farm on Sunday afternoon and was told that the widow was over in the wet west sixteen, poking about with the boy Dirk at her heels.

The Reverend Dekker appeared late Sunday afternoon on his way to evening service. A dour dominie, the Reverend Dekker, and one whose talents were anachronistic. He would have been invaluable in the days when New York was New Amsterdam. But the second and third generations of High Prairie Dutch were beginning to chafe under his old-world regime. A hard blue eye, had the Reverend Dekker, and a fanatic one.

"What is this talk I hear, Mrs. DeJong, that you are going to the Haymarket with the garden stuff, a woman alone?"

"Dirk goes with me."

"You don't know what you are doing, Mrs. DeJong. The Haymarket is no place for a decent woman. As for the boy! There is card-playing, drinking—all manner of wickedness—daughters of Jezebel on the street, going among the wagons."

"Really!" said Selena. It sounded thrilling, after twelve years on the farm.

"You must not go."

"The vegetables are rotting in the ground. And Dirk and I must live."

"Remember the two sparrows. 'One of them shall not fall on the ground without'—Matthew X-29."

"I don't see," replied Selina, simply, "what good that does the sparrow, once it's fallen."

By Monday afternoon the parlour curtains of every High Prairie farmhouse that faced the Halsted road were agitated as though by a brisk wind between the hours of three and five, when the market wagons were to be seen moving toward Chicago. Klaas Pool at dinner that noon had spoken of Selina's contemplated trip with a mingling of pity and disapproval.

"It ain't decent a woman should drive to market."

Mrs. Klaas Pool (they still spoke of her as the Widow Paarlenberg) smiled her slippery crooked smile. "What could you expect! Look how she's always acted."

Klaas did not follow this. He was busy with his own train of thought. "It don't seem hardly possible. Time she come here school teacher I drove her out and she was like a little robin or what, set up on the seat. She says, I remember like yesterday, cabbages was beautiful. I bet she learned different by this time."

But she hadn't. So little had Selina learned in these past eleven years that now, having loaded the wagon in the yard she surveyed it with more sparkle in her eye than High Prairie would have approved in a widow of little more than a week. They had picked and bunched only the best of the late crop—the firmest reddest radishes, the roundest juiciest beets; the carrots that tapered a good seven inches from base to tip; kraut cabbages of the drumhead variety that were flawless green balls; firm juicy spears of cucumber; cauliflower (of her own planting; Pervus had opposed it) that looked like a bride's bouquet. Selina stepped back now and regarded this riot of crimson and green, of white and gold and purple.

"Aren't they beautiful! Dirk, aren't they beautiful!"

Dirk, capering in his excitement at the prospect of the trip before him, shook his head impatiently. "What? I don't see anything beautiful. What's beautiful?"

Selina flung out her arms. "The—the whole wagon load. The cabbages."

"I don't know what you mean," said Dirk. "Let's go, Mother. Aren't we going now? You said as soon as the load was on."

"Oh, Sobig, you're just exactly like your——" She stopped.

"Like my what?"

"We'll go now, son. There's cold meat for your supper, Jan, and potatoes all sliced for frying and half an apple pie left from noon. Wash your dishes—don't leave them cluttering around the kitchen. You ought to get in the rest of the squash and pumpkins by evening. Maybe I can sell the lot instead of taking them in by the load. I'll see a commission man. Take less, if I have to."

She had dressed the boy in his home-made suit cut down from one of his father's. He wore a wide-brimmed straw hat which he hated. Selina had made him an overcoat of stout bean-sacking and this she tucked under the wagon seat, together with an old black fascinator, for though the September afternoon was white-hot she knew that the evenings were likely to be chilly, once the sun, a great crimson Chinese balloon, had burned itself out in a blaze of flame across the prairie horizon. Selina herself, in a full-skirted black-stuff dress, mounted the wagon agilely, took up the reins, looked down at the boy seated beside her, clucked to the horses. Jan Steen gave vent to a final outraged bellow.

"Never in my life did I hear of such a thing!"

Selina turned the horses' heads toward the city. "You'd be surprised, Jan, to know of all the things you're going to hear of some day that you've never heard of before." Still, when twenty years had passed and the Ford, the phonograph, the radio, and the rural mail delivery had dumped the world at Jan's plodding feet he liked to tell of that momentous day when Selina DeJong had driven off to market like a man with a wagon load of hand-scrubbed garden truck and the boy Dirk perched beside her on the seat.

If, then, you had been travelling the Halsted road, you would have seen a decrepit wagon, vegetable-laden, driven by a too-thin woman, sallow, bright-eyed, in a shapeless black dress, a battered black felt hat that looked like a man's old "fedora" and probably was. Her hair was unbecomingly strained away from the face with its high cheek bones, so that unless you were really observant you failed to notice the exquisite little nose or the really fine eyes so unnaturally large now in the anxious face. On the seat beside her you would have seen a farm boy of nine or thereabouts—a brown freckle-faced lad in a comically home-made suit of clothes and a straw hat with a broken and flopping brim which he was forever jerking off only to have it set firmly on again by the woman who seemed to fear the effects of the hot afternoon sun on his close-cropped head. But in the brief intervals when the hat was off you must have noted how the boy's eyes were shining.

At their feet was the dog Pom, a mongrel whose tail bore no relation to his head, whose ill-assorted legs appeared wholly at variance with his sturdy barrel of a body. He dozed now, for it had been his duty to watch the wagon load at night, while Pervus slept.

A shabby enough little outfit, but magnificent, too. Here was Selina DeJong driving up the Halsted road toward the city instead of sitting, black-robed, in the farm parlour while High Prairie came to condole. In Selina, as they jogged along the hot dusty way, there welled up a feeling very like elation. Conscious of this, the New England strain in her took her to task. "Selina Peake, aren't you ashamed of yourself! You're a wicked woman! Feeling almost gay when you ought to be sad. . . . Poor Pervus . . . the farm . . . Dirk . . . and you can feel almost gay! You ought to be ashamed of yourself!"

But she wasn't, and knew it. For even as she thought this the little wave of elation came flooding over her again. More than ten years ago she had driven with Klaas Pool up that same road for the first time, and in spite of the recent tragedy of her father's death, her youth, her loneliness, the terrifying thought of the new home to which she was going, a stranger among strangers, she had been conscious of a warm little thrill of elation, of excitement—of adventure! That was it. "The whole thing's just a grand adventure," her father, Simeon Peake, had said. And now the sensations of that day were repeating themselves. Now, as then, she was doing what was considered a revolutionary and daring thing; a thing that High Prairie regarded with horror. And now, as then, she took stock. Youth was gone, but she had health, courage; a boy of nine; twenty-five acres of wornout farm land; dwelling and out-houses in a bad state of repair; and a gay adventuresome spirit that was never to die, though it led her into curious places and she often found, at the end, only a trackless waste from which she had to retrace her steps painfully. But always, to her, red and green cabbages were to be jade and burgundy, chrysoprase and porphyry. Life has no weapons against a woman like that.

And the wine-red cashmere. She laughed aloud.

"What are you laughing at, Mom?"

That sobered her. "Oh, nothing, Sobig. I don't know I was laughing. I was just thinking about a red dress I had when I first came to High Prairie a girl. I've got it yet."

"What's that to laugh at?" He was following a yellow-hammer with his eyes.

"Nothing. Mother said it was nothing."

"Wisht I'd brought my sling-shot." The yellow-hammer was perched on the fence by the roadside not ten feet away.

"Sobig, you promised me you wouldn't throw at any more birds, ever."

"Oh, I wouldn't hit it. I would just like to aim at it."

Down the hot dusty country road. She was serious enough now. The cost of the funeral to be paid. The doctor's bills. Jan's wage. All the expenses, large and small, of the poor little farm holding. Nothing to laugh at, certainly. The boy was wiser than she.

"There's Mrs. Pool on her porch, Mom. Rocking."

There, indeed, was the erstwhile Widow Paarlenberg on her porch, rocking. A pleasant place to be in mid-afternoon of a hot September day. She stared at the creaking farm wagon, vegetable laden; at the boy perched on the high seat; at the sallow shabby woman who was charioteer for the whole crazy outfit. Mrs. Klaas Pool's pink face creased in a smile. She sat forward in her chair and ceased to rock.

"Where you going this hot day, Mis' DeJong?"

Selina sat up very straight. "To Bagdad, Mrs. Pool."

"To—Where's that? What for?"

"To sell my jewels, Mrs. Pool. And to see Aladdin, and Harun-al-Rashid and Ali Baba. And the Forty Thieves."

Mrs. Pool had left her rocker and had come down the steps. The wagon creaked on past her gate. She took a step or two down the path, and called after them. "I never heard of it. Bag—How do you get there?"

Over her shoulder Selina called out from the wagon seat. "You just go until you come to a closed door. And you say 'Open Sesame!' and there you are."

Bewilderment shadowed Mrs. Pool's placid face. As the wagon lurched on down the road it was Selina who was smiling and Mrs. Pool who was serious.

The boy, round eyed, was looking up at his mother. "That's out of *Arabian Nights,* what you said. Why did you say that?" Suddenly excitement tinged his voice. "That's out of the book. Isn't it? Isn't it! We're not really——"

She was a little contrite, but not very. "Well, not really, perhaps. But 'most any place is Bagdad if you don't know what will happen in it. And this is an adventure, isn't it, that we're going on? How can you tell! All kind of things can happen. All kinds of people. People in disguise in the Haymarket. Caliphs, and princes, and slaves, and thieves, and good fairies, and witches."

"In the Haymarket! That Pop went to all the time! That is just dumb talk."

Within Selina something cried out, "Don't say that, Sobig! Don't say that!"

On down the road. Here a head at a front room window. There a woman's calicoed figure standing in the doorway. Mrs. Vander Sijde on the porch, fanning her flushed face with her apron; Cornelia Snip in the yard pretending to tie up the drooping stalks of the golden-glow and eyeing the approaching team with the avid gossip's gaze. To these Selina waved, bowed, called.

"How d'you do, Mrs. Vander Sijde!"

A prim reply to this salutation. Disapproval writ large on the farm wife's flushed face.

"Hello, Cornelia!"

A pretended start, notable for its bad acting. "Oh, is it you, Mrs. DeJong! Sun's in my eyes. I couldn't think it was you like that."

Women's eyes, hostile, cold, peering.

Five o'clock. Six. The boy climbed over the wheel, filled a tin pail with water at a farmhouse well. They ate and drank as they rode along, for there was no time to lose. Bread and meat and pickles and pie.

There were vegetables in the wagon, ripe for eating. There were other varieties that Selina might have cooked at home in preparation for this meal—German celery root boiled tender and soaked in vinegar; red beets, pickled; onions; coleslaw; beans. They would have regarded these with an apathetic eye all too familiar with the sight of them. Selina knew now why the Pools' table, in her school-teacher days, had been so lacking in the green stuff she had craved. The thought of cooking the spinach which she had planted, weeded, spaded, tended, picked, washed, bunched, filled her with a nausea of distaste such as she might have experienced at the contemplation of cannibalism.

The boy had started out bravely enough in the heat of the day, sitting up very straight beside his mother, calling to the horses, shrieking and waving his arms at chickens that flew squawking across the road. Now he began to droop. Evening was coming on. A cool blanket of air from the lake on the east enveloped them with the suddenness characteristic of the region, and the mist began to drift across the prairie, softening the autumn stubble, cooling the dusty road, misting the parched willows by the roadside, hazing the shabby squat farmhouses.

She brushed away the crumbs, packed the remaining bread and meat thriftily into the basket and covered it with a napkin against the boy's future hunger should he waken in the night.

"Sleepy, Sobig?"

"No. Should say not." His lids were heavy. His face and body, relaxed, took on the soft baby contours that come with weariness. The sun was low. Sunset gloried the west in a final flare of orange and crimson. Dusk. The boy drooped against her heavy, sagging. She wrapped the old black fascinator about him. He opened his eyes, tugged at the wrapping about his shoulders. "Don't want the old thing . . . fas'nator . . . like a girl . . ." drooped again with a sigh and found the soft curve where her side just cushioned his head. In the twilight the dust gleamed white on weeds, and brush, and grass. The far-off mellow sonance of a cowbell. Horses' hoofs clopping up behind them, a wagon passing in a cloud of dust, a curious backward glance, or a greeting exchanged.

One of the Ooms boys, or Jakob Boomsma. "You're never going to market, Mis' DeJong!" staring with china-blue eyes at her load.

"Yes, I am, Mr. Boomsma."

"That ain't work for a woman, Mis' DeJong. You better stay home and let the men folks go."

Selina's men folks looked up at her—one with the asking eyes of a child, one with the trusting eyes of a dog. "My men folks are going," answered Selina. But then, they had always thought her a little queer, so it didn't matter much.

She urged the horses on, refusing to confess to herself her dread of the destination which they were approaching. Lights now, in the houses along the way, and those houses closer together. She wrapped the reins around the whip, and holding the sleeping boy with one hand reached beneath the seat with the other for the coat of sacking. This she placed around him snugly, folded an empty sack for a pillow, and lifting the boy in her arms laid him gently on the lumpy bed formed by the bags of potatoes piled up just behind the seat in the back of the wagon. So the boy slept. Night had come on.

The figure of the woman drooped a little now as the old wagon creaked on toward Chicago. A very small figure in the black dress and a shawl over her shoulders. She had taken off her old black felt hat. The breeze ruffled her hair that was fine and soft, and it made a little halo about the white face that gleamed almost luminously in the darkness as she turned it up toward the sky.

"I'll sleep out with Sobig in the wagon. It won't hurt either of us. It will be warm in town, there in the Haymarket. Twenty-five cents—maybe fifty for the two of us, in the rooming house. Fifty cents just to sleep. It takes hours of work in the fields to make fifty cents."

She was sleepy now. The night air was deliciously soft and soothing. In her nostrils was the smell of the fields, of grass dew-wet, of damp dust, of cattle; the pungent prick of goldenrod, and occasionally a scented wave that meant wild phlox in a near-by ditch. She sniffed all this gratefully, her mind and body curiously alert to sounds, scents, forms even, in the darkness. She had suffered much in the past week; had eaten and slept but little. Had known terror, bewilderment, agony, shock. Now she was relaxed, receptive, a little light-headed perhaps, what with under-feeding and tears and over-work. The racking process had cleared brain and bowels; had washed her spiritually clean; had quickened her perceptions abnormally. Now she was like a delicate and sensitive electric instrument keyed to receive and register; vibrating to every ether wave.

She drove along in the dark, a dowdy farm woman in shapeless garments; just a bundle on the rickety seat of a decrepit truck wagon. The boy slept on his hard lumpy bed like the little vegetable that he was. The farm lights went out. The houses were blurs in the black. The lights of the city came nearer. She was thinking clearly, if disconnectedly, without bitterness, without reproach.

"My father was wrong. He said that life was a great adventure—a fine show. He said the more things that happen to you the richer you are, even if they're not pleasant things. That's living, he said. No matter what happens to you, good or bad, it's just so much—what was that word he used?—so much—oh, yes—'velvet.' Just so much velvet. Well, it isn't true. He had brains, and charm, and knowledge and he died in a gambling house, shot while looking on at some one else who was to have been killed. . . . Now we're on the cobblestones. Will Dirk wake up? My little So Big. . . . No, he's asleep. Asleep on a pile of potato sacks because his mother thought that life was a grand adventure—a fine show—and that you took it as it came. A lie! I've taken it as it came and made the best of it. That isn't the way. You take the best, and make the most of it. . . . Thirty-fifth Street, that was. Another hour and a half to reach the Haymarket. . . . I'm not afraid. After all, you just sell your vegetables for what you can get. . . . Well, it's going to be different with him. I mustn't call him Sobig any more. He doesn't like it. Dirk. That's a fine name. Dirk DeJong. . . . No drifting along for him. I'll see that he starts with a plan, and follows it. He'll have every chance. Every chance. Too late for me, now, but he'll be different. . . . Twenty-second Street . . . Twelfth . . . Look at all the people! . . . I'm enjoying this. No use denying it. I'm enjoying this. Just as I enjoyed driving along with Klaas Pool that evening, years and years ago. Scared, but enjoying it. Perhaps I oughtn't to be—but that's hypocritical and sneaking. Why not, if I really do enjoy it! I'll wake him. Dirk! Dirk, we're almost there. Look at all the people, and the lights. We're almost there."

The boy awoke, raised himself from his bed of sacking, looked about, blinked, sank back again and curled into a ball. "Don't want to see the lights . . . people . . ."

He was asleep again. Selina guided the horses skilfully through the downtown streets. She looked about with wide ambient eyes. Other wagons passed her. There was a line of them ahead of her. The men looked at her curiously. They called to one another, and jerked a thumb in her direction, but she paid no heed. She decided, though, to have the boy on the seat beside her. They were within two blocks of the Haymarket, on Randolph Street.

"Dirk! Come, now. Come up here with mother." Grumbling, he climbed to the seat, yawned, smacked his lips, rubbed his knuckles into his eyes.

"What are we here for?"

"So we can sell the garden truck and earn money."

"What for?"

"To send you to school to learn things."

"That's funny. I go to school already."

"A different school. A big school."

He was fully awake now, and looking about him interestedly. They turned into the Haymarket. It was a tangle of horses, carts, men. The wagons were streaming in from the German truck farms that lay to the north of Chicago as well as from the Dutch farms that lay to the southwest, whence Selina came. Fruits and vegetables—tons of it—acres of it—piled in the wagons that blocked the historic square. An unarmed army bringing food to feed a great city. Through this little section, and South Water Street that lay to the east, passed all the verdant growing things that fed Chicago's millions. Something of this came to Selina as she manoeuvred her way through the throng. She felt a little thrill of significance, of achievement. She knew the spot she wanted for her own. Since that first trip to Chicago with Pervus in the early days of her marriage she had made the journey into town perhaps not more than a dozen times, but she had seen, and heard, and remembered. A place near the corner of Des Plaines, not at the curb, but rather in the double line of wagons that extended down the middle of the road. Here the purchasing pedlers and grocers had easy access to the wagons. Here Selina could display her wares to the best advantage. It was just across the way from Chris Spank-noebel's restaurant, rooming house, and saloon. Chris knew her; had known Pervus for years and his father before him; would be kind to her and the boy in case of need.

Dirk was wide awake now; eager, excited. The lights, the men, the horses, the sound of talk, and laughter, and clinking glasses from the eating houses along the street were bewilderingly strange to his country-bred eyes and ears. He called to the horses; stood up in the wagon; but clung closer to her as they found themselves in the thick of the mêlée.

On the street corners where the lights were brightest there were stands at which men sold chocolate, cigars, collar buttons, suspenders, shoe strings, patent contrivances. It was like a fair. Farther down the men's faces loomed mysteriously out of the half light. Stolid, sun-burned faces now looked dark, terrifying, the whites of the eyes very white, the mustaches very black, their shoulders enormous. Here was a crap game beneath the street light. There stood two girls laughing and chatting with a policeman.

"Here's a good place, Mother. Here! There's a dog on that wagon like Pom."

Pom, hearing his name, stood up, looked into the boy's face, quivered, wagged a nervous tail, barked sharply. The Haymarket night life was an old story to Pom, but it never failed to stimulate him. Often he had guarded the wagon when Pervus was absent for a short time. He would stand on the seat ready to growl at any one who so much as fingered a radish in Pervus's absence.

"Down Pom! Quiet, Pom!" She did not want to attract atten-tion to herself and the boy. It was still early. She had made excellent time. Pervus had often slept in snatches as he drove into town and the horses had lagged, but Selina had urged them on tonight. They had gained a good half hour over the usual time. Halfway down the block Selina espied the place she wanted. From the opposite direction came a truck farmer's cart obviously making for the same stand. For the first time that night Selina drew the whip out of its socket and clipped sharply her surprised nags. With a start and a shuffle they broke into an awkward lope. Ten seconds too late the German farmer perceived her intention, whipped up his own tired team, arrived at the spot just as Selina, blocking the way, prepared to back into the vacant space.

"Heh, get out of there you——" he roared; then, for the first time, perceived in the dim light of the street that his rival was a woman. He faltered, stared open-mouthed, tried other tactics. "You can't go in there, missus."

"Oh, yes, I can." She backed her team dexterously.

"Yes, we can!" shouted Dirk in an attitude of fierce belligerence.

From the wagons on either side heads were lifted. "Where's your man?" demanded the defeated driver, glaring.

"Here," replied Selina; put her hand on Dirk's head.

The other, preparing to drive on, received this with incredulity. He assumed the existence of a husband in the neighbourhood—at Chris Spanknoebel's probably, or talking prices with a friend at another wagon when he should be here attending to his own. In the absence of this, her natural protector, he relieved his disgruntled feelings as he gathered up the reins. "Woman ain't got no business here in Haymarket, anyway. Better you're home night time in your kitchen where you belong."

This admonition, so glibly mouthed by so many people in the past few days, now was uttered once too often. Selina's nerves snapped. A surprised German truck farmer found himself being harangued from the driver's seat of a vegetable wagon by an irate and fluent woman in a mashed black hat.

"Don't talk to me like that, you great stupid! What good does it do a woman to stay home in her kitchen if she's going to starve there, and her boy with her! Staying home in my kitchen won't earn me any money. I'm here to sell the vegetables I helped raise and I'm going to do it. Get out of my way, you. Go along about your business or I'll report you to Mike, the street policeman."

Now she clambered over the wagon wheel to unhitch the tired horses. It is impossible to tell what interpretation the dumfounded northsider put upon her movements. Certainly he had nothing to fear from this small gaunt creature with the blazing eyes. Nevertheless as he gathered up his reins terror was writ large on his rubicund face.

"*Teufel!* What a woman!" Was off in a clatter of wheels and hoofs on the cobblestones.

Selina unharnessed swiftly. "You stay here, Dirk, with Pom. Mother'll be back in a minute." She marched down the street driving the horses to the barns where, for twenty-five cents, the animals were to be housed in more comfort than their owner. She returned to find Dirk deep in conversation with two young women in red shirtwaists, plaid skirts that swept the ground, and sailor hats tipped at a saucy angle over pyramidal pompadours.

"I can't make any sense out of it, can you, Elsie? Sounds like Dirt to me, but nobody's going to name a kid that, are they? Stands to reason."

"Oh, come on. Your name'll be mud first thing you know. Here it's after nine already and not a——" she turned and saw Selina's white face.

"There's my mother," said Dirk, triumphantly, pointing. The three women looked at each other. Two saw the pathetic hat and the dowdy clothes, and knew. One saw the red shirtwaists and the loose red lips, and knew.

"We was just talking to the kid," said the girl who had been puzzled by Dirk's name. Her tone was defensive. "Just asking him his name, and like that."

"His name is Dirk," said Selina, mildly. "It's a Dutch name— Holland, you know. We're from out High Prairie way, south. Dirk DeJong. I'm Mrs. DeJong."

"Yeh?" said the other girl. "I'm Elsie. Elsie from Chelsea, that's me. Come on, Mabel. Stand gabbin' all night." She was blonde and shrill. The other was older, dark-haired. There was about her a paradoxical wholesomeness.

Mabel, the older one, looked at Selina sharply. From the next wagon came loud snores issuing from beneath the seat. From down the line where a lantern swung from the tailboard of a cart came the rattle of dice. "What you doing down here, anyway?"

"I'm here to sell my stuff to-morrow morning. Vegetables. From the farm."

Mabel looked around. Hers was not a quick mind. "Where's your man?"

"My husband died a week ago." Selina was making up their bed for the night. From beneath the seat she took a sack of hay, tight-packed, shook out its contents, spread them evenly on the floor of the wagon, at the front, first having unhinged the seat and clapped it against the wagon side as a headboard. Over the hay she spread empty sacking. She shook out her shawl, which would serve as cover. The girl Mabel beheld these preparations. Her dull eyes showed a gleam of interest which deepened to horror.

"Say, you ain't never going to sleep out here, are you? You and the kid. Like that!"

"Yes."

"Well, for——" She stared, turned to go, came back. From her belt that dipped so stylishly in the front hung an arsenal of jangling metal articles—purse, pencil, mirror, comb—a chatelaine, they called it. She opened the purse now and took from it a silver dollar. This she tendered Selina, almost roughly. "Here. Get the kid a decent roost for the night. You and the kid, see."

Selina stared at the shining round dollar; at Mabel's face. The quick sting of tears came to her eyes. She shook her head, smiled. "We don't mind sleeping out here. Thank you just the same—Mabel."

The girl put her dollar plumply back into her purse. "Well, takes all kinds, I always say. I thought I had a bum deal but, say, alongside of what you got I ain't got it so worse. Place to sleep in, anyways, even if it is—well, good-night. Listen to that Elsie, hollering for me. I'm comin'! Shut up!"

You heard the two on their way up the street, arm in arm, laughing.

"Come Dirk."

"Are we going to sleep here!" He was delighted.

"Right here, all snug in the hay, like campers."

The boy lay down, wriggling, laughing. "Like gypsies. Ain't it, Mom?"

" 'Isn't it,' Dirk—not 'ain't it'." The school teacher.

She lay down beside him. The boy seemed terribly wide awake. "I liked the Mabel one best, didn't you? She was the nicest, h'm?"

"Oh, much the nicest," said Selina, and put one arm around him and drew him to her, close. And suddenly he was asleep, deeply. The street became quieter. The talking and laughter ceased. The lights were dim at Chris Spanknoebel's. Now and then the clatter of wheels and horses' hoofs proclaimed a late comer seeking a place, but the sound was not near by, for this block and those to east and west were filled by now. These men had been up at four that morning, must be up before four the next.

The night was cool, but not cold. Overhead you saw the wide strip of sky between the brick buildings on either side of the street. Two men came along singing. "Shut up!" growled a voice from a wagon along the curb. The singers subsided. It must be ten o'clock and after, Selina thought. She had with her Pervus's nickel watch, but it was too dark to see its face, and she did not want to risk a match. Measured footsteps that passed and repassed at regular intervals. The night policeman.

She lay looking up at the sky. There were no tears in her eyes. She was past tears. She thought, "Here I am, Selina Peake, sleeping in a wagon, in the straw, like a bitch with my puppy snuggled beside me. I was going to be like Jo in Louisa Alcott's book. On my feet are boots and on my body a dyed dress. How terribly long it is going to be until morning. . . . I must try to sleep. . . . I must try to sleep . . ."

She did sleep, miraculously. The September stars twinkled brightly down on them. As she lay there, the child in her arms, asleep, peace came to the haggard face, relaxed the tired limbs. Much like another woman who had lain in the straw with her child in her arms almost two thousand years before.

11

✦

It would be enchanting to be able to record that Selina, next day, had phenomenal success, disposing of her carefully bunched wares to great advantage, driving smartly off up Halsted Street toward High Prairie with a goodly profit jingling in her scuffed leather purse. The truth is that she had a day so devastating, so catastrophic, as would have discouraged most men and certainly any woman less desperate and determined.

She had awakened, not to daylight, but to the three o'clock blackness. The street was already astir. Selina brushed her skirt to rid it of the clinging hay, tidied herself as best she could. Leaving Dirk still asleep, she called Pom from beneath the wagon to act as sentinel at the dashboard, and crossed the street to Chris Spanknoebel's. She knew Chris, and he her. He would let her wash at the faucet at the rear of the eating house. She would buy hot coffee for herself and Dirk to warm and revivify them. They would eat the sandwiches left from the night before.

Chris himself, a pot-paunched Austrian, blond, benevolent, was standing behind his bar, wiping the slab with a large moist cloth. With the other hand he swept the surface with a rubber-tipped board about the size of a shingle. This contrivance gathered up such beads of moisture as might be left by the cloth. Two sweeps of it rendered the counter dry and shining. Later Chris allowed Dirk to wield this rubber-tipped contrivance—a most satisfactory thing to do, leaving one with a feeling of perfect achievement.

Spanknoebel seemed never to sleep, yet his colour was ruddy, his blue eyes clear. The last truckster coming in at night for a beer or a cup of coffee and a sandwich was greeted by Chris, white-aproned, pink-cheeked, wide awake, swabbing the bar's shining surface with the thirsty cloth, swishing it with the sly rubber-tipped board. "Well, how goes it all the while?" said Chris. The earliest morning trader found Chris in a fresh white apron crackling with starch and ironing. He would swab the bar with a gesture of welcome, of greeting. "Well, how goes it all the while?"

As Selina entered the long room now there was something heartening, reassuring about Chris's clean white apron, his ruddy colour, the very sweep of his shirt-sleeved arm as it encompassed the bar-slab. From the kitchen at the rear came the sounds of sizzling and frying, and the gracious scent of coffee and of frying pork and potatoes. Already the market men were seated at the tables eating huge and hurried breakfasts: hunks of ham; eggs in pairs; potatoes cut in great cubes; cups of steaming coffee and chunks of bread that they plastered liberally with butter.

Selina approached Chris. His round face loomed out through the smoke like the sun in a fog. "Well, how goes it all the while?" Then he recognized her. "*Um Gottes!*—why, it's Mis' DeJong!" He wiped his great hand on a convenient towel, extended it in sympathy to the widow. "I heerd," he said, "I heerd." His inarticulateness made his words doubly effective.

"I've come in with the load, Mr. Spanknoebel. The boy and I. He's still asleep in the wagon. May I bring him over here to clean him up a little before breakfast?"

"Sure! Sure!" A sudden suspicion struck him. "You ain't slept in the wagon, Mis' DeJong! *Um Gottes!* ——"

"Yes. It wasn't bad. The boy slept the night through. I slept, too, quite a little."

"Why you didn't come here! Why ——" At the look in Selina's face he knew then. "For nothing you and the boy could sleep here."

"I knew that! That's why."

"Don't talk dumb, Mrs. DeJong. Half the time the rooms is vacant. You and the boy chust as well—twenty cents, then, and pay me when you got it. But any way you don't come in reg'lar with the load, do you? That ain't for womans."

"There's no one to do it for me, except Jan. And he's worse than nobody. Just through September and October. After that, may-be ——" Her voice trailed off. It is hard to be hopeful at three in the morning, before breakfast.

She went to the little wash room at the rear, felt better immediately she had washed vigorously, combed her hair. She returned to the wagon to find a panic stricken Dirk sure of nothing but that he had been deserted by his mother. Fifteen minutes later the two were seated at a table on which was spread what Chris Spanknoebel considered an adequate breakfast. A heartening enough beginning for the day, and a deceptive.

The Haymarket buyers did not want to purchase its vegetables from Selina DeJong. It wasn't used to buying of women, but to selling to them. Peddlers and small grocers swarmed in at four—Greeks, Italians, Jews. They bought shrewdly, craftily, often dishonestly. They sold their wares to the housewives. Their tricks were many. They would change a box of tomatoes while your back was turned; filch a head of cauliflower. There was little system or organization.

Take Luigi. Luigi peddled on the north side. He called his wares through the alleys and side streets of Chicago, adding his raucous voice to the din of an inchoate city. A swarthy face had Luigi, a swift brilliant smile, a crafty eye. The Haymarket called him Loogy. When prices did not please Luigi he pretended not to understand. Then the Haymarket would yell, undeceived, "Heh, Loogy, what de mattah! Spika da Engleesh!" They knew him.

Selina had taken the covers off her vegetables. They were revealed crisp, fresh, colourful. But Selina knew they must be sold now, quickly. When the leaves began to wilt, when the edges of the cauliflower heads curled ever so slightly, turned brown and limp, their value decreased by half, even though the heads themselves remained white and firm.

Down the street came the buyers—little black-eyed swarthy men; plump, shirt-sleeved, greasy men; shrewd, tobacco-chewing men in overalls. Stolid red Dutch faces, sunburned. Lean dark foreign faces. Shouting, clatter, turmoil.

"Heh! Get your horse outta here! What the hell!"

"How much for the whole barrel?"

"Got any beans? No, don't want no cauliflower. Beans!"

"Tough!"

"Well, keep 'em. I don't want 'em."

"Quarter for the sack."

"G'wan, them ain't five-pound heads. Bet they don't come four pounds to a head."

"Who says they don't!"

"Gimme five bushels them."

Food for Chicago's millions. In and out of the wagons. Under horses' hoofs. Bare-footed children, baskets on their arms, snatching bits of fallen vegetables from the cobbles. Gutter Annie, a shawl pinned across her pendulous breasts, scavengering a potato there, an onion fallen to the street, scraps of fruit and green stuff in the ditch. Big Kate buying carrots, parsley, turnips, beets, all slightly wilted and cheap, which she would tie into bunches with her bit of string and sell to the real grocers for soup greens.

The day broke warm. The sun rose red. It would be a humid September day such as frequently came in the autumn to this lake region. Garden stuff would have to move quickly this morning. Afternoon would find it worthless.

Selina stationed herself by her wagon. She saw the familiar faces of a half dozen or more High Prairie neighbours. These called to her, or came over briefly to her wagon, eyeing her wares with a calculating glance. "How you making out, Mis' DeJong? Well, you got a good load there. Move it along quick this morning. It's going to be hot I betcha." Their tone was kindly, but disapproving, too. Their look said, "No place for a woman. No place for a woman."

The peddlers looked at her bunched bouquets, glanced at her, passed her by. It was not unkindness that prompted them, but a certain shyness, a fear of the unaccustomed. They saw her pale fine face with its great sombre eyes; the slight figure in the decent black dress; the slim brown hands clasped so anxiously together. Her wares were tempting but they passed her by with the instinct that the ignorant have against that which is unusual.

By nine o'clock trading began to fall off. In a panic Selina realized that the sales she had made amounted to little more than two dollars. If she stayed there until noon she might double that, but no more. In desperation she harnessed the horses, threaded her way out of the swarming street, and made for South Water Street farther east. Here was the commission houses. The district was jammed with laden carts and wagons exactly as the Haymarket had been, but trading was done on a different scale. She knew that Pervus had sometimes left his entire load with an established dealer here, to be sold on commission. She remembered the name—Talcott— though she did not know the exact location.

"Where we going now, Mom?" The boy had been almost incredibly patient and good. He had accepted his bewildering new surroundings with the adaptability of childhood. He had revelled richly in Chris Spanknoebel's generous breakfast. He had thought the four dusty artificial palms that graced Chris's back room luxuriantly tropical. He had been fascinated by the kitchen with its long glowing range, its great tables for slicing, paring, cutting. He liked the ruddy cheer of it, the bustle, the mouth-watering smells. At the wagon he had stood sturdily next his mother, had busied himself vastly assisting her in her few pitiful sales; had plucked wilted leaves, brought forward the freshest and crispest vegetables. But now she saw that he was drooping a little as were her wares, with the heat and the absence from accustomed soil. "Where we going now, Mom?"

"To another street, Sobig ——"

"Dirk!"

"—Dirk, where there's a man who'll buy all our stuff at once—maybe. Won't that be fine! Then we'll go home. You help mother find his name over the store. Talcott—T-a-l-c-o-double t.''

South Water Street was changing with the city's growth. Yankee names they used to be—Flint—Keen—Rusk—Lane. Now you saw Cuneo—Meleges—Garibaldi—Campagna. There it was: William Talcott. Fruits and Vegetables.

William Talcott, standing in the cool doorway of his great deep shedlike store, was the antithesis of the feverish crowded street which he so calmly surveyed. He had dealt for forty years in provender. His was the unruffled demeanour of a man who knows the world must have what he has to sell. Every week-day morning at six his dim shaded cavern of a store was packed with sacks, crates, boxes, barrels from which peeped ruffles and sprigs of green; flashes of scarlet, plum-colour, orange. He bought the best only; sold at high prices. He had known Pervus, and Pervus's father before him, and had adjudged them honest, admirable men. But of their garden truck he had small opinion. The Great Lakes boats brought him choice Michigan peaches and grapes; refrigerator cars brought him the products of California's soil in a day when out-of-season food was a rare luxury. He wore neat pepper-and-salt pants and vest; shirt sleeves a startling white in that blue-shirted overalled world; a massive gold watch chain spanning his middle; square-toed boots; a straw fedora set well back; a pretty good cigar, unlighted, in his mouth. Shrewd blue eyes he had; sparse hair much the colour of his suit. Like a lean laconic god he stood in his doorway niche while toilers offered for his inspection the fruits of the earth.

"Nope. Can't use that lot, Jake. Runty. H'm. Wa-a-al, guess you'd better take them farther up the street, Tunis. Edges look kind of brown. Wilty."

Stewards from the best Chicago hotels of that day—the Sherman House, the Auditorium, the Palmer House, the Wellington, the Stratford—came to Will Talcott for their daily supplies. The grocers who catered to the well-to-do north-side families and those in the neighbourhood of fashionable Prairie Avenue on the south bought of him.

Now, in his doorway, he eyed the spare little figure that appeared before him all in rusty black, with its strained anxious face, its great deep-sunk eyes.

"DeJong, eh? Sorry to hear about your loss, ma'am. Pervus was a fine lad. No great shakes at truck farming, though. His widow, h'm? Hm." Here, he saw, was no dull-witted farm woman; no stolid Dutch woman truckster. He went out to her wagon, tweaked the boy's brown cheek. "Wa-al now, Mis' DeJong, you got a right smart lot of garden stuff here and it looks pretty good. Yessir, pretty good. But you're too late. Ten, pret' near."

"Oh, no!" cried Selina. "Oh, no! Not too late!" And at the agony in her voice he looked at her sharply.

"Tell you what, mebbe I can move half of 'em along for you. But stuff don't keep this weather. Turns wilty and my trade won't touch it . . . First trip in?"

She wiped her face that was damp and yet cold to the touch. "First—trip in." Suddenly she was finding it absurdly hard to breathe.

He called from the sidewalk to the men within: "George! Ben! Hustle this stuff in. Half of it. The best. Send you check to-morrow, Mis' DeJong. Picked a bad day, didn't you, for your first day?"

"Hot, you mean?"

"Wa-al, hot, yes. But I mean a holiday like this peddlers mostly ain't buying."

"Holiday?"

"You knew it was a Jew holiday, didn't you? Didn't!—Wa-al, my sakes! Worst day in the year. Jew peddlers all at church to-day and all the others not peddlers bought in Saturday for two days. Chicken men down the street got empty coops and will have till to-morrow. Yessir. Biggest chicken eaters, Jews are, in the world . . . Hm . . . Better just drive along home and just dump the rest that stuff, my good woman."

One hand on the seat she prepared to climb up again—did step to the hub. You saw her shabby, absurd side-boots that were so much too big for the slim little feet. "If you're just buying my stuff because you're sorry for me ——" The Peake pride.

"Don't do business that way. Can't afford to, ma'am. My da'ter she's studying to be a singer. In Italy now, Car'line is, and costs like all getout. Takes all the money I can scrape together, just about."

There was a little colour in Selina's face now. "Italy! Oh, Mr. Talcott!" You'd have thought she had seen it, from her face. She began to thank him, gravely.

"Now, that's all right, Mis' DeJong. I notice your stuff's bunched kind of extry, and all of a size. Fixin' to do that way right along?"

"Yes. I thought—they looked prettier that way—of course vegetables aren't supposed to look pretty, I expect ——" she stammered, stopped.

"You fix 'em pretty like that and bring 'em in to me first thing, or send 'em. My trade, they like their stuff kind of special. Yessir."

As she gathered up the reins he stood again in his doorway, cool, remote, his unlighted cigar in his mouth, while hand-trucks rattled past him, barrels and boxes thumped to the sidewalk in front of him, wheels and hoofs and shouts made a great clamour all about him.

"We going home now?" demanded Dirk. "We going home now? I'm hungry."

"Yes, lamb." Two dollars in her pocket. All yesterday's grim toil, and all to-day's, and months of labour behind those two days. Two dollars in the pocket of her black calico petticoat. "We'll get something to eat when we drive out a ways. Some milk and bread and cheese."

The sun was very hot. She took the boy's hat off, passed her tender work-calloused hand over the damp hair that clung to his forehead. "It's been fun, hasn't it?" she said. "Like an adventure. Look at all the kind people we've met. Mr. Spanknoebel, and Mr. Talcott ——"

"And Mabel."

Startled, "And Mabel."

She wanted suddenly to kiss him, knew he would hate it with all the boy and all the Holland Dutch in him, and did not.

She made up her mind to drive east and then south. Pervus had sometimes achieved a late sale to outlying grocers. Jan's face if she came home with half the load still on the wagon! And what of the unpaid bills? She had perhaps, thirty dollars, all told. She owed four hundred. More than that. There were seedlings that Pervus had bought in April to be paid for at the end of the growing season, in the fall. And now fall was here.

Fear shook her. She told herself she was tired, nervous. That terrible week. And now this. The heat. Soon they'd be home, she and Dirk. How cool and quiet the house would seem. The squares of the kitchen tablecloth. Her own neat bedroom with the black walnut bed and dresser. The sofa in the parlour with the ruffled calico cover. The old chair on the porch with the cane seat sagging where warp and woof had become loosened with much use and stuck out in ragged tufts. It seemed years since she had seen all this. The comfort of it, the peace of it. Safe, desirable, suddenly dear. No work for a woman, this. Well, perhaps they were right.

Down Wabash Avenue, with the L trains thundering overhead and her horses, frightened and uneasy with the unaccustomed roar and clangour of traffic, stepping high and swerving stiffly, grotesque and angular in their movements. A dowdy farm woman and a sun-burned boy in a rickety vegetable wagon absurdly out of place in this canyon of cobblestones, shops, street-cars, drays, carriages, bicycles, pedestrians. It was terribly hot.

The boy's eyes popped with excitement and bewilderment.

"Pretty soon," Selina said. The muscles showed white beneath the skin of her jaw. "Pretty soon. Prairie Avenue. Great big houses, and lawns, all quiet." She even managed a smile.

"I like it better home."

Prairie Avenue at last, turning in at Sixteenth Street. It was like calm after a storm. Selina felt battered, spent.

There were groceries near Eighteenth, and at the other cross-streets—Twenty-second, Twenty-sixth, Thirty-first, Thirty-fifth. They were passing the great stone houses of Prairie Avenue of the '90s. Turrets and towers, cornices and cupolas, hump-backed conservatories, porte-cochères, bow windows—here lived Chicago's rich that had made their riches in pork and wheat and dry goods; the selling of necessities to a city that clamoured for them.

"Just like me," Selina thought, humorously. Then another thought came to her. Her vegetables, canvas covered, were fresher than those in the near-by markets. Why not try to sell some of them here, in these big houses? In an hour she might earn a few dollars this way at retail prices slightly less than those asked by the grocers of the neighbourhood.

She stopped her wagon in the middle of the block on Twenty-fourth Street. Agilely she stepped down the wheel, gave the reins to Dirk. The horses were no more minded to run than the wooden steeds on a carrousel. She filled a large market basket with the finest and freshest of her stock and with this on her arm looked up a moment at the house in front of which she had stopped. It was a four-story brownstone, with a hideous high stoop. Beneath the steps were a little vestibule and a door that was the tradesmen's entrance. The kitchen entrance, she knew, was by way of the alley at the back, but this she would not take. Across the sidewalk, down a little flight of stone steps, into the vestibule under the porch. She looked at the bell—a brass knob. You pulled it out, shoved it in, and there sounded a jangling down the dim hallway beyond. Simple enough. Her hand was on the bell. "Pull it!" said the desperate Selina. "I can't! I can't!" cried all the prim dim Vermont Peakes, in chorus. "All right. Starve to death and let them take the farm and Dirk, then."

At that she pulled the knob hard. Jangle went the bell in the hall. Again. Again.

Footsteps up the hall. The door opened to disclose a large woman, high cheek-boned, in a work apron; a cook, apparently.

"Good morning," said Selina. "Would you like some fresh country vegetables?"

"No." She half shut the door, opening it again to ask, "Got any fresh eggs or butter?" At Selina's negative she closed the door, bolted it. Selina, standing there, basket on arm, could hear her heavy tread down the passageway toward the kitchen. Well, that was all right. Nothing so terrible about that, Selina told herself. Simply hadn't wanted any vegetables. The next house. The next house, and the next, and the next. Up one side of the street, and down the other. Four times she refilled her basket. At one house she sold a quarter's worth. Fifteen at another. Twenty cents here. Almost fifty there. "Good morning," she always said at the door in her clear, distinct way. They stared, usually. But they were curious, too, and did not often shut the door in her face.

"Do you know of a good place?" one kitchen maid said. "This place ain't so good. She only pays me three dollars. You can get four now. Maybe you know a lady wants a good girl."

"No," Selina answered. "No."

At another house the cook had offered her a cup of coffee, noting the white face, the look of weariness. Selina refused it, politely. Twenty-first Street—Twenty-fifth—Twenty-eighth. She had over four dollars in her purse. Dirk was weary now and hungry to the point of tears. "The last house," Selina promised him, "the very last one. After this one we'll go home." She filled her basket again. "We'll have something to eat on the way, and maybe you'll go to sleep with the canvas over you, high, fastened to the seat like a tent. And we'll be home in a jiffy."

The last house was a new gray stone one, already beginning to turn dingy from the smoke of the Illinois Central suburban trains that puffed along the lake front a block to the east. The house had large bow windows, plump and shining. There was a lawn, with statues, and a conservatory in the rear. Real lace curtains at the downstairs windows with plush hangings behind them. A high iron grille ran all about the property giving it an air of aloofness, of security. Selina glanced at this wrought-iron fence. And it seemed to bar her out. There was something forbidding about it—menacing. She was tired, that was it. The last house. She had almost five dollars, earned in the last hour. "Just five minutes," she said to Dirk, trying to make her tone bright, her voice gay. Her arms full of vegetables which she was about to place in the basket at her feet she heard at her elbow:

"Now, then, where's your license?"

She turned. A policeman at her side. She stared up at him. How enormously tall, she thought; and how red his face. "License?"

"Yeh, you heard me. License. Where's your peddler's license? You got one, I s'pose."

"Why, no. No." She stared at him, still.

His face grew redder. Selina was a little worried about him. She thought, stupidly, that if it grew any redder ——

"Well, say, where d'ye think you are, peddlin' without a license! A good mind to run you in. Get along out of here, you and the kid. Leave me ketch you around here again!"

"What's the trouble, Officer?" said a woman's voice. A smart open carriage of the type known as a victoria, with two chestnut horses whose harness shone with metal. Spanking, was the word that came to Selina's mind, which was acting perversely certainly; crazily. A spanking team. The spankers disdainfully faced Selina's comic bony nags which were grazing the close-cropped grass that grew in the neat little lawn-squares between curb and sidewalk. "What's the trouble, Reilly?"

The woman stepped out of the victoria. She wore a black silk Eton suit, very modish, and a black hat with a plume.

"Woman peddling without a license, Mrs. Arnold. You got to watch 'em like a hawk. . . . Get along wid you, then." He put a hand on Selina's shoulder and gave her a gentle push.

There shook Selina from head to foot such a passion, such a storm of outraged sensibilities, as to cause street, victoria, silk-clad woman, horses, and policeman to swim and shiver in a haze before her eyes. The rage of a fastidious woman who had had an alien male hand put upon her. Her face was white. Her eyes glowed black, enormous. She seemed tall, majestic even.

"Take your hand off me!" Her speech was clipped, vibrant. "How dare you touch me! How dare you! Take your hand! ——" The blazing eyes in the white mask. He took his hand from her shoulder. The red surged into her face. A tanned weather-beaten toil-worn woman, her abundant hair skewered into a knob and held by a long gray-black hairpin, her full skirt grimed with the mud of the wagon wheel, a pair of old side-boots on her slim feet, a grotesquely battered old felt hat (her husband's) on her head, her arms full of ears of sweet corn, and carrots, and radishes and bunches of beets; a woman with bad teeth, flat breasts—even then Julie had known her by her eyes. And she had stared and then run to her in her silk dress and her plumed hat, crying, "Oh, Selina! My dear! My dear!" with a sob of horror and pity. "My dear!" And had taken Selina, carrots, beets, corn, and radishes in her arms. The vegetables lay scattered all about them on the sidewalk in front of Julie Hempel Arnold's great stone house on Prairie Avenue. But strangely enough it had been Selina who had done the comforting, patting Julie's plump silken shoulder and saying, over and over, soothingly, as to a child, "There, there! It's all right, Julie. It's all right. Don't cry. What's there to cry for! Sh-sh! It's all right."

Julie lifted her head in its modish black plumed hat, wiped her eyes, blew her nose. "Get along with you, do," she said to Reilly, the policeman, using his very words to Selina. "I'm going to report you to Mr. Arnold, see if I don't. And you know what that means."

"Well, now, Mrs. Arnold, ma'am, I was only doing my duty. How cud I know the lady was a friend of yours. Sure, I ——" He surveyed Selina, cart, jaded horses, wilted vegetables. "Well, how *cud* I, now, Mrs. Arnold, ma'am!"

"And why not!" demanded Julie with superb unreasonableness. "Why not, I'd like to know. Do get along with you."

He got along, a defeated officer of the law, and a bitter. And now it was Julie who surveyed Selina, cart, Dirk, jaded horses, wilted left-over vegetables. "Selina, whatever in the world! What are you doing with ——" She caught sight of Selina's absurd boots then and she began to cry again. At that Selina's overwrought nerves snapped and she began to laugh, hysterically. It frightened Julie, that laughter. "Selina, don't! Come in the house with me. What are you laughing at! Selina!"

With shaking finger Selina was pointing at the vegetables that lay tumbled at her feet. "Do you see that cabbage, Julie? Do you remember how I used to despise Mrs. Tebbitt's because she used to have boiled cabbage on Monday nights?"

"That's nothing to laugh at, is it? Stop laughing this minute, Selina Peake!"

"I'll stop. I've stopped now. I was just laughing at my ignorance. Sweat and blood and health and youth go into every cabbage. Did you know that, Julie? One doesn't despise them as food, knowing that. . . . Come, climb down, Dirk. Here's a lady mother used to know—oh, years and years ago, when she was a girl. Thousands of years ago."

12

The best thing for Dirk. The best thing for Dirk. It was the phrase that repeated itself over and over in Selina's speech during the days that followed. Julie Arnold was all for taking him into her gray stone house, dressing him like Lord Fauntleroy and sending him to the north-side private school attended by Eugene, her boy, and Pauline, her girl. In this period of bewilderment and fatigue Julie had attempted to take charge of Selina much as she had done a dozen years before at the time of Simeon Peake's dramatic death. And now, as then, she pressed into service her wonder-working father and bounden slave, August Hempel. Her husband she dismissed with affectionate disregard.

"Michael's all right," she had said on that day of their first meeting, "if you tell him what's to be done. He'll always do it. But Pa's the one that thinks of things. He's like a general, and Michael's the captain. Well, now, Pa'll be out to-morrow and I'll probably come with him. I've got a committee meeting, but I can easily——"

"You said—did you say your father would be out to-morrow! Out where?"

"To your place. Farm."

"But why should he? It's a little twenty-five-acre truck farm, and half of it under water a good deal of the time."

"Pa'll find a use for it, never fear. He won't say much, but he'll think of things. And then everything will be all right."

"It's miles. Miles. Way out in High Prairie."

"Well, if you could make it with those horses, Selina, I guess we can with Pa's two grays that hold a record for a mile in three minutes or three miles in a minute, I forget which. Or in the auto, though Pa hates it. Michael is the only one in the family who likes it."

A species of ugly pride now possessed Selina. "I don't need help. Really I don't, Julie dear. It's never been like to-day. Never before. We were getting on very well, Pervus and I. Then after Pervus's death so suddenly like that I was frightened. Terribly frightened. About Dirk. I wanted him to have everything. Beautiful things. I wanted his life to be beautiful. Life can be so ugly, Julie. You don't know. You don't know."

"Well, now, that's why I say. We'll be out to-morrow, Pa and I. Dirk's going to have everything beautiful. We'll see to that."

It was then that Selina had said, "But that's just it. I want to do it myself, for him. I can. I want to give him all these things myself."

"But that's selfish."

"I don't mean to be. I just want to do the best thing for Dirk."

It was shortly after noon that High Prairie, hearing the unaccustomed chug of a motor, rushed to its windows or porches to behold Selina DeJong in her mashed black felt hat and Dirk waving his battered straw wildly, riding up the Halsted road toward the DeJong farm in a bright red automobile that had shattered the nerves of every farmer's team it had met on the way. Of the DeJong team and the DeJong dog Pom, and the DeJong vegetable wagon there was absolutely no sign. High Prairie was rendered unfit for work throughout the next twenty-four hours.

The idea had been Julie's, and Selina had submitted rather than acquiesced, for by now she was too tired to combat anything or any one. If Julie had proposed her entering High Prairie on the back of an elephant with a mahout perched between his ears Selina would have agreed—rather, would have been unable to object.

"It'll get you home in no time," Julie had said, energetically. "You look like a ghost and the boy's half asleep. I'll telephone Pa and he'll have one of the men from the barns drive your team out so it'll be there by six. Just you leave it all to me. Haven't you ever ridden in one! Why, there's nothing to be scared of. I like the horses best, myself. I'm like Pa. He says if you use horses you get there."

Dirk had accepted the new conveyance with the adaptability of childhood, had even predicted, grandly, "I'm going to have one when I grow up that'll go faster'n this, even."

"Oh, you wouldn't want to go faster than this, Dirk," Selina had protested breathlessly as they chugged along at the alarming rate of almost fifteen miles an hour.

Jan Snip had been rendered speechless. Until the actual arrival of the team and wagon at six he counted them as mysteriously lost and DeJong's widow clearly gone mad. August Hempel's arrival next day with Julie seated beside him in the light spider-phaeton drawn by two slim wild-eyed quivering grays made little tumult in Jan's stunned mind by now incapable of absorbing any fresh surprises.

In the twelve years' transition from butcher to packer Aug Hempel had taken on a certain authority and distinction. Now, at fifty-five, his hair was gray, relieving the too-ruddy colour of his face. He talked almost without an accent; used the idiomatic American speech he heard about the yards, where the Hempel packing plant was situated. Only his d's were likely to sound like t's. The letter j had a slightly ch sound. In the last few years he had grown very deaf in one ear, so that when you spoke to him he looked at you intently. This had given him a reputation for keenness and great character insight, when it was merely the protective trick of a man who does not want to confess that he is hard of hearing. He wore square-toed shoes with soft tips and square-cut gray clothes and a large gray hat with a chronically inadequate sweat-band. The square-cut boots were expensive, and the square-cut gray clothes and the large gray hat, but in them he always gave the effect of being dressed in the discarded garments of a much larger man.

Selina's domain he surveyed with a keen and comprehensive eye. "You want to sell?"

"No."

"That's good." (It was nearly goot as he said it.) "Few years from now this land will be worth money." He had spent a bare fifteen minutes taking shrewd valuation of the property from fields to barn, from barn to house "Well, what do you want to do, heh, Selina?"

They were seated in the cool and unexpectedly pleasing little parlour, with its old Dutch lustre set gleaming softly in the cabinet, its three rows of books, its air of comfort and usage. Dirk was in the yard with one of the Van Ruys boys, surveying the grays proprietorially. Jan was rooting in the fields. Selina clasped her hands tightly in her lap—those hands that, from much grubbing in the soil, had taken on something of the look of the gnarled things they tended. The nails were short, discoloured, broken. The palms rough, calloused. The whole story of the last twelve years of Selina's life was written in her two hands.

"I want to stay here, and work the farm, and make it pay. I can. By next spring my asparagus is going to begin to bring in money. I'm not going to grow just the common garden stuff any more—not much, anyway. I'm going to specialize in the fine things—the kind the South Water Street commission men want. I want to drain the low land. Tile it. That land hasn't been used for years. It ought to be rich growing land by now, if once it's properly drained. And I want Dirk to go to school. Good schools. I never want my son to go to the Haymarket. Never. Never."

Julie stirred with a little rustle and click of silk and beads. Her gentle amiability was vaguely alarmed by the iron quality of determination in the other's tone.

"Yes, but what about you, Selina?"

"Me?"

"Yes, of course. You talk as though you didn't count. Your life. Things to make you happy."

"My life doesn't count, except as something for Dirk to use. I'm done with anything else. Oh, I don't mean that I'm discouraged, or disappointed in life, or anything like that. I mean I started out with the wrong idea. I know better now. I'm here to keep Dirk from making the mistakes I made."

Here Aug Hempel, lounging largely in his chair and eyeing Selina intently, turned his gaze absently through the window to where the grays, a living equine statue, stood before the house. His tone was one of meditation, not of argument. "It don't work out that way, seems. About mistakes it's funny. You got to make your own; and not only that, if you try to keep people from making theirs they get mad." He whistled softly through his teeth following this utterance and tapped the chair seat with his finger nails.

"It's beauty!" Selina said then, almost passionately. Aug Hempel and Julie plainly could make nothing of this remark so she went on, eager, explanatory. "I used to think that if you wanted beauty—if you wanted it hard enough and hopefully enough—it came to you. You just waited, and lived your life as best you could, knowing that beauty might be just around the corner. You just waited, and then it came."

"Beauty!" exclaimed Julie, weakly. She stared at Selina in the evident belief that this work-worn haggard woman was bemoaning her lack of personal pulchritude.

"Yes. All the worth-while things in life. All mixed up. Rooms in candle-light. Leisure. Colour. Travel. Books. Music. Pictures. People—all kinds of people. Work that you love. And growth—growth and watching people grow. Feeling very strongly about things and then developing that feeling to—to make something fine come of it." The word self-expression was not in cant use then, and Selina hadn't it to offer them. They would not have known what she meant if she had. She threw out her hands now in a futile gesture. "That's what I mean by beauty. I want Dirk to have it."

Julie blinked and nodded with the wise amiable look of comprehension assumed by one who has understood no single word of what has been said. August Hempel cleared his throat.

"I guess I know what you're driving at Selina, maybe. About Julie I felt just like that. She should have everything fine. I wanted her to have everything. And she did, too. Cried for the moon she had it."

"I never did have it, Pa, any such thing!"

"Never cried for it, I know of."

"For pity's sake!" pleaded Julie, the literal, "let's stop talking and do something. My goodness, anybody with a little money can have books and candles and travel around and look at pictures, if that's all. So let's *do* something. Pa, you've probably got it all fixed in your mind long ago. It's time we heard it. Here Selina was one of the most popular girls in Miss Fister's school, and lots of people thought the prettiest. And now just look at her!"

A flicker of the old flame leaped up in Selina. "Flatterer!" she murmured.

Aug Hempel stood up. "If you think giving your whole life to making the boy happy is going to make him happy you ain't so smart as I took you for. You go trying to live somebody else's life for them."

"I'm not going to live his life for him. I want to show him how to live it so that he'll get full value out of it."

"Keeping him out of the Haymarket if the Haymarket's the natural place for him to be won't do that. How can you tell! Monkeying with what's to be. I'm out at the yards every day, in and out of the cattle pens, talking to the drovers and herders, mixing in with the buyers. I can tell the weight of a hog and what he's worth just by a look at him, and a steer, too. My son-in-law Michael Arnold sits up in the office all day in our plant, dictating letters. His clothes they never stink of the pens like mine do. . . . Now I ain't saying anything against him, Julie. But I bet my grandson Eugene"—he repeated it, stressing the name so that you sensed his dislike of it—"Eugene, if he comes into the business at all when he grows up, won't go within smelling distance of the yards. His office I bet will be in a new office building on, say Madison Street, with a view of the lake. Life! You'll be hoggin' it all yourself and not know it."

"Don't pay any attention to him," Julie interposed. "He goes on like that. Old yards!"

August Hempel bit off the end of a cigar, was about to spit out the speck explosively, thought better of it and tucked it in his vest pocket. "I wouldn't change places with Mike, not——"

"Please don't call him Mike, Pa."

"Michael, then. Not for ten million. And I need ten million right now."

"And I suppose," retorted Selina, spiritedly, "that when your son-in-law Michael Arnold is your age he'll be telling Eugene how he roughed it in an office over at the yards in the old days. These will be the old days."

August Hempel laughed good-humouredly. "That can be, Selina. That can be." He chewed his cigar and settled to the business at hand.

"You want to drain and tile. Plant high-grade stuff. You got to have a man on the place that knows what's what, not this Rip Van Winkle we saw in the cabbage field. New horses. A wagon." His eyes narrowed speculatively. Shrewd wrinkles radiated from their corners. "I betcha we'll see the day when you truck farmers will run into town with your stuff in big automobile wagons that will get you there in under an hour. It's bound to come. The horse is doomed, that's chust what." Then, abruptly, "I will get you the horses, a bargain, at the yards." He took out a long flat check book. He began writing in it with a pen that he took from his pocket—some sort of marvellous pen that seemed already filled with ink and that you unscrewed at the top and then screwed at the bottom. He squinted through his cigar smoke, the check book propped on his knee. He tore off the check with a clean rip. "For a starter," he said. He held it out to Selina.

"There now!" exclaimed Julie, in triumphant satisfaction. That was more like it. Doing something.

But Selina did not take the check. She sat very still in her chair, her hands folded. "That isn't the regular way," she said.

August Hempel was screwing the top on his fountain pen again. "Regular way? for what?"

"I'm borrowing this money, not taking it. Oh, yes, I am! I couldn't get along without it. I realize that now, after yesterday. Yesterday! But in five years—seven—I'll pay it back." Then, at a half-uttered protest from Julie, "That's the only way I'll take it. It's for Dirk. But I'm going to earn it—and pay it back. I want a——" she was being enormously businesslike, and unconsciously enjoying it—— "a—an I.O.U. A promise to pay you back just as—as soon as I can. That's business, isn't it? And I'll sign it."

"Sure," said Aug Hempel, and unscrewed his fountain pen

again. "Sure that's business." Very serious, he scribbled again, busily, on a piece of paper. A year later, when Selina had learned many things, among them that simple and compound interest on money loaned are not mere problems devised to fill Duffy's Arithmetic in her school-teaching days, she went to August Hempel between laughter and tears.

"You didn't say one word about interest, that day. Not a word. What a little fool you must have thought me."

"Between friends," protested August Hempel.

But—"No," Selina insisted. "Interest."

"I guess I better start me a bank pretty soon if you keep on so businesslike."

Ten years later he was actually the controlling power in the Yards & Rangers' Bank. And Selina had that original I.O.U. with its "Paid In Full. Aug Hempel," carefully tucked away in the carved oak chest together with other keepsakes that she foolishly treasured— ridiculous scraps that no one but she would have understood or val- ued—a small school slate such as little children use (the one on which she had taught Pervus to figure and parse); a dried bunch of trilliums; a bustled and panniered wine-red cashmere dress, absurdly old-fashioned; a letter telling about the Infanta Eulalie of Spain, and signed Julie Hempel Arnold; a pair of men's old side-boots with mud caked on them; a crude sketch, almost obliterated now, done on a torn scrap of brown paper and showing the Haymarket with the wag-ons vegetable-laden and the men gathered beneath the street-flares, and the patient farm horses—Roelf's childish sketch.

Among this rubbish she rummaged periodically in the years that followed. Indeed, twenty years later Dirk, coming upon her smooth-ing out the wrinkled yellow creases of the I.O.U. or shaking the camphor-laden folds of the wine-red cashmere, would say, "At it again! What a sentimental generation yours was, Mother. Pressed flowers! They went out with the attic, didn't they? If the house caught fire you'd probably run for the junk in that chest. It isn't worth two cents, the lot of it."

"Perhaps not," Selina said slowly. "Still, there'd be some money value, I suppose, in an early original signed sketch by Rodin."

"Rodin! You haven't got a——"

"No, but here's one by Pool—Roelf Pool—signed. At a sale in New York last week one of his sketches—not a finished thing at all— just a rough drawing that he'd made of some figures in a group that went into the Doughboy statue—brought one thous——"

"Oh, well, that—yes. But the rest of the stuff you've got there— funny how people will treasure old stuff like that. Useless stuff. It isn't even beautiful."

"Beautiful!" said Selina, and shut the lid of the old chest. "Why, Dirk—Dirk! You don't even know what beauty is. You never will know."

13

If those vague characteristics called (variously) magnetism, manner, grace, distinction, attractiveness, fascination, go to make up that nebulous quality known as charm; and if the possessor of that quality is accounted fortunate in his equipment for that which the class-day orators style the battle of life, then Dirk DeJong was a lucky lad and life lay promisingly before him. Undoubtedly he had it; and undoubtedly it did. People said that things "came easy" for Dirk. He said so himself, not boastfully, but rather shyly. He was not one to talk a great deal. Perhaps that was one of his most charming qualities. He listened so well. And he was so quietly effortless. He listened while other people talked, his fine head inclined just a little to one side and bent toward you. Intent on what you were saying, and evidently impressed by it. You felt him immensely intelligent, appreciative. It was a gift more valuable than any other social talent he might have possessed. He himself did not know how precious an attribute this was to prove in a later day when to be allowed to finish a sentence was an experience all too rare. Older men especially said he was a smart young feller and would make his mark. This, surprisingly enough, after a conversation to which he had contributed not a word other than "Yes," or "No," or, "Perhaps you're right, sir," in the proper places.

Selina thought constantly of Dirk's future. A thousand other thoughts might be racing through her mind during the day—plans for the farm, for the house—but always, over and above and through all these, like the steady beat of a drum penetrating sharper and more urgent sounds—was the thought of Dirk. He did well enough at high school. Not a brilliant student, nor even a very good one. But good enough. Average. And well liked.

It was during those careless years of Dirk's boyhood between nine and fifteen that Selina changed the DeJong acres from a worn-out and down-at-heel truck farm whose scant products brought a second-rate price in a second-rate market to a prosperous and blooming vegetable garden whose output was sought a year in advance by the South Water Street commission merchants. DeJong asparagus with firm white thick stalk bases tapering to a rich green streaked with lavender at the tips. DeJong hothouse tomatoes in February, plump, scarlet, juicy. You paid for a pound a sum Pervus had been glad to get for a bushel.

These six or seven years of relentless labour had been no showy success with Selina posing grandly as the New Woman in Business. No, it had been a painful, grubbing, heart-breaking process as is any project that depends on the actual soil for its realization. She drove herself pitilessly. She literally tore a living out of the earth with her two bare hands. Yet there was nothing pitiable about this small energetic woman of thirty-five or forty with her fine soft dark eyes, her clean-cut jawline, her shabby decent clothes that were so likely to be spattered with the mud of the road or fields, her exquisite nose with the funny little wrinkle across the bridge when she laughed. Rather, there was something splendid about her; something rich, prophetic. It was the splendour and richness that achievement imparts.

It is doubtful that she ever could have succeeded without the money borrowed from August Hempel; without his shrewd counsel. She told him this, sometimes. He denied it. "Easier, yes. But you would have found a way, Selina. Some way. Julie, no. But you, yes. You are like that. Me, too. Say, plenty fellers that was butchers with me twenty years ago over in North Clark Street are butchers yet, cutting off a steak or a chop. 'Good morning, Mrs. Kruger. What'll it be to-day?' "

The Hempel Packing Company was a vast monster now stretching great arms into Europe, into South America. In some of the yellow journals that had cropped up in the last few years you even saw old Aug himself portrayed in cartoons as an octopus with cold slimy eyes and a hundred writhing reaching tentacles. These bothered Aug a little, though he pretended to laugh at them. "What do they want to go to work and make me out like that for? I sell good meat for all I can get for it. That's business, ain't it?"

Dirk had his tasks on the farm. Selina saw to that. But they were not heavy. He left for school at eight in the morning, driving, for the distance was too great for walking. Often it was dark on his return in the late afternoon. Between these hours Selina had accomplished the work of two men. She had two field-helpers on the place now during the busy season and a woman in the house, the wife of Adam Bras, one of the labourers. Jan Snip, too, still worked about the place in the barn, the sheds, tending the coldframes and hothouses, doing odd jobs of carpentering. He distrusted Selina's new-fangled methods, glowered at any modern piece of machinery, predicted dire things when Selina bought the twenty acres that comprised the old Bouts place adjoining the DeJong farm.

"You bit off more as you can chew," he told her. "You choke yet. You see."

By the time Dirk returned from school the rough work of the day was over. His food was always hot, appetizing, plentiful. The house was neat, comfortable. Selina had installed a bathroom—one of the two bathrooms in High Prairie. The neighbourhood was still rocking with the shock of this when it was informed by Jan that Selina and Dirk ate with candles lighted on the supper table. High Prairie slapped its thigh and howled with mirth.

"Cabbages is beautiful," said old Klaas Pool when he heard this. "Cabbages is beautiful I betcha."

Selina, during the years of the boy's adolescence, had never urged him to a decision about his future. That, she decided, would come. As the farm prospered and the pressure of necessity lifted she tried, in various ingenious ways, to extract from him some unconscious sign of definite preference for this calling, that profession. As in her leanest days she had bought an occasional book at the cost of much-needed shoes for herself so now she bought many of them with money that another woman would have used for luxury or adornments. Years of personal privation had not killed her love of fine soft silken things, mellow colouring, exquisite workmanship. But they had made it impossible for her to covet these things for herself. She loved to see them, to feel them. Could not wear them. Years later, when she could well afford a French hat in one of the Michigan Avenue millinery shops, she would look at the silk and satin trifles blooming in the windows like gay brilliant flowers in a conservatory—and would buy an untrimmed "shape" for $2.95 in Field's basement. The habit of a lifetime is strong. Just once she made herself buy one of these costly silk-and-feather extravagances, going about the purchase deliberately and coldly as a man gets drunk once for the experience. The hat had cost twenty-two dollars. She never had worn it.

Until Dirk was sixteen she had been content to let him develop as naturally as possible, and to absorb impressions unconsciously from the traps she so guilefully left about him. Books on the lives of great men—lives of Lincoln, of Washington, Gladstone, Disraeli, Voltaire. History. Books on painting, charmingly illustrated. Books on architecture; law; medicine, even. She subscribed to two of the best engineering magazines. There was a shed which he was free to use as a workshop, fitted up with all sorts of tools. He did not use it much, after the first few weeks. He was pleasantly and mildly interested in all these things; held by none of them. Selina had thought of Roelf when they were fitting up the workshop. The Pools had heard from Roelf just once since his flight from the farm. A letter had come from France. In it was a sum of money for Geertje and Jozina—a small sum to take the trouble to send all the way from an outlandish country, the well-to-do Pool household thought. Geertje was married now to Vander Sijde's son Gerrit and living on a farm out Low Prairie way. Jozina had a crazy idea that the impecunious young Paris art student had had to save it sou by sou. Selina had never heard from him. But one day years later she had come running to Dirk with an illustrated magazine in her hand.

"Look!" she had cried, and pointed to a picture. He had rarely seen her so excited, so stirred. The illustration showed a photographic reproduction of a piece of sculpture—a woman's figure. It was called The Seine. A figure sinuous, snake-like, graceful, revolting, beautiful, terrible. The face alluring, insatiable, generous, treacherous, all at once. It was the Seine that fed the fertile valley land; the Seine that claimed a thousand bloated lifeless floating Things: the red-eyed hag of 1793; the dimpling coquette of 1650. Beneath the illustration a line or two—Roelf Pool . . . Salon . . . American . . . future . . .

"It's Roelf!" Selina had cried. "Roelf. Little Roelf Pool!" Tears in her eyes. Dirk had been politely interested. But then he had never known him, really. He had heard his mother speak of him, but ——

Selina showed the picture to the Pools, driving over there one evening to surprise them with it. Mrs. Klaas Pool had been horrified at the picture of a nude woman's figure; had cried "Og heden!" in disgust, and had seemed to think that Selina had brought it over in a spirit of spite. Was she going to show it to the rest of High Prairie!

Selina understood High Prairie folk better now, though not altogether, even after almost twenty years of living amongst them. A cold people, yet kindly. Suspicious, yet generous. Distrustful of all change, yet progressing by sheer force of thrift and unceasing labour. Unimaginative for generations, only to produce—a Roelf Pool.

She tried now to explain the meaning of the figure Roelf had moulded so masterfully. "You see, it's supposed to represent the Seine. The River Seine that flows through Paris into the countryside beyond. The whole history of Paris—of France—is bound up in the Seine; intertwined with it. Terrible things, and magnificent things. It flows just beneath the Louvre. You can see it from the Bastille. On its largest island stands Notre Dame. The Seine has seen such things, Mrs. Pool! ——"

"What *dom* talk!" interrupted the late widow. "A river can't see. Anybody knows that."

At seventeen Dirk and Selina talked of the year to come. He was going to a university. But to what university? And what did he want to study? We-e-ll, hard to say. Kind of a general course, wasn't there?

Some languages—little French or something—and political economy, and some literature and maybe history.

"Oh," Selina had said. "Yes. General. Of course, if a person wanted to be an architect, why, I suppose Cornell would be the place. Or Harvard for law. Or Boston Tech for engineering, or ——"

Oh, yeh, if a fellow wanted any of those things. Good idea, though, to take a kind of general course until you found out exactly what you wanted to do. Languages and literature and that kind of thing.

Selina was rather delighted than otherwise. That, she knew, was the way they did it in England. You sent your son to a university not to cram some technical course into him, or to railroad him through a book-knowledge of some profession. You sent him so that he might develop in an atmosphere of books, of learning; spending relaxed hours in the companionship of men who taught for the love of teaching; whose informal talks before a study fire were more richly valuable than whole courses of classroom lectures. She had read of these things in English novels. Oxford. Cambridge. Dons. Ivy. Punting. Prints. Mullioned windows. Books. Discussion. Literary clubs.

This was England. An older civilization, of course. But there must be something of that in American universities. And if that was what Dirk wanted she was glad. Glad! A reaching after true beauty.

You heard such wonderful things about Midwest University, in Chicago. On the south side. It was new, yes. But those Gothic buildings gave an effect, somehow, of age and permanence (the smoke and cinders from the Illinois Central suburban trains were largely responsible for that, as well as the soft coal from a thousand neighbouring chimneys). And there actually was ivy. Undeniable ivy, and mullioned windows.

Dirk had suggested it, not she. The entrance requirements were quite mild. Harvard? Yale? Oh, those fellows all had wads of money. Eugene Arnold had his own car at New Haven.

In that case, they decided, Midwest University, in Chicago, on the south side near the lake, would do splendidly. For a general course, sort of. The world lay ahead of Dirk. It was like the childhood game of counting buttons.

> *Rich man, poor man, beggar-man, thief,*
> *Doctor, lawyer, merchant, chief.*

Together they counted Dirk's mental buttons but it never came out twice the same. It depended on the suit you happened to be wearing, of course. Eugene Arnold was going to take law at Yale. He said it would be necessary if he was going into the business. He didn't put it just that way, when talking to Dirk. He said the damned old hog business. Pauline (she insisted that they call her Paula now) was at a girls' school up the Hudson—one of those schools that never advertise even in the front of the thirty-five-cent magazines.

So, at eighteen, it had been Midwest University for Dirk. It was a much more economical plan than would have resulted from the choice of an eastern college. High Prairie heard that Dirk DeJong was going away to college. A neighbour's son said, "Going to Wisconsin? Agricultural course there?"

"My gosh, no!" Dirk had answered. He told this to Selena, laughing. But she had not laughed.

"I'd like to take that course myself, if you must know. They say it's wonderful." She looked at him, suddenly. "Dirk, you wouldn't like to take it, would you? To go to Madison, I mean. Is that what you'd like?"

He stared. "Me! No! . . . Unless you want me to, Mother. Then I would, gladly. I hate your working like this, on the farm, while I go off to school. It makes me feel kind of rotten, having my mother working for me. The other fellows ——"

"I'm doing the work I'm interested in, for the person I love best in the world. I'd be lost—unhappy—without the farm. If the city creeps up on me, as they predict it will, I don't know what I shall do."

But Dirk had a prediction of his own to make. "Chicago'll never grow this way, with all those steel mills and hunkies to the south of us. The north side is going to be the place to live. It is already."

"The place for whom?"

"For the people with money."

She smiled then so that you saw the funny little wrinkle across her nose. "Well, then the south section of Chicago is going to be all right for us yet a while."

"Just you wait till I'm successful. Then there'll be no more working for you."

"What do you mean by 'successful', Sobig?" She had not called him that in years. But now the old nickname came to her tongue perhaps because they were speaking of his future, his success. "What do you mean by 'successful', Sobig?"

"Rich. Lots of money."

"Oh, no, Dirk! No! That's not success. Roelf—the thing Roelf does—that's success."

"Oh, well, if you have money enough you can buy the things he makes, and have 'em. That's almost as good, isn't it?"

Midwest University had sprung up almost literally overnight on the property that had been the site of the Midway Plaisance during the World's Fair in Chicago in '93. One man's millions had been the magic wand that, waved over a bare stretch of prairie land, had produced a seat of learning. The university guide book spoke of him reverently as the Founder, capitalizing the word as one does the Deity. The student body spoke of him with somewhat less veneration. They called him Coal-Oil Johnny. He had already given thirty millions to the university and still the insatiable maw of this institute of learning yawned for more. When oil went up a fraction of a cent they said, "Guess Coal-Oil Johnny's fixing to feed us another million."

Dirk commenced his studies at Midwest University in the autumn of 1909. His first year was none too agreeable, as is usually the case in first years. He got on well, though. A large proportion of the men students were taking law, which accounts for the great number of real-estate salesmen and insurance agents now doing business in and about Chicago. Before the end of the first semester he was popular. He was a natural-born floor committeeman and badges bloomed in his buttonhole. Merely by donning a ready-made dress suit he could give it a made-to-order air. He had great natural charm of manner. The men liked him, and the girls, too. He learned to say, "Got Pol Econ at ten." which meant that he took Political Economy at that hour; and "I'd like to cut Psyk," meant that he was not up on his approaching lesson in Applied Psychology. He rarely "cut" a class. He would have felt that this was unfair and disloyal to his mother. Some of his fellow students joked about this faithfulness to his classes. "Person would think you were an Unclassified," they said.

The Unclassifieds were made up, for the most part, of earnest and rather middle-aged students whose education was a delayed blooming. They usually were not enrolled for a full course, or were taking double work feverishly. The Classifieds, on the other hand, were the regularly enrolled students, pretty well of an age (between seventeen and twenty-three) who took their education with a sprinkling of sugar. Of the Unclassified students the University catalogue said:

> Persons at least twenty-one years of age, not seeking a degree, may be admitted through the office of the University Examiner to the courses of instruction offered in the University, as unclassified students. They shall present evidence of successful experience as a teacher or *other valuable educative experience in practical life*. . . . They are ineligible for public appearance. . . .

You saw them the Cinderellas and the Smikes of this temple of learning.

The Classifieds and the Unclassifieds rarely mixed. Not age alone, but purpose separated them. The Classifieds, boys and girls, were, for the most part slim young lads with caps and pipes and sweaters, their talk of football, baseball, girls; slim young girls in sheer shirtwaists with pink ribbons run through the corset covers showing beneath, pleated skirts that switched delightfully as they strolled across the campus arm in arm, their talk of football games, fudge, clothes, boys. They cut classes whenever possible. The Student Body. Midwest turned them out by the hundreds—almost by the link, one might say, as Aug Hempel's sausage factory turned out its fine plump sausages, each one exactly like the one behind and the one ahead of it. So many hundreds graduated in this year's class. So many more hundreds to be graduated in next year's class. Occasionally an unruly sausage burst its skin and was discarded. They attended a university because their parents—thrifty shopkeepers, manufacturers, merchants, or professional men and their good wives—wanted their children to have an education. Were ambitious for them. "I couldn't have it myself, and always regretted it. Now I want my boy (or girl) to have a good education that'll fit 'em for the battle of life. This is an age of specialization, let me tell you."

Football, fudge, I-said-to-Jim, I-said-to-Bessie.

The Unclassifieds would no more have deliberately cut a class than they would have thrown their sparse weekly budget-allowance into the gutter. If it had been physically possible they would have attended two classes at once, listened to two lectures, prepared two papers simultaneously. Drab and earnest women between thirty and forty-eight, their hair not an ornament, but something to be pinned up quickly out of the way, their clothes a covering, their shoes not even smartly "sensible," but just shoes, scuffed, patched, utilitarian. The men were serious, shabby, often spectacled; dandruff on their coat collars; their lined, anxious faces in curious contrast to the fresh, boyish, care-free countenances of the Classifieds. They said, carefully, almost sonorously, "Political Economy. Applied Psychology." Most of them had worked ten years, fifteen years for this deferred schooling. This one had had to support a mother; that one a family of younger brothers and sisters. This plump woman of thirty-nine, with the jolly kindly face, had had a paralyzed father. Another had known merely poverty, grinding, sordid poverty, with fifteen years of painful penny savings to bring true this gloriously realized dream of a university education. Here was one studying to be a trained Social Service Worker. She had done everything from housework as a servant girl to clerking in a 5- and 10-cent store. She had studied evenings; saved pennies, nickels, dimes, quarters. *Other valuable educative experience in practical life.* They had had it, God knows.

They regarded the university at first with the love-blind eyes of a bridegroom who looks with the passionate tenderness of possession upon his mistress for whom he has worked and waited through the years of his youth. The university was to bring back that vanished youth—and something more. Wisdom. Knowledge. Power. Understanding. They would have died for it—they almost had, what with privation, self-denial, work.

They came with love clasped close in their two hands, an offertory. "Take me!" they cried. "I come with all I have. Devotion, hope, desire to learn, a promise to be a credit to you. I have had experience, bitter-sweet experience. I have known the battle. See, here are my scars. I can bring to your classrooms much that is valuable. I ask only for bread—the bread of knowledge."

And the University gave them a stone.

"Get on to the hat!" said the Classifieds, humorously, crossing the campus. "A fright!"

The professors found them a shade too eager, perhaps; too inquiring; demanding too much. They stayed after class and asked innumerable questions. They bristled with interrogation. They were prone to hold forth in the classroom, "Well, I have found it to be the case in my experience that——"

But the professor preferred to do the lecturing himself. If there was to be any experience related it should come from the teacher's platform, not the student's chair. Besides, this sort of thing interfered with the routine; kept you from covering ground fast enough. The period bell rang, and there you were, halfway through the day's prescribed lesson.

In his first year Dirk made the almost fatal mistake of being rather friendly with one of these Unclassifieds—a female Unclassified. She was in his Pol Econ class and sat next to him. A large, good-humoured, plump girl, about thirty-eight, with a shiny skin which she never powdered and thick hair that exuded a disagreeable odour of oil. She was sympathetic and jolly, but her clothes were a fright, the Classifieds would have told you, and no matter how cold the day there was always a half-moon of stain showing under her armpits. She had a really fine mind, quick, eager, balanced, almost judicial. She knew just which references were valuable, which useless. Just how to go about getting information for next day's class; for the weekly paper to be prepared. Her name was Schwengauer—Mattie Schwengauer. Terrible!

"Here," she would say good-naturedly, to Dirk. "You don't need to read all those. My, no! I'll tell you. You'll get exactly what you want by reading pages 256 to 273 in Blaine's; 549 to 567 in Jaeckel; and the first eleven—no, twelve—pages of Trowbridge's report. That'll give you practically everything you need."

Dirk was grateful. Her notes were always copious, perfect. She never hesitated to let him copy them. They got in the way of walking out of the classroom together, across the campus. She told him something of herself.

"Your people farmers!" Surprised, she looked at his well-cut clothes, his slim, strong, unmarked hands, his smart shoes and cap. "Why, so are mine. Iowa." She pronounced it Ioway. "I lived on the farm all my life till I was twenty-seven. I always wanted to go away to school, but we never had the money and I couldn't come to town to earn because I was the oldest, and Ma was sickly after Emma—that's the youngest—there are nine of us—was born. Ma was anxious I should go and Pa was willing, but it couldn't be. No fault of theirs. One year the summer would be so hot, with no rain hardly from spring till fall, and the corn would just dry up on the stalks, like paper. The next year it would be so wet the seed would rot in the ground. Ma died when I was twenty-six. The kids were all pretty well grown up by that time. Pa married again in a year and I went to Des Moines to work. I stayed there six years but I didn't save much on account of my brother. He was kind of wild. He had come to Des Moines, too, after Pa married. He and Aggie—that's the second wife—didn't get along. I came to Chicago about five years ago. . . . I've done all kinds of work, I guess, except digging in a coal mine. I'd have done that if I'd had to."

She told him all this ingenuously, simply. Dirk felt drawn toward her, sorry for her. His was a nature quick to sympathy. Something she said now stirred him while it bewildered him a little, too.

"You can't have any idea what it means to me to be here . . . All those years! I used to dream about it. Even now it seems to me it can't be true. I'm conscious of my surroundings all the time and yet I can't believe them. You know, like when you are asleep and dream about something beautiful, and then wake up and find it's actually true. I get a thrill out of just being here. 'I'm crossing the campus,' I say to myself. 'I'm a student—a girl student—in Midwest University and now I'm crossing the campus of my university to go to a class.' "

Her face was very greasy and earnest and fine.

"Well, that's great," Dirk replied, weakly. "That's cer'nly great."

He told his mother about her. Usually he went home on Friday nights to stay until Monday morning. His first Monday-morning class was not until ten. Selina was deeply interested and stirred. "Do you think she'd spend some Saturday and Sunday here with us on the farm? She could come with you on Friday and go back Sunday night if she wanted to. Or stay until Monday morning and go back with you. There's the spare room, all quiet and cool. She could do as she liked. I'd give her cream and all the fresh fruit and vegetables she wanted. And Meena would bake one of her fresh cocoanut cakes. I'd have Adam bring a fresh cocoanut from South Water Street."

Mattie came one Friday night. It was the end of October, and Indian summer, the most beautiful time of the year on the Illinois prairie. A mellow golden light seemed to suffuse everything. It was as if the very air were liquid gold, and tonic. The squash and pumpkins next the good brown earth gave back the glow, and the frost-turned leaves of the maples in the sun. About the countryside for miles was the look of bounteousness, of plenty, of prophecy fulfilled as when a beautiful and fertile woman having borne her children and found them good, now sits serene-eyed, gracious, ample-bosomed, satisfied.

Into the face of Mattie Schwengauer there came a certain glory. When she and Selina clasped hands Selina stared at her rather curiously, as though startled. Afterward she said to Dirk, aside, "But I thought you said she was ugly!"

"Well, she is, or—well, isn't she?"

"Look at her!"

Mattie Schwengauer was talking to Meena Bras, the houseworker. She was standing with her hands on her ample hips, her fine head thrown back, her eyes alight, her lips smiling so that you saw her strong square teeth. A new cream separator was the subject of their conversation. Something had amused Mattie. She laughed. It was the laugh of a young girl, care-free, relaxed, at ease.

For two days Mattie did as she pleased, which meant she helped pull vegetables in the garden, milk the cows, saddle the horses; rode them without a saddle in the pasture. She tramped the road. She scuffled through the leaves in the woods, wore a scarlet maple leaf in her hair, slept like one gloriously dead from ten until six; ate prodigiously of cream, fruits, vegetables, eggs, sausage, cake.

"It got so I hated to do all those things on the farm," she said, laughing a little shamefacedly. "I guess it was because I had to. But now it comes back to me and I enjoy it because it's natural to me, I suppose. Anyway, I'm having a grand time, Mrs. DeJong. The grandest time I ever had in my life." Her face was radiant and almost beautiful.

"If you want me to believe that," said Selina, "you'll come again."

But Mattie Schwengauer never did come again.

Early the next week one of the university students approached Dirk. He was a Junior, very influential in his class, and a member of the fraternity to which Dirk was practically pledged. A decidedly desirable frat.

"Say, look here, DeJong, I want to talk to you a minute. Uh, you've got to cut out that girl—Swinegour or whatever her name is—or it's all off with the fellows in the frat."

"What d'you mean! Cut out! What's the matter with her!"

"Matter! She's Unclassified, isn't she! And do you know what the story is? She told it herself as an economy hint to a girl who was working her way through. She bathes with her union suit and white stockings on to save laundry soap. Scrubs 'em on her! 'S the God's truth."

Into Dirk's mind there flashed a picture of this large girl in her tight knitted union suit and her white stockings sitting in a tub half full of water and scrubbing them and herself simultaneously. A comic picture, and a revolting one. Pathetic, too, but he would not admit that.

"Imagine!" the frat brother-to-be was saying. "Well, we can't have a fellow who goes around with a girl like that. You got to cut her out, see! Completely. The fellahs won't stand for it."

Dirk had a mental picture of himself striking a noble attitude and saying, "Won't stand for it, huh! She's worth more than the whole caboodle of you put together. And you can all go to hell!"

Instead he said, vaguely, "Oh. Well. Uh—"

Dirk changed his seat in the classroom, avoided Mattie's eyes, shot out of the door the minute class was over. One day he saw her coming toward him on the campus and he sensed that she intended to stop and speak to him—chide him laughingly, perhaps. He quickened his pace, swerved a little to one side, and as he passed lifted his cap and nodded, keeping his eyes straight ahead. Out of the tail of his eye he could see her standing a moment irresolutely in the path.

He got into the fraternity. The fellahs liked him from the first. Selina said once or twice, "Why don't you bring that nice Mattie home with you again some time soon? Such a nice girl—woman, rather. But she seemed so young and care-free while she was here, didn't she? A fine mind, too, that girl. She'll make something of herself. You'll see. Bring her next week, h'm?"

Dirk shuffled, coughed, looked away. "Oh, I dunno. Haven't seen her lately. Guess she's busy with another crowd, or something."

He tried not to think of what he had done, for he was honestly ashamed. Terribly ashamed. So he said to himself, "Oh, what of it!" and hid his shame. A month later Selina again said, "I wish you'd invite Mattie for Thanksgiving dinner. Unless she's going home, which I doubt. We'll have turkey and pumpkin pie and all the rest of it. She'll love it."

"Mattie?" He had actually forgotten her name.

"Yes, of course. Isn't that right? Mattie Schwengauer?"

"Oh, her. Uh—well—I haven't been seeing her lately."

"Oh, Dirk, you haven't quarrelled with that nice girl!"

He decided to have it out. "Listen, Mother. There are a lot of different crowds at the U, see? And Mattie doesn't belong to any of 'em. You wouldn't understand, but it's like this. She—she's smart and jolly and everything but she just doesn't belong. Being friends with a girl like that doesn't get you anywhere. Besides, she isn't a girl. She's a middle-aged woman, when you come to think of it."

"Doesn't get you anywhere!" Selina's tone was cool and even. Then, as the boy's gaze did not meet hers: "Why, Dirk DeJong, Mattie Schwengauer is one of my reasons for sending you to a university. She's what I call part of a university education. Just talking to her is learning something valuable. I don't mean that you wouldn't naturally prefer pretty young girls of your own age to go around with, and all. It would be queer if you didn't. But this Mattie—why, she's life. Do you remember that story of when she washed dishes in the kosher restaurant over on Twelfth Street and the proprietor used to rent out dishes and cutlery for Irish and Italian neighbourhood weddings where they had pork and goodness knows what all, and then use them next day in the restaurant again for the kosher customers?"

Yes, Dirk remembered. Selina wrote Mattie, inviting her to the farm for Thanksgiving, and Mattie answered gratefully, declining. "I shall always remember you," she wrote in that letter, "with love."

14

Throughout Dirk's Freshman year there were, for him, no heartening, informal, mellow talks before the wood-fire in the book-lined study of some professor whose wisdom was such a mixture of classic lore and modernism as to be an inspiration to his listeners. Midwest professors delivered their lectures in the classroom as they had been delivering them in the past ten or twenty years and as they would deliver them until death or a trustees' meeting should remove them. The younger professors and instructors in natty gray suits and bright-coloured ties made a point of being unpedantic in the classroom and rather overdid it. They posed as being one of the fellows; would dashingly use a bit of slang to create a laugh from the boys and an adoring titter from the girls. Dirk somehow preferred the pedants to these. When these had to give an informal talk to the men before some university even they would start by saying, "Now listen, fellahs ——" At the dances they were not above "rushing" the pretty co-eds.

Two of Dirk's classes were conducted by women professors. They were well on toward middle age, or past it; desiccated women. Only their eyes were alive. Their clothes were of some indefinite dark stuff, brown or drab-gray; their hair lifeless; their hands long, bony, unvital. They had seen classes and classes and classes. A roomful of fresh young faces like round white pencil marks manipulated momentarily on a slate, only to be sponged off to give way to other round white marks. Of the two women one—the elder—was occasionally likely to flare into sudden life; a flame in the ashes of a burned-out grate. She had humour and a certain caustic wit, qualities that had managed miraculously to survive even the deadly and numbing effects of thirty years in the classroom. A fine mind, and iconoclastic, hampered by the restrictions of a conventional community and the soul of a congenital spinster.

Under the guidance of these Dirk chafed and grew restless. Miss Euphemia Hollingswood had a way of emphasizing every third or fifth syllable, bringing her voice down hard on it, thus:

"In the consideration of *all* the facts in the *case* presented be*fore* us we must *first* review the *his*tory and at*tempt* to analyze the *out*standing ——"

He found himself waiting for that emphasis and shrinking from it as from a sledge-hammer blow. It hurt his head.

Miss Lodge droned. She approached a word with a maddening uh-uh-uh-uh. In the uh-uh-uh face of the uh-uh-uh-uh geometrical situation of the uh-uh-uh uh ——

He shifted restlessly in his chair, found his hands clenched into fists, and took refuge in watching the shadow cast by an oak branch outside the window on a patch of sunlight against the blackboard behind her.

During the early spring Dirk and Selina talked things over again, seated before their own fireplace in the High Prairie farmhouse. Selina had had that fireplace built five years before and her love of it amounted to fire-worship. She had it lighted always on winter evenings and in the spring when the nights were sharp. In Dirk's absence she would sit before it at night long after the rest of the weary household had gone to bed. Old Pom, the mongrel, lay stretched at her feet enjoying such luxury in old age as he had never dreamed of in his bastard youth. High Prairie, driving by from some rare social gathering or making a late trip to market as they sometimes were forced to do, saw the rosy flicker of Mrs. DeJong's fire dancing on the wall and warmed themselves by it even while they resented it.

"A good heater in there and yet anyway she's got to have a fire going in a grate. Always she does something funny like that. I should think she'd be lonesome sitting there like that with her dog only."

They never knew how many guests Selina entertained there before her fire those winter evenings—old friends and new. Sobig was there, the plump earth-grimed baby who rolled and tumbled in the fields while his young mother wiped the sweat from her face to look at him with fond eyes. Dirk DeJong of ten years hence was there. Simeon Peake, dapper, soft-spoken, ironic, in his shiny boots and his hat always a little on one side. Pervus DeJong, a blue-shirted giant with strong tender hands and little fine golden hairs on the backs of them. Fanny Davenport, the actress-idol of her girlhood came back to her, smiling, bowing; and the gorgeous spangled creatures in the tights and bodices of the old Extravaganzas. In strange contrast to these was the patient, tireless figure of Maartje Pool standing in the doorway of Roelf's little shed, her arms tucked in her apron for warmth. "You make fun, huh?" she said, wistfully, "you and Roelf. You make fun." And Roelf, the dark vivid boy, misunderstood. Roelf, the genius. He was always one of the company.

Oh, Selina DeJong never was lonely on these winter evenings before her fire.

She and Dirk sat there one fine sharp evening in early April. It was Saturday. Of late Dirk had not always come to the farm for the weekend. Eugene and Paula Arnold had been home for the Easter holidays. Julie Arnold had invited Dirk to the gay parties at the Prairie Avenue house. He had even spent two entire week-ends there. After the brocaded luxury of the Prairie Avenue house his farm bedroom seemed almost startlingly stark and bare. Selina frankly enjoyed Dirk's somewhat fragmentary accounts of these visits: extracted from them as much vicarious pleasure as he had had in the reality—more, probably.

"Now tell me what you had to eat," she would say, sociably, like a child. "What did you have for dinner, for example? Was it grand? Julie tells me they have a butler now. Well! I can't wait till I hear Aug Hempel on the subject."

He would tell her of the grandeurs of the Arnold ménage. She would interrupt and exclaim: "Mayonnaise! On fruit! Oh, I don't believe I'd like *that*. You did! Well, I'll have it for you next week when you come home. I'll get the recipe from Julie."

He didn't think he'd be home next week. One of the fellows he'd met at the Arnolds' had invited him to their place out north, on the lake. He had a boat.

"That'll be lovely!" Selina exclaimed, after an almost unnoticeable moment of silence—silence with panic in it. "I'll try not to fuss and be worried like an old hen every minute of the time I think you're on the water. . . . Now do go on, Sobig. First fruit with mayonnaise, h'm? What kind of soup?"

He was not a naturally talkative person. There was nothing surly about his silence. It was a taciturn streak inherited from his Dutch ancestry. This time, though, he was more voluble than usual. "Paula . . ." came again and again into his conversation. "Paula . . . Paula . . ." and again ". . . Paula." He did not seem conscious of the repetition, but Selina's quick ear caught it.

"I haven't seen her," Selina said, "since she went away to school the first year. She must be—let's see—she's a year older than you are. She's nineteen going on twenty. Last time I saw her I thought she was a dark scrawny little thing. Too bad she didn't inherit Julie's lovely gold colouring and good looks, instead of Eugene, who doesn't need 'em."

"She isn't!" said Dirk, hotly. "She's dark and slim and sort of—uh—sensuous"—Selina started visibly, and raised her hand quickly to her mouth to hide a smile—"like Cleopatra. Her eyes are big and kind of slanting—not squinty I don't mean, but slanting up a little at the corners. Cut out, kind of, so that they look bigger than most people's."

"My eyes used to be considered rather fine," said Selina, mischievously; but he did not hear.

"She makes all the other girls look sort of blowzy." He was silent a moment. Selina was silent, too, and it was not a happy silence. Dirk spoke again, suddenly, as though continuing aloud a train of thought, "—all but her hands."

Selina made her voice sound natural, not sharply inquisitive. "What's the matter with her hands, Dirk?"

He pondered a moment, his brows knitted. At last, slowly, "Well, I don't know. They're brown, and awfully thin and sort of— grabby. I mean it makes me nervous to watch them. And when the rest of her is cool they're hot when you touch them."

He looked at his mother's hands that were busy with some sewing. The stuff on which she was working was a bit of satin ribbon; part of a hood intended to grace the head of Geertje Pool Vander Sijde's second baby. She had difficulty in keeping her rough fingers from catching on the soft surface of the satin. Manual work, water, sun, and wind had tanned those hands, hardened them, enlarged the knuckles, spread them, roughened them. Yet how sure they were, and strong, and cool and reliable—and tender. Suddenly, looking at them, Dirk said, "Now your hands. I love your hands, Mother."

She put down her work hastily, yet quietly, so that the sudden rush of happy grateful tears in her eyes should not sully the pink satin ribbon. She was flushed, like a girl. "Do you, Sobig?" she said.

After a moment she took up her sewing again. Her face looked young, eager, fresh, like the face of the girl who had found cabbages so beautiful that night when she bounced along the rutty Halsted road with Klaas Pool, many years ago. It came into her face, that look, when she was happy, exhilarated, excited. That was why those who loved her and brought that look into her face thought her beautiful, while those who did not love her never saw the look and consequently considered her a plain woman.

There was another silence between the two. Then: "Mother, what would you think of my going East next fall, to take a course in architecture?"

"Would you like that, Dirk?"

"Yes, I think so—yes."

"Then I'd like it better than anything in the world. I—it makes me happy just to think of it."

"It would—cost an awful lot."

"I'll manage. I'll manage. . . . What made you decide on architecture?"

"I don't know, exactly. The new buildings at the university—Gothic, you know—are such a contrast to the old. Then Paula and I were talking the other day. She hates their house on Prairie—terrible old lumpy gray stone pile, with the black of the I.C. trains all over it. She wants her father to build north—an Italian villa or French château. Something of that sort. So many of her friends are moving to the north shore, away from these hideous south-side and north-side Chicago houses with their stoops, and their bay windows, and their terrible turrets. Ugh!"

"Well, now, do you know," Selina remonstrated mildly, "I like 'em. I suppose I'm wrong, but to me they seem sort of natural and solid and unpretentious, like the clothes that old August Hempel wears, so squarecut and baggy. Those houses look dignified to me, and fitting. They may be ugly—probably are—but anyway they're not ridiculous. They have a certain rugged grandeur. They're Chicago. Those French and Italian gimcracky things they—they're incongruous. It's as if Abraham Lincoln were to appear suddenly in pink satin knee breeches and buckled shoes, and lace ruffles at his wrists."

Dirk could laugh at that picture. But he protested, too. "But there's no native architecture, so what's to be done! You wouldn't call those smoke-blackened old stone and brick piles with their iron fences and their conservatories and cupolas and gingerbread exactly native, would you?"

"No," Selina admitted, "but those Italian villas and French châteaux in north Chicago suburbs are a good deal like a lace evening gown in the Arizona desert. It wouldn't keep you cool in the daytime, and it wouldn't be warm enough at night. I suppose a native architecture is evolved from building for the local climate and the needs of the community, keeping beauty in mind as you go. We don't need turrets and towers any more than we need draw-bridges and moats. It's all right to keep them, I suppose, where they grew up, in a country where the feudal system meant that any day your next-door neighbour might take it into his head to call his gang around him and sneak up to steal your wife and tapestries and gold drinking cups."

Dirk was interested and amused. Talks with his mother were likely to affect him thus. "What's your idea of a real Chicago house, Mother?"

Selina answered quickly, as if she had thought often about it; as if she would have liked just such a dwelling on the site of the old DeJong farmhouse in which they now were seated so comfortably. "Well, it would need big porches for the hot days and nights so's to catch the prevailing southwest winds from the prairies in the summer—a porch that would be swung clear around to the east, too—or a terrace or another porch east so that if the precious old lake breeze should come up just when you think you're dying of the heat, as it sometimes does, you could catch that, too. It ought to be built—the house, I mean—rather squarish and tight and solid against our cold winters and northeasters. Then sleeping porches, of course. There's a grand American institution for you! England may have its afternoon tea on the terrace, and Spain may have its patio, and France its courtyard, and Italy its pergola, vine-covered; but America's got the sleeping porch—the screened-in open-air sleeping porch, and I shouldn't wonder if the man who first thought of that would get precedence, on Judgment Day, over the men who invented the aeroplane, the talking machine, and the telephone. After all, he had nothing in mind but the health of the human race." After which grand period Selina grinned at Dirk, and Dirk grinned at Selina and the two giggled together there by the fireplace, companionably.

"Mother, you're simply wonderful!—only your native Chicago dwelling seems to be mostly porch."

Selina waved such carping criticism away with a careless hand. "Oh, well, any house that has enough porches, and two or three bathrooms and at least eight closets can be lived in comfortably, no matter what else it has or hasn't got."

Next day they were more serious. The eastern college and the architectural career seemed to be settled things. Selina was content, happy. Dirk was troubled about the expense. He spoke of it at breakfast next mornng (Dirk's breakfast; his mother had hers hours before and now as he drank his coffee, was sitting with him a moment and glancing at the paper that had come in the rural mail delivery). She had been out in the fields overseeing the transplanting of young tomato seedlings from hotbed to field. She wore an old gray sweater buttoned up tight, for the air was still sharp. On her head was a battered black felt soft hat (an old one of Dirk's) much like the one she had worn to the Haymarket that day ten years ago. Selina's cheeks were faintly pink from her walk across the fields in the brisk morning air.

She sniffed. "That coffee smells wonderful. I think I'll just ———" She poured herself a half cup with the air of virtue worn by one who really longs for a whole cup and doesn't take it.

"I've been thinking," he began, "the expense ———"

"Pigs," said Selina, serenely.

"Pigs!" He looked around, bewildered; stared at his mother.

"Pigs'll do it," Selina explained, calmly. "I've been wanting to put them in for three or four years. It's August Hempel's idea. Hogs, I should have said."

Again, as before, he echoed, "Hogs!" rather faintly.

"High-bred hogs. They're worth their weight in silver this minute, and will be for years to come. I won't go in for them extensively. Just enough to make an architect out of Mr. Dirk DeJong." Then, at the expression in his face: "Don't look so pained, son. There's nothing revolting about a hog—not my kind, brought up in a pen as sanitary as a tiled bathroom and fed on corn. He's a handsome, impressive-looking animal, the hog, when he isn't treated like one."

He looked dejected. "I'd rather not go to school on—hogs."

She took off the felt hat and tossed it over to the old couch by the window; smoothed her hair back with the flat of her palm. You saw that the soft dark hair was liberally sprinkled with gray now, but the eyes were bright and clear as ever.

"You know, Sobig, this is what they call a paying farm—as vegetable farms go. We're out of debt, the land's in good shape, the crop promises well if we don't have another rainy cold spring like last year's.

But no truck garden is going to make its owner rich these days, with labour so high and the market what it is, and the expense of hauling and all. Any truck farmer who comes out even thinks he's come out ahead."

"I know it." Rather miserably.

"Well. I'm not complaining, son. I'm just telling you. I'm having a grand time. When I see the asparagus plantation actually yielding, that I planted ten years ago, I'm as happy as if I'd stumbled on a gold mine. I think, sometimes, of the way your father objected to my planting the first one. April, like this, in the country, with everything coming up green and new in the rich black loam—I can't tell you. And when I know that it goes to market as food—the best kind of food, that keeps people's bodies clean and clear and flexible and strong! I like to think of babies' mothers saying: 'Now eat your spinach, every scrap, or you can't have any dessert! . . . Carrots makes your eyes bright. . . . Finish your potato. Potatoes make you strong!' "

Selina laughed, flushed a little.

"Yes, but how about hogs? Do you feel that way about hogs?"

"Certainly!" said Selina, briskly. She pushed toward him a little blue-and-white platter that lay on the white cloth near her elbow. "Have a bit more bacon, Dirk. One of these nice curly slivers that are so crisp."

"I've finished my breakfast, Mother." He rose.

The following autumn saw him a student of architecture at Cornell. He worked hard, studied even during his vacations. He would come home to the heat and humidity of the Illinois summers and spend hours each day in his own room that he had fitted up with a long work table and a drawing board. His T-square was at hand; two triangles—a 45 and a 60; his compass; a pair of dividers. Selina sometimes stood behind him watching him as he carefully worked on the tracing paper. His contempt for the local architecture was now complete. Especially did he hold forth on the subject of the apartment-houses that were mushrooming on every street in Chicago from Hyde Park on the south to Evanston on the north. Chicago was very elegant in speaking of these; never called them "flats"; always apartments. In front of each of these (there were usually six to a building), was stuck a little glass-enclosed cubicle known as a sun-parlour. In these (sometimes you heard them spoken of, grandly, as solariums) Chicago dwellers took refuge from the leaden skies, the heavy lake atmosphere, the gray mist and fog and smoke that so frequently swathed the city in gloom. They were done in yellow or rose cretonnes. Silk lamp shades glowed therein, and flower-laden boxes. In these frank little boxes Chicago read its paper, sewed, played bridge, even ate its breakfast. It never pulled down the shades.

"Terrible!" Dirk fumed. "Not only are they hideous in themselves, stuck on the front of those houses like three pairs of spectacles; but the lack of decent privacy! They do everything but bathe in 'em. Have they never heard the advice given people who live in glass houses!"

By his junior year he was talking in a large way about the Beaux Arts. But Selina did not laugh at this. "Perhaps," she thought. "Who can tell! After a year or two in an office here, why not another year of study in Paris if he needs it."

Though it was her busiest time on the farm Selina went to Ithaca for his graduation in 1913. He was twenty-two and, she was calmly sure, the best-looking man in his class. Undeniably he was a figure to please the eye; tall, well-built, as his father had been, and blond, too, like his father, except for his eyes. These were brown—not so dark as Selina's, but with some of the soft liquid quality of her glance. They strengthened his face, somehow; gave him an ardent look of which he was not conscious. Women, feeling the ardour of that dark glance turned upon them, were likely to credit him with feelings toward themselves of which he was quite innocent. They did not know that the glance and its effect were mere matters of pigmentation and eye-conformation. Then, too, the gaze of a man who talks little is always more effective than that of one who is loquacious.

Selina, in her black silk dress, and her plain black hat, and her sensible shoes was rather a quaint little figure amongst all those vivacious, bevoiled, and beribboned mammas. But a distinctive little figure, too. Dirk need not be ashamed of her. She eyed the rather paunchy, prosperous, middle-aged fathers and thought, with a pang, how much handsomer Pervus would have been than any of these, if only he could have lived to see this day. Then, involuntarily, she wondered if this day would ever have occurred, had Pervus lived. Chided herself for thinking thus.

When he returned to Chicago, Dirk went into the office of Hollis & Sprague, Architects. He thought himself lucky to work with this firm, for it was doing much to guide Chicago's taste in architecture away from the box car. Already Michigan Boulevard's skyline soared somewhat above the grimly horizontal. But his work there was little more than that of draughtsman, and his weekly stipend could hardly be dignified by the term of salary. But he had large ideas about architecture and he found expression for his suppressed feelings on his week-ends spent with Selina at the farm. "Baroque" was the word with which he dismissed the new Beachside Hotel, north. He said the new Lincoln Park band-stand looked like an igloo. He said that the city council ought to order the Potter Palmer mansion destroyed as a blot on the landscape, and waxed profane on the subject of the east face of the Public Library Building, down town.

"Never mind," Selina assured him, happily. "It was all thrown up so hastily. Remember that just yesterday, or the day before, Chicago was an Indian fort, with tepees where towers are now, and mud wallows in place of asphalt. Beauty needs time to perfect it. Perhaps we've been waiting all these years for just such youngsters as you. And maybe some day I'll be driving down Michigan Boulevard with a distinguished visitor—Roelf Pool, perhaps. Why not? Let's say Roelf Pool, the famous sculptor. And he'll say, 'Who designed that building—the one that is so strong and yet so light? So gay and graceful, and yet so reticent!' And I'll say, 'Oh, that! That's one of the earlier efforts of my son, Dirk DeJong.' "

But Dirk pulled at his pipe moodily; shook his head. "Oh, you don't know, Mother. It's so damned slow. First thing you know I'll be thirty. And what am I! An office boy—or little more than that—at Hollis's."

During his university years Dirk had seen much of the Arnolds,

Eugene and Paula, but it sometimes seemed to Selina that he avoided these meetings—these parties and week-ends. She was content that this should be so, for she guessed that the matter of money held him back. She thought it was well that he should realize the difference now. Eugene had his own car—one of five in the Arnold garage. Paula, too, had hers. She had been one of the first Chicago girls to drive a gas car; had breezed about Chicago's boulevards in one when she had been little more than a child in short skirts. At the wheel she was dexterous, dare-devil, incredibly relaxed. Her fascination for Dirk was strong. Selina knew that, too. In the last year or two he had talked very little of Paula and that, Selina knew, meant that he was hard hit.

Sometimes Paula and Eugene drove out to the farm, making the distance from their new north-shore house to the DeJong place far south in some breath-taking number of minutes. Eugene would appear in rakish cap, loose London coat, knickers, queer brogans with an English look about them, a carefully careless looseness about the hang and fit of his jacket. Paula did not affect sports clothes for herself. She was not the type, she said. Slim, dark, vivacious, she wore slinky clothes—crêpes, chiffons. Her feet were slim in sheer silk stockings and slippers with buckles. Her eyes were languorous, lovely. She worshipped luxury and said so.

"I'll have to marry money," she declared. "Now that they've finished calling poor Grandpa a beef-baron and taken I don't know how many millions away from him, we're practically on the streets."

"You look it!" from Dirk; and there was bitterness beneath his light tone.

"Well, it's true. All this silly muckraking in the past ten years or more. Poor Father! Of course Grand-dad was pur-ty rough, let me tell you. I read some of the accounts of that last indictment—the 1910 one—and I must say I gathered that dear old Aug made Jesse James look like a philanthropist. I should think, at his age, he'd be a little scared. After all, when you're over seventy you're likely to have some doubts and fears about punishment in the next world. But not a grand old pirate like Grandfather. He'll sack and burn and plunder until he goes down with the ship. And it looks to me as if the old boat had a pretty strong list to starboard right now. Father says himself that unless a war breaks, or something, which isn't at all likely, the packing industry is going to spring a leak."

"Elaborate figure of speech," murmured Eugene. The four of them—Paula, Dirk, Eugene, and Selina—were sitting on the wide screened porch that Selina had had built at the southwest corner of the house. Paula was, of course, in the couch-swing. Occasionally she touched one slim languid foot to the floor and gave indolent impetus to the couch.

"It is, rather, isn't it? Might as well finish, it, then. Darling Aug's been the grand old captain right through the vi'age. Dad's never been more than a pretty bum second mate. And as for you, Gene my love, cabin boy would be, y'understand me, big." Eugene had gone into the business a year before.

"What can you expect," retorted Eugene, "of a lad that hates salt pork? And every other kind of pig meat?" He despised the yards and all that went with it.

Selina now got up and walked to the end of the porch. She looked out across the fields, shading her eyes with her hand. "There's Adam coming in with the last load for the day. He'll be driving into town now. Cornelius started an hour ago." The DeJong farm sent two great loads to the city now. Selina was contemplating the purchase of one of the large automobile trucks that would do away with the plodding horses and save hours of time on the trip. She went down the steps now on her way to oversee the loading of Adam Bras's wagon. At the bottom of the steps she turned. "Why can't you two stay to supper? You can quarrel comfortably right through the meal and drive home in the cool of the evening."

"I'll stay," said Paula, "thanks. If you'll have all kinds of vegetables, cooked and uncooked. The cooked ones smothered in cream and oozing butter. And let me go out into the fields and pick 'em myself like Maud Muller or Marie Antoinette or any of those make-believe rustic gals."

In her French-heeled slippers and her filmy silk stockings she went out into the rich black furrows of the fields, Dirk carrying the basket.

"Asparagus," she ordered first. Then, "But where is it? Is *that* it!"

"You dig for it, idiot," said Dirk, stooping, and taking from his basket the queerly curved sharp knife or spud used for cutting the asparagus shoots. "Cut the shoots three or four inches below the surface."

"Oh, let me do it!" She was down on her silken knees in the dirt, ruined a goodly patch of the fine tender shoots, gave it up and sat watching Dirk's expert manipulation of the knife. "Let's have radishes, and corn, and tomatoes and lettuce and peas and artichokes and——"

"Artichokes grow in California, not Illinois." He was more than usually uncommunicative, and noticeably moody.

Paula remarked it. "Why the Othello brow?"

"You didn't mean that rot, did you? about marrying a rich man."

"Of course I meant it. What other sort of man do you think I ought to marry?" He looked at her, silently. She smiled. "Yes, wouldn't I make an ideal bride for a farmer!"

"I'm not a farmer."

"Well, architect then. Your job as draughtsman at Hollis & Sprague's must pay you all of twenty-five a week."

"Thirty-five," said Dirk, grimly. "What's that got to do with it!"

"Not a thing, darling." She stuck out one foot. "These slippers cost thirty."

"I won't be getting thirty-five a week all my life. You've got brains enough to know that. Eugene wouldn't be getting that much if he weren't the son of his father."

"The grandson of his grandfather," Paula corrected him. "And I'm not so sure he wouldn't. Gene's a born mechanic if they'd just let him work at it. He's crazy about engines and all that junk. But no—'Millionaire Packer's Son Learns Business from Bottom Rung of Ladder.' Picture of Gene in workman's overalls and cap in the Sunday papers. He drives to the office on Michigan at ten and leaves at four and he doesn't know a steer from a cow when he sees it."

"I don't care a damn about Gene. I'm talking about you. You were joking, weren't you?"

"I wasn't. I'd hate being poor, or even just moderately rich. I'm used to money—loads of it. I'm twenty-four. And I'm looking around."

He kicked an innocent beet-top with his boot. "You like me better than any man you know."

"Of course I do. Just my luck."

"Well, then!"

"Well, then, let's take these weggibles in and have 'em cooked in cream, as ordered."

She made a pretense of lifting the heavy basket. Dirk snatched it roughly out of her hand so that she gave a little cry and looked ruefully down at the red mark on her palm. He caught her by the shoulder—even shook her a little. "Look here, Paula. Do you mean to tell me you'd marry a man simply because he happened to have a lot of money?"

"Perhaps not simply because he had a lot of money. But it certainly would be a factor, among other things. Certainly he would be preferable to a man who knocked me about the fields as if I were a bag of potatoes."

"Oh, forgive me. But—listen, Paula—you know I'm—gosh! ——And there I am stuck in an architect's office and it'll be years before I——"

"Yes, but it'll probably be years before I meet the millions I require, too. So why bother? And even if I do, you and I can be just as good friends."

"Oh, shut up. Don't pull that ingénue stuff on me, please. Remember I've known you since you were ten years old."

"And you know just how black my heart is, don't you, what? You want, really, some nice hearty lass who can tell asparagus from peas when she sees 'em, and who'll offer to race you from here to the kitchen."

"God forbid!"

Six months later Paula Arnold was married to Theodore A. Storm, a man of fifty, a friend of her father's, head of so many companies, stockholder in so many banks, director of so many corporations that even old Aug Hempel seemed a recluse from business in comparison. She never called him Teddy. No one ever did. Theodore Storm was a large man—not exactly stout, perhaps, but flabby. His inches saved him from grossness. He had a large white serious face, fine thick dark hair, graying at the temples, and he dressed very well except for a leaning toward rather effeminate ties. He built for Paula a town house on the Lake Shore drive in the region known as the Gold Coast. The house looked like a restrained public library. There was a country place beyond Lake Forest far out on the north shore, sloping down to the lake and surrounded by acres and acres of fine woodland, expertly parked. There were drives, ravines, brooks, bridges, hothouses, stables, a racetrack, gardens, dairies, fountains, bosky paths, keeper's cottage (twice the size of Selina's farmhouse). Within three years Paula had two children, a boy and a girl. "There! That's done," she said. Her marriage was a great mistake and she knew it. For the war, coming in 1914, a few months after her wedding, sent the Hempel-Arnold interests skyrocketing. Millions of pounds of American beef and pork were shipped to Europe. In two years the Hempel fortune was greater than it ever had been. Paula was up to her eyes in relief work for Bleeding Belgium. All the Gold Coast was. The Beautiful Mrs. Theodore A. Storm in her Gift Shop Conducted for the Relief of Bleeding Belgium.

Dirk had not seen her in months. She telephoned him unexpectedly one Friday afternoon in his office at Hollis & Sprague's.

"Come out and spend Saturday and Sunday with us, won't you? We're running away to the country this afternoon. I'm sick of Bleeding Belgium, you can't imagine. I'm sending the children out this morning. I can't get away so early. I'll call for you in the roadster this afternoon at four and drive you out myself."

"I am going to spend the week-end with Mother. She's expecting me."

"Bring her along."

"She wouldn't come. You know she doesn't enjoy all that velvet-footed servitor stuff."

"Oh, but we live quite simply out there, really. Just sort of rough it. Do come, Dirk. I've got some plans to talk over with you . . . How's the job?"

"Oh, good enough. There's very little building going on, you know."

"Will you come?"

"I don't think I——"

"I'll call for you at four. I'll be at the curb. Don't keep me waiting, will you? The cops fuss so if you park in the Loop after four."

15

"Run along!" said Selina, when he called her on the farm telephone.
"It'll do you good. You've been as grumpy as a gander for weeks.
How about shirts? And you left one pair of flannel tennis pants out
here last fall—clean ones. Won't you need . . ."

In town he lived in a large front room and alcove on the third
floor of a handsome old-fashioned three-story-and-basement house in
Deming Place. He used the front room as a living room, the alcove as
a bedroom. He and Selina had furnished it together, discarding all of
the room's original belongings except the bed, a table, and one fat
comfortable faded old armchair whose brocade surface hinted a past
grandeur. When he had got his books ranged in open shelves along
one wall, soft-shaded lamps on table and desk, the place looked more
than livable; lived in. During the process of furnishing Selina got into
the way of coming into town for a day or two to prowl the auction
rooms and the second-hand stores. She had a genius for this sort of
thing; hated the spick-and-span varnish and veneer of the new furniture to be got in the regular way.

"Any piece of furniture, I don't care how beautiful it is, has got
to be lived with, and kicked about, and rubbed down, and mistreated
by servants, and repolished, and knocked around and dusted and sat
on or slept in or eaten off of before it develops its real character,"
Selina said. "A good deal like human beings. I'd rather have my old
maple table, mellow with age and rubbing, that Pervus's father put

together himself by hand seventy years ago, than all the mahogany library slabs on Wabash Avenue."

She enjoyed these rare trips into town; made a holiday of them. Dirk would take her to the theatre and she would sit entranced. Her feeling for this form of entertainment was as fresh and eager as it had been in the days of the Daly Stock Company when she, a little girl, had been seated in the parquet with her father, Simeon Peake. Strangely enough, considering the lack of what the world calls romance and adventure in her life, she did not like the motion pictures. "All the difference in the world," she would say, "between the movies and the thrill I get out of a play at the theatre. My, yes! Like fooling with paper dolls when you could be playing with a real live baby."

She developed a mania for nosing into strange corners of the huge sprawling city; seemed to discover a fresh wonder on each visit. In a short time she was more familiar with Chicago than was Dirk—for that matter, than old Aug Hempel who had lived in it for over half a century but who never had gone far afield in his pendulum path between the yards and his house, his house and the yards.

The things that excited her about Chicago did not seem to interest Dirk at all. Sometimes she took a vacant room for a day or two in Dirk's boarding house. "What do you think!" she would say to him, breathlessly, when he returned from the office in the evening. "I've been way over on the northwest side. It's another world. It's—it's Poland. Cathedrals and shops and men sitting in restaurants all day long reading papers and drinking coffee and playing dominoes or something like it. And what do you think I found out! Chicago's got the second largest Polish population of any city in the world. In the world!"

"Yeh?" Dirk would reply, absently.

There was nothing absent-minded about his tone this afternoon as he talked to his mother on the telephone. "Sure you don't mind? Then I'll be out next Saturday. Or I may run out in the middle of the week to stay over night . . . Are you all right?"

"I'm fine. Be sure and remember all about Paula's new house

so's you can tell me about it. Julie says it's like the kind you read of in the novels. She says old Aug saw it just once and now won't go near it even to visit his grandchildren."

The day was marvellously mild for March in Chicago. Spring, usually so coy in this region, had flung herself at them head first. As the massive revolving door of Dirk's office building fanned him into the street he saw Paula in her long low sporting roadster at the curb. She was dressed in black. All feminine fashionable and middle-class Chicago was dressed in black. All feminine fashionable and middle-class America was dressed in black. Two years of war had robbed Paris of its husbands, brothers, sons. All Paris walked in black. America, untouched, gayly borrowed the smart habiliments of mourning and now Michigan Boulevard and Fifth Avenue walked demurely in the gloom of crêpe and chiffon; black hats, black gloves, black slippers. Only black was "good" this year.

Paula did not wear black well. She was a shade too sallow for these sombre swathings even though relieved by a pearl strand of exquisite colour, flawlessly matched; and a new sly face-powder. Paula smiled up at him, patted the leather seat beside her with one hand that was absurdly thick-fingered in its fur-lined glove.

"It's cold driving. Button up tight. Where'll we stop for your bag? Are you still in Deming Place?"

He was still in Deming Place. He climbed into the seat beside her—a feat for the young and nimble. Theodore Storm never tried to double his bulk into the jack-knife position necessary to riding in his wife's roadster. The car was built for speed, not comfort. One sat flat with the length of one's legs stretched out. Paula's feet, pedalling brake and clutch so expertly, were inadequately clothed in sheer black silk stockings and slim buckled patent-leather slippers.

"You're not dressed warmly enough," her husband would have said. "Those shoes are idiotic for driving." And he would have been right.

Dirk said nothing.

Her manipulation of the wheel was witchcraft. The roadster slid in and out of traffic like a fluid thing, an enamel stream, silent as a swift current in a river. "Can't let her out here," said Paula. "Wait till we get past Lincoln Park. Do you suppose they'll ever really get rid of this terrible Rush Street bridge?" When his house was reached, "I'm coming up," she said. "I suppose you haven't any tea?"

"Gosh, no! What do you think I am! A young man in an English novel!"

"Now, don't be provincial and Chicago-ish, Dirk." They climbed the three flights of stairs. She looked about. Her glance was not disapproving. "This isn't so bad. Who did it? She did! Very nice. But of course you ought to have your own smart little apartment, with a Jap to do you up. To do that for you, for example."

"Yes," grimly. He was packing his bag—not throwing clothes into it, but folding them deftly, neatly, as the son of a wise mother packs. "My salary'd just about keep him in white linen house-coats."

She was walking about the living room, picking up a book, putting it down, fingering an ash tray, gazing out of the window, examining a photograph, smoking a cigarette from the box on his table. Restless, nervously alive, catlike. "I'm going to send you some things for your room, Dirk."

"For God's sake don't!"

"Why not?"

"Two kinds of women in the world. I learned that at college. Those who send men things for their rooms and those that don't."

"You're very rude."

"You asked me. There! I'm all set." He snapped the lock of his bag. "I'm sorry I can't give you anything. I haven't a thing. Not even a glass of wine and a—what is it they say in books?—oh, yeh—a biscuit."

In the roadster again they slid smoothly out along the drive, along Sheridan Road, swung sharply around the cemetery curve into Evanston, past the smug middle-class suburban neatness of Wilmette and Winnetka. She negotiated expertly the nerve-racking curves of the Hubbard Woods hills, then maintained a fierce and steady speed for the remainder of the drive.

"We call the place Stormwood," Paula told him. "And nobody

outside the dear family knows how fitting that is. Don't scowl. I'm not going to tell you my marital woes. And don't you say I asked for it. . . . How's the job?"

"Rotten."

"You don't like it? The work?"

"I like it well enough, only—well, you see we leave the university architectural course thinking we're all going to be Stanford Whites or Cass Gilberts, tossing of a Woolworth building and making ourselves famous overnight. I've spent all yesterday and to-day planning how to work in space for toilets on every floor of the new office building, six stories high and shaped like a drygoods box, that's going up on the corner of Milwaukee Avenue and Ashland, west."

"And ten years from now?"

"Ten years from now maybe they'll let me do the plans for the dry-goods box all alone."

"Why don't you drop it?"

He was startled. "Drop it! How do you mean?"

"Chuck it. Do something that will bring you quick results. This isn't an age of waiting. Suppose, twenty years from now, you do plan a grand Gothic office building to grace this new and glorified Michigan Boulevard they're always shouting about! You'll be a middle-aged man living in a middle-class house in a middle-class suburb with a middle-class wife."

"Maybe"—slightly nettled. "And maybe I'll be the Sir Christopher Wren of Chicago."

"Who's he?"

"Good G——, how often have you been in London?"

"Three times."

"Next time you find yourself there you might cast your eye over a very nice little structure called St. Paul's Cathedral. I've never seen it but it has been very well spoken of."

They turned in at the gates of Stormwood. Though the trees and bushes were gaunt and bare the grass already showed stretches of vivid green. In the fading light one caught glimpses through the shrubbery of the lake beyond. It was a dazzling sapphire blue in the sunset. A final turn of the drive. An avenue of trees. A house, massive, pillared, porticoed. The door opened as they drew up at the entrance. A maid in cap and apron stood in the doorway. A man appeared at the side of the car, coming seemingly from nowhere, greeted Paula civilly and drove the car off. The glow of an open fire in the hall welcomed them. "He'll bring up your bag," said Paula. "How're the babies, Anna? Has Mr. Storm got here?"

"He telephoned, Mrs. Storm. He says he won't be out till late—maybe ten or after. Anyway, you're not to wait dinner."

Paula, from being the limp, expert, fearless driver of the high-powered roadster was now suddenly very much the mistress of the house, quietly observant, giving an order with a lift of the eyebrow or a nod of the head. Would Dirk like to go to his room at once? Perhaps he'd like to look at the babies before they went to sleep for the night, though the nurse would probably throw him out. One of those stern British females. Dinner at seven-thirty. He needn't dress. Just as he liked. Everything was very informal here. They roughed it. (Dirk had counted thirteen servants by noon next day and hadn't been near the kitchen, laundry, or dairy.)

His room, when he reached it, he thought pretty awful. A great square chamber with narrow leaded windows, deep-set, on either side. From one he could get a glimpse of the lake, but only a glimpse. Evidently the family bedrooms were the lake rooms. In the DeJong code and class the guest had the best but evidently among these moneyed ones the family had the best and the guest was made comfortable, but was not pampered. It was a new angle for Dirk. He thought it startling but rather sensible. His bag had been brought up, unpacked, and stowed away in a closet before he reached his room. "Have to tell that to Selina," he thought, grinning. He looked about the room, critically. It was done in a style that he vaguely defined as French. It gave him the feeling that he had stumbled accidentally into the chamber of a Récamier and couldn't get out. Rose brocade with gold net and cream lace and rosebuds. "Swell place for a man," he thought, and kicked a footstool—a *fauteuil* he supposed it was called, and was secretly glad that he could pronounce it faultlessly. Long mirrors, silken hanging, cream walls. The bed was lace hung. The coverlet was rose satin, feather-light. He explored his bathroom. It actually was a room, much larger than his alcove bedroom on Deming Place—as large as his own bedroom at home on the farm. The bath was done dazzlingly in blue and white. The tub was enormous and as solid as if the house had been built around it. There were towels and towels and towels in blue and white, ranging in size all the way from tiny embroidered wisps to fuzzy all-enveloping bath towels as big as a carpet.

He was much impressed.

He decided to bathe and change into dinner clothes and was glad of this when he found Paula in black chiffon before the fire in the great beamed room she had called the library. Dirk thought she looked very beautiful in that diaphanous stuff, with the pearls. Her heart-shaped face, with its large eyes that slanted a little at the corners; her long slim throat; her dark hair piled high and away from her little ears. He decided not to mention it.

"You look extremely dangerous," said Paula.

"I am," replied Dirk, "but it's hunger that brings this look of the beast to my usually mild Dutch features. Also, why do you call this the library?" Empty shelves gaped from the wall on all sides. The room was meant to hold hundreds of volumes. Perhaps fifty or sixty in all now leaned limply against each other or lay supine.

Paula laughed. "They do look sort of sparse, don't they? Theodore bought this place, you know, as is. We've books enough in town, of course. But I don't read much out here. And Theodore!—I don't believe he ever in his life read anything but detective stories and the newspapers."

Dirk told himself that Paula had known her husband would not be home until ten and had deliberately planned a tête-à-tête meal. He would not, therefore, confess himself a little nettled when Paula said, "I've asked the Emerys in for dinner; and we'll have a game of bridge afterward. Phil Emery, you know, the Third. He used to have it on his visiting card, like royalty."

The Emerys were drygoods; had been drygoods for sixty years;

were accounted Chicago aristocracy; preferred England; rode to hounds in pink coats along Chicago's prim and startled suburban prairies. They had a vast estate on the lake near Stormwood. They arrived a trifle late. Dirk had seen pictures of old Phillip Emery ("Phillip the First," he thought, with an inward grin) and decided, looking at the rather anaemic third edition, that the stock was running a little thin. Mrs. Emery was blonde, statuesque, and unmagnetic. In contrast Paula seemed to glow like a sombre jewel. The dinner was delicious but surprisingly simple; little more than Selina would have given him, Dirk thought, had he come home to the farm this week-end. The talk was desultory and rather dull. And this chap had millions, Dirk said to himself. Millions. No scratching in an architect's office for this lad. Mrs. Emery was interested in the correct pronunciation of Chicago street names.

"It's terrible," she said. "I think there ought to be a Movement for the proper pronunciation. The people ought to be taught; and the children in the schools. They call Goethe Street 'Gerty'; and pronounce all the s's in Des Plaines. Even Illinois they call 'Illi*noise*.'" She was very much in earnest. Her breast rose and fell. She ate her salad rapidly. Dirk thought that large blondes oughtn't to get excited. It made their faces red.

At bridge after dinner Phillip the Third proved to be sufficiently the son of his father to win from Dirk more money than he could conveniently afford to lose. Though Mrs. Phil had much to do with this, as Dirk's partner. Paula played with Emery, a bold shrewd game.

Theodore Storm came in at ten and stood watching them. When the guests had left the three sat before the fire. "Something to drink?" Storm asked Dirk. Dirk refused but Storm mixed a stiff highball for himself, and then another. The whiskey brought no flush to his large white impassive face. He talked almost not at all. Dirk, naturally silent, was loquacious by comparison. But while there was nothing heavy, unvital about Dirk's silence this man's was oppressive, irritating. His paunch, his large white hands, his great white face gave the effect of bleached bloodless bulk. "I don't see how she stands him," Dirk thought. Husband and wife seemed to be on terms of polite friendliness. Storm excused himself and took himself off with a word about being tired, and seeing them in the morning.

After he had gone: "He likes you," said Paula.

"Important," said Dirk, "if true."

"But it is important. He can help you a lot."

"Help me how? I don't want——"

"But I do. I want you to be successful. I want you to be. You can be. You've got it written all over you. In the way you stand, and talk, and don't talk. In the way you look at people. In something in the way you carry yourself. It's what they call force, I suppose. Anyway, you've got it."

"Has your husband got it?"

"Theodore! No! That is——"

"There you are. I've got the force, but he's got the money."

"You can have both." She was leaning forward. Her eyes were bright, enormous. Her hands—those thin dark hot hands—were twisted in her lap. He looked at her quietly. Suddenly there were tears in her eyes. "Don't look at me that way, Dirk." She huddled back in her chair, limp. She looked a little haggard and older, somehow. "My marriage is a mess, of course. You can see that."

"You knew it would be, didn't you?"

"No. Yes. Oh, I don't know. Anyway, what's the difference, now? I'm not trying to be what they call an Influence in your life. I'm just fond of you—you know that—and I want you to be great and successful. It's maternal, I suppose."

"I should think two babies would satisfy that urge."

"Oh, I can't get excited about two pink healthy lumps of babies. I love them and all that, but all they need is to have a bottle stuffed into their mouths at proper intervals and to be bathed, and dressed and aired and slept. It's a mechanical routine and about as exciting as a treadmill. I can't go round being maternal and beating my breast over two nice firm lumps of flesh."

"Just what do you want me to do, Paula?"

She was eager again, vitally concerned in him. "It's all so ridiculous. All these men whose incomes are thirty—forty—sixty—a hundred thousand a year usually haven't any qualities, really, that the five-thousand-a-year man hasn't. The doctor who sent Theodore a bill for four thousand dollars when each of my babies was born didn't do a thing that a country doctor with a Ford wouldn't do. But he knew he could get it and he asked it. Somebody has to get the fifty-thousand-dollar salaries—some advertising man, or bond salesman or—why, look at Phil Emery! He probably couldn't sell a yard of pink ribbon to a schoolgirl if he had to. Look at Theodore! He just sits and blinks and says nothing. But when the time comes he doubles up his fat white fist and mumbles, 'Ten million,' or 'Fifteen million,' and that settles it."

Dirk laughed to hide his own little mounting sensation of excitement. "It isn't quite as simple as that, I imagine. There's more to it than meets the eye."

"There isn't! I tell you I know the whole crowd of them. I've been brought up with this moneyed pack all my life, haven't I? Pork packers and wheat grabbers and peddlers of gas and electric light and dry goods. Grandfather's the only one of the crowd that I respect. He has stayed the same. They can't fool him. He knows he just happened to go into wholesale beef and pork when wholesale beef and pork was a new game in Chicago. Now look at him!"

"Still, you will admit there's something in knowing when," he argued.

Paula stood up. "If you don't know I'll tell you. Now is when. I've got Grandfather and Dad and Theodore to work with. You can go on being an architect if you want to. It's a fine enough profession. But unless you're a genius where'll it get you? Go in with them, and Dirk, in five years——"

"What!" They were both standing, facing each other, she tense, eager; he relaxed but stimulated.

"Try it and see what, will you? Will you, Dirk?"

"I don't know, Paula. I should say my mother wouldn't think much of it."

"What does she know! Oh, I don't mean that she isn't a fine, wonderful person. She is. I love her. But success! She thinks success is another acre of asparagus or cabbage; or a new stove in the kitchen now that they've brought gas out as far as High Prairie."

He had a feeling that she possessed him; that her hot eager hands held him though they stood apart and eyed each other almost hostilely.

As he undressed that night in his rose and satin room he thought, "Now what's her game? What's she up to? Be careful, Dirk, old boy." On coming into the room he had gone immediately to the long mirror and had looked at himself carefully, searchingly, not knowing that Paula, in her room, had done the same. He ran a hand over his close-shaved chin, looked at the fit of his dinner coat. He wished he had had it made at Peter Peel's, the English tailor on Michigan Boulevard. But Peel was so damned expensive. Perhaps next time . . .

As he lay in the soft bed with the satin coverlet over him he thought, "Now what's her lit-tle game!"

He awoke at eight, enormously hungry. He wondered, uneasily, just how he was going to get his breakfast. She had said his breakfast would be brought him in his room. He stretched luxuriously, sprang up, turned on his bath water, bathed. When he emerged in dressing gown and slippers his breakfast tray had been brought him mysteriously and its contents lay appetizingly on a little portable table. There were flocks of small covered dishes and a charming individual coffee service. The morning papers, folded and virgin, lay next this. A little note from Paula: "Would you like to take a walk at about half-past nine? Stroll down to the stables. I want to show you my new horse."

The distance from the house to the stables was actually quite a brisk little walk in itself. Paula, in riding clothes, was waiting for him. She looked boyish and young standing beside the sturdy bulk of Pat, the head stableman. She wore tan whipcord breeches, a coat of darker stuff, a little round felt hat whose brim curved away from her face.

She greeted him. "I've been out two hours. Had my ride."

"I hate people who tell you, first thing in the morning, that they've been out two hours."

"If that's the kind of mood you're in we won't show him the horse, will we, Pat?"

Pat thought they would. Pat showed him the new saddle mare as a mother exhibits her latest offspring, tenderly, proudly. "Look at her back," said Pat. "That's the way you tell a horse, sir. By the length of this here line. Lookut it! There's a picture for you, now!"

Paula looked up at Dirk. "You ride, don't you?"

"I used to ride the old nags, bareback, on the farm."

"You'll have to learn. We'll teach him, won't we, Pat?"

Pat surveyed Dirk's lean, flexible figure. "Easy."

"Oh, say!" protested Dirk.

"Then I'll have some one to ride with me. Theodore never rides. He never takes any sort of exercise. Sits in that great fat car of his."

They went into the coach house, a great airy white-washed place with glittering harness and spurs and bridles like jewels in glass cases. There were ribbons, too, red and yellow and blue in a rack on the wall; and trophy cups. The coach house gave Dirk a little hopeless feeling. He had never before seen anything like it. In the first place, there were no motors in it. He had forgotten that people rode in anything but motors. A horse on Chicago's boulevards raised a laugh. The sight of a shining brougham with two sleek chestnuts driving down Michigan Avenue would have set that street to staring and sniggering as a Roman chariot drawn by zebras might have done. Yet here was such a brougham, glittering, spotless. Here was a smart cream surrey with a cream-coloured top hung with fringe. There were two-wheeled carts high and slim and chic. A victoria. Two pony carts. One would have thought, seeing this room, that the motor vehicle had never been invented. And towering over all, dwarfing the rest, out-glittering them, stood a tally-ho, a sheer piece of wanton insolence. It was in perfect order. Its cushions were immaculate. Its sides shone. Its steps glistened. Dirk, looking up at it, laughed outright. It seemed too splendid, too absurd. With a sudden boyish impulse he swung himself up the three steps that led to the box and perched himself on the fawn cushioned seat. He looked very handsome there. "A coach and four—isn't that what they call it? Got any Roman juggernauts?"

"Do you want to drive it?" asked Paula. "This afternoon? Do

you think you can? Four horses, you know." She laughed up at him, her dark face upturned to his.

Dirk looked down at her. "No." He climbed down. "I suppose that at about the time they drove this hereabouts my father was taking the farm plugs into the Haymarket."

Something had annoyed him, she saw. Would he wait while she changed to walking things? Or perhaps he'd rather drive in the roadster. They walked up to the house together. He wished that she would not consult his wishes so anxiously. It made him sulky, impatient.

She put a hand on his arm. "Dirk, are you annoyed at me for what I said last night?"

"No."

"What did you think when you went to your room last night? Tell me. What did you think?"

"I thought: 'She's bored with her husband and she's trying to vamp me. I'll have to be careful.' "

Paula laughed delightedly. "That's nice and frank . . . What else?"

"I thought my coat didn't fit very well and I wished I could afford to have Peel make my next one."

"You can," said Paula.

16

As it turned out, Dirk was spared the necessity of worrying about the fit of his next dinner coat for the following year and a half. His coat, during that period, was a neat olive drab as was that of some millions of young men of his age, or thereabouts. He wore it very well, and with the calm assurance of one who knows that his shoulders are broad, his waist slim, his stomach flat, his flanks lean, and his legs straight. Most of that time he spent at Fort Sheridan, first as an officer in training, then as an officer training others to be officers. He was excellent at this job. Influence put him there and kept him there even after he began to chafe at the restraint. Fort Sheridan is a few miles outside Chicago, north. No smart North Shore dinner was considered complete without at least a major, a colonel, two captains, and a sprinkling of first lieutenants. Their boots shone so delightfully while dancing.

In the last six months of it (though he did not, of course, know that it was to be the last six months) Dirk tried desperately to get to France. He was suddenly sick of the neat job at home; of the dinners; of the smug routine; of the olive-drab motor car that whisked him wherever he wanted to go (he had a captaincy); of making them "snap into it"; of Paula; of his mother, even. Two months before the war's close he succeeded in getting over; but Paris was his headquarters.

Between Dirk and his mother the first rift had appeared.

"If I were a man," Selina said, "I'd make up my mind straight about this war and then I'd do one of two things. I'd go into it the way Jan Snip goes at forking the manure pile—a dirty job that's got to be cleaned up; or I'd refuse to do it altogether if I didn't believe in it as a job for me. I'd fight, or I'd be a conscientious objector. There's nothing in between for any one who isn't old or crippled, or sick."

Paula was aghast when she heard this. So was Julie whose wailings had been loud when Eugene had gone into the air service. He was in France now, thoroughly happy. "Do you mean," demanded Paula, "that you actually want Dirk to go over there and be wounded or killed!"

"No. If Dirk were killed my life would stop. I'd go on living, I suppose, but my life would have stopped."

They were all doing some share in the work to be done.

Selina had thought about her own place in this war welter. She had wanted to do canteen work in France but had decided against this as being selfish. "The thing for me to do," she said, "is to go on raising vegetables and hogs as fast as I can." She supplied countless households with free food while their men were gone. She herself worked like a man, taking the place of the able-bodied helper who had been employed on her farm.

Paula was lovely in her Red Cross uniform. She persuaded Dirk to go into the Liberty Bond selling drive and he was unexpectedly effective in his quiet, serious way; most convincing and undeniably thrilling to look at in uniform. Paula's little air of possession had grown until now it enveloped him. She wasn't playing now; was deeply and terribly in love with him.

When, in 1918, Dirk took off his uniform he went into the bond department of the Great Lakes Trust Company in which Theodore Storm had a large interest. He said that the war had disillusioned him. It was a word you often heard uttered as a reason or an excuse for abandoning the normal. "Disillusioned."

"What did you think war was going to do?" said Selina. "Purify! It never has yet."

It was understood, by Selina at least, that Dirk's abandoning of his profession was a temporary thing. Quick as she usually was to arrive at conclusions, she did not realize until too late that this son of hers had definitely deserted building for bonds; that the only structures he would rear were her own castles in Spain. His first two months as a bond salesman netted him more than a year's salary at his old post at Hollis & Sprague's. When he told this to Selina, in triumph, she said, "Yes, but there isn't much fun in it, is there? This selling things on paper? Now architecture, that must be thrilling. Next to writing a play and seeing it acted by real people—seeing it actually come alive before your eyes architecture must be the next most fun. Putting a building down on paper—little marks here, straight lines there, figures, calculations, blueprints, measurements—and then, suddenly one day, the actual building itself. Steel and stone and brick, with engines throbbing inside it like a heart, and people flowing in and out. Part of a city. A piece of actual beauty conceived by you! Oh, Dirk!" To see her face then must have given him a pang, it was so alive, so eager.

He found excuses for himself. "Selling bonds that make that building possible isn't so dull, either."

But she waved that aside almost contemptuously. "What nonsense, Dirk. It's like selling seats at the box office of a theatre for the play inside."

Dirk had made many new friends in the last year and a half. More than that, he had acquired a new manner; an air of quiet authority, of assurance. The profession of architecture was put definitely behind him. There had been no building in all the months of the war; probably would be none in years. Materials were prohibitive, labour exorbitant. He did not say to Selina that he had put the other work from him. But after six months in his new position he knew that he would never go back.

From the start he was a success. Within one year he was so successful that you could hardly distinguish him from a hundred other successful young Chicago business and professional men whose clothes were made at Peel's; who kept their collars miraculously clean in the soot-laden atmosphere of the Loop; whose shoes were bench-made; who lunched at the Noon Club on the roof of the First National Bank where Chicago's millionaires ate corned-beef hash whenever that plebeian dish appeared on the bill of fare. He had had a little thrill out of his first meal at this club whose membership was made up of the "big men" of the city's financial circle. Now he could even feel a little flicker of contempt for them. He had known old Aug Hempel, of course, for years, as well as Michael Arnold, and, later, Phillip Emery, Theodore Storm, and others. But he had expected these men to be different.

Paula had said, "Theodore, why don't you take Dirk up to the Noon Club some day? There are a lot of big men he ought to meet."

Dirk went in some trepidation. The great grilled elevator, as large as a room, whisked them up to the roof of the fortress of gold. The club lounge furnished his first disappointment. It looked like a Pullman smoker. The chairs were upholstered in black leather or red plush. The woodwork was shiny red imitation mahogany. The carpet was green. There were bright shining brass cuspidors in the hall near the cigar counter. The food was well cooked. Man's food. Nine out of every ten of these men possessed millions. Whenever corned beef and cabbage appeared on the luncheon menu nine out of ten took it. These were not at all the American Big Business Man of the comic papers and of fiction—that yellow, nervous, dyspeptic creature who lunches off milk and pie. They were divided into two definite types. The older men of between fifty and sixty were great high-coloured fellows of full habit. Many of them had had a physician's warning of high blood pressure, hardening arteries, overworked heart, rebellious kidneys. So now they waxed cautious, taking time over their substantial lunches, smoking and talking. Their faces were impassive, their eyes shrewd, hard. Their talk was colloquial and frequently illiterate. They often said "was" for "were." "Was you going to see Baldwin about that South American stuff or is he going to ship it through without?" Most of them had known little of play in their youth and now they played ponderously and a little sadly and yet eagerly as does one to whom the gift of leisure had come too late. On Saturday afternoon you saw them in imported heather green golf stockings and Scotch tweed suits making for the links or the lake. They ruined their palates and livers with strong cigars, thinking cigarette smoking undignified and pipes common. "Have a cigar!" was their greeting, their password, their open sesame. "Have a cigar!" Only a few were so rich, so assured as to smoke cheap light panatellas. Old Aug Hempel was one of these. Dirk noticed that when he made one of his rare visits to the Noon Club his entrance was met with a little stir, a deference. He was nearing seventy-five now; was still straight, strong, zestful of life; a magnificent old buccaneer among the pettier crew. His had been the direct and brutal method—swish! swash! and his enemies walked the plank. The younger men eyed him with a certain amusement and respect.

These younger men whose ages ranged from twenty-eight to forty-five were disciples of the new system in business. They were graduates of universities. They had known luxury all their lives. They were the second or third generation. They used the word "psychology." They practised restraint. They knew the power of suggestion. Where old Aug Hempel had flown the black flag they resorted to the periscope. Dirk learned that these men did not talk business during meal time except when they had met definitely for that purpose. They wasted a good deal of time, Dirk thought, and often, when they were supposed to be "in conference" or when their secretaries said primly that they were very busy and not to be disturbed until three, they were dozing off for a comfortable half hour in their private offices. They were the sons or grandsons of those bearded, rugged, and rather terrible old boys who, in 1835 or 1840, had come out of County Limerick or County Kilkenny or out of Scotland or the Rhineland to mold this new country in their strong hairy hands; those hands whose work had made possible the symphony orchestras, the yacht clubs, the golf clubs through which their descendants now found amusement and relaxation.

Dirk listened to the talk of the Noon Club.

"I made it in eighty-six. That isn't so bad for the Tippecanoe course."

". . . boxes are going pretty well but the Metropolitan grabs up all the big ones and the house wants names. Garden dosen't draw the way she used to, even in Chicago. It's the popular subscription that counts."

". . . grabbed the Century out of New York at two-forty-five and got back here in time to try out my new horse in the park. She's a little nervous for city riding but we're opening the house at Lake Forest next week ——"

". . . pretty good show but they don't send the original companies here, that's the trouble . . ."

". . . in London. It's a neat shade of green, isn't it? You can't get ties like this over here, I don't know why. Got a dozen last time I was over. Yeah, Plumbridge in Bond Street."

Well, Dirk could talk like that easily enough. He listened quietly, nodded, smiled, agreed or disagreed. He looked about him carefully, appraisingly. Waist lines well kept in; carefully tailored clothes; shrewd wrinkles of experience radiating in fine sprays in the skin around the corners of their eyes. The president of an advertising firm lunching with a banker; a bond salesman talking to a rare book collector; a packer seated at a small table with Horatio Craft, the sculptor.

Two years and Dirk, too, had learned to "grab the Century" in order to save an hour or so of time between Chicago and New York. Peel said it was a pleasure to fit a coat to his broad, flat tapering back, and trousers to his strong sturdy legs. His colour, inherited from his red-cheeked Dutch ancestors brought up in the fresh sea-laden air of the Holland flats, was fine and clear. Sometimes Selina, in pure sensuous delight, passed her gnarled, work-worn hand over his shoulders and down his fine, strong, straight back. He had been abroad twice. He learned to call it "running over to Europe for a few days." It had all come about in a scant two years, as is the theatrical way in which life speeds in America.

Selina was a little bewildered now at this new Dirk whose life was so full without her. Sometimes she did not see him for two weeks, or three. He sent her gifts which she smoothed and touched delightedly and put away; fine soft silken things, hand-made—which she could not wear. The habit of years was too strong upon her. Though she had always been a woman of dainty habits and fastidious tastes the grind of her early married life had left its indelible mark. Now, as she dressed, you might have seen that her petticoat was likely to be black sateen and her plain, durable corset cover neatly patched where it had worn under the arms. She employed none of the artifices of a youth-mad day. Sun and wind and rain and the cold and heat of the open prairie had wreaked their vengeance on her flouting of them. Her skin was tanned, weather-beaten; her hair rough and dry. Her eyes, in that frame, startled you by their unexpectedness, they were so calm, so serene, yet so alive. They were the beautiful eyes of a wise young girl in the face of a middle-aged woman. Life was still so fresh to her.

She had almost poignantly few personal belongings. Her bureau drawers were like a nun's; her brush and comb, a scant stock of plain white underwear. On the bathroom shelf her toothbrush, some vase-line, a box of talcum powder. None of those aids to artifice with which the elderly woman deludes herself into thinking that she is hoodwink-ing the world. She wore well-made walking oxfords now, with sensible heels the kind known as Field's special; plain shirtwaists and neat dark suits, or a blue cloth dress. A middle-aged woman approaching elder-liness; a woman who walked and carried herself well; who looked at you with a glance that was direct but never hard. That was all. Yet there was about her something arresting, something compelling. You felt it.

"I don't see how you do it!" Julie Arnold complained one day as Selina was paying her one of her rare visits in town. "Your eyes are as bright as a baby's and mine look like dead oysters." They were up in Julie's dressing room in the new house on the north side—the new house that was now the old house. Julie's dressing table was a bewil-dering thing. Selina DeJong, in her neat black suit and her plain black hat, sat regarding it and Julie seated before it, with a grim and lively interest.

"It looks," Selina said, "like Mandel's toilette section, or a hos-pital operating room just before a major operation." There were great glass jars that contained meal, white and gold. There were rows and rows of cream pots holding massage cream, vanishing cream, cleansing cream. There were little china bowls of scarlet and white and yellowish pastes. A perforated container spouted a wisp of cotton. You saw toilet waters, perfumes, atomizers, French soaps, unguents, tubes. It wasn't a dressing table merely, but a laboratory.

"This!" exclaimed Julie. "You ought to see Paula's. Compared to her toilette ceremony mine is just a splash at the kitchen sink." She rubbed cold cream now around her eyes with her two forefingers, using a practised upward stroke.

"It looks fascinating," Selina exclaimed. "Some day I'm going to try it. There are so many things I'm going to try some day. So many things I've never done that I'm going to do for the fun of it. Think of it, Julie! I've never had a manicure! Some day I'm going to have one. I'll tell the girl to paint my nails a beautiful bright vermilion. And I'll tip her twenty-five cents. They're so pretty with their bobbed hair and their queer bright eyes. I s'pose you'll think I'm crazy if I tell you they make me feel young."

Julie was massaging. Her eyes had an absent look. Suddenly: "Listen, Selina. Dirk and Paula are together too much. People are talking."

"Talking?" The smile faded from Selina's face.

"Goodness knows I'm not strait-laced. You can't be in this day and age. If I had ever thought I'd live to see the time when —— Well, since the war of course anything's all right, seems. But Paula has no sense. Everbody knows she's insane about Dirk. That's all right for Dirk, but how about Paula! She won't go anywhere unless he's invited. Of course Dirk is awfully popular. Goodness knows there are few enough young men like him in Chicago—handsome and successful and polished and all. Most of them dash off East just as soon as they can get their fathers to establish an Eastern branch or something. . . . They're together all the time, everywhere. I asked her if she was going to divorce Storm and she said no, she hadn't enough money of her own and Dirk wasn't earning enough. His salary's thousands, but she's used to millions. Well!"

"They were boy and girl together," Selina interrupted, feebly.

"They're not any more. Don't be silly, Selina. You're not as young as that."

No, she was not as young as that. When Dirk next paid one of his rare visits to the farm she called him into her bedroom—the cool, dim shabby bedroom with the old black walnut bed in which she had lain as Pervus DeJong's bride more than thirty years ago. She had a little knitted jacket over her severe white nightgown. Her abundant hair was neatly braided in two long plaits. She looked somehow girlish there in the dim light, her great soft eyes gazing up at him.

"Dirk, sit down here at the side of my bed the way you used to."

"I'm dead tired, Mother. Twenty-seven holes of golf before I came out."

"I know. You ache all over—a nice kind of ache. I used to feel like that when I'd worked in the fields all day, pulling vegetables, or planting." He was silent. She caught his hand. "You didn't like that. My saying that. I'm sorry. I didn't say it to make you feel bad, dear."

"I know you didn't, Mother."

"Dirk, do you know what that woman who writes the society news in the Sunday *Tribune* called you today?"

"No. What? I never read it."

"She said you were on the *jeunesse dorée.*"

Dirk grinned. "Gosh!"

"I remember enough of my French at Miss Fister's school to know that that means gilded youth."

"Me! That's good! I'm not even spangled."

"Dirk!" her voice was low, vibrant. "Dirk, I don't want you to be a gilded youth, I don't care how thick the gilding. Dirk, that isn't what I worked in the sun and cold for. I'm not reproaching you; I didn't mind the work. Forgive me for even mentioning it. But, Dirk, I don't want my son to be known as one of the *jeunesse dorée.* No! Not my son!"

"Now, listen, Mother. That's foolish. If you're going to talk like that. Like a mother in a melodrama whose son's gone wrong. . . . I work like a dog. You know that. You get the wrong angle on things, stuck out here on this little farm. Why don't you come into town and take a little place and sell the farm?"

"Live with you, you mean?" Pure mischievousness.

"Oh, no. You wouldn't like that," hastily. "Besides, I'd never be there. At the office all day, and out somewhere in the evening."

"When do you do your reading, Dirk?"

"Why—uh ——"

She sat up in bed, looking down at the thin end of her braid as she twined it round and round her finger. "Dirk, what is this you sell in that mahogany office of yours? I never did get the hang of it."

"Bonds, Mother. You know that perfectly well."

"Bonds." She considered this a moment. "Are they hard to sell? Who buys them?"

"That depends. Everybody buys them—that is . . ."

"I don't. I suppose because whenever I had any money it went back into the farm for implements, or repairs, or seed, or stock, or improvements. That's always the way with a farmer—even on a little truck farm like this." She pondered again a moment. He fidgeted, yawned. "Dirk DeJong—Bond Salesman."

"The way you say it, Mother, it sounds like a low criminal pursuit."

"Dirk, do you know sometimes I actually think that if you had stayed here on the farm ——"

"Good God, Mother! What for!"

"Oh, I don't know. Time to dream. Time to—no, I suppose that isn't true any more. I suppose the day is past when the genius came from the farm. Machinery has cut into his dreams. He used to sit for hours on the wagon seat, the reins slack in his hands, while the horses plodded into town. Now he whizzes by in a jitney. Patent binders, ploughs, reapers—he's a mechanic. He hasn't time to dream. I guess if Lincoln had lived to-day he's have split his rails to the tune of a humming, snarling patent wood cutter, and in the evening he'd have whirled into town to get his books at the public library, and he'd have read them under the glare of the electric light bulb instead of lying flat in front of the flickering wood fire. . . . Well. . . ."

She lay back, looked up at him. "Dirk, why don't you marry?"

"Why—there's no one I want to marry."

"No one who's free, you mean?"

He stood up. "I mean no one." He stooped and kissed her lightly. Her arms went round him close. Her hand with the thick gold wedding band on it pressed his head to her hard. "Sobig!" He was a baby again.

"You haven't called me that in years." He was laughing.

She reverted to the old game they had played when he was a child. "How big is my son! How big?" She was smiling, but her eyes were sombre.

"So big!" answered Dirk, and measured a very tiny space between thumb and forefinger. "So big."

She faced him, sitting up very straight in bed, the little wool shawl hunched about her shoulders. "Dirk, are you ever going back to architecture? The war is history. It's now or never with you. Pretty soon it will be too late. Are you ever going back to architecture? To your profession?"

A clean amputation. "No, Mother."

She gave an actual gasp, as though icy water had been thrown full in her face. She looked suddenly old, tired. Her shoulders sagged. He stood in the doorway, braced for her reproaches. But when she spoke it was to reproach herself. "Then I'm a failure."

"Oh, what nonsense, Mother. I'm happy. You can't live somebody else's life. You used to tell me, when I was a kid I remember, that life wasn't just an adventure, to be taken as it came, with the hope that something glorious was always hidden just around the corner. You said you had lived that way and it hadn't worked. You said ——"

She interrupted him with a little cry. "I know I did. I know I did." Suddenly she raised a warning finger. Her eyes were luminous, prophetic. "Dirk, you can't desert her like that!"

"Desert who?" He was startled.

"Beauty! Self-expression. Whatever you want to call it. You wait!

She'll turn on you some day. Some day you'll want her, and she won't be there.''

Inwardly he had been resentful of this bedside conversation with his mother. She made little of him, he thought, while outsiders appreciated his success. He had said, "So big," measuring a tiny space between thumb and forefinger in answer to her half-playful question, but he had not honestly meant it. He thought her ridiculously old-fashioned now in her viewpoint, and certainly unreasonable. But he would not quarrel with her.

"You wait, too, Mother," he said now, smiling. "Some day your wayward son will be a real success. Wait till the millions roll in. Then we'll see.''

She lay down, turned her back deliberately upon him, pulled the covers up about her.

"Shall I turn out your light, Mother, and open the windows?"

"Meena'll do it. She always does. Just call her. . . . Good-night.''

He knew that he had come to be a rather big man in his world. Influence had helped. He knew that, too. But he shut his mind to much of Paula's manoeuvring and wire pulling—refused to acknowledge that her lean, dark, eager fingers had manipulated the mechanism that ordered his career. Paula herself was wise enough to know that to hold him she must not let him feel indebted to her. She knew that the debtor hates his creditor. She lay awake at night planning for him, scheming for his advancement, then suggested these schemes to him so deftly as to make him think he himself had devised them. She had even realized of late that their growing intimacy might handicap him if openly commented on. But now she must see him daily, or speak to him. In the huge house on Lake Shore Drive her own rooms—sitting room, bedroom, dressing room, bath—were as detached as though she occupied a separate apartment. Her telephone was a private wire leading only to her own bedroom. She called him the first thing in the morning; the last thing at night. Her voice, when she spoke to him, was an organ transformed; low, vibrant, with a timbre in its tone that would have made it unrecognizable to an outsider.

Her words were commonplace enough, but pregnant and meaningful for her.

"What did you do to-day? Did you have a good day? . . . Why didn't you call me? . . . Did you follow up that suggestion you made about Kennedy? I think it's a wonderful idea, don't you? You're a wonderful man, Dirk; did you know that? . . . I miss you. . . . Do you? . . . When? . . . Why not lunch? . . . Oh, not if you have a business appointment . . . How about five o'clock? . . . No, not there . . . Oh, I don't know. It's so public . . . Yes . . . Good-bye. . . . Good-night. . . . Good-night. . . ."

They began to meet rather furtively, in out-of-the-way places. They would lunch in department store restaurants where none of their friends ever came. They spent off afternoon hours in the dim, close atmosphere of the motion picture palaces, sitting in the back row, seeing nothing of the film, talking in eager whispers that failed to annoy the scattered devotees in the middle of the house. When they drove it was on obscure streets of the south side, as secure there from observation as though they had been in Africa, for to the north sider the south side of Chicago is the hinterland of civilization.

Paula had grown very beautiful, her world thought. There was about her the aura, the glow, the roseate exaltation that surrounds the woman in love.

Frequently she irritated Dirk. At such times he grew quieter than ever; more reserved. As he involuntarily withdrew she advanced. Sometimes he thought he hated her—her hot eager hands, her glowing asking eyes, her thin red mouth, her sallow heart-shaped exquisite face, her perfumed clothing, her air of ownership. That was it! Her possessiveness. She clutched him so with her every look and gesture, even when she did not touch him. There was about her something avid, sultry. It was like the hot wind that sometimes blew over the prairie—blowing, blowing, but never refreshing. It made you feel dry, arid, irritated, parched. Sometimes Dirk wondered what Theodore Storm thought and knew behind that impassive flabby white mask of his.

Dirk met plenty of other girls. Paula was clever enough to see to that. She asked them to share her box at the opera. She had them at her dinners. She affected great indifference to their effect on him. She suffered when he talked to one of them.

"Dirk, why don't you take out that nice Farnham girl?"

"Is she nice?"

"Well, isn't she! You were talking to her long enough at the Kirks' dance. What were you talking about?"

"Books."

"Oh. Books. She's awfully nice and intelligent, isn't she? A lovely girl." She was suddenly happy. Books.

The Farnham girl was a nice girl. She was the kind of girl one should fall in love with and doesn't. The Farnham girl was one of the many well-bred Chicago girls of her day and class. Fine, honest, clear-headed, frank, capable, good-looking in an indefinite and unarresting sort of way. Hair-coloured hair, good teeth, good enough eyes, clear skin, sensible medium hands and feet; skated well, danced well, talked well. Read the books you have read. A companionable girl. Loads of money but never spoke of it. Travelled. Her hand met yours firmly—and it was just a hand. At the contact no current darted through you, sending its shaft with a little zing to your heart.

But when Paula showed you a book her arm, as she stood next you, would somehow fit into the curve of yours and you were conscious of the feel of her soft slim side against you.

He knew many girls. There was a distinct type known as the North Shore Girl. Slim, tall, exquisite; a little fine nose, a high, sweet, slightly nasal voice, earrings, a cigarette, luncheon at Huyler's. All these girls looked amazingly alike, Dirk thought; talked very much alike. They all spoke French with a pretty good accent; danced intricate symbolic dances; read the new books; had the same patter. They prefaced, interlarded, concluded their remarks to each other with, "My deah!" It expressed, for them, surprise, sympathy, amusement, ridicule, horror, resignation. "My *deah!* You should have seen her! My *deeah!*"—horror. Their slang was almost identical with that used by the girls working in his office. "She's a good kid," they said, speaking in admiration of another girl. They made a fetish of frankness. In a

day when everyone talked in screaming headlines they knew it was
necessary to red-ink their remarks in order to get them noticed at all.
The word rot was replaced by garbage and garbage gave way to the
ultimate swill. One no longer said "How shocking!" but, "How perfectly obscene!" The words, spoken in their sweet clear voices, fell
nonchalantly from their pretty lips. All very fearless and uninhibited
and free. That, they told you, was the main thing. Sometimes Dirk
wished they wouldn't work so hard at their play. They were forever
getting up pageants and plays and large festivals for charity; Venetian
fêtes, Oriental bazaars, charity balls. In the programme performance
of these many of them sang better, acted better, danced better than
most professional performers, but the whole thing always lacked the
flavour, somehow, of professional performance. On these affairs they
lavished thousands in costumes and decorations, receiving in return
other thousands which they soberly turned over to the Cause. They
found nothing ludicrous in this. Spasmodically they went into business or semi-professional ventures, defying the conventions. Paula did
this, too. She or one of her friends were forever opening blouse shops;
starting Gifte Shoppes; burgeoning into tea rooms decorated in crude
green and vermilion and orange and black; announcing their affilia-
tion with an advertising agency. These adventures blossomed, withered, died. They were the result of post-war restlessness. Many of
these girls had worked indefatigably during the 1917–1918 period;
had driven service cars, managed ambulances, nursed, scrubbed, conducted canteens. They missed the excitement, the satisfaction of
achievement.

They found Dirk fair game, resented Paula's proprietorship.
Susans and Janes and Kates and Bettys and Sallys—plain old-fashioned
names for modern, erotic misses—they talked to Dirk, danced with
him, rode with him, flirted with him. His very unattainableness gave
him piquancy. That Paula Storm had him fast. He didn't care a hoot
about girls.

"Oh, Mr. DeJong," they said, "your name's Dirk, isn't it? What
a slick name! What does it mean?"

"Nothing, I suppose. It's a Dutch name. My people—my father's people—were Dutch, you know."

"A dirk's a sort of sword, isn't it, or poniard? Anyway, it sounds very keen and cruel and fatal—Dirk."

He would flush a little (one of his assets) and smile, and look at them, and say nothing. He found that to be all that was necessary.

He got on enormously.

17

Between these girls and the girls that worked in his office there existed a similarity that struck and amused Dirk. He said, "Take a letter, Miss Roach," to a slim young creature as exquisite as the girl with whom he had danced the day before; or ridden or played tennis or bridge. Their very clothes were faultless imitations. They even used the same perfume. He wondered, idly, how they did it. They were eighteen, nineteen, twenty, and their faces and bodies and desires and natural equipment made their presence in a business office a paradox, an absurdity. Yet they were capable, too, in a mechanical sort of way. Theirs were mechanical jobs. They answered telephones, pressed levers, clicked buttons, tapped typewriters, jotted down names. They were lovely creatures with the minds of fourteen-year-old children. Their hair was shining, perfectly undulated, as fine and glossy and tenderly curling as a young child's. Their breasts were flat, their figures singularly sexless like that of a very young boy. They were wise with the wisdom of the serpent. They wore wonderful little sweaters and flat babyish collars and ridiculously sensible stockings and oxfords. Their legs were slim and sturdy. Their mouths were pouting, soft, pink, the lower lip a little curled back, petal-wise, like the moist mouth of a baby that has just finished nursing. Their eyes were wide apart, empty, knowledgeous. They managed their private affairs like generals. They were cool, remote, disdainful. They reduced their boys to desperation. They were brigands, desperadoes, pirates, taking all, giving little. They came, for the most part, from sordid homes, yet they knew, in some miraculous way, all the fine arts that Paula knew and practised. They were corsetless, pliant, bewildering, lovely, dangerous. They ate lunches that were horrible mixtures of cloying sweets and biting acids yet their skin was like velvet and cream. Their voices were thin, nasal, vulgar; their faces like those in a Greuze or a Fragonard. They said, with a twang that racked the listener, "I wouldn't of went if I got an invite but he could of give me a ring, anyways. I called him right. I was sore."

"Yeh? Wha'd he say?"

"Oh, he laffed."

"Didja go?"

"Me! No! Whatcha think I yam, anyway?"

"Oh, he's a good kid."

Among these Dirk worked immune, aloof, untouched. He would have been surprised to learn that he was known among them as Frosty. They approved his socks, his scarfs, his nails, his features, his legs in their well-fitting pants, his flat strong back in the Peel coat. They admired and resented him. Not one that did not secretly dream of the day when he would call her into his office, shut the door, and say, "Loretta" (their names were burbankian monstrosities born of grafting the original appellation onto their own idea of beauty in nomenclature—hence Loretta, Imogene, Nadine, Natalie, Ardella), "Loretta, I have watched you for a long, long time and you must have noticed how deeply I admire you."

It wasn't impossible. Those things happen. The movies had taught them that.

Dirk, all unconscious of their pitiless, all-absorbing scrutiny, would have been still further appalled to learn how fully aware they were of his personal and private affairs. They knew about Paula, for example. They admired and resented her, too. They were fair in granting her the perfection of her clothes, drew immense satisfaction from the knowledge of their own superiority in the matters of youth and colouring; despised her for the way in which she openly displayed her feeling for him (how they knew this was a miracle and a mystery, for she almost never came into the office and disguised all her telephone talks with him). They thought he was grand to his mother. Selina had been in his office twice, perhaps. On one of these occasions she had spent five minutes chatting sociably with Ethelinda Quinn who had the face of a Da Vinci cherub and the soul of a man-eating shark. Selina always talked to everyone. She enjoyed listening to street car conductors, washwomen, janitors, landladies, clerks, doormen, chauffeurs, policemen. Something about her made them talk. They opened to her as flowers to the sun. They sensed her interest, her liking. As they talked Selina would exclaim, "You don't say! Well, that's terrible!" Her eyes would be bright with sympathy.

Selina had said, on entering Dirk's office, "My land! I don't see how you can work among those pretty creatures and not be a sultan. I'm going to ask some of them down to the farm over Sunday."

"Don't, Mother! They wouldn't understand. I scarcely see them. They're just part of the office equipment."

Afterward, Ethelinda Quinn had passed expert opinion. "Say, she's got ten times the guts that Frosty's got. I like her fine. Did you see her terrible hat! But say, it didn't look funny on her, did it? Anybody else in that getup would look comical, but she's the kind that could walk off with anything. I don't know. She's got what I call an air. It beats style. Nice, too. She said I was a pretty little thing. Can you beat it! At that she's right. I cer'nly yam."

All unconscious, "Take a letter, Miss Quinn," said Dirk half an hour later.

In the midst, then, of this fiery furnace of femininity Dirk walked unscorched. Paula, the North Shore girls, well-bred business and professional women he occasionally met in the course of business, the enticing little nymphs he encountered in his own office, all practised on him their warm and perfumed wiles. He moved among them cool and serene. Perhaps his sudden success had had something to do with this; and his quiet ambition for further success. For he really was accounted successful now, even in the spectacular whirl of Chicago's meteoric financial constellation. North-side mammas regarded his income, his career, and his future with eyes of respect and wily speculation. There was always a neat little pile of invitations in the mail that lay on the correct little console in the correct little apartment ministered by the correct little Jap on the correct north-side street near (but not too near) the lake, and overlooking it.

The apartment had been furnished with Paula's aid. Together she and Dirk had gone to interior decorators. "But you've got to use your own taste, too," Paula had said, "to give it the individual touch." The apartment was furnished in a good deal of Italian furniture, the finish a dark oak or walnut, the whole massive and yet somehow unconvincing. The effect was sombre without being impressive. There were long carved tables on which an ash tray seemed a desecration; great chairs roomy enough for lolling, yet in which you did not relax; dull silver candlesticks; vestments; Dante's saturnine features sneering down upon you from a correct cabinet. There were not many books. Tiny foyer, large living room, bedroom, dining room, kitchen, and a cubby-hole for the Jap. Dirk did not spend much time in the place. Sometimes he did not sit in a chair in the sitting room for days at a time, using the room only as a short cut in his rush for the bedroom to change from office to dinner clothes. His upward climb was a treadmill, really. His office, the apartment, a dinner, a dance. His contacts were monotonous, and too few. His office was a great splendid office in a great splendid office building in LaSalle Street. He drove back and forth in a motor car along the boulevards. His social engagements lay north. LaSalle Street bounded him on the west, Lake Michigan on the east, Jackson Boulevard on the south, Lake Forest on the north. He might have lived a thousand miles away for all he knew of the rest of Chicago—the mighty, roaring, sweltering, pushing, screaming, magnificent hideous steel giant that was Chicago.

Selina had had no hand in the furnishing of his apartment. When it was finished Dirk had brought her in triumph to see it. "Well," he had said, "what do you think of it, Mother?"

She had stood in the centre of the room, a small plain figure in the midst of these massive sombre carved tables, chairs, chests. A little smile had quirked the corner of her mouth. "I think it's as cosy as a cathedral."

Sometimes Selina remonstrated with him, though of late she had taken on a strange reticence. She no longer asked him about the furnishings of the houses he visited (Italian villas on Ohio Street), or the exotic food he ate at splendid dinners. The farm flourished. The great steel mills and factories to the south were closing in upon her but had not yet set iron foot on her rich green acres. She was rather famous now for the quality of her farm products and her pens. You saw "DeJong asparagus" on the menu at the Blackstone and the Drake hotels. Sometimes Dirk's friends twitted him about this and he did not always acknowledge that the similarity of names was not a coincidence.

"Dirk, you seem to see no one but just these people," Selina told him in one of her infrequent rebukes. "You don't get the full flavour of life. You've got to have a vulgar curiosity about people and things. All kinds of people. All kinds of things. You revolve in the same little circle, over and over and over."

"Haven't time. Can't afford to take the time."

"You can't afford not to."

Sometimes Selina came into town for a week or ten days at a stretch, and indulged in what she called an orgy. At such times Julie Arnold would invite her to occupy one of the guest rooms at the Arnold house, or Dirk would offer her his bedroom and tell her that he would be comfortable on the big couch in the living room, or that he would take a room at the University Club. She always declined. She would take a room in a hotel, sometimes north, sometimes south. Her holiday before her she would go off roaming gaily as a small boy on a Saturday morning, with the day stretching gorgeously and adventuresomely ahead of him, sallies down the street without plan or appointment, knowing that richness in one form or another lies before him for the choosing. She loved the Michigan Boulevard and State Street shop windows in which haughty waxed ladies in glittering evening gowns postured, fingers elegantly crooked as they held a fan, a rose, a programme, meanwhile smiling condescendingly out upon an envious world flattening its nose against the plate glass barrier. A sociable woman, Selina, savouring life, she liked the lights, the colour, the rush, the noise. Her years of grinding work, with her face pressed down to the very soil itself, had failed to kill her zest for living. She prowled into the city's foreign quarters—Italian, Greek, Chinese, Jewish. She penetrated the Black Belt, where Chicago's vast and growing Negro population shifted and moved and stretched its great limbs ominously, reaching out and out in protest and overflowing the bounds that irked it. Her serene face and her quiet manner, her bland interest and friendly look protected her. They thought her a social worker, perhaps; one of the uplifters. She bought and read the *Independent,* the Negro newspaper in which herb doctors advertised magic roots. She even sent the twenty-five cents required for a box of these, charmed by their names——Adam and Eve roots, Master of the Woods, Dragon's Blood, High John the Conqueror, Jezebel Roots, Grains of Paradise.

"Look here, Mother," Dirk would protest, "you can't wander around like that. It isn't safe. This isn't High Prairie, you know. If you want to go round I'll get Saki to drive you."

"That would be nice," she said, mildly. But she never availed herself of this offer. Sometimes she went over to South Water Street, changed now, and swollen to such proportions that it threatened to burst its confines. She liked to stroll along the crowded sidewalks, lined with crates and boxes and barrels of fruits, vegetables, poultry. Swarthy foreign faces predominated now. Where the red-faced overalled men had been she now saw lean muscular lads in old army shirts and khaki pants and scuffed puttees wheeling trucks, loading boxes, charging down the street in huge rumbling auto vans. Their faces were hard, their talk terse. They moved gracefully, with an economy of gesture. Any one of these, she reflected, was more vital, more native, functioned more usefully and honestly than her successful son, Dirk DeJong.

"Where 'r' beans?"

"In th' ol' beanery."

"Tough."

"Best you can get."

"Keep 'em."

Many of the older men knew her, shook hands with her, chatted a moment friendlily. William Talcott, a little more dried up, more wrinkled, his sparse hair quite gray now, still leaned up against the side of his doorway in his shirt sleeves and his neat pepper-and-salt pants and vest, a pretty good cigar, unlighted, in his mouth, the heavy gold watch chain spanning his middle.

"Well, you certainly made good, Mrs. DeJong. Remember the day you come here with your first load?"

Oh, yes. She remembered.

"That boy of yours has made his mark, too, I see. Doing grand, ain't he? Wa-al, great satisfaction having a son turn out well like that. Yes, sirree! Why, look at my da'ter Car'line——"

Life at High Prairie had its savour, too. Frequently you saw strange visitors there for a week or ten days at a time—boys and girls whose city pallor gave way to a rich tan; tired-looking women with sagging figures who drank Selina's cream and ate her abundant vegetables and tender chickens as though they expected these viands to be momentarily snatched from them. Selina picked these up in odd corners of the city. Dirk protested against this, too. Selina was a member of the High Prairie school board now. She often drove about the roads and into town in a disreputable Ford which she manipulated with imagination and skill. She was on the Good Roads Committee and the Truck Farmers' Association valued her opinion. Her life was full, pleasant, prolific.

18

Paula had a scheme for interesting women in bond buying. It was a good scheme. She suggested it so that Dirk thought he had thought of it. Dirk was head now of the bond department in the Great Lakes Trust Company's magnificent new white building on Michigan Boulevard north. Its white towers gleamed pink in the lake mists. Dirk said it was a terrible building, badly proportioned, and that it looked like a vast vanilla sundae. His new private domain was more like a splendid bookless library than a business office. It was finished in rich dull walnut and there were great upholstered chairs, soft rugs, shaded lights. Special attention was paid to women clients. There was a room for their convenience fitted with low restful chairs and couches, lamps, writing desks, in mauve and rose. Paula had selected the furnishings for this room. Ten years earlier it would have been considered absurd in a suite of business offices. Now it was a routine part of the equipment.

Dirk's private office was almost as difficult of access as that of the nation's executive. Cards, telephones, office boys, secretaries stood between the caller and Dirk DeJong, head of the bond department. You asked for him, uttering his name in the ear of the six-foot statuesque detective who, in the guise of usher, stood in the centre of the marble rotunda eyeing each visitor with a coldly appraising gaze. This one padded softly ahead of you on rubber heels, only to give you over to the care of a glorified office boy who took your name. You waited. He returned. You waited. Presently there appeared a young woman with inquiring eyebrows. She conversed with you. She vanished. You waited. She reappeared. You were ushered into Dirk DeJong's large and luxurious inner office. And there formality fled.

Dirk was glad to see you; quietly, interestly glad to see you. As you stated your business he listened attentively, as was his charming way. The volume of business done with women clients by the Great Lakes Trust Company was enormous. Dirk was conservative, helpful—and he always got the business. He talked little. He was amazingly effective. Ladies in the modish black of recent bereavement made quite a sombre procession to his door. His suggestions (often originating with Paula) made the Great Lakes Trust Company's discreet advertising rich in results. Neat little pamphlets written for women on the subjects of saving, investments. "You are not dealing with a soulless corporation," said these brochures. "May we serve you? You need more than friends. Before acting, you should have your judgment vindicated by an organization of investment specialists. You may have relatives and friends, some of whom would gladly advise you on investments. But perhaps you rightly feel that the less they know about your financial affairs, the better. To handle trusts, and to care for the securities of widows and orphans, is our business."

It was startling to note how this sort of thing mounted into millions. "Women are becoming more and more used to the handling of money," Paula said, shrewdly. "Pretty soon their patronage is going to be as valuable as that of men. The average woman doesn't know about bonds—about bond buying. They think they're something mysterious and risky. They ought to be educated up to it. Didn't you say something, Dirk, about classes in finance for women? You could make a sort of semi-social affair of it. Send out invitations and get various bankers—big men, whose names are known—to talk to these women."

"But would the women come?"

"Of course they'd come. Women will accept any invitation that's engraved on heavy cream paper."

The Great Lakes Trust had a branch in Cleveland now, and one in New York, on Fifth Avenue. The drive to interest women in bond buying and to instruct them in finance was to take on almost national proportions. There was to be newspaper and magazine advertising.

The Talks for Women on the Subject of Finance were held every two weeks in the crystal room of the Blackstone and were a great success. Paula was right. Much of old Aug Hempel's shrewdness and business foresight had descended to her. The women came—widows with money to invest; business women who had thriftily saved a portion of their salaries; moneyed women who wanted to manage their own property, or who resented a husband's interference. Some came out of curiosity. Others for lack of anything better to do. Others to gaze on the well-known banker or lawyer or business man who was scheduled to address the meeting. Dirk spoke three or four times during the winter and was markedly a favourite. The women, in smart crêpe gowns and tailored suits and small chic hats, twittered and murmured about him, even while they sensibly digested his well-thought-out remarks. He looked very handsome, clean-cut, and distinguished there on the platform in his admirably tailored clothes, a small white flower in his buttonhole. He talked easily, clearly, fluently; answered the questions put to him afterward with just the right mixture of thoughtful hesitation and confidence.

It was decided that for the national advertising there must be an illustration that would catch the eye of women, and interest them. The person to do it, Dirk thought, was this Dallas O'Mara whose queer hentrack signature you saw scrawled on half the advertising illustrations that caught your eye. Paula had not been enthusiastic about this idea.

"M-m-m, she's very good," Paula had said, guardedly, "but aren't there others who are better?"

"She!" Dirk had exclaimed. "Is it a woman? I didn't know. That name might be anything."

"Oh, yes, she's a woman. She's said to be very—very attractive."

Dirk sent for Dallas O'Mara. She replied, suggesting an appointment two weeks from that date. Dirk decided not to wait, consulted other commercial artists, looked at their work, heard their plans outlined, and was satisfied with none of them. The time was short. Ten days had passed. He had his secretary call Dallas O'Mara on the telephone. Could she come down to see him that day at eleven?

No: she worked until four daily at her studio.

Could she come to his office at four-thirty, then?

Yes, but wouldn't it be better if he could come to her studio where he could see something of the various types of drawings—oils, or black-and-white, or crayons. She was working mostly in crayons now.

All this relayed by his secretary at the telephone to Dirk at his desk. He jammed his cigarette-end viciously into a tray, blew a final infuriated wraith of smoke, and picked up the telephone connection on his own desk. "One of those damned temperamental near-artists trying to be grand," he muttered, his hand over the mouthpiece. "Here, Miss Rawlings——I'll talk to her. Switch her over."

"Hello, Miss—uh—O'Mara. This is Mr. DeJong talking. I much prefer that you come to my office and talk to me." (No more of this nonsense.)

Her voice: "Certainly, if you prefer it. I thought the other would save us both some time. I'll be there at four-thirty." Her voice was leisurely, low, rounded. An admirable voice. Restful.

"Very well. Four-thirty," said Dirk, crisply. Jerked the receiver into the hook. That was the way to handle 'em. These females of forty with straggling hair and a bundle of drawings under their arm.

The female of forty with straggling hair and a bundle of drawings under her arm was announced at four-thirty to the dot. Dirk let her wait five minutes in the outer office, being still a little annoyed. At four-thirty-five there entered his private office a tall slim girl in a smart little broadtail jacket, fur-trimmed skirt, and a black hat at once so daring and so simple that even a man must recognize its French nativity. She carried no portfolio of drawings under her arms.

Through the man's mind flashed a series of unbusinesslike thoughts such as: "Gosh! . . . Eyes! . . . That's the way I like to see a girl dress . . . Tired looking . . . No, guess it's her eyes—sort of fatigued. . . . Pretty . . . No, she isn't . . . yes, she . . ." Aloud he said, "This is very kind of you, Miss O'Mara." Then he thought that sounded pompous and said, curtly. "Sit down."

Miss O'Mara sat down. Miss O'Mara looked at him with her tired deep blue eyes. Miss O'Mara said nothing. She regarded him pleasantly, quietly, composedly. He waited for her to say that usually she did not come to business offices; that she had only twenty minutes to give him; that the day was warm, or cold; his office handsome; the view over the river magnificent. Miss O'Mara said nothing, pleasantly. So Dirk began to talk, rather hurriedly.

Now, this was a new experience for Dirk DeJong. Usually women spoke to him first and fluently. Quiet women waxed voluble under his silence; voluble women chattered. Paula always spoke a hundred words to his one. But here was a woman more silent than he; not sullenly silent, nor heavily silent, but quietly, composedly, restfully silent.

"I'll tell you the sort of thing we want, Miss O'Mara." He told her. When he had finished she probably would burst out with three or four plans. The others had done that.

When he had finished she said, "I'll think about it for a couple of days while I'm working on something else. I always do. I'm doing an olive soap picture now. I can begin work on yours Wednesday."

"But I'd like to see it—that is, I'd like to have an idea of what you're planning to do with it." Did she think he was going to let her go ahead without consulting his judgment!

"Oh, it will be all right. But drop into the studio if you like. It will take me about a week, I suppose. I'm over on Ontario in that old studio building. You'll know it by the way most of the bricks have fallen out of the building and are scattered over the sidewalk." She smiled a slow wide smile. Her teeth were good but her mouth was too big, he thought. Nice big warm kind of smile, though. He found himself smiling, too, sociably. Then he became businesslike again. Very businesslike.

"How much do you—what is your—what would you expect to get for a drawing such as that?"

"Fifteen hundred dollars," said Miss O'Mara.

"Nonsense." He looked at her then. Perhaps that had been humour. But she was not smiling. "You mean fifteen hundred for a single drawing?"

"For that sort of thing, yes."

"I'm afraid we can't pay that, Miss O'Mara."

Miss O'Mara stood up. "That is my price." She was not at all embarrassed. He realized that he had never seen such effortless composure. It was he who was fumbling with the objects on his flat-topped desk—a pen, a sheet of paper, a blotter. "Good-bye, Mr.— DeJong." She held out a friendly hand. He took it. Her hair was gold—dull gold, not bright—and coiled in a single great knot at the back of her head, low. He took her hand. The tired eyes looked up at him.

"Well, if that's your price, Miss O'Mara. I wasn't prepared to pay any such—but of course I suppose you top-notchers do get crazy prices for your work."

"Not any crazier than the prices you top-notchers get."

"Still, fifteen hundred dollars is quite a lot of money."

"I think so, too. But then, I'll always think anything over nine dollars is quite a lot of money. You see, I used to get twenty-five cents apiece for sketching hats for Gage's."

She was undeniably attractive. "And now you've arrived. You're successful."

"Arrived! Heavens, no! I've started."

"Who gets more money than you do for a drawing?"

"Nobody, I suppose."

"Well, then?"

"Well, then, in another minute I'll be telling you the story of my life." She smiled again her slow wide smile; turned to leave. Dirk decided that while most women's mouths were merely features this girl's was a decoration.

She was gone. Miss Ethelinda Quinn *et al.*, in the outer office, appraised the costume of Miss Dallas O'Mara from her made-to-order foot-gear to her made-in-France millinery and achieved a lightning mental reconstruction of their own costumes. Dirk DeJong in the inner office realized that he had ordered a fifteen-hundred-dollar drawing, sight unseen, and that Paula was going to ask questions about it.

"Make a note, Miss Rawlings, to call Miss O'Mara's studio on Thursday."

In the next few days he learned that a surprising lot of people knew a surprisingly good deal about this Dallas O'Mara. She hailed from Texas, hence the absurd name. She was twenty-eight—twenty-five—thirty-two—thirty-six. She was beautiful. She was ugly. She was an orphan. She had worked her way through art school. She had no sense of the value of money. Two years ago she had achieved sudden success with her drawings. Her ambition was to work in oils. She toiled like a galley-slave; played like a child; had twenty beaux and no lover; her friends, men and women, were legion and wandered in and out of her studio as though it were a public thoroughfare. You were likely to find there at any hour any one from Bert Colson, the black-face musical comedy star, to Mrs. Robinson Gilman of Lake Forest and Paris; from Leo Mahler, first violin with the Chicago Symphony Orchestra, to Fanny Whipple who designed dresses for Carson's. She supported an assortment of unlucky brothers and spineless sisters in Texas and points west.

Miss Rawlings made an appointment for Thursday at three. Paula said she'd go with him and went. She dressed for Dallas O'Mara and the result was undeniably enchanting. Dallas sometimes did a crayon portrait, or even attempted one in oils. Had got a prize for her portrait of Mrs. Robinson Gilman at last spring's portrait exhibit at the Chicago Art Institute. It was considered something of an achievement to be asked to pose for her. Paula's hat had been chosen in deference to her hair and profile, and the neck line of her gown in deference to hat, hair, and profile, and her pearls with an eye to all four. The whole defied competition on the part of Miss Dallas O'Mara.

Miss Dallas O'Mara, in her studio, was perched on a high stool before an easel with a large tray of assorted crayons at her side. She looked a sight and didn't care at all. She greeted Dirk and Paula with a cheerful friendliness and went right on working. A model, very smartly gowned, was sitting for her.

"Hello!" said Dallas O'Mara. "This is it. Do you think you're going to like it?"

"Oh," said Dirk. "Is that it?" It was merely the beginning of a drawing of the smartly gowned model. "Oh, that's it, is it?" Fifteen hundred dollars!

"I hope you didn't think it was going to be a picture of a woman buying bonds." She went on working. She squinted one eye, picked up a funny little mirror thing which she held to one side, looked into, and put down. She made a black mark on the board with a piece of crayon then smeared the mark with her thumb. She had on a faded all-enveloping smock over which French ink, rubber cement, pencil marks, crayon dust and wash were so impartially distributed that the whole blended and mixed in a rich mellow haze like the Chicago atmosphere itself. The collar of a white silk blouse, not especially clean, showed above this. On her feet were soft kid bedroom slippers, scuffed, with pompons on them. Her dull gold hair was carelessly rolled into that great loose knot at the back. Across one cheek was a swipe of black.

"Well," thought Dirk, "she looks a sight."

Dallas O'Mara waved a friendly hand toward some chairs on which were piled hats, odd garments, bristol board and (on the broad arm of one) a piece of yellow cake. "Sit down." She called to the girl who had opened the door to them: "Gilda, will you dump some of those things. This is Mrs. Storm, Mr. DeJong—Gilda Hanan." Her secretary, Dirk later learned.

The place was disorderly, comfortable, shabby. A battered grand piano stood in one corner. A great skylight formed half the ceiling and sloped down at the north end of the room. A man and a girl sat talking earnestly on the couch in another corner. A swarthy foreign-looking chap, vaguely familiar to Dirk, was playing softly at the piano. The telephone rang. Miss Hanan took the message, transmitted it to Dallas O'Mara, received the answer, repeated it. Perched atop the stool, one slippered foot screwed in a rung, Dallas worked on concentratedly, calmly, earnestly. A lock of hair straggled over her eyes. She pushed it back with her wrist and left another dark splotch on her forehead. There was something splendid, something impressive, something magnificent about her absorption, her indifference to appearance, her unawareness of outsiders, her concentration on the work before her. Her nose was shiny. Dirk hadn't seen a girl with a shiny nose in years. They were always taking out those little boxes and things and plastering themselves with the stuff in 'em.

"How can you work with all this crowd around?"

"Oh," said Dallas in that deep restful leisurely voice of hers, "there are always between twenty and thirty"—she slapped a quick scarlet line on the board, rubbed it out at once—"thousand people in and out of here every hour, just about. I like it. Friends around me while I'm slaving."

"Gosh!" he thought, "she's——I don't know—she's——"

"Shall we go?" said Paula.

He had forgotten all about her. "Yes. Yes, I'm ready if you are."

Outside, "Do you think you're going to like the picture?" Paula asked. They stepped into her car.

"Oh, I don't know. Can't tell much about it at this stage, I suppose."

"Back to your office?"

"Sure."

"Attractive, isn't she?"

"Think so?"

So he was going to be on his guard, was he! Paula threw in the clutch viciously, jerked the lever into second speed. "Her neck was dirty."

"Crayon dust," said Dirk.

"Not necessarily," replied Paula.

Dirk turned sideways to look at her. It was as though he saw her for the first time. She looked brittle, hard, artificial—small, somehow. Not in physique but in personality.

The picture was finished and delivered within ten days. In that time Dirk went twice to the studio in Ontario Street. Dallas did not seem to mind. Neither did she appear particularly interested. She was working hard both times. Once she looked as he had seen her on her first visit. The second time she had on a fresh crisp smock of faded yellow that was glorious with her hair; and high-heeled beige kid slippers, very smart. She was like a little girl who had just been freshly scrubbed and dressed in a clean pinafore, Dirk thought.

He thought a good deal about Dallas O'Mara. He found himself talking about her in what he assumed to be a careless offhand manner. He liked to talk about her. He told his mother of her. He could let himself go with Selina and he must have taken advantage of this for she looked at him intently and said: "I'd like to meet her. I've never met a girl like that."

"I'll ask her if she'll let me bring you up to the studio some time when you're in town."

It was practically impossible to get a minute with her alone. That irritated him. People were always drifting in and out of the studio— queer, important, startling people; little, dejected, shabby people. An impecunious girl art student, red-haired and wistful, that Dallas was taking in until the girl got some money from home; a pearl-hung grand-opera singer who was condescending to the Chicago Opera for a fortnight. He did not know that Dallas played until he came upon her late one afternoon sitting at the piano in the twilight with Bert Colson, the blackface comedian. Colson sang those terrible songs about April showers bringing violets, and about mah Ma-ha-ha-ha-ha-ha-ha-my but they didn't seem terrible when he sang them. There was about this lean, hollow-chested, sombre-eyed comedian a poignant pathos, a gorgeous sense of rhythm—a something unnameable that bound you to him, made you love him. In the theatre he came out to the edge of the runway and took the audience in his arms. He talked like a bootblack and sang like an angel. Dallas at the piano, he leaning over it, were doing "blues." The two were rapt, ecstatic. I got the blues—I said the blues—I got the this or that—the somethingorother—blue—hoo-hoos. They scarcely noticed Dirk. Dallas had nodded when he came in, and had gone on playing. Colson sang the cheaply sentimental ballad as though it were the folksong of a tragic race. His arms were extended, his face rapt. As Dallas played the tears stood in her eyes. When they had finished, "Isn't it a terrible song?" she said. "I'm crazy about it. Bert's going to try it out to-night."

"Who—uh—wrote it?" asked Dirk politely.

Dallas began to play again. 'H'm? Oh, I did." They were off once more. They paid no more attention to Dirk. Yet there was nothing rude about their indifference. They simply were more interested in what they were doing. He left telling himself he wouldn't go there again. Hanging around a studio. But next day he was back.

"Look here, Miss O'Mara," he had got her alone for a second. "Look here, will you come out to dinner with me some time? And the theatre?"

"Love to."

"When?" He was actually trembling.

"To-night." He had an important engagement. He cast it out of his life.

"To-night! That's grand. Where do you want to dine? The Casino?" The smartest club in Chicago; a little pink stucco Italian box of a place on the Lake Shore Drive. He was rather proud of being in a position to take her there as his guest.

"Oh, no, I hate those arty little places. I like dining in a hotel full of all sorts of people. Dining in a club means you're surrounded by people who're pretty much alike. Their membership in the club means they're there because they are all interested in golf, or because they're university graduates, or belong to the same political party or write, or paint, or have incomes of over fifty thousand a year, or something. I like 'em mixed up, higgledy-piggledy. A dining room full of gamblers, and insurance agents, and actors, and merchants, thieves, bootleggers, lawyers, kept ladies, wives, flaps, travelling men, millionaires—everything. That's what I call dining out. Unless one is dining at a friend's house, of course." A rarely long speech for her.

"Perhaps," eagerly, "you'll dine at my little apartment some time. Just four or six of us, or even——"

"Perhaps."

"Would you like the Drake to-night?"

"It looks too much like a Roman bath. The pillars scare me. Let's go to the Blackstone. I'll always be sufficiently from Texas to think the Blackstone French room the last word in elegance."

They went to the Blackstone. The head waiter knew him. "Good evening, Mr. DeJong." Dirk was secretly gratified. Then, with a shock, he realized that the head waiter was grinning at Dallas and Dallas was grinning at the head waiter. "Hello, André," said Dallas.

"Good evening, Miss O'Mara." The text of his greeting was correct and befitting the head waiter of the French room at the Blackstone. But his voice was lyric and his eyes glowed. His manner of seating her at a table was an enthronement.

At the look in Dirk's eyes, "I met him in the army," Dallas explained, "when I was in France. He's a grand lad."

"Were you in—what did you do in France?"

"Oh, odd jobs."

Her dinner gown was very smart, but the pink ribbon strap of an under-garment showed untidily at one side. Her silk brassiere, probably. Paula would have—but then, a thing like that was impossible in Paula's perfection of toilette. He loved the way the gown cut sharply away at the shoulder to show her firm white arms. It was dull gold, the colour of her hair. This was one Dallas. There were a dozen—a hundred. Yet she was always the same. You never knew whether you were going to meet the gamin of the rumpled smock and the smudged face or the beauty of the little fur jacket. Sometimes Dirk thought she looked like a Swede hired girl with those high cheek bones of hers and her deep-set eyes and her large capable hands. Sometimes he thought she looked like the splendid goddesses you saw in paintings— the kind with high pointed breasts and gracious gentle pose—holding out a horn of plenty. There was about her something genuine and earthy and elemental. He noticed that her nails were short and not well cared for—not glittering and pointed and cruelly sharp and horridly vermilion, like Paula's. That pleased him, too, somehow.

"Some oysters?" he suggested. "They're perfectly safe here. Or fruit coctail? Then breast of guinea hen under glass and an artichoke——"

She looked a little worried. "If you—suppose you take that. Me, I'd like a steak and some potatoes au gratin and a salad with Russian——"

"That's fine!" He was delighted. He doubled that order and they consumed it with devastating thoroughness. She ate rolls. She ate butter. She made no remarks about the food except to say, once, that it was good and that she had forgotten to eat lunch because she had been so busy working. All this Dirk found most restful and refreshing. Usually, when you dined in a restaurant with a woman she said, "Oh, I'd love to eat one of those crisp little rolls!"

You said, "Why not?"

Invariably the answer to this was, "I daren't! Goodness! A half pound at least. I haven't eaten a roll with butter in a year."

Again you said, "Why not?"

"Afraid I'll get fat."

Automatically, "You! Nonsense. You're just right."

He was bored with these women who talked about their weight, figure, lines. He thought it in bad taste. Paula was always rigidly refraining from this or that. It made him uncomfortable to sit at the table facing her; eating his thorough meal while she nibbled fragile curls of Melba toast, a lettuce leaf, and half a sugarless grapefruit. It lessened his enjoyment of his own oysters, steak, coffee. He thought that she always eyed his food a little avidly, for all her expressed indifference to it. She was looking a little haggard, too.

"The theatre's next door," he said. "Just a step. We don't have to leave here until after eight."

"That's nice." She had her cigarette with her coffee in a mellow sensuous atmosphere of enjoyment. He was talking about himself a good deal. He felt relaxed, at ease, happy.

"You know I'm an architect—at least, I was one. Perhaps that's why I like to hang around your shop so. I get sort of homesick for the pencils and the drawing board—the whole thing."

"Why did you give it up, then?"

"Nothing in it."

"How do you mean—nothing in it?"

"No money. After the war nobody was building. Oh, I suppose if I'd hung on——"

"And then you became a banker, h'm? Well, there ought to be money enough in a bank."

He was a little nettled. "I wasn't a banker—at first. I was a bond salesman."

Her brows met in a little frown. Her eyebrows were thick and strongly marked and a little uneven and inclined to meet over her nose. Paula's brows were a mere line of black—a carefully traced half-parenthesis above her unmysterious dark eyes. "I'd rather," Dallas said, slowly, "plan one back door of a building that's going to help make this town beautiful and significant than sell all the bonds that ever floated a—whatever it is that bonds are supposed to float."

He defended himself. "I felt that way, too. But you see my mother had given me my education, really. She worked for it. I couldn't go dubbing along, earning just enough to keep me. I wanted to give her things. I wanted——"

"Did she want those things? Did she want you to give up architecture and go into bonds?"

"Well—she—I don't know that she exactly——" He was too decent—still too much the son of Selina DeJong—to be able to lie about that."

"You said you were going to let me meet her."

"Would you let me bring her in? Or perhaps you'd even—would you drive out to the farm with me some day? She'd like that so much."

"So would I."

He leaned toward her, suddenly. "Listen, Dallas. What do you think of me, anyway?" He wanted to know. He couldn't stand not knowing any longer.

"I think you're a nice young man."

That was terrible. "But I don't want you to think I'm a nice young man. I want you to like me—a lot. Tell me, what haven't I got that you think I ought to have? Why do you put me off so many times? I never feel that I'm really near you. What is it I lack?" He was abject.

"Well, if you're asking for it. I do demand of the people I see often that they possess at least a splash of splendour in their makeup. Some people are nine tenths splendour and one tenth tawdriness, like Gene Meran. And some are nine tenths tawdriness and one tenth splendour, like Sam Huebch. But some people are all just a nice even pink without a single patch of royal purple."

"And that's me, h'm?"

He was horribly disappointed, hurt, wretched. But a little angry, too. His pride. Why, he was Dirk DeJong, the most successful of Chicago's younger men; the most promising; the most popular. After all, what did she do but paint commercial pictures for fifteen hundred dollars apiece?"

"What happens to the men who fall in love with you? What do they do?"

Dallas stirred her coffee thoughtfully. "They usually tell me about it."

"And then what?"

"Then they seem to feel better and we become great friends."

"But don't you ever fall in love with them?" Pretty damned sure of herself. "Don't you ever fall in love with them?"

"I almost always do," said Dallas.

He plunged. "I could give you a lot of things you haven't got, purple or no purple."

"I'm going to France in April. Paris."

"What d'you mean! Paris. What for?"

"Study. I want to do portraits. Oils."

He was terrified. "Can't you do them here?"

"Oh, no. Not what I need. I have been studying here. I've been taking life-work three nights a week at the Art Institute, just to keep my hand in."

"So that's where you are, evenings." He was strangely relieved. "Let me go with you some time, will you?" Anything. Anything.

She took him with her one evening, steering him successfully past the stern Irishman who guarded the entrance to the basement classrooms; to her locker, got into her smock, grabbed her brushes. She rushed down the hall. "Don't talk," she cautioned him. "It bothers them. I wonder what they'd think of my shop." She turned into a small, cruelly bright, breathlessly hot little room, its walls whitewashed. Every inch of the floor space was covered with easels. Before them stood men and women, brushes in hand, intent. Dallas went directly to her place, fell to work at once. Dirk blinked in the strong light. He glanced at the dais toward which they were all gazing from time to time as they worked. On it lay a nude woman.

To himself Dirk said in a sort of panic: "Why, say, she hasn't got any clothes on! My gosh! this is fierce. She hasn't got anything on!" He tried, meanwhile, to look easy, careless, critical. Strangely enough, he succeeded, after the first shock, not only in looking at ease, but feeling so. The class was doing the whole figure in oils.

The model was a moron with a skin like velvet and rose petals. She fell into poses that flowed like cream. Her hair was waved in wooden undulations and her nose was pure vulgarity and her earrings were drugstore pearls in triple strands but her back was probably finer than Helen's and her breasts twin snowdrifts peaked with coral. In twenty minutes Dirk found himself impersonally interested in tone, shadows, colours, line. He listened to the low-voice instructor and squinted carefully to ascertain whether that shadow on the model's stomach really should be painted blue or brown. Even he could see that Dallas's canvas was almost insultingly superior to that of the men and women about her. Beneath the flesh on her canvas there were muscles and beneath those muscles blood and bone. You felt she had a surgeon's knowledge of anatomy. That, Dirk decided, was what made her commercial pictures so attractive. The drawing she had done for the Great Lakes Trust Company's bond department had been conventional enough in theme. The treatment, the technique, had made it arresting. He thought that if she ever did portraits in oils they would be vital and compelling portraits. But oh, he wished she didn't want to do portraits in oils. He wished——

It was after eleven when they emerged from the Art Institute doorway and stood a moment together at the top of the broad steps surveying the world that lay before them. Dallas said nothing. Suddenly the beauty of the night rushed up and overwhelmed Dirk. Gorgeousness and tawdriness; colour and gloom. At the right the white tower of the Wrigley building rose wraithlike against a background of purple sky. Just this side of it a swarm of impish electric lights grinned their message in scarlet and white. In white:

TRADE AT

then blackness, while you waited against your will. In red:

THE FAIR

Blackness again. Then, in a burst of both colours, in bigger letters, and in a blaze that hurled itself at your eyeballs momentarily shutting out tower, sky, and street:

SAVE MONEY

Straight ahead the hut of the Adams Street L station in midair was a Venetian bridge with the black canal of asphalt flowing sluggishly beneath. The reflection of cafeteria and cigar-shop windows on either side were slender shafts of light along the canal. An enchanting sight. Dirk thought suddenly that Dallas was a good deal like that—like Chicago. A mixture of grandeur and cheapness; of tawdriness and magnificence; of splendour and ugliness.

"Nice," said Dallas. A long breath. She was a part of all this.

"Yes." He felt an outsider. "Want a sandwich? Are you hungry?"

"I'm starved."

They had sandwiches and coffee at an all-night one-arm lunch room because Dallas said her face was too dirty for a restaurant and she didn't want to bother to wash it. She was more than ordinarily companionable that night; a little tired; less buoyant and independent than usual. This gave her a little air of helplessness—of fatigue—that aroused all his tenderness. Her smile gave him a warm rush of pure happiness—until he saw her smile in exactly the same way at the pimply young man who lorded it over the shining nickel coffee container, as she told him that his coffee was grand.

19

The things that had mattered so vitally didn't seem to be important, somehow, now. The people who had seemed so desirable had become suddenly insignificant. The games he had played appeared silly games. He was seeing things through Dallas O'Mara's wise, beauty-loving eyes. Strangely enough, he did not realize that this girl saw life from much the same angle as that at which his mother regarded it. In the last few years his mother had often offended him by her attitude toward these rich and powerful friends of his—their ways, their games, their amusements, their manners. And her way of living in turn offended them. On his rare visits to the farm it seemed to him there was always some drab dejected female in the kitchen or living room or on the porch—a woman with broken teeth and comic shoes and tragic eyes—drinking great draughts of coffee and telling her woes to Selina—Sairey Gampish ladies smelling unpleasantly of peppermint and perspiration and poverty. "And he ain't had a lick of work since November ——"

"You don't say! That's terrible!"

He wished she wouldn't.

Sometimes old Aug Hempel drove out there and Dirk would come upon the two snickering wickedly together about something that he knew concerned the North Shore crowd.

It had been years since Selina had said, sociably, "What did they have for dinner, Dirk? H'm?"

"Well—soup ——"

"Nothing before the soup?"

"Oh, yeh. Some kind of a—one of those canapé things, you know. Caviare."

"My! Caviare!"

Sometimes Selina giggled like a naughty girl at things that Dirk had taken quite seriously. The fox hunts, for example. Lake Forest had taken to fox hunting, and the Tippecanoe crowd kept kennels. Dirk had learned to ride—pretty well. An Englishman—a certain Captain Stokes-Beatty—had initiated the North Shore into the mysteries of fox hunting. Huntin'. The North Shore learned to say nec's'ry and conservat'ry. Captain Stokes-Beatty was a tall, bow-legged, and somewhat horse-faced young man, remote in manner. The nice Farnham girl seemed fated to marry him. Paula had had a hunt breakfast at Stormwood and it had been very successful, though the American men had balked a little at the devilled kidneys. The food had been patterned as far as possible after the pale flabby viands served at English hunt breakfasts and ruined in an atmosphere of lukewarm steam. The women were slim and perfectly tailored but wore their hunting clothes a trifle uneasily and self-consciously like girls in the first low-cut party dresses. Most of the men had turned stubborn on the subject of pink coats, but Captain Stokes-Beatty wore his handsomely. The fox—a worried and somewhat dejected-looking animal—had been shipped in a crate from the south and on being released had a way of sitting sociably in an Illinois corn field instead of leaping fleetly to cover. At the finish you had a feeling of guilt, as though you had killed a cockroach.

Dirk had told Selina about it, feeling rather magnificent. A fox hunt.

"A fox hunt! What for?"

"For! Why, what's any fox hunt for?"

"I can't imagine. They used to be for the purpose of ridding a fox-infested country of a nuisance. Have the foxes been bothering 'em out in Lake Forest?"

"Now, Mother, don't be funny." He told her about the breakfast.

"Well, but it's so silly, Dirk. It's smart to copy from another country the things that that country does better than we do. England does gardens and wood-fires and dogs and tweeds and walking shoes and pipes and leisure better than we do. But those luke-warm steamy breakfasts of theirs! It's because they haven't gas, most of them. No Kansas or Nebraska farmer's wife would stand for one of their kitchens—not for a minute. And the hired man would balk at such bacon." She giggled.

"Oh, well, if you're going to talk like that."

But Dallas O'Mara felt much the same about these things. Dallas, it appeared, had been something of a fad with the North Shore society crowd after she had painted Mrs. Robinson Gilman's portrait. She had been invited to dinners and luncheons and dances, but their doings, she told Dirk, had bored her.

"They're nice," she said, "but they don't have much fun. They're all trying to be something they're not. And that's such hard work. The women were always explaining that they lived in Chicago because their husband's business was here. They all do things pretty well—dance or paint or ride or write or sing—but not well enough. They're professional amateurs, trying to express something they don't feel; or that they don't feel strongly enough to make it worth while expressing."

She admitted, though, that they did appreciate the things that other people did well. Visiting and acknowledged writers, painters, lecturers, heroes, they entertained lavishly and hospitably in their Florentine or English or Spanish or French palaces on the north side of Chicago, Illinois. Especially foreign notables of this description. Since 1918 these had descended upon Chicago (and all America) like a plague of locusts, starting usually in New York and sweeping westward, devouring the pleasant verdure of greenbacks and chirping as they came. Returning to Europe, bursting with profits and spleen, they thriftily wrote of what they had seen and the result was more clever than amiable; bearing, too, the taint of bad taste.

North Shore hostesses vied for the honour of entertaining these notables. Paula—pretty, clever, moneyed, shrewd—often emerged from these contests the winner. Her latest catch was Emile Goguet— General Emile Goguet, hero of Champagne—Goguet of the stiff white beard, the empty left coat-sleeve, and the score of medals. He was coming to America ostensibly to be the guest of the American Division which, with Goguet's French troops, had turned the German onslaught at Champagne, but really, it was whispered, to cement friendly relations between his country and a somewhat diffident United States.

"And guess," trilled Paula, "guess who's coming with him, Dirk! That wonderful Roelf Pool, the French sculptor! Goguet's going to be my guest. Pool's going to do a bust, you know, of young Quentin Roosevelt from a photograph that Mrs. Theodore Roosevelt ——"

"What d'you mean—French sculptor! He's no more French than I am. He was born within a couple of miles of my mother's farm. His people were Dutch truck farmers. His father lived in High Prairie until a year ago, when he died of a stroke."

When he told Selina she flushed like a girl, as she sometimes still did when she was much excited. "Yes, I saw it in the paper. I wonder," she added, quietly "if I shall see him."

That evening you might have seen her sitting, cross-legged, before the old carved chest, fingering the faded shabby time-worn objects the saving of which Dirk had denounced as sentimental. The crude drawing of the Haymarket; the wine-red cashmere dress; some faded brittle flowers.

Paula was giving a large—but not too large—dinner on the second night. She was very animated about it, excited, gay. "They say," she told Dirk, "that Goguet doesn't eat anything but hard-boiled eggs and rusks. Oh, well, the others won't object to squabs and mushrooms and things. And his hobby is his farm in Brittany. Pool's stunning—dark and sombre and very white teeth."

Paula was very gay these days. Too gay. It seemed to Dirk that her nervous energy was inexhaustible—and exhausting. Dirk refused to admit to himself how irked he was by the sallow heart-shaped exquisite face, the lean brown clutching fingers, the air of ownership. He had begun to dislike things about her as an unfaithful spouse is irritated by quite innocent mannerisms of his unconscious mate. She scuffed her heels a little when she walked, for example. It maddened him. She had a way of biting the rough skin around her carefully tended nails when she was nervous. "Don't *do* that!" he said.

Dallas never irritated him. She rested him, he told himself. He would arm himself against her, but one minute after meeting her he would sink gratefully and resistlessly into her quiet depths. Sometimes he thought all this was an assumed manner in her.

"This calm of your—this effortlessness," he said to her one day, "is a pose, isn't it?" Anything to get her notice.

"Partly," Dallas had replied, amiably. "It's a nice pose though, don't you think?"

What are you going to do with a girl like that!

Here was the woman who could hold him entirely, and who never held out a finger to hold him. He tore at the smooth wall of her indifference, though he only cut and bruised his own hands in doing it.

"Is it because I'm a successful business man that you don't like me?"

"But I do like you."

"That you don't find me attractive, then."

"But I think you're an awfully attractive man. Dangerous, that's wot."

"Oh, don't be the wide-eyed ingénue. You know damned well what I mean. You've got me and you don't want me. If I had been a successful architect instead of a successful business man would that have made any difference?" He was thinking of what his mother had said just a few years back, that night when they had talked at her bedside. "Is that it? He's got to be an artist, I suppose, to interest you."

"Good Lord, no! Some day I'll probably marry a horny-handed son of toil, and if I do it'll be the horny hands that will win me. If you want to know, I like 'em with their scars on them. There's something about a man who has fought for it—I don't know what it is—a look in his eye—the feel of his hand. He needn't have been successful—though he probably would be. I don't know. I'm not very good at this analysis stuff. I only know he—well, you haven't a mark on you. Not a mark. You quit being an architect, or whatever it was, because architecture was an uphill disheartening job at the time. I don't say that you should have kept on. For all I know you were a bum architect. But if you had kept on—if you had loved it enough to keep on—fighting, and struggling, and sticking it out—why, that fight would show in your face today—in your eyes and your jaw and your hands and in your way of standing and walking and sitting and talking. Listen. I'm not criticizing you. But you're all smooth. I like 'em bumpy. That sounds terrible. It isn't what I mean at all. It isn't ——"

"Oh, never mind," Dirk said, wearily. "I think I know what you mean." He sat looking down at his hands—his fine strong unscarred hands. Suddenly and unreasonably he thought of another pair of hands—his mother's—with the knuckles enlarged, the skin broken—expressive—her life written on them. Scars. She had them. "Listen, Dallas. If I thought—I'd go back to Hollis & Sprague's and begin all over again at forty a week if I thought you'd ——"

"Don't."

20

General Goguet and Roelf Pool had been in Chicago one night and part of a day. Dirk had not met them—was to meet them at Paula's dinner that evening. He was curious about Pool but not particularly interested in the warrior. Restless, unhappy, wanting to see Dallas (he admitted it, bitterly), he dropped into her studio at an unaccustomed hour almost immediately after lunch and heard gay voices and laughter. Why couldn't she work alone once in a while without that rabble around her!

Dallas in a grimy smock and the scuffed kid slippers was entertaining two truants from Chicago society—General Emile Goguet and Roelf Pool. They seemed to be enjoying themselves immensely. She introduced Dirk as casually as though their presence were a natural and expected thing—which it was. She had never mentioned them to him. Yet now: "This is Dirk DeJong—General Emile Goguet. We were campaigners together in France. Roelf Pool. So were we, weren't we, Roelf?"

General Emile Goguet bowed formally, but his eyes were twinkling. He appeared to be having a very good time. Roelf Pool's dark face had lighted up with such a glow of surprise and pleasure as to transform it. He strode over to Dirk, clasped his hand. "Dirk DeJong! Not—why, say, don't you know me? I'm Roelf Pool!"

"I ought to know you," said Dirk.

"Oh, but I mean I'm—I knew you when you were a kid. You're

Selina's Dirk. Aren't you? My Selina. I'm driving out to see her this afternoon. She's one of my reasons for being here. Why, I'm ——" He was laughing, talking excitedly, like a boy. Dallas, all agrin, was enjoying it immensely.

"They've run away," she explained to Dirk, "from the elaborate programme that was arranged for them this afternoon. I don't know where the French got their reputation for being polite. The General is a perfect boor, aren't you? And scared to death of women. He's the only French general in captivity who ever took the trouble to learn English."

General Goguet nodded violently and roared. "And you?" he said to Dirk in his careful and perfect English. "You, too, are an artist?"

"No," Dirk said, "not an artist."

"What, then?"

"Why—uh—bonds. That is, the banking business. Bonds."

"Ah, yes," said General Goguet, politely. "Bonds. A very good thing, bonds. We French are very fond of them. We have great respect for American bonds, we French." He nodded and twinkled and turned away to Dallas.

"We're all going" announced Dallas, and made a dash for the stuffy little bedroom off the studio.

Well, this was a bit too informal. "Going where?" inquired Dirk. The General, too, appeared bewildered.

Roelf explained, delightedly. "It's a plot. We're all going to drive out to your mother's. You'll go, won't you? You simply must."

"Go?" now put in General Goguet. "Where is it that we go? I thought we stayed here, quietly. It is quiet here, and no reception committees." His tone was wistful.

Roelf attempted to make it clear. "Mr. DeJong's mother is a farmer. You remember I told you all about her in the ship coming over. She was wonderful to me when I was a kid. She was the first person to tell me what beauty was—is. She's magnificent. She raises vegetables."

"Ah! A farm! But yes! I, too, am a farmer. Well!" He shook

Dirk's hand again. He appeared now for the first time to find him interesting.

"Of course I'll go. Does Mother know you're coming? She has been hoping she'd see you but she thought you'd grown so grand ——"

"Wait until I tell her about the day I landed in Paris with five francs in my pocket. No, she doesn't know we're coming, but she'll be there, won't she? I've a feeling she'll be there, exactly the same. She will, won't she?"

"She'll be there." It was early spring; the busiest of seasons on the farm.

Dallas emerged in greatcoat and a new spring hat. She waved a hand to the faithful Gilda Hanan. "Tell any one who inquires for me that I've felt the call of spring. And if the boy comes for that clay pack picture tell him to-morrow was the day."

They were down the stairs and off in the powerful car that seemed to be at the visitors' disposal. Through the Loop, up Michigan Avenue, into the south side. Chicago, often lowering and gray in April, was wearing gold and blue to-day. The air was sharp but beneath the brusqueness of it was a gentle promise. Dallas and Pool were very much absorbed in Paris plans, Paris reminiscences. "And do you remember the time we . . . only seven francs among the lot of us and the dinner was . . . you're surely coming over in June, then . . . oils . . . you've got the thing, I tell you . . . you'll be great, Dallas . . . remember what Vibray said . . . study . . . work . . ."

Dirk was wretched. He pointed out objects of interest to General Goguet. Sixty miles of boulevard. Park system. Finest in the country. Grand Boulevard. Drexel Boulevard. Jackson Park. Illinois Central trains. Terrible, yes, but they were electrifying. Going to make 'em run by electricity, you know. Things wouldn't look so dirty, after that. Halsted Street. Longest street in the world.

And, "Ah, yes," said the General, politely. "Ah, yes. Quite so. Most interesting."

The rich black loam of High Prairie. A hint of fresh green things just peeping out of the earth. Hot-houses. Coldframes. The farm.

It looked very trim and neat. The house, white with green shutters (Selina's dream realized), smiled at them from among the willows that were already burgeoning hazily under the wooing of a mild and early spring.

"But I thought you said it was a small farm!" said General Goguet, as they descended from the car. He looked about at the acreage.

"It is small," Dirk assured him. "Only about forty acres."

"Ah, well, you Americans. In France we farm on a very small scale, you understand. We have not the land. The great vast country." He waved his right arm. You felt that if the left sleeve had not been empty he would have made a large and sweeping gesture with both arms.

Selina was not in the neat quiet house. She was not on the porch, or in the yard. Meena Bras, phlegmatic and unflustered, came in from the kitchen. Mis' DeJong was in the fields. She would call her. This she proceeded to do by blowing three powerful blasts and again three on a horn which she took from a hook on the wall. She stood in the kitchen doorway facing the fields, blowing, her red cheeks puffed outrageously. "That brings her," Meena assured them; and went back to her work. They came out on the porch to await Selina. She was out on the west sixteen—the west sixteen that used to be unprolific, half-drowned muckland. Dirk felt a little uneasy, and ashamed that he should feel so.

Then they saw her coming, a small dark figure against the background of sun and sky and fields. She came swiftly yet ploddingly, for the ground was heavy. They stood facing her, the four of them. As she came nearer they saw that she was wearing a dark skirt pinned up about her ankles to protect it from the wet spring earth and yet it was spattered with a border of mud spots. A rough heavy gray sweater was buttoned closely about the straight slim body. On her head was a battered soft black hat. Her feet, in broad-toed sensible boots, she lifted high out of the soft clinging soil. As she came nearer she took off her hat and holding it a little to one side against the sun, shaded her eyes with it. Her hair blew a little in the gentle spring breeze. Her cheeks were faintly pink. She was coming up the path now. She could distinguish their faces. She saw Dirk; smiled, waved. Her glance went inquiringly to the others—the bearded man in uniform, the tall girl, the man with the dark vivid face. Then she stopped, suddenly, and her hand went to her heart as though she had felt a great pang, and her lips were parted, and her eyes enormous. As Roelf came forward swiftly she took a few quick running steps toward him like a young girl. He took the slight figure in the mud-spattered skirt, the rough gray sweater, and the battered old hat into his arms.

21

They had had tea in the farm sitting room and Dallas had made a little moaning over the beauty of the Dutch lustre set. Selina had entertained them with the shining air of one who is robed in silk and fine linen. She and General Goguet had got on famously from the start, meeting on the common ground of asparagus culture.

"But how thick?" he had demanded, for he, too, had his pet asparagus beds on the farm in Brittany. "How thick at the base?"

Selina made a circle with thumb and forefinger. The General groaned with envy and despair. He was very comfortable, the General. He partook largely of tea and cakes. He flattered Selina with his eyes. She actually dimpled, flushed, laughed like a girl. But it was to Roelf she turned; it was on Roelf that her eyes dwelt and rested. It was with him she walked when she was silent and the others talked. It was as though he were her one son, and had come home. Her face was radiant, beautiful.

Seated next to Dirk, Dallas said, in a low voice: "There, that's what I mean. That's what I mean when I say I want to do portraits. Not portraits of ladies with a string of pearls and one lily hand half hidden in the folds of a satin skirt. I mean character portraits of men and women who are really distinguished looking—distinguishedly American, for example—like your mother."

Dirk looked up at her quickly, half smiling, as though expecting to find her smiling, too. But she was not smiling. "My mother!"

"Yes, if she'd let me. With that fine splendid face all lit up with the light that comes from inside; and the jaw-line like that of the women who came over in the *Mayflower*, or crossed the continent in a covered wagon; and her eyes! And that battered funny gorgeous bum old hat and the white shirtwaist—and her hands! She's beautiful. She'd make me famous at one leap. You'd see!"

Dirk stared at her. It was as though he could not comprehend. Then he turned in his chair to stare at his mother. Selina was talking to Roelf.

"And you've done all the famous men of Europe, haven't you, Roelf! To think of it! You've seen the world, and you've got it in your hand. Little Roelf Pool. And you did it all alone. In spite of everything."

Roelf leaned toward her. He put his hand over her rough one. "Cabbages are beautiful," he said. Then they both laughed as at some exquisite joke. Then, seriously: "What a fine life you've had, too, Selina. A full life, and a rich one and successful."

"I!" exclaimed Selina. "Why, Roelf, I've been here all these years, just where you left me when you were a boy. I think the very hat and dress I'm wearing might be the same I wore then. I've been nowhere, done nothing, seen nothing. When I think of all the places I was going to see! All the things I was going to do!"

"You've been everywhere in the world," said Roelf. "You've seen all the places of great beauty and light. You remember you told me that your father had once said, when you were a little girl, that there were only two kinds of people who really mattered in the world. One kind was wheat and the other kind emeralds. You're wheat, Selina."

"And you're emerald," said Selina, quickly.

The General was interested but uncomprehending. He glanced now at the watch on his wrist and gave a little exclamation. "But the dinner! Our hostess, Madame Storm! It is very fine to run away but one must come back. Our so beautiful hostess." He had sprung to his feet.

"She is beautiful, isn't she?" said Selina.

"No," Roelf replied, abruptly. "The mouth is smaller than the eyes. With Mrs. Storm from here to here"—he illustrated by turning to Dallas, touching her lips, her eyes, lightly with his slender powerful brown fingers—"is smaller than from here to here. When the mouth is smaller than the eyes there is no real beauty. Now Dallas here——"

"Yes, me," scoffed Dallas, all agrin. "There's a grand mouth for you. If a large mouth is your notion of beauty then I must look like Helen of Troy to you, Roelf."

"You do," said Roelf, simply.

Inside Dirk something was saying, over and over, "You're nothing but a rubber stamp, Dirk DeJong. You're nothing but a rubber stamp." Over and over.

"These dinners!" exclaimed the General. "I do not wish to seem ungracious, but these dinners! Much rather would I remain here on this quiet and beautiful farm."

At the porch steps he turned, brought his heels together with a sharp smack, bent from the waist, picked up Selina's rough work-worn hand and kissed it. And then, as she smiled a little, uncertainly, her left hand at her breast, her cheeks pink, Roelf, too, kissed her hand tenderly.

"Why," said Selina, and laughed a soft tremulous little laugh, "Why, I've never had my hand kissed before."

She stood on the porch steps and waved at them as they were whirled swiftly away, the four of them. A slight straight little figure in the plain white blouse and the skirt spattered with the soil of the farm.

"You'll come out again?" she had said to Dallas. And Dallas had said yes, but that she was leaving soon for Paris, to study and work.

"When I come back you'll let me do your portrait?"

"*My* portrait!" Selina had exclaimed, wonderingly.

Now as the four were whirled back to Chicago over the asphalted Halsted road they were relaxed, a little tired. They yielded to the narcotic of spring that was in the air.

Roelf Pool took off his hat. In the cruel spring sunshine you saw that the black hair was sprinkled with gray. "On days like this I refuse to believe that I'm forty-five. Dallas, tell me I'm not forty-five."

"You're not forty-five," said Dallas in her leisurely caressing voice.

Roelf's lean brown hand reached over frankly and clasped her strong white one. "When you say it like that, Dallas, it sounds true."

"It is true," said Dallas.

They dropped Dallas first at the shabby old Ontario Street studio, then Dirk at his smart little apartment, and went on.

Dirk turned his key in the lock. Saki, the Japanese houseman, slid silently into the hall making little hissing noises of greeting. On the correct little console in the hall there was a correct little pile of letters and invitations. He went through the Italian living room and into his bedroom. The Jap followed him. Dirk's correct evening clothes (made by Peel the English tailor on Michigan Boulevard) were laid correctly on his bed—trousers, vest, shirt, coat; fine, immaculate.

"Messages, Saki?"

"Missy Stlom telephone."

"Oh. Leave any message?"

"No. Say s'e call 'gain."

"All right, Saki." He waved him away and out of the room. The man went and closed the door softly behind him as a correct Jap servant should. Dirk took off his coat, his vest, threw them on a chair near the bed. He stood at the bedside looking down at his Peel evening clothes, at the glossy shirtfront that never bulged. A bath, he thought, dully, automatically. Then, quite suddenly, he flung himself on the fine silk-covered bed, face down, and lay there, his head in his arms, very still. He was lying there half an hour later when he heard the telephone's shrill insistence and Saki's gentle deferential rap at the bedroom door.

EDNA FERBER

"I didn't want to be a writer," Edna Ferber admitted in her 1939 autobiography *A Peculiar Treasure.* "I never had wanted to be a writer. I couldn't even use a typewriter, never having tried. The stage was my one love. . . . I go to the theater because I love it; I write plays for the theater because I love it. I am still wrapped in my childish dream [of being an actress, but]. . . . At seventeen my writing career accidentally began."

That accidental career, of course, was an astounding success. Beginning as a "Girl Reporter" for the Appleton, Wisconsin, *Crescent* at age seventeen, Ferber parlayed a short stint as a journalist into a long career as a writer of short stories, novels, and plays—a career that lasted more than sixty years and brought her great fame and wealth.

Ferber was born on August 15, 1885 in Kalamazoo, Michigan, to Jacob and Julia Ferber, a Hungarian-born Jewish merchant and his American-born wife. Throughout Edna's childhood, the family moved several times throughout the Midwest before settling in Appleton, where the Ferbers ran a general store. When Jacob began losing his sight to a degenerative eye disease, Julia took control of the family fortunes, running the store with indefatigable shrewdness. A formidable woman, Julia would later appear, fictionalized, in many of her daughter's novels.

For financial reasons, Ferber set aside her plans to study for a career on the stage and took a job right after high school on the *Crescent*. After a year and a half covering every imaginable type of story, she was fired by a new editor who disdained her "feminine" writing style, but she was hired immediately by the *Milwaukee Journal*. Young and enthusiastic, she took her job seriously, neglecting her personal well-being. When she collapsed from exhaustion, she returned to Appleton for what was supposed to be a temporary leave. Except for some freelance assignments during political conventions, however, Ferber never returned to newspaper work. While she was recuperating she wrote her first short story, "The Homely Heroine." It was published in *Everybody's Magazine* and Edna Ferber's career as a writer of fiction took off.

More stories followed, and a novel, *Dawn O'Hara*, was published in 1911. In a short story called "Representing T.A. Buck," Ferber introduced the unusual character of Mrs. Emma McChesney, a divorced traveling saleswoman with a young son, who worked for the T.A. Buck Featherloom Petticoat Company. *American Magazine* published the story and asked for a second installment. Without having planned it, Ferber embarked on a string of Emma McChesney stories that appeared in *American Magazine* and *Cosmopolitan*, were collected into three volumes, and had a huge following (Theodore Roosevelt was a fan). When a reviewer of the third volume, *Emma McChesney & Co.* (1915) accused Ferber of beating a dead horse, Ferber realized "I had been sliding to oblivion on a path greased by Emma McChesney." She immediately stopped writing the stories, despite an offer from *Cosmopolitan* to name her own price. Nonetheless, Ferber did dramatize the stories for the stage, working in collaboration with George V. Hobart. The play, *Our Mrs. McChesney* was produced in 1915 and starred Ethel Barrymore.

Ferber's second novel, *Fanny Herself*, was published in 1917, her third, *The Girls*, in 1921. It was Ferber's next novel, *So Big* (1924), that established her as a major writer. It won the Pulitzer Prize and became the first of many best sellers she would produce.

While she worked on novels, Ferber continued to publish short stories in magazines and books. One story, "Old Man Minick," caught the attention of playwright George S. Kaufman, who asked her to collaborate with him on adapting it for the stage. The play, *Minick*, was the first in an impressive list of collaborations between the two writers. After *Minick*, Ferber topped the success of *So Big* with the novel *Show Boat* (1926), which served as the basis for the now-classic 1927 Broadway musical and three film versions. In what was surely a coup for any writer, *Show Boat* opened on Broadway December 27, 1927 and another Ferber hit, *The Royal Family*, written with Kaufman, opened the next day.

By this time, Ferber was living full time in New York and hanging around with the legendary wits of the Algonquin Round Table, including Kaufman, Alexander Woollcott, Marc Connelly, Robert Sherwood, Heywood Broun, and Dorothy Parker. But her rigorous work schedule precluded social lunches, and she admitted that she managed to grace these legendary gatherings only three or four times a year.

After *Show Boat*, many of Ferber's novels were large-scale social histories that dealt with regional America. *Cimarron* (1930) recreates the Oklahoma land rush of 1889, *American Beauty* (1931) is based on a wave of immigration of industrious Polish farmers to New England in the late Nineteenth Century, *Come and Get It* (1935) exposes the rape of Wisconsin and Michigan forests by the Robber Barons. Other novels include *Saratoga Trunk* (1941) and *Great Son* (1945); her other plays with Kaufman include *Dinner at Eight* (1932), and *Stage Door* (1936).

Ferber's 1952 novel *Giant*, a sprawling contemporary satire of the newly wealthy in Texas, caused quite an uproar in the Lone Star State, but was a huge commercial success. The 1956 film version of the book, famous for being the last film of screen legend James Dean, was nominated for seven Academy Awards, winning the Oscar for its director, George Stevens. *Ice Palace* (1958), her last novel, was set in

Alaska. She published two volumes of her memoirs, *A Peculiar Treasure* (1939) and *A Kind of Magic* (1963). Ferber, who never married, died of cancer on April 16, 1968.

Hugely successful in her day, Ferber's novels have fallen out of favor, perhaps because commercial success often breeds contempt among the intelligentsia. Ferber was a quintessentially American writer, choosing American settings—often huge panoramas—and themes for her work. "Each one of them had been written with a definite underlying theme in mind, and this had, for some baffling reason, been almost entirely overlooked by the average reader," Ferber once complained. "I found myself regarded as a go-getting best seller and a deft writer of romantic and colorful American novels."

In her obituary, *The New York Times* said, "Her books were not profound, but they were vivid and had a sound sociological basis. She was among the best-read novelists in the nation, and critics of the 1920s and '30s did not hesitate to call her the greatest American woman novelist of her day."

Ferber herself once wrote, "Those critics or well-wishers who think that I could have written better than I have are flattering me. Always I have written at the top of my bent at that particular time. It may be that this or that, written five years later or one year earlier, or under different circumstances, might have been the better for it. But one writes as the opportunity and the material and the inclination shape themselves. This is certain: I never have written a line except to please myself. I never have written with an eye to what is called the public or the market or the trend or the editor or the reviewer. Good or bad, popular or unpopular, lasting or ephemeral, the words I have put down on paper were the best words I could summon at the time to express the thing I wanted more than anything else to say."

So Big

1924

If ever an author failed to anticipate the public's response to one of her own books, it was Edna Ferber when she was writing *So Big*. Fourteen years after its remarkable success, she confessed, "I never dreamed that *So Big* would be [popular]. I wrote it against my judgment. . . . I wrote my book because I wanted to write it more than anything else in the world. . . . Not only did I not plan to write a best seller when I wrote *So Big*; I thought, when I had finished it, that I had written the world's worst seller. Not that alone, I thought I had written a complete Non-Seller."

In fact, when Ferber submitted the final manuscript to her publisher, her cover letter to Russell Doubleday said, "I feel very strongly that I should not publish it as a novel. It will, as you know, appear serially in the *Woman's Home Companion*. I think its publication as a book would hurt you, as publishers, and me as an author."

Doubleday did publish the book, and the critical response was overwhelmingly positive. Reviewing *So Big* for *The New York Times*, L.M. Field called it "a thoughtful book, clean and strong, dramatic at times, interesting always, clear-sighted, sympathetic, a novel to read and to remember." In the *Literary Review*, J.J. Smertenko went further, noting that "with all its flaws and crudities it has the completeness, and finality, that grips and exalts and convinces. By virtue of these qualities *So Big* is a masterpiece."

Not for the last time in her career, Ferber was singled out for the distinctly American quality of her prose and subject matter. "There can be no question that *So Big* gets close to the life of its chosen bit of American soil, or that it is persuasively human in its touch," said the *Springfield Republican*. And C.H. Towne, writing in the *International Book Review*, said, "Here is a young woman who knows the power of the sharp, incisive phrase, dipping her pen into the blood of humanity, bringing us news of life, as she sees it, with no thought of 'serialization' and 'movie rights'. . . . We need this sort of writing and editing in these United States."

But no one surpassed Burton Rascoe in his praise. "To Miss Ferber's narrative and descriptive powers I genuflect in homage," he wrote in the *New York Tribune*. "Her vocabulary is rich and vital; she sees material objects with a penetrating and delightful vision; she has portrayed aspects of Chicago more vividly and with greater distinction than any writer I know; she knows the history of the development of Chicago in the industrial age and she is able to convey in a few words the import of that development; she can describe flappers and debutantes, shop girls and stenographers, tell you how they dress, how they talk, what their working philosophy is, with illuminating flashes."

Ferber was never happy with the title *So Big*, intending to use it only as a tentative working one. When it was serialized in the *Woman's Home Companion*, it was titled *Selina*, after its heroine, but when it came time to publish in book form, the author could think of no better title, so she reluctantly returned to *So Big*. "I still didn't like it," she wrote in her 1939 autobiography, *A Peculiar Treasure*, "but it had stuck somehow. I now think that those two short words, their familiar ring, and all the fat round curves in the S, the O, the B and the G helped to make the book a selling success."

She attributed much of its success to a young staffer at Doubleday, Dan Longwell, who championed the book and mapped out a campaign for selling it. He reputedly made a substantial bet that the book would sell fifty thousand copies—an estimate it certainly surpassed many times over. Whatever Longwell did, it worked. Shortly after the publication date, Ferber embarked on a trip to Europe. On the voyage she encountered so many passengers reading *So Big* that she knew instinctively that she had a best seller on her hands.

Ferber's fourth novel, *So Big*, won the Pulitzer Prize, and was published in Germany, England, Holland, Finland, Sweden, Norway, Hungary, Poland, Russia, and Denmark. It quickly became required reading for English courses at many high schools and colleges.

Given its critical and commercial triumph, it was inevitable that Hollywood would adapt *So Big* into a movie. But the novel's narrative success has not translated so well to the screen, despite three attempts. The first was a 1925 silent film starring Colleen Moore. Barbara Stanwyck assayed the role of Selina in William Wellman's 1932 film, Jane Wyman in Robert Wise's 1953 remake. Ferber herself called the first two efforts "very bad indeed."

After *So Big*, Ferber's next novel was *Show Boat*, which proved even more popular and enduring. While she would never again win a Pulitzer for one of her novels, she lived and wrote for another forty-two years. Her prolific output as novelist, short story writer, and playwright proved to have great popular appeal around the world, making her among the most commercially successful writers of her day.

PERENNIAL ▪ CLASSICS

Books by Edna Ferber:

SO BIG
ISBN 0-06-095669-0 (paperback)
The Pulitzer Prize–winning novel about the life of a gambler's daughter and of her son, Dirk. A critically acclaimed masterpiece that deals with such contemporary issues as poverty, sexism, and success.

"A thoughtful book, clean and strong, dramatic at times, interesting always, clear-sighted, sympathetic, a novel to read and to remember."
—The New York Times

GIANT
ISBN 0-06-095670-4 (paperback)
A tale of power, love, cattle barons, and oil tycoons in a place racked by noise and heat, big men and bourbon, and the high shrill voices of Texas women.
    Giant was the basis for the epic 1956 motion picture starring Elizabeth Taylor, Rock Hudson, and James Dean.

"A powerful story . . . truly as big as its subject." *—Los Angeles Times*

SARATOGA TRUNK
ISBN 0-06-095671-2 (paperback)
A classic novel about a New Orleans vixen and a handsome Texan who are so obsessed with acquiring everything they have ever wanted, they fail to realize they already have all they will ever need . . . each other.
    Saratoga Trunk was the basis for the classic film starring Ingrid Bergman and Gary Cooper.

"The greatest American woman novelist of her day." *—The New York Times*

Available wherever books are sold, or call 1-800-331-3761 to order.